# Bedtime Stories

*A Novel of*
*Cinematic Wanderlust*

Joseph Emil Blum

Illustrated by David Campbell

SAWMILL BALLROOM PUBLISHING
29251 Ham Road
Eugene, Oregon 97405

Library of Congress Control Number: 2007907655

Blum, Joseph Emil
    Bedtime Stories: Tales of a Cinematic Wanderer / Joseph Emil Blum.
    Eugene, Oregon: Sawmill Ballroom Publishing, 2008
    p. cm.

    Trade Paperback
      ISBN 13: 978-0-9799816-3-0

Printed in the United States of America by Vaughan Printing, Inc.
First Printing

Book interior and dustjacket design by Didona Design

Disclaimer
This is a work of fiction. Names, characters, places and incidents
either are the product of the author's imagination
or are used fictitiously, and any resemblance to any actual persons,
living or dead, events or locales is entirely coincidental.

# DEDICATION

---

*To all the little voices in faraway places.*
*You know who you are and what role*
*you have played in my life.*
*I would be nothing without you.*

# TABLE OF CONTENTS

*continued on next page*

# PROLOGUE

---

What follows is an account of a life released
from the constraints of gravity and time…

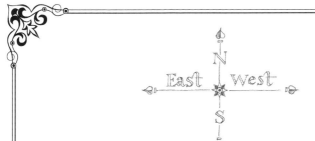

## SECTION 1

# One Road Starts At The End Of Another

CHAPTER 1

# One Road Starts At
# The End Of Another

**In Which** we are introduced to Eva and Emil's boy, our protagonist, Jake Spinner (also known as A. L. Janus when writing about films) and we learn of the events which will propel him away from his home, of his two beloved uncles, Fred and Julian, and of The Lost Sons of Zhitomir -- a rolling film theater.

My name is Jake Spinner and I was born with the wanderer's gene. I know early memories are unreliable, but one memory is clear to me. At the age of five a ringing telephone allowed me to elude the watchful eyes of my mother and the rural, picketed confines of our apple-orchard yard. As my mother walked inside our home to answer the telephone, I responded to my own calling by mounting my bicycle and pedaling carefree through the pastoral surroundings leading to the center of my ancestral hometown of Larch.

In those days Larch was nothing more than a polite grid of tree-lined streets and simple commerce, but with one radiant jewel shining in those streets: the Larch Regal Movie Theater. That's where I stopped. The Regal was where my mother and I spent most Saturday afternoons. Seeing me unattended on a Thursday afternoon, Verna, the dreamy eyed ticket clerk, came out from her glass-enclosed booth and after piecing together why I was alone, she sat me down inside the theater for a detention that was more reward than punishment. I sat eating a box of yesterday's popcorn watching Katharine Hepburn and Humphrey Bogart until my mother arrived. More for show than for any displeasure, when Mom arrived, she gave me a playful swat on the behind and told Verna, "It looks like Jake's got the family wanderlust." When I asked Mom what wanderlust was, she sighed and said, "You'll find out in due time." Then she laughed and added, "At least you knew where to stop," and seeing the movie on the big screen, added, "*The African Queen*, this is supposed to be good." At that point Mom ran out to the lobby and came back with a Fanta and a box of Raisinets, and together we watched the rest of the film.

It may have taken a few decades after that bicycle trip for my wanderer's gene to blossom, but once it did, there was no turning back. I know I'm inclined to look beyond the horizon and there always seems to be something else around the corner. Fortunately, I get to follow that inclination more than most people because I travel the country living out of a large cargo truck painted with the inside of an elegant, movie theater draped in crimson curtains and ornate gold tassels on both sides of its stage. Written above each panel is the legend: "*The Lost Sons of Zhitomir Rolling Film Society.*" Zhitomir is the town in Russia that my paternal grandparents came from in the early 20th century. The name honors the grandfather I never met who, according to family lore, told anyone who asked where he was from, "I'm a lost son of Zhitomir." By the way: you pronounce Zhitomir like this: ZHUH TUM MIR. Below The Lost Sons of Zhitomir Rolling Film Society, in a fine calligrapher's lettering, is written: "*For Hire: All Occasions.*" My trade, if I dare say it, is showing and writing about movies. Is it my profession? I can't honestly say I have a profession, but I do have a purpose: to be a purveyor and collector of stories. Movies are the stories of my time and I use them to light the eyes around me and to collect the stories and souls behind each set of eyes I meet.

This book is about how my life changed after my guardian Uncle Fred Tolliver died. With Fred's death, the few remaining things holding me to one place suddenly departed and my "urge to go" took on a life of its own. Fred left me an unlikely inheritance that both defined and has supported my rather strange purpose in life. Though I never met my father and I lost my mother at a young age, I seldom considered myself an orphan. I was fortunate to have two uncles who cared for and shaped me in ways for which I am endlessly grateful. After my mother died, I lived with her only brother, Fred, whose eulogy ends this chapter. Fred lived in our hometown of Larch where three generations of Tollivers had forged the town's now mostly forgotten legacy. Fred was the Gary Cooper of our family, including six foot two inches of rustic good looks and ferocious erudition artfully welded into a natural balance between the practical and the philosophical aspects of life. Fred taught me how to talk to anyone about anything.

My other influence was my late father's brother, Julian Spinner. Julian was a well-regarded film critic for a newspaper in New York City. He's still alive and continues to be a hero and patron to me. People who know us both have said we have more in common than our compact physiques and dark hair. I'm not sure why, because Julian is like an aging Mickey Rooney. He's five feet seven inches tall, has electric hazel eyes radiating intensity, and once Julian's eyes lock onto you, you're engaged. He's like a fireball coming right at you. Julian would never survive in a poker game because his face reveals everything he feels and he has a piercing way of speaking. I'm a few inches taller than Julian, have dark brown eyes, which more than a few people have described as sad and puppy-like, and I'm inclined to be shy. I'm also more inclined to listen than to speak and too often retreat into a solitude I wish I could escape. As for poker, I can hold a pair of deuces and run the stakes up. The thing about Julian is, at the same time he's turning your world on end, he's charming you. He makes friends as easy as he breathes and he has no reverse gear. As for what we have in common, I've never thought I shared much of Julian's charm, but I do have a healthy dose of his curiosity and interest in people.

Fred and Julian admired each other. Fred said once, "You always know when Julian has picked your pocket because he leaves a piece of candy behind." Julian has said he hopes there is reincarnation so that he can come back as solid and rooted as Fred. "The man was an oak tree."

I spent my school years with Fred in rural western Larch. I spent my summers with Julian who lived two blocks from Carnegie Hall in New York City. Though they inhabited different worlds, there was one thing my two uncles shared: they loved to lecture their nephew. Fred's lectures were about physics, firewood, and automobiles, while Julian's were about the history and craft of movies. One plane ride and I shifted 180 degrees from the world of Fred's wrenches and gaskets to a world of theaters, film, and conversations in restaurants with people who spoke, with no doubts, about the importance of their lives. Julian bestowed upon me his love of movies. Each summer with Julian was a film festival. If we weren't in theaters, taking in revivals at the Thalia or Waverly, we'd be at new releases all over town. Julian didn't have to go to the movies. He received preview copies of most of the films and could have watched them in the comfort of his own living room that he dubbed "The Little Paradise Theater." Julian had two cardinal rules for watching movies. The first: films should be seen in theaters. The second, which was odd for a film critic: don't read anything about any film until you've seen it.

Julian and I spent many a New York summer evening watching films from his extensive collection of shorts, cartoons, and classic films long out of circulation. There was a fitting irony, that Julian had bought his apartment years ago from another sort of connoisseur, a flamboyant Italian wine merchant who had outfitted an expansive walk-in cooler to hold his self-proclaimed "finest wine collection this side of Bordeaux." The wine merchant could not have known that Julian would use the perfectly acclimatized wine cooler to store films or that his French drapes would conceal two 16mm projectors. "Good wine, good women, and good films all get better with age," said Julian once while tracing circles with his feet into a vintage Persian rug he'd worn thin over the years.

As the revival houses began their decline and film began its march to video, Julian continued expanding his archives and eventually started a journal of classic film called *The Tattered Edge. The Tattered Edge* sustained itself for years with features like obituaries of faded film celebrities or pieces by Julian's enormous list of film industry people about techniques and history. When it became harder and harder to see older films in theaters, Julian had the idea that I could screen films in Larch and then write a monthly column about a classic film's impact on a modern audience. When I protested that I wasn't a good enough writer to handle a column, Julian said, "They're words, Jake; they don't bite. You can do it." Thus, with two projectors, a small collection of 16mm classic films, and a collapsible movie screen, I began both my writing and film-screening careers.

Once a month, in Larch or another nearby town, I'd haul my projectors to a community center, church, school, or suitable business with wall space to throw up an image. I even bought some dark black curtains and had a stand built to flank the screen trying to replicate the ambiance of Julian's "Little Paradise Theater." The film archives reflected another one of Julian's film commandments: "Put them to bed with a good story." On this matter, Julian was emphatic. "Jake, we're living in a time when our dreams are fed not by singing mothers but writers and storytellers. When you look at the stories that send so many people off to sleep, is it any wonder things can seem crazy? Put them to bed with a good story!" Julian was right. Before too long there was an established and eagerly anticipated event every month under the banner of *The Larch Film Society.*

If showing films was easy, writing about them was not. My column for *The Tattered Edge* is called "Fade Out," in which I write under the cover of film writer A.L. Janus. Julian and I selected the pseudonym, deriving it from the names of my favorite president and Julian's favorite collection of classic films. At first, I balked at the idea of a pseudonym, but Julian convinced me, saying, "Pseudonyms are good, Jake. You can hide when you want to, spy when you need to, and you can be two people at the same time." The persona of Abraham Lincoln Janus provided me some money to make ends meet, and occasionally the rather unlikely answer to the "What do you do?" question. After each film show I'd write up a piece about the film evening and the audience's response and then drop it in the closest mailbox. Julian would do whatever editing he thought necessary at his end. *The Tattered Edge* was no more than a cult magazine until Julian sold it to *Time Life* and they gave it a makeover. With *Time Life* clout and marketing, four million people now read A.L. Janus's pieces every month. Fortunately, in Larch, only a handful of people knew or cared about the real identity of A.L. Janus.

There was nothing to foreshadow any eventual change, so it may be fairly asked, as it often is now: What set me on the road? I wish I could say it came from me, that I grew and changed, and found a new passion. In fact, like many things in my life, it was the guidance of others that directed me outward. In this, Fred would play a large part.

It seems funny now that Fred, who had cared for me when my mother died and had been my anchor through a blur of decades, needed me less than I needed him. Even as he grew older and closer to death he was most comfortable by himself. He was that way. Visitors, often more in need of repair themselves than the cars they brought to him, provided him with enough human contact. There was no getting around that Fred chose to pull out of the world and never thought it necessary to look back at that decision. You can probe the soul of a loner for clues to their isolation, but when all is said and done, it simply came down to the fact that Fred enjoyed his own company. It was only when he died that I saw how much I had needed him, and how I had remained a moon to the planet of his life for the better part of three decades.

There were only eight people at Fred's funeral beside myself: Clara Spengler, the owner of *The Sonnet: Rare and Used Bookstore.* Clara had been Fred's high school English teacher and later mine as well. The others present were his neighbor of thirty years, Cattie Pinkard; his dogs' veterinarian, Dr. David Hilger, an occasional chess companion; retired *Larch Post* editor, Don Goforth; Leon Finster, who came once a year to tune Fred's piano, and other neighbors, Nora and Billy Sullivan, with their seven-year-old daughter, Louise.

It was an odd gathering with so few people. After Fred's eulogy there was a few minutes of silence. Fred hadn't specified details of his funeral service, except that it would be nice if those attending might stop for a few minutes to feel the Earth spinning. In that silence, I thought about all the people who had passed out of my life, the people I'd lost. I was embarrassed to do so, but I was so numb to my own feelings that I glanced around the room at the others, hoping I might see in them something that I could feel. I couldn't feel anything except a pain in my heart. A pull like the weight of a heavy load, a thousand small deaths tugged at my heart. I wanted to run from the pain. I wanted to run out of the room, and I might have, had not Clara Spengler, seeing me falter, taken my hand firmly into hers.

I've only known the pain of losing someone I loved once before. That pain came when my mother died. I was never certain whether that memory was my own or simply the repeated stories of others that had left such a deep impression. There was no such doubt about Fred, and I felt his death deep in my heart as an inexplicable ache that removed any doubt that the heart is the seat of the human soul. It was only the touch of Clara's hand that settled my grief. It would be many years later that I would come to know how my hand had steadied hers well. After Fred's memorial I was numb with loss. I heard my sobs and felt the gasping air move in and out of my lungs. I wanted Fred back. I wanted to find the sacrifice I might offer in exchange for Fred's return, but in the end, there was no bargain to be made, and I simply cried until I realized I was crying for myself, not for Fred, who would have had more than a few things to say about all the sobbing. Once the tears stopped, I rattled around for hours looking for something to fill the awkward void. Nothing worked, especially with the coffee from the memorial service surging through my blood. I needed something to slow me down and finally found it in the television schedule of the paper. Over the next twenty minutes I made some eggs and toast, ate, then turned on the television as *Variety Lights* was beginning. The film was one of my mother's favorites. I remember watching it with her on television when I was a small child and her telling me, "You may be too young now, Jake, but someday you'll understand this." Even though it's old and fading into history like a poorly stored sepia photograph, that night *Variety Lights* was my comfort and companion. I watched as Fellini showed us how powerful the urge is to find another pathway that gives a life meaning.

I woke up the next morning in a skin that no longer fit, surrounded by memories. What started as a subtle and quiet reminder grew louder and more persistent. Fred's death was like coarse rock to a snake shedding its skin. Soon the snake is rubbing itself against that rock until the dry, brittle, and obsolete containment of its body is completely removed. My wanderer's gene, far from atrophying with neglect, had gained force and now insisted on expression. I felt the rumblings, but had no idea what forces or form would be expressed in the coming days. Yesterday's stagnant surroundings were now vibrating. When I touched the patchwork quilt my grandmother had made for my parents' bed, there was a memory. The smell of the aging wool she had cut from old clothing formed a memory of her sitting and tearing old coats for woolen strips to braid into rugs. When my eyes fell on the wormwood frame which held a tattered black-and-white photograph of my father and Julian sitting on the granite stairs leading into the Manhattan apartment building of their childhood, I heard them speaking as young brothers. Everything around me held a living memory, but the people who forged those memories were all gone.

I walked around the house and it seemed like everything anybody had ever touched had a story to tell. They were all talking at the same time. My grandfather's currycomb from his WWI cavalry days started telling me about his horse. When I held the comb to my nose, I could actually smell Grisha, a horse that had died more than eighty years ago. My mother used to sculpt ceramic heads, and these too were speaking about the movement of her thumbs in the supple clay. An unglazed pitcher with a spray of fresh-cut lavender, my mother's favorite plant, emitted its scent as her voice spoke to me from the room where she'd lived. I touched the coat hanger by the front door and imagined something I had never heard: my mother telling my father to take off his shoes and get into the bath before the water got cold. They were all there, and it was as if they were preparing a big reunion to welcome Fred back home from the army. Of course I'd known the dead could speak, but I didn't know how loudly or for how long. They carried on all that day until they disappeared again, along with the smells, the sounds, the music and the tastes.

You never know what innocent catalyst will tip your life from stationary to rolling, but suddenly there it was. When I walked out to the mailbox that afternoon I found a notice from the Tolliver County Court summoning me to jury duty. I had lived in Larch for forty-five years, and in that entire time I could never recall a sense of urgency about anything. There was something about the jury summons that felt strange, especially the part that commanded, "You must appear in person." More rumblings: things were feeling ominous.

---

*Larch Post*, February 6th, 1999

On a sad note, we report the passing of one of Larch's pioneer citizens this week at the age of 77. Fred Tolliver was born on June 8th, 1922, into a different Larch than exists today. It can be fairly said that the town of Larch and Fred grew up together. Fred's life and the lives of his ancestors are woven into our town's legacy. Fred was a wise and private man and he would not have wanted us to "waste ink" on his passing. For those of you who knew him, there is nothing that needs to be said. For those of you who didn't: we only hope you may be lucky enough to cross paths with someone like Fred Tolliver at least once in your life. In Fred's honor, we print the text of the eulogy delivered by his sole remaining relative, nephew, Jake Spinner, at the memorial service held for him last Saturday at Larch's own Sonnet: Rare and Used Bookstore.

### Living at the End of the Road
#### by Jake Spinner

*Fred Tolliver was my mother's brother. Uncle Fred was a tall, good-looking man with warm fluid eyes and a sturdy, treelike posture, which led people to remark on his resemblance to Gary Cooper. Fred was born at the end of a dirt road in a town with no sidewalks, and where hardly anyone came to visit. He went through college on the GI bill and handled course-work the same way he handled cars: with great ease and skill. But Fred grew tired of what he called, "the aberrant condition of academia." He quit school and came home to a solitary life as a mechanic and poet.*

*Fred was not your everyday mechanic, but rather, he understood and spoke as a passionate philosopher about things that crossed his mind. Those of you who knew him understood that Fred indeed was a philosopher-mechanic; that fixing machines was simply the disguise he wore to involve you in a deeper engagement with life. Some thought Fred was wasting his life and needed to get out more, but Fred always said that eventually, the world would spin on its axis and arrive at your door. He further asserted he could prove it mathematically, a claim of which no one had ever dared to challenge him.*

*The simple truth was that the world never came to Fred's door, and he went on fixing cars, writing poetry, and talking to anyone who drifted in, which generally were those people who couldn't afford to take their cars to the shops in town. Decades passed, a larger town grew up around him, and like all vestigial organs, Fred became another strange character people who didn't know him told stories about, and few knew or cared to discover. When Fred died, his house was donated to a grateful fire department for a training burn. Up in smoke went fifty years of unread poetry, and calendars with the high and low temperature for every day written on them. Fred was not a man of possessions and he would have enjoyed the warmth of a good fire.*

*I'd like to believe that the ashes of Fred's life were caught by the wind and that a little of those ashes have settled on all of us, because Fred Tolliver was a kind guardian, a wise teacher, and an unpretentious observer of life.*

*I will miss him.*

CHAPTER 2

# This Is Not Inherit The Wind

In Which we are dismissed at the feet of justice, see a glowing light, have a vision interpreted by a former high-school English teacher, meet "the truck," and describe "The Howler," a storm spent comfortably with my mother.

One week later, I walked to the Samuel Tolliver Courthouse to report for jury duty. As a child that three-mile walk was through farms and woods, and often accompanied by a swelling crescendo of amorous frogs. Now it was a continuous grid of homes and roads filled with the steady hum and sputter of machinery. In the year I was born, 1952, there were one hundred seventy-six people in Larch. I know, because they used to include the population statistic in your birth announcement in the weekly paper, *The Larch Post.* Mine had read: "Jacob Oscar Spinner was born to Eva and Emil Spinner, bringing our lovely town's population to an even 176 residents." They stopped doing that a while ago, but I noticed walking into town that morning the town-limits sign read thus: Entering Larch: Population 16,769.

It was strange to be in the Courthouse, a building I knew well, but now the center of a town full of people whose names and faces were mostly foreign to me. At nine o'clock a group of forty potential jurors were seated in one of the courtrooms awaiting the arrival of the two principal attorneys. First to enter was Howard Deggles, a frumpy and distracted public defender for the accused who often browsed the shelves of *The Sonnet* looking for cheap copies of detective stories. A minute later, for the county appeared assistant prosecutor, Katrina Lating, a sinewy young woman with a voice like the shrill alarm of a smoke detector. The two attorneys took their turns trying to gain some advantage from this small pool of people. When it came to my turn, I answered their questions routinely, until the ermine-like prosecutor asked me an odd thing.

"One last question, Mr. Spinner: Do you have any bumper stickers on your car?"

When I told her no, she rolled her eyes as if some great snare trap had been sprung.

"None?"

"No, Ma'am."

Now she exchanged glances with the public defender, who seemed to be more focused on why he had forgotten to shave that morning than on the pending "Felony Auto-Theft II" case now before him. There was something about my lack of bumper stickers that was igniting the lithe, and now energetic, prosecutor, and for a second I drifted into images of Katharine Hepburn trumping Spencer Tracy in *Adam's Rib*. That faded quickly, however, as Miss Lating was certainly no Hepburn, and I soon grinned to myself as I imagined her donning an English barrister's wig. She pressed closer now.

"Hmm? No bumper sticker you say, you've never had any bumper stickers on your car?"

Then she touched and splayed her hands palms out, as if the final card had been played. I wondered why she was making such a big deal of this as I answered the question.

"No, Ma'am, never."

Lating believed I was lying. She rolled her eyes again as if in a pact with the other possible jurors and then continued.

"You're quite certain of this? Most people have, sir."

"Yes, ma'am, I am sure. I did drive a vegetable delivery truck one summer when I was a teenager that had an old bumper sticker on it. I think it said "I Like Ike," but anyway it was the owner's truck. You see, ma'am, it's one of my rules."

Now, Lating turned her back to my chair confident of having proven some mysterious point while aiming an intimidating stare into the worried eyes of the other prospective jurors. I glanced at the overmatched Deggles, hoping he would rise from his whiskey-filled thermos like Charles Laughton in *Witness for the Prosecution* and intone "Your honor, haven't we had enough of this foolishness?"

It didn't happen. Instead, Deggles silently ruffled through some papers as if trying to find a lost homework assignment while Miss Lating continued her inquisition.

"You have a rule about bumper stickers?"

"Yes, ma'am, I do."

"Any other personal rules we should know about here?"

"That depends, ma'am. If I had a moment to think, there might be more than a few, but the only one coming to mind is that I don't wear T-shirts with logos on them."

That, apparently, was all that Miss Lating needed to know and she waved her hand in the air, before saying "You're dismissed. Next!"

It's not that I felt any great desire to stick around but I was expecting something a little more *Inherit the Wind* before my peremptory dismissal.

"You're dismissing me because I don't have bumper stickers on my car?" I said, which caught Lating by surprise.

"Your honor, the people have exercised their right and would like to proceed. Shouldn't you direct the bailiff to please escort Mr. Spinner out of the courtroom."

I should have let it go, but something about Lating's arrogance egged me on.

"So, Madam counselor, if my car was pasted with I Heart Chihuahuas, or I'm A Square Dancer and I Vote, you'd seat me on your jury?"

The judge, to my great pleasure, seemed to enjoy seeing Lating defied, and smiled as Lating became annoyed."

"Your honor, must the people ask again that Mr. Spinner depart from this court so we can get on with the people's business?"

"Counselor Lating, there are days I'm not sure exactly what the people's business is. For instance, today the people are being asked to settle a dispute over a stolen chain saw and its subsequent use in removing a decrepit fence."

"Your honor!" Lating blurted with an overblown sense of indignation before the judge decided it was best to move on.

"Mr. Spinner, I too am curious what the bumper stickers have to do with any of this, but I'm afraid the assistant district attorney is well within her legal authority. If you would do us all the kind favor of leaving, sir, I'm sure the people will call upon you again in the future."

"Thank you your honor. Had I known I needed a bumper sticker on my car to serve the cause of justice I would have done so."

This remark sent Lating over the edge and she began ranting about the rightful prerogative of the people as the bailiff, barely controlling her own laughter, gently guided me out of the courtroom.

I felt cheated. If not Clarence Darrow and William Jennings Bryan, I was hoping for a little Spencer Tracy and Frederick March. I was shocked that in the mind of this so-called representative of justice, there was some know-able connection between my not sporting bumper stickers and her sporting desire to convict a man for stealing a car. Even worse, had I been dismissed because I didn't wear T-shirts with designer logos like Calvin Klein written on them? If I had placed a *Stumps Don't Lie* "or "*Nixon's the One*" across the rusted fender of my car would I be better suited to her need to predict my opinions? Had I been dismissed because I might change my mind? Might think? Because I might consider that things can have more than one side and that the world wasn't so awfully goddamn tidy that you can arrange it into perfect little categories? For the first time in years I was actually angry!

If the tightly wound Miss Lating, along with the rest of the people in the courthouse didn't know or care that in 1915 my great-grandfather, Sam Tolliver -- the man whose name was etched into the building in which we all sat -- had sheltered, fought for, and finally been shot to death defending two Nez Perce Indians who were then lynched by an angry mob -- it mattered to me. This mob had accused them of stealing a set of carpenter's tools from a white man, only to find out three days later that the man's brother had borrowed the tools to repair a church damaged by a windstorm. Katrina Lating's cluelessness and the potential jurors' pervasive numbness were the last straw that finally set this camel in motion (before its back broke or its spirit snapped).

I hadn't been dismissed, no; Katrina Lating had unknowingly cut free the last tether holding this hot air balloon to the ground. In that moment, I felt the pull of the wind and the updraft of the warm sun creating thermals. I experienced the joy a soaring bird must have while floating in the ether between heaven and earth. I sensed the liberating presence of the far-too-dormant wanderer's gene.

I floated out of the courtroom carried by something outside of my

body. A huge smile formed on my face. As I exited the room, the clerk reached for the dismissal form in my hand.

"You can go home now, sir."

I looked at her with a wild and indiscernible grin she could never in a million years understand. I'm sure it made her nervous. In a decent impression of W. C. Fields I said, "No, my gentle canary, I don't think I can."

As I stepped out of that building, the courthouse clock chimed the first of the twelve noon bells. The clock chimes pealed like a glorious proclamation as I descended the steps into blinding, low angle sunlight. Above me the light shone on the Samuel Tolliver County Courthouse Scales of Justice and despite the winter chill, a warm and shimmering light hovered above my eyes and held me captive in its glow. Feeling like a black cat walking the streets of Rome in a Fellini film, I strolled through Larch in my newly felt freedom. Each step, each sight was vivid, and time slowed in what I became aware was a geographical farewell tour of a big part of my life.

I headed down Ida Street, floating past the office windows of lawyers, accountants, computer stores, and emporiums selling clothing, shoes, paper supplies, doughnuts, candy, wedding dresses, lawnmowers, cell phones, compact discs, tax returns, and games. It was as if I were awakening from a coma and beginning to comprehend the reality that a long period of time had passed. As of now, it was no longer my world. I continued until I arrived in front of *The Sonnet: Rare and Used Bookstore.*

As I entered, the bells hanging from the doorknob alerted Clara. She looked up, barely nodding an acknowledgment of my entrance, while continuing to examine the handwritten Bible before her. Clara often got lost in a book. After years of teaching writing, Clara, had found a way to live in the words she loved. Fulfilled by decades of inspiring high school students, she felt free to retire and live out her final dream in an untidy little bookstore where the books were good, the shelves densely packed, and tables covered with un-shelved acquisitions awaiting their places in Clara's literary fortress. Clara spent her days buried in stories, first editions, and on-line in a passionate Internet chat-room romance with a man she suspected was Kurt Vonnegut. The books were all priced too high, no doubt to preserve them for the shelves and cases that were the erudite ramparts comprising *The Sonnet's* walls.

She waved me over and showed me the leather bound Bible, saying that it had been intended as a gift to Eleanor Roosevelt from the citizens of

Larch after the President's death. Clara explained that it had been returned unopened, with one addition -- it bore the Presidential Seal of the United States on the package.

"Look at this inscription, Jake. *To our great woman in respect for the passing of a great man.*" Clara read. "I'll bet your grandmother had something to do with this." Then, setting aside the book, Clara asked, "To what honor do we owe this visit?"

"Well me sweet dear"(Clara and I had a running gag -- foreign accents today -- I was attempting a poor Irish brogue), "I have been dismissed."

"Dismissed, what on earth are you talking about, Jake Spinner?"

"Dismissed, Clara, like Jesus by the Jews, or like Copernicus by the church, or even like MacArthur by Truman, like so many things that start their lives from rejection.

"I see you do not intend to let me in on your joke?"

With a brief explanation, I told her about my epiphany: the golden light, the bells, all the unusual conversations and visitations taking place back home since Fred had died.

"Yes, that sounds like your family. Tollivers, for certain, and Spinners I suspect were nothing if not clever and persistent."

"I'm not sure what you mean by that, Clara."

"You didn't think death could stop them, did you? I know your uncle shared some of his pet theories with you. Did you not pay him any attention? Or did you think he was nuts?"

Then, Clara, who after six decades of analyzing literature could find the crux of any story, said, "Vision, old son. You've been handed a vision! Get your head out of the sand and see it for what it is. Hah! Right now you think you're going to walk around floating in golden light for the rest of your life. You like the feeling of floating and the heady scent of insight, but a vision isn't a dispensation Jake, it's a passkey. You're the one who has to take the initiative to turn the lock and walk through that golden door."

Clara was right. Since Fred's death there had been so many strange surprises. When I returned home, would I find Fred, Mom, Dad, Grandma and Grandpa sitting at the table having a cup of coffee and playing cribbage or would I come home to echoes and solitude? Radiant light transformed me, forced me to see myself, pushed me into thinking and feeling things I didn't want to think or feel. The adrenaline surge of the morning's events was gone, leaving me numb. When I left *The Sonnet* my Fellini walk had ceased.

Arriving home, I found a letter stuck in the door from Clark, Meyers, and Tollefson, Attorneys at Law. They were handling Fred's estate. Inside the printed envelope was a smaller tattered envelope. A paper contained a hand-written message to me.

*Dear Jake,*

*Here's some money, and the keys to that piano mover. Hope the money means more to you than it did to me. The truck is big but it's a hummer and will run forever if you treat her right. It starts a little cold, so be patient, and it'll be good to you. It's time that you had a go at life. Thanks for looking after me.*

*Uncle Fred*

*PS. Here's a copy of that story you wrote. I always liked it. Fred.*

Wow. Though I had always loved the truck, my first reaction to the gift was that I thought Fred was handing me a white elephant. At 30,000 pounds, the thought of taking it on was a bit daunting. But very little Fred ever did was without some esoteric calculation and so it was to be with his truck.

If you like trucks, and Fred did, his "Piano Mover" is a beautiful thing. It's not a piano mover at all, but a big delivery truck, a white 1992 International with a 230-horsepower diesel and a twenty-foot-long by eight-and-one-half-foot-tall by eight-and-one-half-foot-wide box. In the vernacular of the truck world: "Stout." It has a tall step-up cab, with room to seat three comfortably, and four in a pinch. The driver's seat is plush. Fred took the truck in lieu of six months work he did for an artisan cabinetmaker in Larch who customized it to show off his skill. The night before he skipped out of town to dodge his creditors, the cabinetmaker signed the truck over to Fred saying, "After they sort through the ashes somebody's going to get this thing, Fred. It might as well be you."

The thing you would never imagine in a million years is how the inside of the cargo box had been customized. Like the hidden crystal of a geological thunder egg, when you crack things open you get a big surprise. Instead of metal walls of sweating steel, the box is lined with wooden plank panels of aged cherry. Fred said once it reminded him of the wood of an ornate nineteenth-century saloon. Originally designed for what International calls "medium usage," it was meant to haul stuff like furniture, deli meats, or cartons of beer. Fred used it once to haul two Steinway Concert Grand Pianos when their original truck broke down near Larch in transit from Cleve-

land to Seattle. With a pressing delivery date to the *American/Soviet Friends of Perestroika* in jeopardy, the driver was relieved when he found Fred. Fred said he'd haul the pianos for the cost of the diesel, two front row seats at the upcoming concert, and an autographed photo of Mikhail Gorbachev. He also hauled an elephant once, but that was a sore spot with Fred because the elephant did a lot of damage to the wooden floors which needed refinishing. There's more to the truck, but I'm saving some of that for later.

As for the copy of my story, it was neatly preserved in a manila folder. I had written it when I was fifteen for the *Regional Youth Mother's Day Writing Contest*. For winning the contest I received $15 and publication in *The Larch Post* with my picture beside the essay. I was also invited to read it on the radio, making me a mini-celebrity for a few weeks in spite of Clara Spengler's critique, (which I didn't understand) that the fourth paragraph was confusing. I hadn't seen that story in nearly thirty years but it didn't take me long to see how great a gift were these two last things from Fred. I opened it and read.

---

*The Larch Post.* December 12, 1967

### The Howler: A Double Feature at the Larch Regal Theater.

### A Memory of My Mother.
By Jake Spinner.

Mother's Day is never my happiest day of the year. My mother is dead. Most of my memories of her are faded like old black-and-white photos with brittle edges, slowly dissolving away to time. I wonder whether they are real, or recreations of stories told to me about her over the years.

My last clear memory of her is in the Larch Regal Movie Theater on a winter Saturday afternoon. She had bundled me up in my thick wool coat and wrapped a scarf around my face to keep me warm for the walk to the movie house. It was so cold the air blasted against my eyes like cracking glass. The walk seemed long, but at last we arrived to the comforting warmth and stillness of the theater lobby. Those who had braved the cold shared an excited satisfaction and Mom told another woman, "They say this is going to be the biggest storm since the Blast of 1947!" I loved the way that sounded - - the Blast! The other woman said, "Yes, they're calling this one the Howler!" I loved the way that sounded even more -- the Howler!

Mom found two seats on the center aisle and she laid my coat open on the chair like a nest. "Jake, I'll be right back," she said, and left for a few minutes before returning with a box of Raisinets and the smell of cigarette smoke when she exhaled. When she pressed against me I heard the crinkle of the Pall Malls in her sweater pocket. She wrapped her coat over the two of us, and then leaned over to me as the curtain drew back and in her pre-film whisper said, "Jake, this is a Barbara Stanwyck film. If there's anything you don't understand, close your eyes, pop a Raisinet in your mouth, and hold my hand." I answered, "Mom, I'm five years old now and I understand everything!" Hearing that, Mom started to laugh aloud and said, "Well, little man, there are a few things that may still surprise you, so give that box a shake and have it ready. Okay?"

There was a lot of eye closing and Raisinet-popping that day. But Mom would give my hand a squeeze and in her quieter film-whisper say things from time to time like "Jake, that's Marilyn Monroe." "Jake, look at those fishing boats." "Jake, don't you think Joe looks like your Uncle Fred." Mom loved to whisper in the movies and she'd get annoyed if someone shushed her. I probably fell asleep in the film because all I remember is the end when the woman comes back to her husband. That seemed odd, because it didn't seem like she loved him even though he was such a nice guy. I didn't want to leave because there was a movie they called "the feature" about to start, but Mom said she thought we'd better get home, so we bundled up again. Then, she wrapped my scarf around my face and it was wet. Yecch!

When we got to the lobby there were only a few people who were standing and staring out of the window to the street, which was covered with snow. The storm was so fierce you couldn't see the other side because the snow was coming down so hard. It was beautiful and I was hoping we'd get to make snowmen later. A small group of people came in from the outside with snow on their coats. One of them was a friend of my mother's and when she said hello, I leaned against her wool coat and smelled the melting snow mingling with the warming wool.

I remember Harry Goforth, the theater owner, shouting across to Mom, "Eva, no point you two heading out now. Might as well stay for the second show. It's got Paul Newman; handsome fellow, and there sure won't be a lot of people here today. I'm going to close down as soon as this show is over and I'll run you two home in the car if you'd like. Jake, you can have all the free popcorn you want." So we unbundled and went back to our seats. Before the feature started, Mom, gave me a little kiss on the head and whispered "Don't you love the movies, Jake."

Happy Mother's Day, Mom.

CHAPTER 3

# How One Becomes
# A Circus Painter

**In Which** we learn that heaven can wait, and are drawn to a circus painter while vapors rise from a woolen blanket.

Since Fred's death many things happened to set my life in motion but none was more important than the metamorphosis of the truck.

In late February, Fred's spirit lingered until his favorite flower, Daphne, bloomed to offer its fragrant hope of the coming of spring. My friends Trace and Lucy Toussaint, whose six-year-old son, Peter, had been diagnosed with leukemia, asked me to do them a favor. The family needed to raise money for Peter to get the help he needed and they were looking at ways to rally people to contribute something. I took a portion of the inheritance from Fred and gave it to the family, but more was needed. It was Trace who came up with the idea of showing a movie, and he subsequently arranged for a dinner and movie banquet at the Rapid Falls Community Center.

Rapid Falls, forty miles from Larch, is not so much a town as a gas stop along the road. The Community Center wasn't much more than a covered space with a passable kitchen built out of massive old beams. Without a stage or screen to work with, I needed to pack an entire theater into Fred's truck. Since the weather forecast that day would have started Noah building the ark, and I knew the program would run late, I threw a fold-up bed in the van. I didn't want to drive home on such a wild night and at the

last minute I thought to include a sleeping bag and a couple of wool blankets. Alongside the screen I loaded up a gearbox with the projectors, cords, speakers, and anything else I might need for the showing, including a large flashlight. Stepping back, I took notice of the nice little scene I had created with all the gear stowed and the bed set up. It felt so cozy I was inspired to throw in a small rug and a pair of fold-up chairs. The van was filled with a sweet musty smell and you could detect the aroma of the cherries emanating from the aged red planks, completing its homey ambiance. Acting out of some strange impulse, I pinned a small picture of two intertwined sleeping puppies that I had cut from a Life Magazine, and which for some reason made me happy, on to the wall beside the cot. At that moment, it seemed like the most comfortable spot on earth. It was as though I could feel my future.

I drove the forty miles to Rapid Falls in a driving rainstorm, and when I arrived there, was amazed by all the activity. People were rallying around the event, as they will do for children or for those unfairly afflicted, rolling out their money and generosity. Little Peter had most of the town working for him and if any of that outpouring of loving energy translated into his struggling body he'd live to a ripe old age. Rapid Falls didn't have more than two hundred people in its boundaries, but the Community Center was overflowing with people full of energy and having a good time. Most had been working since early in the morning setting up chairs, cooking, cleaning, making phone calls, painting signs, taking care of children, and shopping for food. Kids were making popcorn and selling raffle tickets. It seemed as though everyone who showed up had brought some kind of door prize or contribution.

The center's makeshift stage, barely more than a plywood platform that dipped when you walked on it, suddenly caught my eye. An imaginative and enchanting painted background of five plywood panels detailed the stage like an elaborate carnival. Even the Ferris wheel was detailed with excited little faces in each car. Amazing! When I hung the screen in place in the center of this vibrant masterpiece, people stood and stared with anticipation, as if the blank silver fabric were a window through which one could pass into the scene painted around it.

It only took about an hour to place the projectors, check the focus and sound levels, and then to tape down cords and connectors. With the movie reels in place there wasn't anything left to do except take a few minutes to

appreciate what was going on around me. I can't imagine the Rapid Falls Community Center had ever had a standing room only crowd before, but there weren't enough chairs in the room, so quite a few people were standing in the back. It was clear that no one in town planned to let Peter go without a fight. Before starting the movie, Trace and Lucy got up on stage and thanked everyone for coming. They tried to get Peter to join them, but he was too busy being what remained of a healthy six-year-old and the last thing he wanted to do was stop scurrying around with his friends and stand in front of a big crowd.

When we had first planned the evening, Lucy's mother, Esther, suggested that we show the 1943 version of *Heaven Can Wait* with Don Ameche and Gene Tierney. I was uncomfortable evoking even a cinematic reference to the afterlife when we were trying to save Peter's life, so I asked if I might watch the film again before showing it. And when I did, it was amply clear that Esther was right. *Heaven Can Wait* is tender and kind, and filled with an innocence that only someone without a heart could miss. In short, it was an Ernst Lubitsch film. Perfect.

Before the feature, the film opened with an eleven minute trade short *Careers in Hotel Management*, leaving the audience with an unexpected appreciation of what "an exciting new career has to offer." More than any other era in film, the "Fifties" has a comic book quality about it for those who didn't live in it and, I sense, relief that it has passed for those who did. People shouted out comments like "You'll never see that again" and, "Get a load of those shiny shoes" as the parade of well-dressed hotel managers offered crisp, efficient service to all their guests. But once the feature started the crowd settled in and was swept away by the ever-delightful Lubitsch's storytelling. If the purpose of the evening was to help save a life, the film was a reminder of all a life can hold.

The audience offered an appreciative round of applause at the end of the movie. That's special. Movies aren't live performances and audiences know this. Even though most film screenings are without the writers, actors, or any production crew in attendance, occasionally audiences are touched and moved to applaud. It's a powerful urge, a way they share their appreciation of the film with each other, and in a very direct way, it is the highest honor they can give to the creators of the film. It was also the moment of realizing why everyone had come, and as soon as the applause ended people quietly rose from their chairs and filed out, relaxed and con-

tent, pleased to have been part of the evening. Amazingly, we raised close to eleven thousand dollars that night, a big part of that coming from Dr. Brewster Patent, the retired physician who had presided over the births of both Lucy Toussaint and her son Peter, and who left a most generous pledge of $5000.

A flurry of activity ensued as the few of us who remained helped tear down the makeshift theater. Lucy stood by holding her young son, who two hours ago had sat on my lap enthralled with the flutter of the projectors throwing the film on the screen before him, oblivious to the appeal for money to chase away his disease. Peter now rested heavy and sleeping against Lucy, held firmly in the way mothers hold their sleeping children with a mysterious strength. Lucy came up to me and said, "You must be hungry. I made food for our crew and you're welcome to join us for dinner at the house. I can't tell you how much we appreciate what you did for us, Jake. I hope you'll come."

An hour later, in Lucy and Trace's home, we sat at a dinner table lit by candles and covered with vases of flowers; the napkins embroidered with violets. The centerpiece was an extraordinary dish topped with shrimp, slices of red pepper, and olives, all arranged in a mosaic over yellow rice. The heady fragrance of saffron filled the air. Wine bottles flanked the dish and in the amber midnight light of the room we sat down to eat.

Sitting beside me at the table was Lucy's sister, Sophie. We'd been introduced at the show earlier, she being the painter of the remarkable stage panels. Sophie tells me she lives in Paris, but has come home to help since Peter is sick. Sophie is one of those people you can't take your eyes away from. Even at the movie I had found myself scanning the room to catch a glimpse of her. Watching her is a little like getting drafted into the tail wind of a fast car that blows by you on the highway. Between enthusiastic sips of wine she tells me,

"I've been back in America for two months. This was a good time for me to get away because I'm on hiatus from my work."

"What kind of work do you do?"

"I'm a circus painter. I paint sets. We're between shows right now. Lucy and Trace are trying to keep things normal, but with Peter so sick they need all the help they can get. Lucy told me about the money you gave them. That was very kind of you."

I explain to Sophie how the money came to me and how I thought Fred

would have approved. After another glass of wine the other voices at the table begin to recede as I listen to Sophie.

"I've been imagining something for that truck of yours today. It may sound nuts, but I see everything as a blank canvas. Can you imagine it with something other than white metal and rivets on it? If you can stay here for a few days, no longer than a week, I can paint it for you. We can pull it into the barn, set up some lights, and have at it. After all you've done for Peter, it would make me happy to do something for you. "

It was one of those moments when the air around you gets thin and your heart starts racing. It was all I could do to look directly at her.

"I could use a little color in my life, Sophie. Have at it!"

"All right, Jake. You won't regret it. Never underestimate what a good painting can do for your life. I have some ideas for designs already, but if you tell me more about your life perhaps I can create something that might better represent this rolling theater of yours. What an idea! A box-on-wheels showing movies around the country. You have something special with that, you know?"

In that expression, Sophie changed my life into a box-on-wheels showing movies around the country!

At the late hour of three-thirty I finally climbed into the back of the truck and slept a deep, nurturing sleep. Dreams came -- full, melodic, and colorful, only to evaporate upon awakening. They were the kind of dreams that, although you can't remember their stories or their details, create a shift in your soul that you feel forever, waking up a different person from when you went to sleep. The theme of tonight's dreams circled around the echoing words, "You have something special in that, you know . . ." I drifted in the satisfying tug between sleep and wakefulness until I heard footsteps on the tailgate, and a knocking at the door finally pierced my dreams. I remembered where I was. The creaky, need-to-be-oiled doors swung open, and Sophie stepped into the van holding two cups of coffee.

"Cream and sugar, yes?" she says handing me my cup.

"Yes, of course." I'm speaking, but still tired.

My memory of that morning is one of comfort. Sophie holds a cup in her hand. Sits in the folding chair beside the bed. She unfolds one of the woolen blankets at the foot of the mattress and drapes her body with the pleats falling to the floor. The steam from her coffee rises through the folds of the blanket, wafting across her face in a moist vapor.

"They're all still asleep inside, Jake. Last night was a big release for everyone. Peter's illness has been wearing them down. They'll be asleep for hours. I was hoping you'd be awake. It didn't matter though; I was going to wake you anyway because if I'm going to paint your truck I need to get to know you better. Not all set painters work this way, but this is my way."

"No problem, it's your work, fire away," I say as I yawn and stretch from my slumber while Sophie notices the sleeping puppies and traces their forms with her fingers.

"Before we lift a brush or stir any paint there's a story meeting. We work hard to invent a world filled with pictures and flavors, and flowers and light and music. We are the only circus in the world that has its own candy. Can you imagine? Every show opens a hidden door into a private world -- acrobatics, animals or clowns. We are *The Circus of the Lost Worlds: Le Cirque Des Mondes Perdus*! Have you ever heard of us? No? Well, that's what we do and we're very popular. There aren't many lost worlds left in our century are there?"

Now Sophie speaks as if she were a Master of Ceremonies, her hand set like a bullhorn against her mouth as she speaks to an imaginary audience.

"You sit there thinking there are no more lost worlds. Yes, you of the modern century, progeny of an age of discovery: no mysteries remaining to be uncovered. But, are you certain? Each night when you sleep you create exotic worlds in your dreams. You fly, you swim beneath oceans, you jump from island to island in an uncertain crimson sea, or you play music resplendent and grand. So you think there are no more worlds? Hah! How mistaken you are. May we have the privilege of showing you?"

Sophie removes the makeshift bullhorn from her mouth and sips on her coffee, shifting beside me, and close enough that I can feel her body and capture the scent of her breathing. She lets out a deep sigh and falls against my side.

"That's who we are, Jake; *The Circus of the Lost Worlds*. Every year, two shows, one old, one new so there is at least one new set to create. The painting is very detailed and requires a lot of research, focused time, and attention. It consumes our lives for months, until the day of the grand premiere. There is always a line stretching around the block. It's not a tent like here, but a large ornate building adorned with iron, art nouveau latticework and high windows, which are covered during performances by thick black curtains. Like everywhere else in Paris, if nothing took place at all, the architecture would be enough.

"An hour before the show begins, the doors open and people scurry inside. No late arrivals; most everyone is in their seats half an hour before the show begins. With fifteen minutes to go, the room goes completely dark and after precisely ninety seconds the first spotlight reveals one of the stage paintings. It's a little hard to imagine, but since you're a film guy, Jake, let me cover your eyes and you can imagine a series of fade-ins and fade-outs connecting one panel to the next."

Sophie breathed warmth onto her hands and placed them over my eyes and spoke.

"Each panel represents one of the chapters in the story. We begin in darkness, Jake, then fade into Rousseau's *Sleeping Gypsy*; you know the lion and the lamb. Fade out/fade in to the basement of a Parisian nightclub where two lovers embrace in secrecy. Fade out/fade in to a cave with bats hanging upside down. Fade out/fade in to a large book unfolded to Sanskrit text. Fade out/fade in to a coral reef underwater with luminescent schools of fish. Fade out/fade in to an erupting volcano with glowing rivers of hot lava running down its slope. Fade out/fade in to a muddy river lined with elephants and hippopotami backs covered with white cattle egrets. Fade out/fade in to a crowd of protesters on the 1914 streets of Moscow." Sophie presses her thumbs, gently massaging my temples, while continuing to cover my eyes. "Stay with me, Jake. Fade out/fade in to women washing garments on the banks of the Nile River. Fade out/fade in to the strong, clay-covered but feminine hands of Camille Claudel sculpting two large feet. Fade out/fade in to three enormous weight lifters in a gym with gargantuan balls of iron thrust over their heads. Fade out/fade in to a migrating herd of bison in the great western plains of America. Fade out/fade in to salmon seen swimming up the face of a waterfall. Fade out/fade in to streaming beneath icebergs floating off the coast of Antarctica." Sophie releases her hands at last, and she leans her back against mine and we speak while seated against each other. "Our director, Fabian Sabatier, reminds us 'The show starts before the show begins.' His family once created spectacles for all the royal houses in Europe. He's right, Jake. Before anyone appears on the stage the audience has a story embedded in their mind and then the show commences. You can do that in Paris. France is a place where you can tell stories without words. Silence and color are powerful storytellers."

"You are the powerful storyteller, Sophie. How do you do that?"

"Do what?"

"How do you bring so much to life? Gosh, I can barely mumble my name when asked, but you can evoke the Serengeti plains."

Then, in what was a rare and freakish act for me, I embraced Sophie and kissed her.

In the movies, forced kisses draw slaps or submission, and it's that moment of unknowing that holds the audience. Sophie neither slapped nor submitted, but she did say in a voice reminiscent of a sultry Bette Davis, "My sister said I would like you. I'll tell you what, how about you slow that down and we can do some more of it?"

"Mademoiselle, Sophie, it will be a pleasure."

Three hours later, before we return to the house I ask Sophie, "How does one become a circus painter?"

"It sounds odd, Jake, but it was simple for me. I pursued what I wanted to be. I wanted to live in Paris, knew I was a painter, and wanted to work where life would be free from the mundane. So I pursued what I wanted."

"But how does one become a circus painter, Sophie?"

"By painting for a circus, of course!" said Sophie and she kissed her fingers, placed them on my lips, then pressed and held them against my forehead.

A few minutes later we dash from the truck through the continuing rain to the house where people are sitting around the table drinking coffee, eating French toast and bacon. Sophie runs her finger across the back of my hand as we take our seats. I'm embarrassed when Lucy sees her sister's affection. Lucy stands behind us and pours another cup of coffee, then she smiles and asks,

"And what have you two been talking about?"

"French circuses," answers Sophie.

# CHAPTER 4

# Illusion And
# The Physics Of Fire

In Which we watch a painter work, learn of scrim, say good-bye to
a friend, remember one fire and forget about another.

Too many questions; there were too many questions coming from Sophie as we prepared Fred's truck, my truck now, for its overhaul. Maybe the new paint job would make it seem more like mine.

"It's your world we're painting here, Jake. You need to give me a little
inspiration."

"Inspiration isn't my strong point, Sophie."

"Right, kissy boy! How about digging deep and giving me something,
anything? Any idea can turn out to be a good launching point. A few years
ago we did a show about Simone de Beauvoir and Jean Paul Sartre: as I
said, our circus is different than most. Our producer gave us books to read
by both writers, to get inspiration. It wasn't working; it's not easy material
you know. But then one day I latched onto the whole *Being and Nothingness*
thing and thought I might be able to translate that into paintings. Opposing symbols work well in paintings. One side of the stage became "Being"
and the other was "Nothingness." I angled two massive walls to face each
other like wings of an open book and painted vibrant red on the "Being"
side. That contrasted with a massive wall of white on the "Nothingness"
side. François didn't like it -- his concept of "Nothingness" was black and

he thought that would work better with the performers' costumes. I argued that black is mysterious and intriguing so that it does not convey nothing-ness, whereas white is boring, and even though it holds anticipation, it is true nothingness. It's the opposite of color theory if you think about it, so please don't think about it. That conversation was one of the occasions where I appreciated being in France. Can you imagine spending so much time anywhere else in the world discussing this?"

"How did it turn out?"

"Though he thought it was strange, if you must persist, François yields to you:  in the end we worked with the costumer to dress the performers for white."

"Right now I feel like I'm the white stage and you're the color . . ."

Sophie interrupted, "But you're not, Jake. Most people don't drive around in trucks showing movies to save my nephew's life."

"Most people would if they had the chance."

Then Sophie erupted like a thunderbolt that shakes the windows of your house with a little sarcasm, a little ridicule, and a lot of persuasion.

"Jake, when are you going to get that you're not like every one else? Okay, maybe you're a bit slow on the uptake. I mean, how cold was that coffee going to get before you made a move on me? But listen, you have to give me something to work with." Then she paused and the air settled and we sat down leaning comfortably against each other's backs the way we had the morning after the benefit for Peter. We sat that way for a few minutes before I apologized.

"I guess I'm not much help."

"No, you're doing fine, Jake, but you still haven't told me what this is all about. What are you about? Where are you from? What is your pur-pose in life? Where do you want to live? What started you writing? And if you can't answer that, tell me about your parents. What were you like as a child? What do you want people to think when they see the truck roll by?"

It continued that way for the three days we spent sanding away at the truck's enamel. With each question the truck changed, shedding its white surface, revealing a beckoning luster amidst the sparks grinding wheels made against metallic rivets to form a perfect canvas for a circus painter. On the fifth morning Sophie said, "I need to be back in Paris next week, Jake. There's a good break in the weather, enough to lay some paint, so we'll have to go with what we have so far." Then she began to paint. Sophie outlined a massive theater on the side panels -- the view of a grand old theater you'd get if you sat in the middle of the first balcony. There was a great stage flanked by billowed curtains, and the backs of orchestra seats with tassels hanging in braided strands:  Renaissance splendor -- opulence, in a word.

"Theaters are the world of fantasy, Jake. They should never be places of reality. Nothing is more disappointing than walking into a theater and having reality thrown in your face. Can you imagine paying for reality?"

By the end of that day the outline was complete. The next morning Sophie began to add color and the truck came alive -- the theater vibrant, the texture of the velvets on the curtains, the gold braided cord dangling, the warm luminescence of a theater lit by candles.

"Of course, there was no electricity in this era," Sophie said as she painted light into the candelabras on the theater walls and lit the hall with their amber light, little pulses of wax incandescence. She painted the heads of people in their seats, the backs of their heads, their hats, their messily parted hair, upturned collars, feathers on the women's hats and extended fingers of children's hands. Stiff postures, bored postures, some sleeping, some knowing the music, all captured in the tilt of a head, a hand, a slouch. It is the view of a theater seen only from above and behind. As a final element, adding a stark and anachronistic element to this pre-modern world, Sophie filled the stage with a regal movie screen.

Last of all, she created the finishing touch of magic. Hour after hour she dappled gray paint across the entire stage until the entire stage faded deep into the flanks of the crimson curtains, behind an opaque screen.

"That's the scrim. Scrim is like being invited into someone's house. You arrive at the door, they take your coat, you have a drink placed in your hand and you're starting to talk and feel relaxed -- then surprise, they open a bigger door and usher you into the real party which is twice as magnificent as the one you're already in. So for the rest of the evening, you never quite trust that it may not happen again, that another world may be transformed into something even more vivid. That's scrim. When the scrim lifts you are both amazed and held in suspension:  clarity and uncertainty. We use it for dream scenes all the time. Has that woo-woo feel to it."

Between painting sessions, we'd head inside to get away from the cold. Trace and Lucy had needed to take Peter to Seattle for some tests so the

house was empty. I started a fire in the woodstove and we stood beside it to warm up.

"Good fire, Jake. I can never get one going."

Hearing that made me think of the last full conversation I had with Fred, and I told Sophie about it.

It had been cold that morning, one of those November days when you understand the Earth is moving away from the sun. Arriving early to Fred's house, I didn't see any smoke coming from the chimney. It was getting harder and harder for Fred to haul wood and keep the house warm so I wheel-barrowed a couple of loads of wood onto the porch. I opened the door and entered the house, which was cool and dank. I heard snoring coming from the open bedroom door and I wanted him to awaken to a warm home, so I started a fire in the stove and went into the kitchen to make some coffee. As the smell of the coffee started to fill the house, Fred hobbled out of his bedroom smiling at the blast of heat coming from the woodstove. Despite his age and frailty, he was still an imposing man filling the doorway between the two rooms.

"You make a good fire, Jake. Not everyone does, you know."

Spying the coffee pot on the stove, he moved nearer, pouring a cup of coffee while turning his back to warm his body in the column of heat coming from the box.

"You're one of the few who understands the flow of fire."

Fred had a lot of lectures on things, and "The Flow of Fire" was a notorious one. Anyone who entered Fred's world eventually received it, and Fred's lectures were like prayers; the more they were repeated the deeper they became. As his failing body absorbed the heat from the burning logs, yielding the energy of so many sunny summer days, he went on.

"Why is it so hard to understand that fire is an upward flow of heat. Heat is like water flowing over rocks, but upward? How many people stack wood into a stove in pretty little constructions like in some nursery book illustration? That's their image of how a fire is supposed to look, like a little kid's drawing of a tree? They stand there watching their fires go out, never understanding why their pretty little pyramid doesn't ignite. It's simple science, Jake. Three faces in opposition: fuel, temperature, and oxygen. Fire! The wood is the fuel, the spark from the match is the temperature, and the oxygen comes from the air. But, here is the secret: you have to let those three faces of wood talk to each other. That's the key. They start to burn, start to release their energy together, all at once, and the whole thing starts burning hotter and hotter. But no, people will make that pyramid even though it never yields fire. Then they mess with it, stuffing papers on top, stirring it, as if all of a sudden the laws of physics are going to shift and heat will settle and gravity will repel.

"Not everybody sees things the way you do, Fred."

But Fred never suffered ignorance very well.

"Jake, how can a man do something over and over and over again and continue to believe his actions are correct when the outcome is a failure? Simple or not simple, you'd think any sonofabitch would figure it out. "Well, there won't be any problems torching off this place when I'm gone. Plenty of fuel here." Then he got rolling, pleased with himself, laughing a little and in part, I'm sure, because the coffee kicked in. "It's like hull speed, Jake. You know, boats. All boats have an optimal speed based on their shape. That speed is the most efficient use of energy to propel that boat, and though you can make it go faster, it takes an awful lot of energy to do so. It's all about flow, Jake; fire, boats, water, or life, Jake; all the same principle. Get away from the flow and it takes a lot of energy to make things happen. It takes more energy to waste a life than to do something good with one!" Then he sat down and I'm not sure he said anything for the rest of the day. A few months later the last remaining Tolliver, except me, was dead. Good-bye Fred.

At the end of the story Sophie held my hand. There wasn't a lot that needed saying.

Three days of outlining, painting, and dotting scrim yielded two exactly identical images on the sides of Fred's truck. To call it Fred's truck is unfair, for now it had been transformed into two theaters, two enchanted worlds for all to see as it passed by on the road.

When those were complete, Sophie said, "Now for the back. It's still not clear how you're going to do whatever you're going to do with this truck, but you may want to consider putting some kind of information on the sides in case they want to hire you. People are strange that way, they don't trust images, and so they'll need words for clarification. At least a telephone number, an address, or something that explains why some nut is driving a massive gypsy wagon down the road." Sophie laughed as she said this and threw her arms around me in a big bear hug.

So, as you see, I had very little to do with the creation of my life's work.

I owe it completely to the creativity and vision of others. A circus painter with lovely green eyes conceived of the work of *The Lost Sons Of Zhitomir Rolling Film Society*. The words she painted read:

# LOST SONS OF ZHITOMIR
## ROLLING FILM SOCIETY
*Lighting the world one film at a time.*

FOR HIRE: ALL OCCASIONS, ANY LOCATION

The morning Sophie left for the airport, I hopped into my new skin and headed back to Larch. The past week had been timeless, but now there was something eating at me, something I knew I was supposed to be part of but I couldn't remember what. Reaching under the driver's seat to retrieve my keys, there was an envelope waiting for me from Sophie.

*Dear Jake,*

*I know you're on to something special. You don't believe it yet but you're every bit the circus painter I am, you just don't use the same brushes. You need to spend some time sitting and watching people come and go at a video store. Watch their faces, their postures, how they browse and dance around the Light - the promises contained in the little boxes and discs. Watch them leave holding the promise of contentment in their hands, their story for the evening. Those are powerful little boxes, but they pale in strength when compared with the experience of sitting with others in a theater and seeing the Light dance with larger-than-life-characters. Larger-than-life is a literal saying: the images _are_ larger than people in real life, but the meaning is deeper now. Remember, Jake: be inspired when you play with things that are larger-than-life."*

*A bientot, j' èspere Sophie*

Sometimes the world is filled with lots of trick questions such as: "Can you tell us about yourself?" But then there are those few occasions when the time is right and your story wells up as if some single iridescent thread were stitching it all together. I knew it was all being stitched together, but I wasn't sure how. I've often wondered whether I should have gone after Sophie instead of helping her fly away, but it wasn't shyness that stopped me. Sophie came into my life for a reason but it wasn't that she was meant to be my companion in life. All I thought of was what she said that night, "That's who we are Jake, The Circus of the Lost Worlds."

As I entered Larch an hour later, I saw a plume of smoke in the distance and at once knew what had been gnawing at me. I'd completely forgotten about the fire department burning Fred's house! By the time I drove to it, the flames were dancing red and hot and feeding on a hundred years of Tolliver history.  First-hand, a dozen eager trainees learned Fred's lessons about fire. My heart burned as well with a strange pain until all was reduced to a smoldering pile of ash and embers.

Harley Johnson, the fire chief, came over to me, and all he said was, "Jake, what the hell have you gone and done to that truck?"

My new life had begun.

I know you must be curious how I picked up and left my home. There are a lot of things that happened, and I wish I could say it all happened smoothly and simply, that I tied up all the loose ends and gracefully said goodbye, but it didn't happen that way. Even when you're born with a wanderer's gene, sometimes the wind catches you.

If there was any prophesy that a longer voyage was beginning, it was by Clara. The day I left Larch, I stopped into *The Sonnet* to check in with her, say goodbye, but with no hint of finality. Clara was in the back sorting through a collection of old novels given to her by the husband of a former colleague of hers who had died. Stopping for a few minutes to chat, Clara told me to stay in touch, and asked for Julian's address so she could be sure to find me. I thought that was odd, but she insisted, saying you never know what lies ahead. Then, she suggested I do another thing which seemed odd: she told me I should pick some flowers to place on my mother's grave, and she made me promise I wouldn't leave town until I did. Once I made the promise, Clara gave me a warm hug and said; "I knew you weren't going to sit on a shelf like these books for the rest of your life."

Going to my mother's grave had always been sad and confusing to me. Ever since she died I've never exactly known  what I feel when I visit her grave. Even the few memories I had of her had grown and changed into things I was uncertain about. Entering the small section of the Larch Common Cemetery occupied by all the Tollivers, I soon came face to face with the stones marking the lives and deaths of Samuel Sr. and Rose Tolliver, my great-grandparents; Samuel Jr. and Ariella, my grandparents, and finally Eva Marie, my mother. One thing for certain about Tollivers, with the exception of Fred, is we don't seem to live very long. Not that we try to die young, after all, my great-grandfather was lynched, my great-grandmother died of the flu, my grandparents died from meningitis, and my mother died of sadness. There's a little dose of bad luck accounting for our short lives, but Fred had told me not to think about all of that. One thing Fred believed in was personal destiny and he had repeatedly told me that no Tolliver had ever spent a minute complaining about their lot in life. "You get what you get, Jake, so don't screw it up." That said, by all accounts there wasn't a single thing any Tolliver had ever done to hurt anyone, and yet, they never seemed to live very long. Once again, I was a little confused, but I placed the first purple lilacs of spring on her barely weathered tombstone and sat on the cool earth for almost an hour before leaving on a road trip that would last far longer than I ever could have imagined.

CHAPTER 5

# The Sleeping Mother

In Which we learn of Eric and his sleeping mother and the techniques of reel changes.

I adopted Eric, or more honestly he adopted me, soon after I departed Larch. I was staying in his hometown of Veneta, Oregon, doing a few shows for a collective of organic farmers raising money to buy a tractor. It was the second of three midweek shows and since it was the first time I'd shown films in a horse arena, I had decided to take pictures of the set-up. I thought the truck and the screen looked interesting flanked by a matched pair of Belgian draft horses happily eating hay. Needless to say, those kinds of things aren't seen in regular theaters. The first night, we had to shut the film off for a few minutes when a cloud of bats flew across the screen as Bette Davis was coming down the steps to her party in *All About Eve.*

As I was taking the photos, a young kid comes into the horse arena with a camcorder on a tripod and says hello from across the barn. He carefully sets up the camcorder and stands staring, with his arms hanging from a loose-fitting blue jean jacket. With his long red hair hanging over his shoulders he could be a redheaded Jesus Christ. When he finally turned, the back of the jacket revealed a large embroidered patch that read "I'm Looking At You!" He then walked over to me and when I asked him what he was doing with the camcorder, he took a card out of his breast pocket and handed it to me.

He tells me that he's studying film at the local community college and taking a few shots of the barn for a project he's working on.

"Arenas are tough," he says, "bad light, especially a bad balance between natural and artificial light. The camera goes crazy trying to figure it out and you can't add any light when the horses are around cause they get spooked."

I'm intrigued by his competence.

"How do you solve it?"

He laughs with a hint of irony.

"Mainly, I take a lot of close-ups of the riders and their horses, and then an action shot or two. People love to see themselves, and they love to see their horses, so I deal with it." Then he adds, "You're the film guy with that incredible truck, right? I was here last night. Great show." He stares out at the arena again and then says, "I was thinking last night you might want me to do a piece on your scene. The truck's a natural. What an amazing rig! Somebody told me you actually live in it. That's awesome."

I ask him what he charges.

"I get ten dollars an hour plus twenty flat for any editing and five dollars for the tape. If that's too much I can do it cheaper." I bust out laughing and assure him the price is fair and I'd be happy if he'd do a video about the shows. I don't think he expected me to go for it and when I do, a melt-your-soul smile comes from him and he reaches out his hand and says, "My name is Eric Mariette. I'm going to be a filmmaker." I shake his hand and say, "Jake Spinner, I show movies." Then Eric adds as if to make things clear: "The video stuff, the horse shows and weddings; that's how I make money, but I'm serious about making films."

Eric tells me he actually has finished a six-minute short which he'd like to show me.

"Is it good?"

"I think so, but you can see for yourself."

"No, I'll take your word for it. I'll show it tonight before the feature."

"Sweet!"

Eric asks how long I'll be around for him to do the piece. When I tell him only a few more days, he asks me how he can get it to me and I tell him he can send it care of Julian, whose address I scribble on another one of his cards for him. When he sees the name written down he looks confused.

"Julian Spinner is your uncle?"

"That's right."

"This is freaking me," he says. "I've been reading him for years." Then he adds what I will learn is Eric's trademark saying, "Sweet!" With one last afterthought he asks, "Where are you headed after this?" It's unusual for me to know where I'm headed next, but it so happens I'm doing a benefit in two weeks in Wenatchee and I tell him so.

I kept my word and showed his film that night.

It's a simple piece of his mother sleeping, and her awakening in morning light. The film is done in real time and opens with diffuse light coming through a window that slowly illuminates her tranquil face.

During the opening shot, Eric says to me, "I modeled that after Rodin's sculpture, Le Sommeil. I love his stuff. I'd like to do a series of shorts based on his work." From her face he slowly pans around the walls to show little things in it; close-ups of a dresser and a few of the photos on it -- one of a mother turned to the side and kneeling by the smiling face of her toddler son. Then he slowly pulls closer to the figure of the sleeping woman on the bed, and closer yet. What starts in gray and shadow gradually yields to color and the details of his mother's face. As the sunlight finally breaks across the room you see she has a large wine-stain birthmark covering a portion of her beautiful face.

Eric elbows me in the side and whispers, "I tried to get subject, context, and tension all into the opening shots, but I think I may have missed a little."

Most of the crowd that night didn't get any of those because they were busy settling in, digging for snacks, milling around outside swapping baskets of produce, or smoking cigarettes while waiting for the feature to start. However, the few who paid attention were held in the enchanting way only moving pictures can hold you. It was also the first time Eric had seen the film on something larger than a television screen and he was justly proud of himself.

"That's how I planned those extreme close-ups; they can be very affecting when they're enlarged." Then, as an afterthought he says, "I can babysit the projectors for a reel or two if you want to sit and watch the movie." Seeing my obvious apprehension, he says, "Don't worry, I ran these things for years in school." Then he winks and asks, "Are the reel breaks clean?" I liked Eric from the start.

Two weeks later I'm in Wenatchee having dinner in a restaurant two hours before a show when in walks Eric with a big smile on his face. I'm not surprised because he's got a look on his face I've seen before. I get it from young writers, or painters, or from film students who have the passion that lets them see romance where others see reality. Eric reminds me of the scene in *Field Of Dreams* when the vision -driven Ray seeks out his reluctant idol, Terence Mann, only to have Mann fend him off with bug spray. Eric hands me the tape and says, "I'll wave the fee if you let me tag along for a few weeks?"

The problem with youthful energy is that it often overwhelms aged caution, so if I didn't say it in words, I know my look said, "I'm a guy who rolls around the country showing movies."

"Jake, I'm not looking for a father. I want to learn about movies. I'm not exactly tied down at the moment. My parents pre-empted me, they blew out of the nest before I could. They've been teaching in Asia the past three years. They left a year after I got out of high school. And my girlfriend -- she's away at college and things are a little loose there, so why not let me tag along for a few weeks and see how it goes?" Then he points outside to his own little Toyota van.

"Look, I can cook and sleep in it. I won't be any bother to you. I want to see the movies and learn a few things about how audiences react. I'm tired of sitting at home. I'll even start calling the Toyota the Noti if you want."

"Why the Noti?"

"That's where my grandparents came from."

I never stood a chance.

There's one more thing worth telling about that first show with Eric. Standing watch over the projectors, there is a confounding buzz coming from the speakers and it's bugging me, but no one else can hear it because they're into the film. The buzz is getting to me because I know there's a quiet scene coming and I don't want them to notice it. I want to check the power cords, thinking the polarity is off, but I can't do that until after the reel switch. It's driving me nuts. I ask Eric if he can run out to Zhitomir and bring a replacement cord in case that's the problem.

The show is for a man who raises money for an orphanage in Romania. He's a sweet guy who sells RVs for a living. He doesn't know the first thing about films or fund-raisers, but his heart is in the right place. After a customer of his saw Zhitomir on the road a few months ago, he called me. When I first spoke to him he said he wanted to show *The Great Escape*, because he was a big Steve McQueen fan, but I told him it was a little too much of a guy movie and we'd lose money for the orphanage if we did. So instead, we've got *Some Like It Hot* and the crowd loves it. Some films work, some don't. Occasionally, you watch a film that changes your life, transforms your outlook, shoots you into another orbit, makes you change your look or your hair, makes you leave home or fall in love. Years later you try to return to that special space you've held in your heart for all those years. Which can be dangerous. You may walk away disappointed, or worse. You may have a film that has reached deep inside of you, but it may not happen the same way when you watch it again, and worse it may not have the same effect on others. You don't show one of those when you're raising money for an orphanage in Romania. When you need something reliable, go with something from the American Film Institute's Top 100.

Looking at the audience tonight, I hope someone is feeling something good enough for them to give a lot of cash to the orphanage. The buzz is getting worse and I'm wondering what's taking Eric so long with the cord. By the time he gets back with it the reel change is over and fortunately the buzz is gone. I make a note to check the projector in the morning.

It wasn't until a few weeks later that I was in Zhitomir and turned on the VCR to preview a video copy of some film Julian suggested about the Turkish-Armenian war. There was another video already in the VCR and when I turned it on to see what it was, the words "A Glimpse of Jake" appeared. An establishing shot captures my profile against an illuminated screen as I stand working the projectors at the evening for the orphanage fund-raiser. The next shot frames one of Zhitomir's theater side panels and then cuts to the inside and pans the cabinet holding my film archive can by can, stopping on each title. I believe there are 128. It's a long pan. From there, in one constant shot, it shows the orderly cables, screen hooks, pro-jector case, and then rests there before pulling back to show my incongru-ous bed fitted in amidst this little film diorama. He zooms to an extreme close up of a note stuck to the cork board on the wall beside my pillow, an old post-it note with wrinkled edges, no stick remaining, attached with a tack, holding the words Physical, Spiritual, Creative, Service, Humor, Discipline, Sacrifice, Joy. The next shot is from the lying position on the bed, focused on the ceiling above the eyes where I look before falling asleep each night looking up through the skylight on top of the box. Next he pulls close to an embroidered cloth in a wooden frame that my mother did years ago and which is screwed into the wall. Then he dissolves and fades into a black-and-white photo of my parents standing together at a train station beneath a sign that reads Budapest, hand scribbled beneath the real one in Hungarian. Then, he ends with a few cut-in shots of dirty clothes thrown into the corner, my kitchen -- some silverware, two cups, a few plates, and the portable shower that I use when I can't find a public one. He didn't mean to do so, but it leaves me a little embarrassed at my paltry domestic life.  That's all there is. I rewind the tape and later hand it to Eric who is surprised and embarrassed.

"Oops, you have it? I've been wondering where it went. I hope you don't mind, Jake. It's not a film, more a sketch. Your whole world is so odd and interesting."

I'm not upset. I see Eric wants to ask me something but is holding back. I gesture for him to speak and he does. "Jake, a few weeks ago you asked me about being missed by my parents or girlfriend. Don't you ever miss anyone or need someone else in your life?"

Insincerity has never touched Eric's lips and if I had an answer to his questions I would have given it. Instead, I reach into my shelf and draw out Who The Devil Made It, the fine collection of interviews Peter Bogdonov-ich did with some of the most accomplished filmmakers of all time. I have a page marked in the interview with George Cukor where he talks about clothes being a wonderful invention not to be removed so easily. I read the passage to Eric.

"I'm not sure I get it, Jake. Cukor is talking about on-screen nudity."

"It's a little deeper than that, Eric."

"How's it deeper, Jake?"

"Cukor was talking about the difficulty in revealing yourself. You asked me if I ever miss anyone or need someone else in my life . . ."

"You know what I mean, Jake, living like a nomad. Don't you miss people? I mean, come on Jake, I may be younger than you but I know you need a woman in your life to take the edge off."

It's hard learning lessons from a twenty-year-old, but, Eric has the gift of speaking his mind and he has nailed me.

"Sure, I miss people, and I'd like to have a woman in my life, but it's never been my strong suit. You're a lot different than I was, Eric. You're in motion and attacking life with all you've got. I wasn't like that. It took me half a life to set my life in any sort of motion and I enjoy what I have now. I know there's more in me but right now I enjoy rolling around taking it all in. I miss my Uncle Fred, and even though I never met my father, I miss him. With my mother, it's different, because, though she died when I was young, I have warm memories of her even if many are tainted with sadness."

"All the more reason to have a woman in your life. Sadness overcome is sadness no more. Right?"

Eric stops and we sit in silence for a moment. Words mean nothing to Eric so much as their tone. As he exhales, his eyes grow bright and his irrepressible curiosity takes over.

"Jake, how did they die?"

"The odd thing, Eric, is I'm not entirely sure."

"Man, that must be weird. What's that all about?"

"All I know is that my mother died of sadness and my father died while he was in the army. I've never known more than that."

Then, perhaps remembering what started this conversation in the first place, Eric says to me, "I'm sorry about the film. I should stay out of your private life."

"No, Eric, you don't need to apologize to me. I wish I could tell you more. I wish I knew more about all the things that sit inside of me that I never understand. I'd give anything to have a little of your spark and spontaneity but I'm not that way. Please, please don't take it personally."

"Oh, man, Jake, I don't mean to trample on your space. It's that I get so eager sometimes. I want to do what you've done:  chuck it all and head out into the world. I want to do what I'm supposed to do but I'm not sure how. I want to make movies, Jake; I want to make *real* movies, like the ones we show. I don't know how to make real movies.

"I think you do, Eric. You're already doing it."

"No, Jake, when we show these films everything stops. Nothing happens but the movie. The audience is in a trance. They're floating. Jake, they float for hours. I want to know how to make a perfect movie. How do you do it?"

"Eric, I once asked a circus painter friend of mine how one becomes a circus painter, and she said, 'One paints for a circus.'"

"Great, now I've got to think about that deeper meaning all night. Was she hot?"

"Who?"

"The circus painter. Was she hot?"

Eric can pull something out of you, even more so when he has a camera in his hands, but this time it's the two of us, no camera, no record for history.

"Well, movie man, was she hot?"

"Totally hot, Eric. Hotter than you could ever imagine."

Then he raised his hand with a high five, slapped mine, and offered his patented two-syllable, "Swee-eet!"

Eric goes about his life as he sees fit. Sometimes he stays around for a while, other times he takes off with a girlfriend and I won't see him for months. If he's short of money he finds a horse show job or a wedding. It amazes me that he can get these jobs when he wants to, but he does. Half the time he has more money than I do, but money doesn't mean a lot to him. A few times I've seen him reach into his pocket and pull out a crumpled twenty-dollar bill or two he's forgotten about. I never know when something or someone else may capture him for good. He's been working on a full-length documentary for the last year since he got his 16mm Bolex, and he carries his camera with him everywhere. He even sleeps with it next to his bed, loaded and ready to go. As Eric would say, "It's sweet." Eric will make the perfect movie someday.

---

## Reel Changes and Personal Projections, by A.L. Janus

From the *Tattered Edge*, Volume 6 # 4.

I run two 16mm projectors at shows. Today, the films are all wound onto reels of about forty minutes so a typical 120-minute film has two reel changes. Most films are plotted along a theatrical three act structure, so if the film company is careful, the reel changes come at natural stopping points, like closing theatrical curtains. Because those are large shifts in the viewer's attention, even if the projectionist isn't perfect it won't matter. Act changes are like deep exhales, they let you pause and recharge before gearing up for some more action without disorienting the audience. The best thing to do is to preview your films and identify the images leading up to the reel change and write those down. The real problem is this -- some movies are so good that even the experienced projectionist can get swept away and forget to be ready for the change.

Every show is different, but whether projecting from a booth, a table, or a countertop, the ritual is the same to create a smoother and more professional show. First, I clean the sound drum with a cotton swab dipped in alcohol. Sound is the invisible partner of all films, and two seconds to clean the drum so the sound is the best it can be is vital. Next, I clean the lens with lens paper, both outside and inside. The constant movement of the machine and the changes in humidity, and accumulation of dust all have a way of invading the lens housing. You don't want your audience to feel like they've spent the evening swimming through skimmed milk. Also, when I clean the lens I blow a little canned air around the housing in case a fly has died inside. Most of us have seen the dead fly on the movie screen and it makes it hard to concentrate on the action. Fifteen seconds to clean the lens and operate the focus mechanism eliminates skimmed milk and dancing flies. Next, I take out my handy can of compressed lubricant to blow the film tracks and ratchet spools. When you thread film into a projector, whether automatic ones where all the tensions are set, or hand threads, which are better but more finicky, you have to have a slight loop of film in the path. That loop acts as a spring for the film making its way through the projection path and keeps the tension equalized. It's less technical than it sounds. But if you've ever sat in a film when the film starts to flutter; that's from that loop not being right.

The most important thing inside a projector is the channel guiding the film past the illuminated lens. Frame by frame the light shines through the film; there can be little grooves in the side of this flat area where dust and hair, brittle film fragments, or popcorn hulls can settle. I take the time to clean this pathway. Dancing hairs or dancing flies can kill a show. Some people tell me they love it when the hair does its dance -- it reminds them that things aren't perfect -- but it bugs me to think that cinematographers spend all that time getting the lighting perfect and then have a jitterbugging hair destroy their work. Two or three seconds of compressed gas takes care of that.

The last projector routine is to make sure there's an extra bulb on hand for each projector. Five minutes of attention and all is well. Once I've secured the projectors, I make sure the film reels are lined up in order. That's easy with three reels because all we have to do is cue up the first two, then replace reel one with reel three during the change. Simple. If it's a long film, how-ever, and there are four reels, that's two changes. It's not complicated, unless you mistake reel four for reel three. The audience will not only be confused, but they'll get annoyed when you have to stop the film and reset the reels. I call that cinematic aphasia; something a little preparation avoids.

The upper right hand corner of most films has a secret code burned into it. Small white marks, called cigarette burns because that's what they are, mark the passage of segments of film. Five seconds before the reel runs out you get a large white burn mark to alert you, followed by a second mark which tells you to start the other reel. If you see these marks and hit your switches, the audience will never know you made the change. Audiences become deeply involved in the story, so even if you miss a little, it's okay. But if you take too long, the illusion, the magic, the immersion in the story is gone. A person can do reel changes alone, but it's better to have an extra pair of hands around.

If the show is in a community center, or a church, or some other place where they don't have a house sound system, the last thing I do is walk around with a big roll of duct tape and fasten everything down. Boots, chil-dren's hands, dog leashes, wheelchairs, canes, I imagine every possible way a cord can be dislodged, and try to secure it. Cords are the bane of all theater. I met a rock and roll soundman on tour with The Dave Matthew's Band, who told me, "Tape is cheap. Use a lot of it."

Watching films over projectors is different than watching from the audi-ence. One ear is tuned to the pleasant chatter of the film gliding around the gears and rollers that make up the projector. The other ear is tuned to the sound in the viewing hall, and when you love a movie, you listen to the reac-tion from the audience. You can tell by silences and laughter and coughing how deeply engaged the audience is. There's no fooling an audience. If they start coughing early, you know it's going to be a long night.

Every projection is nerve-wracking, especially with older prints which may have poor sound, worn-out thread tracks, and often washed-out im-ages. Sitting above the projectors, I adjust the sound or the focus, hopefully without anyone noticing anything before the story grabs them. If you ever walk away from the projectors you're asking for trouble because the lenses can change as the projector heats up and entire segments can go out of focus. It's good to know that once the audience is engaged in the story there isn't so much of a need to change anything and it's best to avoid changing the sound or focus too much. But I'm never calm until the last reel is safely running through the projector and I know the screening is unlikely to be interrupted. Attention to the little things is what lets it all go without a hitch. I'm not there to watch the movie. My job is to watch the audience watch the movie. When the house lights come up and audience members have that dream-like gaze on their faces, then I know I've done my job.

C H A P T E R   6

# Anchovies, Andy Warhol, Alien Barter, And Cowboys

**In Which** we discover the life of the Fritz Lang Café, receive a general delivery package from Julian, learn of Andy Warhol and Lumen Desire, and spend an evening with a man who wears an extraordinary set of boots.

A hand-painted sign above the outside facade of the Fritz Lang Café shows a movie projector casting its images onto a screen. The images are of a fleet of anchovy boats heading to sea and the wooden plank sign is weather-worn from years of salt-laden Pacific air.

Inside, the Fritz Lang is redolent with the fading smell of anchovy as if the stolid rustic beams, impregnated with decades of the once numerous fish, are breathing. Each time the café's doors open, a gust of cold ocean air carries the plaintive barking of scores of sea lions hauled out on the rocks below. The walls of the Fritz Lang are adorned with film studio black-and-white photos pinned to draped fishnets and floats. The café's eight tables are surrounded by canvas director's stools bearing the names Lang, Fellini, Hitchcock, Bergman, Preminger, Hawks, Aldrich, and Capra on their backs. The mixed motif reflects its owner's two obsessions -- as he likes to call them -- fish and films. The cinematic side is further represented by a collection of movie posters and ticket stubs mounted on posterboard and preserved in glass cases, as if he had started forming the narrative of his life at a very young age and now, befitting a prideful small-business owner with enough money to preserve things, has done that:  created a thematic

attempt to preserve and elevate his life of attending movies. The theater
names on the old stubs read like a list of revival-house dinosaurs; Lido,
Orpheum, Paradise, Cinematique, Waverly, Grammercy, Guild, and be-
neath are handwritten names of the theater's homes: Seattle, San Francisco,
Portland, Los Angeles, Anchorage, New York, Chicago. The actual original
Chuck-a-Luck wheel (from *Rancho Notorious,* a Lang film with Marlene
Dietrich) sits on a small podium, beneath it a sign declaring its origins.
There's a signed picture of Spencer Tracy from *Fury* as his character, Joe
Wheeler, stares out from the damning fire holding him captive. The coffee
cups are promotional mugs with pictures of Marilyn Monroe, Robert Ryan,
and Barbara Stanwyck on them. The chalkboard coffee menu continues the
theme in its specialties:

*The Western Actor: Straight shot of espresso.*
*The Peter Lorre: Single shot of espresso with cardamom liqueur. Served*
*on foggy nights.*
*The Anchovy Net: House coffee with two sugars.*
*The Barbara Stanwyck: Twelve ounces of fresh, hot, black coffee.*
*One free refill.*
*The Marlene Dietrich: Two shots of espresso, nutmeg, and scalding water.*
*The Fury: Four shots of espresso and a dash of Jalapeño sugar. Beware!*
*The Metropolis: Three shots of espresso infused with anisette and*
*mysterious spices.*
*The Chuck-a-Luck: Whatever we want to give you. Always hot,*
*sometimes fresh.*

A double set of wide wooden doors separates the modest café from the
movie lounge where the Fritz, as its regular patrons know it, offers a film
program every third weekend between September and May. Once opened,
the doors reveal a large room about sixty feet long by thirty feet wide with a
stage and screen set up behind a deep blue curtain. The room is heated by a
big woodstove in the back. There's a small sign that reads: Free Coffee For
Fire Wood. But the best part of the screening lounge is its fabulous collection of worn, if not tattered, vintage couches and comfortable chairs which
make watching a movie a pleasure.

The Fritz Lang Café sits across the street from a rock cliff on the Pacific
Ocean. The redwood planked building, once the packed fish warehouse for
the anchovies that were the lifeblood of the town, is owned by Patrick and

Lydia Dugan, she the former Lydia Valderama. I met Patrick nine years ago when he was 19 and on his way to Alaska for one last season of crab fishing, after which he planned to convert wages from "the world's most dangerous profession" into film school tuition. He had heard of my Larch film showings in a chance conversation with Julian while attending a workshop for aspiring filmmakers. Hearing Patrick's plans, Julian told him to look me up since he'd be close to Larch. I later learned from Patrick that during the same workshop a slightly inebriated producer cautioned the would-be directors they were entering a "high risk profession," to which Patrick, anticipating a winter of chopping ice off his boat, *The Bering Destroyer*, to keep it from capsizing in thirty-foot seas, responded sarcastically, "You've never gone crab fishing, have you?" The producer had no idea what Patrick was talking about, but despite his lack of depth, later went on to win an Academy Award for a documentary about the Shining Path Marxist Guerrillas in Peru.

Patrick never made it to film school. Instead, he fell in love with Lydia Valderama, a pretty girl from De Luces who had come north to work for a season unloading crab in the town of Dutch Harbor. While he was working in the turbulent Bering Sea, Patrick held the face of this young woman in his mind for comfort. Lydia now jokes: "At least he wasn't singing 'Brandy' all the time." After the tangle of crabs was off-loaded under the young señorita's watchful eye, Patrick would ask her out. But, perhaps because there was such a limit on places to be asked out to in Dutch Harbor, or because he didn't speak Spanish and her parents would be "disappointed" if she took up with a "stranger," Lydia refused. "My parents called anyone who didn't speak Spanish a stranger." However, Lydia finally succumbed to Patrick's advances. One day when she was covered with fish slime from the plant, Patrick suggested they take a hike in the beckoning treeless hills above the world of fish, crabs, and diesel fumes. It was the first time anyone in Alaska had suggested an activity to her that didn't include alcohol. Lydia blushes now whenever Patrick refers to this as his first appreciation of "Catch and Release Fishing." He usually has to explain this strange metaphor to nonfishing types, and often bogs down when he gets to the barbed-versus-barbless hook details.

At the pinnacle of their hike, as they were standing in bright yellow rain slickers overlooking the subtle beauty of the Aleutian landscape, Lydia grasped the following things: that she was covered with fish slime and bits of crustaceans and the man standing next to her had never seen her any

other way; that every time the two had previously spoken, the air was infused with fish or crabs in some state of decay, and despite all of it, this man
standing beside her was speaking from another world. He was describing
the challenge of capturing the various "colors of gray" from a cinematogra-
pher's viewpoint. "Love is born in strange places, but seldom over fish totes
on a colorless gray day in the Aleutian Islands," says Lydia. Patrick claims
his affection for Lydia was the inspiration for the tee shirt hanging on the
wall behind the espresso machine that reads, "Don't be fooled by slime."

The two grew closer each time Patrick came to shore for the few days
between fishing trips, but Lydia returned home in the early fall, while Patrick remained to finish his season and secure his bonus. Heady with a decent
season's wages in his wallet and on his way to film school, Patrick stopped
in De Luces to visit Lydia, hoping perhaps she might be persuaded to join
him. Lydia's powers of persuasion proved greater than Patrick's.

There was no film school in De Luces, but there was the ocean, and the
remnants of California's faded anchovy-fishing industry. There was also a
funky little warehouse/café for sale where local legend has it that Fritz Lang
holed up in 1951 while working on his classic noir film *Clash by Night*. Lydia tells the story of how Patrick knocked at her door, surprising Raul and
Dolores Valderama. "Yes," says Lydia, "it took a while for Patrick to win my
parents over. My father was asking Patrick questions. You know, protective-
papa - to-daughter's-suitor questions. That night he asked Patrick about
film school and he was impressed with how passionate Patrick was about
it. So my Papa asked him would he give up film school for a woman, and
Patrick said, never. He'd never give up film school for a woman, but he'd
give up anything for Lydia and never look back." With Lydia's father now
on his side, he bought the café with his savings for film school, and though
he didn't become a director, he did marry Lydia and infuse De Luces with
superb baked goods and a forum for cinematic life. Patrick's passion for
films and a wall in a café large enough to show them brought an entire
world to a place that otherwise would have been more concerned with can-
ning techniques and diesel mechanics.

If it weren't for people like Patrick, most of these classic cinematic stories would never get shown. At least there are a few cable channels on television that show them, but it's not the same as seeing a film on screen, larger
than life and with an audience feeling it all around you. They're meant to
be a group experience. When that light gets dancing and the people stop

breathing or get excited, that's what films are! Years ago Julian and I saw *The Godfather* during its opening week. The line stretched around the block, and the anticipatory energy for that movie was tingling in everyone. We all sat in the theater for three hours and when we came out we were exhausted by the whole experience. No one could speak. I think the best part of seeing the film was walking out afterwards and looking at the new line for the next show. You can only imagine what they were thinking as they stared at our worn out faces. They didn't know what we had seen, but they knew it was something powerful. That doesn't happen when you're at home.

Arriving at the Fritz Lang, I see Patrick and Eric aren't doing much to prepare the café for the evening's showings. Instead of placing chairs, running cables, or setting up projectors in the screening lounge, they're discussing films from what they refer to as the *Aliens-Rule-the-World-Genre*. I'm not sure if the films are talking louder than the effects from the empty shots of espresso cups sitting in front of them, but the count looks like Eric - three, and Patrick - four. The two are trading images and scenes back and forth across the table and take no notice of me when I walk past their table. Eric says, "In *Contact*, the Commission represents universal spiritual need. That's the whole point about whether or not she believes in God. Humans have a spiritual dimension that supersedes their intellect."

"Yes, but what about the non-reptilian alien structure? Ridley Scott says aliens have to look alien or we don't believe it. Humanoid forms are not alien. They have to be reptiles."

"Wait, *Contact* is a metaphor for the inner self: it's not about aliens. It's about finding everything she lost: her dad, her mother, and her family."

Patrick counters with, "Right, but that's where the film breaks down. You've got this amazing mathematical construction, a phenomenal decoding of history and time, an E=MC squared transcendence, and then it all turns into "Woo-woo, I found my Daddy again?" How about she lands in some strange galaxy and the aliens look like liquid aluminum zygotes and have an IQ of 8000?"

"Exactly my point, then it would be like *Predator*; you wouldn't like them."

"That's my point - they wouldn't be aliens if we liked them! Who says we have to like the aliens?"

It's not a conversation I want any part of and I'm relieved there's no room at their table for me and I find a seat on the other side of the café.

Movies are like music; they travel with generations. My soul films are *Wings of Desire, The Children of Paradise, Broadway Danny Rose, Car Wash, Dr. Strangelove, Babette's Feast, Night of The Iguana, The French Connection, The Secret of Roan Innish, Madame Rosa, Swept Away*, and *Z*, to name a few. I happen to know that Eric's are The *Star Wars Trilogy, Chasing Amy*, and anything with Johnny Depp. We do have a common list which includes all of Hitchcock, John Sayles, Spike Lee, and Neil Jordan, plus *Magnolia, Tin Men* and any films based on Philip Dick novels like *Blade Runner* and *Total Recall*. Since movies are like language, the great thing is you can learn any generation's films simply by watching them at a young age. There needn't be any generational separation, but it often is easier to look back than to keep moving forward. I spent a winter once watching all the great silent films by D.W. Griffith and Sergei Eisenstein. It took a while to get past the look of the films, but as far as being able to tell a story, their ability surpassed most of what's been done since. With only the little scene descriptions, or the occasional dialog box to tell you "three months later" or "that same day," those films tell powerful stories which reach into your unconscious. The first time I saw *Birth of a Nation* I was stunned by Griffith's manipulation of emotion. It's a dangerous film, but today nobody watches it except film scholars. It's like the little vials of smallpox they keep in vaults.

I'm sure Eric and Patrick are heading for a big crash after the coffee wears off, but clearly that's going to be a while. Patrick sets them up with another round as they turn to a "sexual politics" character analysis of the James Bond films. The scary thing is the more they talk, the more what they say makes sense, but my days of watching James Bond films are long gone, so I head into the screening lounge to run a sound check. A few minutes later, the phone rings in the café and Lydia shouts to tell me the post office has called and there's a package waiting for me there.

I leave the Fritz Lang and walk down to the post office where I retrieve a package from Julian. Since Julian and I are the last of the Spinners, we have a little "Stay in Touch" agreement:  I let him know where I'm headed and he sends me various items like forwarded letters, and frequently parcels of films, thanks to one of the last institutions to respect a nomadic existence: General Postal Delivery. When he's taking a break from his retirement schedule -- a pace a person half his age couldn't maintain -- he browses the Internet looking for old movies. Real movies:  real film, in cans, weighing enough that I'm glad I have twin axles and a strong truck. Julian loves the auctions: he likes mucking around the world and seeing who's collecting what. Since he has enough money, when he finds something interesting he buys it, watches it, and sends it on to me. He spends thousands of dollars a year salvaging the discard heap, an endangered-species list of a century of film that might otherwise vanish. He finds old television shows from the days before videotape and digital storage, commercials with Mickey Mantle and Lucille Ball pitching cigarettes, and the old promotional excerpts from features. They even used to have abbreviated versions of all the major films, like *Readers Digest* condensed books, and Julian has many of those. He says that nobody wants film anymore. They don't want the inconvenience of history if it's bulky and out-of-date. They don't care or understand that film technique evolved around film process. Today, everyone thinks it's about the information, the story, but if anyone thinks it's the same to watch a movie on a tiny computer screen or in your home with the phone ringing and the refrigerator begging for a visit every ten minutes, if they think that's the same as sitting in a theater with a giant screen and five hundred other people who quit breathing all at the same moment, they're nuts. And I agree with him.

There are probably a thousand collectors left in the world with some kind of emotional connection to the films, and then another thousand who are speculators filling out their "diversified collectable" portfolios. Julian told me there's even a guy in Wisconsin with a climate-controlled vault housing over fifty-five thousand films. Julian met him in a film-interest chat room on the Internet. The guy claims he has every major film made before 1960, and entire bodies of shorts from Sennet, Keaton, Disney and the Chuck Jones crowd.

A few years ago one of the big distributors called it quits, and overnight an entire collection of the best shorts ever amassed went out of circulation. I told Julian about it one evening, and the next day he was on the horn to the company. Julian is a master of charm, even on the phone, and he chatted up the secretary responsible for closing up shop. He found out that all the titles were going onto the Internet for auction very shortly. Thanks to this bit of insider advice, Julian can still boast to owning a film print, even if I do have it in my truck, of one of the few remaining 16mm copies of *Quasi at the Quackadero* by the visionary animator Sally Cruikshank.

Julian gets excited about stuff like cartoons from Hungary, psychedelic shorts, newsreels with tribal fighting in Laos, serials of Tarzan and Buck

Rogers, or Laurel and Hardy, and Buster Keaton shorts. Julian must have the largest collection of *Betty Boop* and *Follow the Bouncing Ball* cartoons in the world. My uncle loves music, especially guys like Cab Calloway and Fats Waller, and a lot of their work was used in these old cartoons.

Shortly after the tip from the secretary, the films began to appear on auction lists under e-bay pseudonyms, so as not to reveal the source of the collection. Julian started bidding on one thing after another, and then, boom! All of a sudden every one of the things he was bidding on disappeared from the auction. Every single one! It took him a while to figure what was going on. He discovered that a collector whose bidding name was "Lumen Desire" had made an entire-collection offer for over two thousand films and the bid was accepted. Julian was so intrigued, he found Lumen's address, and wrote him a note on a card with a brooding portrait of Marlon Brando asking him who he was and what he was going to do with all those films. Julian learned that Lumen Desire, a.k.a. Irving Beckman, lives in Mukwonago, Wisconsin, where he collects and stores films. Later, Julian and Irving hit it off on the phone, first talking about films, then discovering how many people they had in common from Irving's CBS days in New York.

Lumen "Please don't call me Irving" Desire invites Julian to Wisconsin to see the vault and sure enough, Lumen Desire and the vault are both real. Lumen lives on a dairy farm under which he has constructed a vast subterranean film depository, ventilated to maintain constant temperature and humidity. In his Irving Beckman days, during the fifties and sixties, Lumen was a producer at CBS living a conventional life until he produced a small feature on Andy Warhol for CBS and things, as Irving said, "Began to change."

They were shooting a segment of Warhol explaining some of his work when suddenly Warhol shouts, "Stop!" and starts ordering every one around. As Lumen Desire told it to Julian, Warhol snatched the camera and told Irving to peel off his shirt and stand absolutely still. Warhol was still barking orders, which woke up Joe Dallesandro who walked in completely naked and saw Irving standing frozen with his shirt off. Warhol oozes, "Joe, I want you to meet Lumen Desire. I think he'll be perfect for *Flesh.*" Lumen Desire tells Julian that things were never quite the same at CBS after his appearance in *Flesh,* so he left CBS to assist Warhol with films. When he wasn't making movies, he worked distributing them until he set aside enough money to retire in Mukwonago, to be closer to his sister, Rose, who lived in Milwaukee with her husband. Lumen Desire gave Julian an extremely rare copy of *Quasi at the Quackadero*. He told Julian he had another one from the time he met Cruikshank at an animator's convention. Julian told me that Lumen was a little nuts, but innocent and charming. Lumen now holds to the belief that alien colonizers of the Earth will need a record of human culture and thinks with his film collection he'll have a bargaining chip once they find out about him. The entire vault is wired for detonation in case, as Lumen Desire put it to Julian, "They try to get it from me before I get immunity."

I never know what sorts of films Julian may send. This one is pretty light; must be shorts and there's something rattling around inside that has me curious. Before leaving the post office, I open the package and a Laundromat detergent box falls out. Funny guy, Julian. There's a note written (as are all his notes) on a postcard of interesting people or paintings. He loves cards with musicians on them and keeps an impressive stack of them pre-stamped and ready to go in his desk. The big upsets in his life come from postage increases when he has to add another stamp to his cards. The one I get today is of Dizzy Gillespie, whom Julian knew well. Dizzy has his trumpet in his mouth and the glint of light off the shiny upturned bell radiates to the heavens.

*Dear Jake,*          *Today*

*Nothing interesting on the Internet for a while, but found these a few weeks ago at a church auction. The church used to raise money by showing films and over the years amassed a pretty good collection. Unfortunately most were too far-gone, but these four are still good. Don't blink, or you'll miss the unlikely appearance of John Garfield. He's the doorman in the film about taking care of your hunting dogs. The credits list him as Howard France, but it's Garfield. The other three are Aesop's Fables with narration by Richard Nixon. Turns out Nixon was asked to do these after the election in 1960 for some warped Hollywood producer who thought Moral Education Films were going to be hot. Oh, yeah, look closely at the character voice credits: they're all aliases used by blacklisted writers during the McCarthy Witch Hunts. Turns out, someone was playing a strange joke on Mr. Nixon. I should sell these to the Nixon Library but thought you could get some mileage out of them first. The next box should be interesting, wherever it ends up being sent. I'm chasing down some shorts of Irish singers in London pubs. Never know what we'll find there.*

*Onward, Julian*

*P.S. Knock yourself out with the detergent. Can't send bleach or I would. J.*

Julian would never live anywhere where he can't send his laundry out.

But -- Onward: that's how Julian signs everything. Julian never looks back. Fred used to say that Julian was like an old truck that had lost its reverse gear long ago. That was high praise from Fred, who loved trucks, but to most people, Julian is far too elegant to be compared to a truck. Julian is more like an aging concert pianist played by Jack Lemmon out for an invigorating stroll in his fitted overcoat. Considering that he's in his early eighties, Julian has more life and savvy than most people. Everyone wants a piece of Julian, either for his knowledge, connections, or his humor. When Julian is interested in you there's no need to ask for his help and when he's not, he deflects you with a charm that leaves you feeling honored -- "I'd love to, but I've got an appointment with the European paintings curator at the Met."

As I finish reading the note, the postmistress shouts out, "Those movies for tonight?" I answer that I'm not sure, but maybe. She's a slight woman in her late forties, not unpleasant to look at, and she's wearing an oversized button on her uniform lapel that I doubt is USPS issue. It reads, "I'm available." Her nameplate says "Lilly," and with her darting eyes, Lilly is sorting through a stack of letters before efficiently pulling and snapping a rubber band around them. That finished, she looks up and says, "You know, they want to get rid of General Delivery what with all the problems with the terrorists and stuff. It sure would be a shame. There are quite a few of you who use it. Well, I hope I get to see you later." Before she starts with the next stack of letters, and with a rubber band dangling from her mouth, Lilly says, "You know what they're showing tonight?"

"No, I don't know yet, but I'm sure it will be good."

It's four o'clock when I get back to the truck. Zhitomir is parked behind the Fritz Lang in the lea of the sea breeze, which is a forceful and buffeting thing. The sky and sea are both gray and it's hard to tell them apart except for the whitecaps dashing about on the water. I walk up the ramp to Zhitomir and go inside where it's warm thanks to the little heater plugged into a heavy-duty extension cord leading to an outlet inside the Fritz Lang. I set the films down and am about to head for the café when Eric pops his head in the door and says, "Hey, Jake, it's all set up and ready to go. No need to worry. Patrick and I ran the sound, reels are cued, cords are taped; you don't need to do a thing." I thank Eric and then lie down for a short nap.

Inside Zhitomir I have a few moments to appreciate the sound of the ocean roiling outside while I'm warm and comfortable in bed. I'd like to take a nap but I notice the floor has gotten caked with little pieces of dried mud from the street so I take the broom fastened to the wall and do a little sweeping. At least when you live in a cargo box of a truck it doesn't take long to clean up and in a few minutes I've got Zhitomir nice and tidy. Now I can take my nap. Borrowing an expression I hear Eric use from time to time: it's all good.

A little before seven I'm awakened by the sounds of people buzzing from inside the café. No time to heat hot water so I settle for a cold wash cloth and clean my face. Now I'm awake. When I step from Zhitomir the wind is groaning through a strong rain. It's a perfect night -- dark, windy, and wet -- to fill the piercing darkness with cinematic color.

Inside the Fritz Lang, Lydia and Patrick are rolling out pizzas and the place is packed. The screening room doors are open and there's a current of warm air flowing from the café's woodstove. As I get to Eric, Lilly, the post-mistress, waves, winks, and shouts, "If you need a place to use that laundry soap you can use my washer and dryer" and she points to the "I'm available" button now pinned on the shoulder of her orange velour blouse.

Once Lilly is out of earshot, Eric says, "What the hell is that all about?"

"I think she likes me."

"Yeah, you think? I got that part, but what's the laundry thing and what's with the orange velour? Jake, man, is there something you need to tell me?"

"Yes, Eric, it's all about the spin cycle. I'll tell you later, okay."

Eric gives an approving smile and says, "Yeah, that's my man, Maytag Jake!"

The espresso machine is working hard, steaming and frothing and dripping out all the Fritz Lang concoctions while Raul and Dolores tend to the popcorn machine. It's forty-five minutes to show time and all is well.

Patrick has done a good job of keeping the feature a secret up to now when I walk over to the projectors and see *The Petrified Forest* is cued up. It's a great film with an innocent Bette Davis, a brutish Humphrey Bogart, and a deeply contemplative Leslie Howard. It's equal parts gangster film and existentialist stage play stuff, and despite its age the star appeal is strong. Patrick breaks away from pizza duty long enough to check in with me. "Jake, what do you think about skipping the shorts and getting right into the feature? It's not that long a film and I've got a surprise second feature."

Eric throws a knowing glance to Patrick but when I ask him what the second film is he won't tell me. "It's a surprise, Jake, but I think you'll like it." I know they're up to something, especially when Eric volunteers to work the second reel. *Petrified Forest* is only eighty-three minutes so it is on two reels instead of the usual three. That means he doesn't want me to see what the surprise is.

Precisely at 7:55 Patrick comes from behind the counter slapping the flour from his apron as he strides to the front of the room and welcomes everyone. "I'd like to say how happy I am that this room which was once used for gutting fish *is* now warm, dry, and filled with all of you instead." He gives a brief introduction to *The Petrified Forest* before hinting at the surprise second feature, assuring everyone that house coffee is free once the second film starts. He tells everyone about the films for the rest of the month, and then thanks Lydia, Dolores, Raul and a long list of other supporters who help to bring the films to the Fritz Lang.

Now we're rolling and within minutes the audience is immersed in the story of an unlikely confluence of humanity thrust together by a robbery. The crowd is silent except for a few whispered observations about how young Bette Davis is. Bogart is young too, but he's the bad guy and bad guys seem older than they look. There are even a few hisses for the actions of the rich coward. If it's a little strange to hear the espresso machine fire off from time to time, by the time the second reel begins no one notices. One of the great things about any gangster film, even one as sophisticated as *Petrified Forest*, is the audience knows right away things will not turn out well for everyone. Moral certainty holds audiences and the only people who stir are a small cluster of patrons sitting beside the woodstove who occasionally rise and leave the room for a few minutes before returning with a strange aroma on them. Patrick joins me at the back of the room and whispers "Isn't this incredible, Jake? Look at them. Teenagers to geezers; the film is over sixty years old and except for the dopers they can't take their eyes off the screen."

A few minutes before the end of *The Petrified Forest*, I notice Patrick slips away to greet somebody at the door. I can't see the person's face, but in the shadowy silhouette cast against the wall I can see he's wearing a cowboy hat.

When the lights come up, there's a tall, slender, and handsome man who looks like Liberace at a rodeo! He reflects light like a ballroom crystal and his red leather cowboy boots are polished to the high luster of radiant embers in a hot fire. He's dressed in the most over-the-top cowboy outfit imaginable and he radiates more energy than the sun to the patrons who surround him like he's Elvis Presley. It's only in the seconds before Eric and Patrick bring him over to introduce me that I remember Gerry Gaxiola, better known as *The Maestro, King of The Cowboy Artists*. Now I understand what Eric and Patrick were concealing. This cowboy is the featured subject of the evening's second feature, an entertaining documentary by Les Blank.

Les Blank is simply one of the best filmmakers ever. Whether telling a story about garlic or Latin percussion, he can take any subject and turn it into an amazing film. He did a trade film about the chicken industry that would please Colonel Sanders, Frank Perdue, and at the same time, every card-carrying member of People for the Ethical Treatment of Animals. You may not know his name but most feature and documentary filmmakers know his work and they all worship him. There are simply no better movies, of any genre, of any subject than the ones made by Les Blank.

It turns out Raul and The Maestro went to high school together and they're good friends. Also the film will lend the perfect balance to the rest of the evening.

I get to shake The Maestro's hand and swap a few words before he is swept away into an adoring crowd.

Patrick and Eric are both grinning ear to ear. Patrick says, "You thought we were going to show *Species* or something like that, didn't you?" Then Eric bolts out of the room to fetch his camera.

"Eric says he hopes he can make something half as good as Les Blank someday," I tell Patrick.

"Is he good?" asks Patrick.

"We'll be showing his stuff here someday."

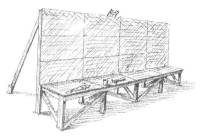

CHAPTER 7

# Drive-In

In Which we meet one fine woman who serves a good breakfast, and make a small contribution to the lives of displaced chicken workers.

This week is special. It's the second annual Starling Ranch Drive-In Movie in Driggs, Idaho. Seraphina Starling (whose name used to be Martha Gordon) runs the Driggs Bakery Café, and she's been putting on this event since we met last year. Seraphina is devoted to her town, and to being that rare hybrid of visionary and maintainer. Even though she doesn't hold office, run a bank, or have a massive pile of discretionary money, it's pretty clear in Driggs that she runs the place. Zoning changes, school funding, elderly housing, and migrant workers' rights -- all roads lead to the Bakery Café, where there is an engraved brass sign above the service counter which says "Control coffee and rule the world!"

Seraphina Starling is one of those rare people with no darkness inside. She proudly boasts she's like the transplanted bird she changed her name to honor:  overwhelming!  Blessed with a big heart, the will to work hard, and the best darn coffee in Idaho, she gets things done. There may be a lot of people who disagree with her, but there isn't anyone who doesn't respect her. I met Seraphina while attending the Teton Valley Film Symposium. I was parked on the street in Jackson, with Eric parked behind me in his van, and I was resting inside awaiting the evening program, when someone started knocking on the side of Zhitomir. When I opened the back door, it was Seraphina, and she alerted me to the fact that I was about to get a ticket for vagrant parking if I didn't move the truck. She introduced herself and told me she had a parking area behind her place in Driggs, across the pass between Wyoming and Idaho, and that I was welcome to set the truck there, as well as Eric's van. Accepting her generosity, I scribbled a note and placed it on Eric's windshield explaining the plan to Eric who was inside the symposium hall shooting footage. While I did that, Seraphina chatted with the policeman who put away his citation pad and said, "No problem, Seraphina. See you Sunday at breakfast." Seraphina then rode with me over the pass, to Driggs, pressing me the entire way for details about the Lost Sons of Zhitomir. When I told her the story of it, I got my first inkling of the genius that is Seraphina Starling, "You know, I've got an idea for a new pastry about you."

"What's that, a giant trucker's donut?"

"No, don't be silly. I'm going to top a bear claw with tons of nuts and ice it to four little donuts."

"And what are you going to call it?"

"I could call it, Jake but better, I'll call it the Nut Job On Wheels!"

By the time we got to the café parking lot, Seraphina had cooked up an-other great idea. She told me she didn't have much money, but she did have a large field on her farm where lots of parties were held, and occasionally a concert. Said she'd feed us for a week if the Lost Sons of Zhitomir would put on a show. It sounded like a great idea but I knew it would take a lot of preparation. I told her if she would set things up we could come back next year. "Next year?" she said, "I was thinking about this Saturday."

Early the next morning, Eric, whose failing muffler made his late night arrival in Driggs less than anonymous, joined me inside the Bakery Café where we enjoyed a full plate of eggs, homefries, and bacon. The Bakery Café is pure Americana: checkered red-and-white table cloths covering stout hand-hewn wooden tables made of local Ponderosa Pine trees set with sturdy porcelain coffee cups and sparkling silverware. The place holds about thirty at the nine tables and another eight can sit at the counter, which is flanked by fresh pies on either side bearing handwritten labels that say things like "Local Blackberry, Lucia Brocknow's Apple, and Chocolate Crème." It's 7:45 am and the tables are full. One table has a group of boister-ous mountain climbers wearing elfish hats that dangle over their unshaven faces and who cannot seem to drink their coffee fast enough. Another table has four uniformed road builders for the Bureau of Land Management. They too are drinking coffee while swapping sections of the newspaper. The other tables are filled with regulars, easily identified because they claim their personal cups from a wall of cups before taking their seats.

The place is electric, as Seraphina's crew serves a full restaurant to the accompaniment of Jane's Addiction blaring from the kitchen.

"Jiminy Ding-Dang Christmas, Seraphina, can you have them turn that down," shouts a man in his fifties as he walks into the restaurant clad in a dirty set of mechanic's coveralls. Seraphina throws her arms up in the air in a futility.

"Sorry, Tim, can't change a thing until the baking crew gets done at eight. If you want people to get up that early and bust their butts for these wages, then they get to choose their own music. It's like in *Car Wash*, Tim. You're old enough to know that one. Wanna see some slow motion? They instantly downshift to granny gear if I put on Van Morrison. Can you imagine that? They think Van Morrison is tame. They'd go comatose if I put on James Taylor."

Seraphina points to her watch and shouts, "See that? Ten more minutes and it's my turn to choose. Stick with me and you'll get to hear some vintage Danny O'Keefe." Tim nods his head. Apparently the best breakfast in town is worth a few more minutes of screaming rock-and-roll. Seraphina sets his place at the counter, and brings him a cup of coffee, saying, "On the house this morning, Tim."

One has to wonder if Seraphina ever sleeps, because since the night before she has had most of eastern Idaho and western Wyoming plastered with leaflets advertising a Drive-In movie at Starling Ranch Theater. She's handing leaflets to everyone in the restaurant and when she gets to us says, "With a computer and a copy machine you can do anything!" Overhearing this in the next booth is a man who chimes in, "Yeah, and a brother who delivers *The Jackson Hole News* and *The Idaho Statesman* to every locale within fifty miles." Seraphina then wraps her arms around the neck of the man and says, "Jake and Eric, this is my brother, Ted. As you may have surmised by that witty comment, he is both my brother and a rather tired delivery driver who doesn't need a second cup of coffee." Seraphina snatches away his steaming cup to his displeasure, then says "He's easy to buy off; for an extra slice of bacon he'll add a few flyers to every bundle of papers."

Incredibly, by Thursday afternoon, we're actually able to begin setting up as Seraphina's crew, including quite a few of the Jane's-Addiction-loving bakers, have built us a magnificent plywood screen painted with reflective silver paint. Seraphina keeps everybody jumping from one task to another with a natural ease and everyone's having fun. We set the projectors atop a flatbed hay truck about a hundred feet away from the screen, and then start up a 5000-watt generator which we've set three hundred feet away in the other direction, surrounded by hay bales to muffle its noise. People keep driving by on the county road slowing down to shout across to us, "What are you guys doing?" When they heard the words "Drive-In," smiles creep across their faces and most promise they'll be back on Saturday for the show.

In a little while it's dark enough and we're ready to light the screen and see if we have enough sound to fill a twenty-acre pasture. The twelve sheets of plywood -- sixteen feet tall by twenty-four feet long -- sit like a strange vacant billboard in the sky. There are still a handful of people around, helping to fasten the remaining stays and securing the plywood to the elaborate framework while their children play nearby. Finally, all is settled, the ladders are removed and Eric flips on the first projector. Filling the blankness is a column and panel of light that is unforgettable. When the projector lights up that gigantic screen the magic begins. You simply cannot imagine what it's like until you're standing in a hay field watching a twelve-foot tall Marlon Brando! The little kids are stunned, never having seen anything like it before. The adults are only slightly less mesmerized. Both young and old stand whipping their heads back and forth between the screen and the distant source of the emanating light.

One little girl of about five comes up to me and asks, "Mister, how do you get all those people inside that little machine?"

The kids start jumping up in the air trying to grab the light out of the sky. One of them grabs two fists of light, then taunts the others, "I caught the big man, I caught the big man!" Another one snatches his own fistful and quickly stuffs it into his mouth and runs around with his eyes bright and excited, pretending that he's going to open his mouth and let it out. The other kids cover their heads every time he gestures with his free arm. The sounds coming through the speakers are scratchy and disconnected at first, especially because the focus is off a little, but when Eric adjusts the focus, the kids freeze and begin to recognize the connection between the images of the people on the screen and the words they're hearing. The adults, though they haven't started jumping around, stand collectively muttering, "Amazing!"

Friday morning I'm eating at The Bakery Café awaiting the arrival of a reporter from *The Jackson Hole News and Guide,* whom Seraphina has arranged for me to talk with to promote the show. After a while the door opens and in walks a young woman barely old enough to drive, carrying a note pad in one hand and a small tape recorder in the other. Seraphina points her my way and she sits right down across the table without introducing herself. She sets her note pad down, then starts fumbling to put a tape into her recorder. When the tape is in, she looks up from behind a terribly bloodshot pair of eyes and says, "Oh, I'm sorry, you must think I'm terribly rude. My name is Kristin Faulkner. I'm the reporter."

"Yes, I believe I had that figured out."

"You must be Mr. Spinner. There was a fatal car accident last night and I haven't had much sleep. I wear a lot of hats at the paper. Last night, local tragedy; today, human interest. I'm really intrigued by the Drive-In."

"Great, how about something to drink.? Maybe something without caffeine."

"Right, good idea. Maybe some herb tea, mint please, would be great. If I drink any more coffee I'll forget my own name."

After the tea comes, Kristin starts the interview.

"I assume you're connected to that marvelous truck outside. I'm a bit confused, Mr. Spinner,"

"Please, call me Jake. What's the confusion?"

"Okay, Jake. What exactly is it you do? And what on earth is a Zhitomir?" She pronounces it Zee toe murr. Over the next half an hour we manage to cover enough of the details before it becomes clear that the exhausted reporter needs to get some sleep. Checking her notes one last time before leaving, she says, "Tell me if I have this right. You drive around the country showing movies from your truck?" I nod yes. "And you live in the truck?" I nod yes again. "And you've been doing this for a few years?" Another nod yes. "And you earn money from doing the shows and by writing for a magazine?" I nod yes one more time. "Journalism school, what a waste of time. I'm still paying off the loans," exclaims the weary reporter as she leaves for a well-earned rest.

The next morning when I enter The Bakery Café, Eric is inside reading the front page of the *Jackson Hole News* that has a large color photo of him fussing with the projectors. The headline reads: "Local Café Enlists Film Gypsies to Revive Drive-In. Film buffs expected to turn out in droves."

Eric is wide-awake from the temptation of free coffee, and he gushes, "Get a load of this, Jake. I've always wanted to be a gypsy. Check it out. Sweet!" Then, while continuing to look at the picture of himself, says, "Not a bad shot, huh? I set it up for her. See how I set Zhitomir, the projectors, and the screen on intersecting focal planes." It's way too early for intersecting focal planes, so I don't respond. Fortunately, before Eric can elaborate on photo technique (without me having the benefit of a cup of coffee first), Seraphina comes over to tell us she thinks there are going to be more people than expected. "This thing is catching on. I've got extra crew on for the food, and someone told me there's going to be a horse trailer loaded with kegs of beer. I've got to run and pick up a roll of tickets but I'll see you guys later. Listen, you ought to try the strawberry pie. We got the berries and it's fantastic. You guys better rest up. Big night ahead."

We're not expecting to throw light on the screen until after nine o'clock but people start rolling in as early as five! By seven o'clock the field is packed with as many cars as can fit and still have an unimpeded line of sight to the screen. The rest park in the adjacent field and those people will have to sit on blankets at the front. A rested Kristin Faulkner is walking around interviewing people and asking them to share their memories about drive-ins. She comes over and plays me the tape of one woman who says in a languid Texas drawl, "I spent a lot of Saturday nights at drive-ins. Friday nights was football, Saturday nights was drive-ins. Hello, east Texas! My boyfriend, Argent, he looked a lot older than he was, and he'd wear a dark trench coat to the movies. He carried a flashlight in his pocket so that once the film started and all us teenagers started making out, he could wander around to all the cars making like he was the security guard. He'd flash the light in their eyes and bark, 'Do you kids have any beer in there?' while continuing to blind them with his flashlight. No one could tell who it was and they'd get so scared they'd hand the beer out the window to him and then we'd drink it."

I notice a lot of people driving in with their trunks filled with more people, even though we're charging by the car. Eric sees this too and shoots some footage of a few cars before coming over confused and curious what that's all about. He's too young to remember families sneaking in a few unpaid admissions but, hearing about it, roars a big "Sweet, oh so sweet!" in approval before heading back to do some more filming before the light fades.

Luck was with us this evening. As a looming dark sky obscured the last light of the day, we fired up the projectors for a remarkable crowd of at least three hundred people, before nine o'clock. Betty Boop started dancing to a Cab Calloway song and the crowd loved it! Little kids pointed at the screen and a bunch of them came back repeating the scene from the first night we tested things. A band of coyotes howled in the night, probably confused about the sounds bouncing into their hills from the loudspeakers. And the rain stayed away. The people in that field knew they were part of the most amazing thing going on in these parts for a very long way around that night, and Seraphina and her crew were clearly happy. Before the last shout out of Brando, Seraphina comes over to the projectors and says, "The minute I saw that truck of yours over in Jackson, I knew something good was going to happen. This is a good thing, fellas."

In only its second year, the Starling Ranch Drive-In has grown tremendously. There's a drawing to see who gets car privileges, as there's only room for about one hundred of them, but altogether there will be close to a thousand people sitting in that field. There'll be food booths and craft areas, people will have small folding chairs lined up in rows, and picnics. The local microbrewery has its own sitting area and even a shuttle bus to take people home in case they overdo it. Berrigan Cadillac lends a cherry red vintage 1966 Eldorado convertible to the event and they run a raffle for four seats in the car. The winners are crowned the "Drive-In Kings and Queens."

Seraphina works her crew and her own tail off for two months in advance making sure everything goes smoothly, and she donates every single penny beyond expenses to the local elementary school. It's a big event.

Today I'm sitting with my annual pre-film breakfast: a delicious helping of home fries, four crisp and perfect pieces of bacon, and two over-easy eggs, and I'm reading a flyer for tonight's "All-1940 Program at Starling Ranch." The program is a Universal Newsreel, *which* includes the invasion of Holland and Norway by the Third Reich, a big-band musical short, *Pinky Tomlin and His Orchestra*, and a *Paramount Unusual Occupations* short featuring a chewing-gum painter, trouser cutter, and a system for controlling beavers. Topping off the all-1940 program is Frank Capra's *The Philadel-*

*phia Story* with Cary Grant, Katharine Hepburn, and Jimmy Stewart. It's a great film and one I carry with me at all times. It's going to be fun, but once I finish breakfast, it's also going to be pretty crazy until we throw the switch and the show begins. We have a three-hour, four-reel-change program, and we need to do a good job of it so that three hundred elementary school kids will have art and music classes in school next year. And so that a thousand people will go home happy, and we can celebrate with the annual midnight feast put on at the Café by Seraphina for the volunteers.

Eric comes in with a copy of a glossy Starling Ranch Drive-In poster featuring an image of the west face of the Grand Teton mountain. Drawn on top is a projector casting light onto a movie screen below. It's fantastic. They make as much on the sales of the poster as on admissions to the film now. Seraphina is working the counter, calm and friendly, but you can tell when she's thinking. Her voice takes on an airy tone and her eyes get that shine which alerts you that she's thinking hard about something. Seeing Eric, she draws a cappuccino from the new addition to her café -- "Need to move with the times," she often says, and brings it to the table. Then she begins to talk.

She tells us about a community of Guatemalans living nearby Sugar City who work in the poultry processing plant. It's one of those miserable places where everyone knows that the workers are illegal, even the INS, but no one else wants the work so there's a wink-and-nod understanding. The Guatemalans have been there for the past ten years and though they mainly keep to themselves, the kids are in the schools and seem to be pretty well accepted.

"I've got a favor to ask you, Jake," says Seraphina. "The INS raided the plant the other day. They were being pressured by some pompous legislator who's running for congress under the slogan 'America for Americans.' They had to do something or he was going to blow the whistle. Ray Caldwell was the INS agent on the case; he's in here all the time and he says his hands were tied but I think his hands were tied when he tried to find his heart. He says he had no options. About half the workers are legal, half not, and their kids are a mix of citizens and non-citizens. The raid was during the night shift so most of the kids should still have at least one parent at home, but at the time a bunch of the families alerted their relatives at home to scatter. Now they've got kids hiding all over the place, parents on planes to Guatemala, and everybody scrambling to calm things down. It's a huge mess.

Every church around here has an appeal out, and people give what they can, but it's going to cost a bundle. They'll need money for attorneys, court costs, and plane tickets, and there won't be nearly enough in donations. "

Eric is all over it. "We could do a bunch of shows in the Moose Basin Park. I know the naturalist who works there and the place is jammed with tourists. You know parents will gladly pay for their kids to have something to do at night. That amphitheater holds plenty of people. We can even use the wall behind it if they'll let us paint it. It's perfect, Jake, they've got power there. We can tap into their sound system. Seraphina gets the popcorn crew together, dollar a bag, and bingo!"

Eric's got it all worked out except for what movies we're going to show. We've got a truck full of films, and the shorts will be easy, but we need something with a big name, and something we don't have to pay rights fees on. Ironic that with our biggest show of the year starting in ten hours, our minds are already beginning to shift gears to our next program. I remember Julian telling me that every time Samuel Goldwyn heard he had a big hit on his hands after its premiere, he'd say, "So, what are we doing tomorrow?"

As expected, the Driggs Drive-In is great fun. Our part of the program comes off with flying colors. No technical problems, smooth reel changes, good sound. Seraphina is pretending to be annoyed that a small group of belly dancers took center stage without asking permission between the shorts and the feature. Fortunately, their topless performance was cloaked in the night, saving any controversy. When you get that many people together you never know what will happen. As usual, the ever-prepared Eric happens to have his camera loaded with high-speed film and is able to capture the dancers' stunning performance, including a slow-motion sequence that borders on the erotic as he slowly zooms in on each dancer and explores the motions of her body. Some people say they "don't get" belly dancing, but should they ever be so fortunate as to see Eric's footage, that lack of comprehension will be put to rest.

But my mind is already elsewhere, trying to solve the dilemma of the Guatemalans. Under the circumstances, I know it is time to call in the big guns. It is time to contact Julian. My uncle Julian knows everybody. Julian knew Picasso, JFK, and Churchill, and Julian knows Bob Dylan and Bernardo Bertolucci. So I send him a note asking for suggestions about the Guatemalan benefit. A few days later a postcard arrives of Annie Oakley sitting bareback atop a horse and brandishing two pistols.

*Dear Jake -*                                                    *Today*

*Here's your festival:*

*The Black Stallion, The Bear, Into the West, My Life As a Dog, and Close Encounters of the Third Kind. Animals, aliens, and kids, Jake, you can never go wrong with animals and aliens. Kids love them. I know you're worried about the price tags, but don't. I've called in some old favors in the name of a good cause and I've already received performance permissions from Spielberg and Coppola on their films. On top of that, they're each sending through a generous donation. I've got calls into Lasse Hallestrom, Jean Jacques, Jim's in New York working on something and said Mike will give his okay, so I've already booked their films as well . . . Shall I send the checks to the café in care of Seraphina?*

*Onward, Julian*

While the rest of us had been out-thinking ourselves with the details of the harsh lives of immigrants and displaced people, Julian got the big picture in an instant. Julian has a way of closing his eyes and seeing the world the way it is instead of complaining about what it should be. Julian instantly envisioned the park, and the night, and the families on vacation. He also knows families don't travel with older kids.

Julian delivered a small talk twenty-five years ago entitled "There Are No Important Films." The piece was part of a film series at the Museum of Modern Art called "Film and Society." The panel was a heavyweight selection of film critics and historians, and Julian quickly found himself the target of a lot of barbs when he rejected the notion that films are vital forces of social change. Julian, the son of European immigrants, grew up poor and smart, believing in a fair fight and in helping the underdog. Finding himself surrounded by a well-heeled crowd of old-fashioned snobs, he did what Julian does so well, dismantling pomposity and intellectual snobbery wherever he finds it. He made a strong statement declaring that film is entertainment and although it may influence individuals, it rarely shapes society. He discussed his belief that the power of film is in making you feel, but that it is that very power which leads you to the false sense that because you feel something, you've done something. I doubt anyone there felt comforted by Julian's ideas. He could easily have withheld these ideas, especially from an audience invested in the belief that their work is significant beyond entertainment. Instead, Julian smiled, went home and wrote a review of *Caddyshack* for the *Washington Post,* titled *"The Most Important*

*Film of the Year."* You get what you get from Julian, who is equal parts angel and oracle.

The following Tuesday at around five-thirty we arrive at the Moran Amphitheater to set up. We have shows planned for the next five nights, and even have flyers posted around describing the quickly named *Grand Teton Film Festival*! It's the same poster we used for the Drive-In with a few modifications. Seraphina has changed the text and had an artist friend draw a border of animal characters around the original. The show is set to start at eight-thirteen. Eric gets exact sunset times from a website run by the government. I prefer calling it "dusk" but Eric's generation likes to have the details.

Latecomers will have to sit on the ground because all the chairs are covered already with jackets and blankets to reserve people's seats. Seraphina has enlisted all the Guatemalan families to bring food and help with the set-up so there's a group of children running around and people drifting in. Each family brings a potluck dish with them to a table filled with food for after the show. I instruct the volunteers about duct-taping all the cords and securing every and any thing someone could trip over. Once the sun is gone you can't see a thing, and long experience leads me to believe that Murphy's Law was named after a movie projectionist.

The little kids surround Eric as he sets up the projectors. When he turns on the bulbs and images of people appear on the screen, two of them jump back and tumble over each other in their haste to flee. An older boy tells them there's nothing to be afraid of, but the youngest asks, "Do you have to feed them?" "Feed who?" asks Eric. "Them, says the boy, pointing directly at the lens. "The ones inside there." "They're not alive," says Eric. "They're pictures." He takes a reel of film and holds out a length of it for the kids to look at. "See, there they are, and when we turn the light on, it makes them appear up on the screen. That's what movies are." The kids spend the next few minutes lingering around Eric, very proud of their newly acquired knowledge. As more kids come by to stare at the projectors and ask what they are, the two boastfully repeat Eric's words, "That's what movies are." Eric asks them if they want to sit behind his table during the film and "run the projectors." Excited, they run quickly to the outside to ask their parents if it's okay, and come soon back with permission.

After the movie, the father of one of the boys thanks us for doing the show. I ask him if he enjoyed the movie, and he says yes, but wants to know if any of the other movies will be newer. He asks me why I show old films. It gets me thinking, because not one of the films we're showing in this series is over twenty years old. Although Julian had made the actual choices, I couldn't agree with them more. I explain that it isn't that I don't like new films, but that films need to age for a while before I show them. New movies have too much buzz around them and I think films can be better appreciated once the buzz subsides. Nodding his head, he tells me he'll be here tomorrow, then walks off to explain what we were talking about in Spanish to his wife, who asks, "¿Que es 'buzz?' He answers, "Buzz, como moscas. ¿Entiendes? Buzzzzz buzzzzz, buzzzzz." I speak enough Spanish to know I'm an idiot.

I'm pretty tired after we pack up for the night, but when I climb into the truck, into my bed, all I can think about is what I said to the man. My thoughts shift from "buzzzzz, buzzzzz, buzzzzz," to *Bye Bye Brazil*, the story of a touring theater troupe, The Caravana Rolidei, making their way, via dirt and mud roads, through a rapidly modernizing Brazil. They're a tattered troupe led by a guy who is part magician, part seducer, and part pimp. They perform in little towns where the future hasn't yet arrived, towns that have nothing going on, the way so many places were for hundreds of years. We can hardly believe there was once a world with no movies, no stereos, no video games, and no television. Can you imagine how quiet the world was for thousands and thousands of years in a time when all music was live? Looking at the instruments -- the trumpets shepherds used to make from goat horns, the bells and the drums, makes it easy to imagine where yodeling came from.

The Caravana Rolidei has only a strongman and a few musical numbers, but the owner's girlfriend is a good-looking gypsy woman, and if ticket sales are too small they get their money another way. She turns tricks for all the local dignitaries, or anyone else who can pay. One day this troupe of gypsies pulls into a little town and picks up a naive and sadly innocent young couple that is looking for a way out of their remote village life. They are so desperate to escape that they don't see that Caravana Rolidei is a funky little fly-by-night operation. They only see the glamour of the road. Meanwhile, Brazil is growing and leaping into the modern world so fast it's blinding. Every time they get to a town which displays a spate of antenna covered rooftops -- meaning televisions -- they know they won't make any money, because sadly television shows offer grander things than the Caravana Rolidei's rolling Chautauqua show.

Naturally, my favorite scene is when Rolidei comes into this village and there's another guy there who travels around showing movies. He rolls from town to town carrying a few tattered film prints, and he sets up in a town hall or an old tent and shows his pictures. The two old-world impresarios confer like salesmen selling different products on the same route. They sit on a stoop sharing stories about life on the road, and lamenting the changing Brazil that will soon be lost forever. (I've often wondered if Sophie the circus painter had something to do with that film?)

The *Grand Teton Film Festival* makes thirty-nine thousand dollars for the chicken plant families. It's not enough, but it's a start. Every night the audience grows, and the night we show *The Bear*, a naturalist brings a live bear cub to the show! Half the families have been separated by the bust, but almost everybody is in contact, and once the "right honorable legislator" gets his news coverage, the heat will subside and hopefully all the exiles can return.

We'll be back too, but not for another year. It's moving day for us with one last meal courtesy of Seraphina. We're exhausted, but Seraphina is a constant, filling coffee cups and moving quickly on to her next project. There's been a big mess in the community fire department over some spending issues and Seraphina has invited all the "principal parties" to hash it out tonight at the café. I suspect no one's going to escape the room until some agreement is made. I'm about out the door when Seraphina gives me one more of her "sure gonna miss you hugs" and a card that arrived from Julian for me.

*Jake,*                                                                       *Today*

    *How did the festival go? I'm off to Rome for a few weeks. American Film Institute wants me to represent them at a celebration of Fellini. Drop me a note so I have something to read when I get home.*

                                                        *Onward, Julian*

    *PS  If you have a copy of that short script you wrote about Uncle Schlomo, send it to me. I've finally found a use for it. J.*

CHAPTER 8

# "Always Cut On Movement."
# Howard Hawks

**In Which** two travelers leave the comfort of full breakfasts and good coffee for the unknown, and we learn of great uncle Schlomo.

Until the infatuating force of the unknown overpowers the familiar, every leaving feels like leaving home. Once I saw Magellan's charts of the world's oceans. Those charts were called mappamundis, maps of the world, and they looked nothing like ours today. Mappamundis portrayed world mythologies as much as they did navigational marks. They detailed floating angels in the heavens and demon beasts to deter the voyagers from entering various hells. The old parchment charts shaded vast areas with ether and phlogiston (a nonexistent chemical that prior to the discovery of oxygen was thought to be released during combustion). There were no straight lines between destinations, no longitude or latitude, but epic and formless portrayals of profound physical and spiritual unknowns. Oceans were not neutral bodies of water but mystical realms holding danger and treasure. It wasn't as it is today, when (punching in coordinates) we assume a finite destination and certainty of arrival.

In today's world, we think we know where we're going and how to get there, and what we'll see along the way. We hop on the interstate and begin ticking off clicks, tenth-mile markers all the way to the inevitable. Everything is so familiar that we're in a trance half the time, or scanning the radio looking for distraction from the tedious voyage.

But it isn't that way when you have no destination, when you have no home holding you, no place that you're from and to which you will return. So when I leave an area, after staying a while, one part of me feels sad about cutting the connection, while another is excited about the freedom ahead. Flight and gravity have an exhilarating (but tense) conversation until the distance cuts the tether and all that remains is open road. Better to leave a place while the action is hot than to suffer through the letdown from loss of interest when the fire goes out.

Eric has managed to extract a small concession from me. Eric has asked me to carry a cell phone. It took Eric over a year to extract this concession. Every reason for carrying a telephone had been rejected by me until one day, Eric simply said this: "Jake, there are times I need to talk to you to know you're okay." Who could resist that?

Most days when we're on the road Eric calls me to arrange our rendez-vous points. Last night though, he told me he was going to have to stay on in Driggs for a few days to get some work done on his van, though I suspect a belly dancer is more the cause. No worries though. He'll be catching up to me soon.

I have a few errands to run before leaving Driggs. The road may be great for the soul but it is tough for doing laundry, bathing, and cooking. In Driggs all my meals have been taken at The Bakery Café and we used Seraphina's house for laundry and showers. You miss showers on the road and I'm not sure why. Most people who've lived on this Earth haven't had showers and didn't clean themselves every day, but then again, most people who've lived on this Earth haven't lived in the back of a large diesel truck. There is nothing I like so much as showering and falling into clean sheets when I go to bed. Though many small towns have Laundromats and you can often find a public shower, believe me, they are not the high points of civilization.

After stopping at the grocery store for what Fred called "canned provi-sions" like bottled water, chili, and hearty packets of dried soups, I stop at the gas station to top off my propane tank. Finally, before leaving Driggs I stop at the local print shop to run a copy of "Schlomo" to send to Julian. One manila envelope and five stamps later, I drop it in the box in front of the Driggs Post Office.

My mother lived in the Larch Town Hospital for two years before she died. I didn't get to see her often, but from time to time she'd get out of the hospital and take me out for an afternoon. On most of those Saturday occasions she'd take me to the movies and then we'd have lunch in Larch afterwards. One of the last times I saw her, before my seventh birthday, I asked her about my father. I'd figured out that most kids didn't live with their uncles, but I was still confused about the "mom in the hospital, Dad killed in the war" parts of my life. While we waited for the cheeseburgers and French fries, I asked my mother about my father. She stared off with an odd blankness, like she was suspended in time. She could be like that. It was a little scary, but finally she caught herself and started talking again.

She told me that she was sorry I never got to meet my father, and that he would have loved me. She told me that I looked a lot like him, and then she fumbled in her purse to find a picture, before giving up and saying it must be back at her room in the hospital. Then she laughed which was a little weird because nothing funny had happened, but she did have a good laugh, and then she told me the Schlomo story, the one my father had told her about his life. She said my father had enjoyed that story, had even told it to my grandparents when they wanted to know how a kid from New York had made his way to Larch.

Later, when Mom went back to the hospital, I went home and wrote down every detail I could remember from that story. I must have been a funny little six-year-old kid, huh? Years later, when I found that little kid's chicken scratch tale, I used it to write the small screenplay. I showed it to Julian once and he said that every detail in it was exactly as he had been told. Julian said that story was repeated often in the Spinner household, especially after bathing time.

I hope you will enjoy reading it.

---

## Welcome To America, Great-Uncle Schlomo

The entire story is narrated in a voice-over.

**Establishing shot of steamer ship in NY Harbor with the Statue of Liberty followed by a long shot of a European immigrant in his twenties walking down a gangway.**

*Narrator:* "Almost one hundred years ago my great-uncle Schlomo, full of hope, clambered down the steerage class gangway of a European ocean liner onto the promising soil of America."

**We see throngs of people rushing to the new arrivals, and small family reunions breaking out.**

**Next we see a man in his mid-twenties, then his feet and worn shoes, landing for the first time on the wharf that is American soil.**

**We see him alone amongst family gatherings.**

*Narrator:* "Schlomo couldn't speak a word of English, barely knew a soul in his new land, had not an inkling of what the future held, but he stopped at the bottom of the gangway and knelt upon the ground to kiss the first patch of soil he touched in America, somehow knowing its promise was true."

**We see Schlomo rising from his knees . . . he is surrounded by a small group of men who enthusiastically shake his hand and embrace him.**

*Narrator:* " 'Official Greeters said their badges, and they spoke to him in a familiar tongue, Yiddish, welcome words to an immigrant. They spoke to Schlomo in kind reassuring tones, and soon had his rapt ear as they told him of the great land. 'Yes, friend, welcome to America. In this great country, you will need a few things, and with those things America will treat you well.' Schlomo was all ears as the men told him, 'Schlomo, in America you need to dress well to make a good impression. You don't want Americans to think you are another Jew from the old country. No, of course you don't, Schlomo.'"

**One of the greeters reaches into a satchel and produces a garment.**

*Narrator:* "'See this suit, my friend?' asked one of the greeters, producing a garment from a bag. 'Let me offer this suit to you. It's what real Americans wear, and it will show them that you, Schlomo, are a force to be reckoned with.' Schlomo, praising God for his good fortune, took the suit, paying for it with several of the few dollars he had tucked into his pocket. His new friends were excited for him and looked on admiringly.

"'Look Schlomo, you are now an American.'"

**Slowly dissolving shots of Schlomo walking the streets of New York City.**

**Schlomo's hands unravel a crumpled, hand-scrawled map.**

*Narrator:* "Proudly wearing his new suit, in his new city, in his new country, Schlomo set out across unfamiliar streets with only an address and a hand-scrawled map of Manhattan. The map to guide him to his sole relative in America, Schlamie (a cousin from his home village near Kiev), had sent him. Schlomo is eager to find his relative Schlamie and his wife, Reva, who have been in the new country for three years. Schlomo knows they will be impressed that he, Schlomo, barely ten minutes off the boat, is already clad in the latest fashion."

**We see a small tenement building on the Lower East Side, followed by Schlomo checking the letter with Schlamie's address.**

*Narrator:* "Finding his cousin's home, he strides up the steps of the three-story brown tenement, and raps his laborer's knuckles against the door."

**We see Schlomo's hands knocking on the door.**

*Narrator:* "Inside he hears the playful voices of children."

**The door opens to Schlamie and a warm greeting.**

*Narrator:* "And when the door opens there are Schlamie and Reva, and three children: Samuel, Sonia, and Bernard, all at the kitchen table. They fed him, offered him drink, embraced him in joy and then sat at the modest table for hours, swapping stories in Yiddish, catching up on relatives, on the hometown, and hearing stories of the Czar's cruelty and how the entire village of Zhitomir had been dispersed across much of the globe. Schlomo said so to Schlamie and Reva. 'Can you imagine? The lost sons of Zhitomir living in some of the most unlikely places in the world! Who can believe Jews are living in such places? And Schlamie nodded his head with the same wonder, adding, Who knows in the vastness of this Earth where a Jew can now live, Schlomo?' "

**We see the sleeping children and empty wine bottles on the festive dinner table.**

*Narrator:* "The evening wore on until finally, the children asleep, they accepted that some stories would have to wait until the next day. Reva had set aside clean sheets for Schlomo and she cleared the table and prepared the sofa for him to sleep. Crammed into this small apartment, Schlomo would spend his first night in the dining room. He would remain there until he could find work and make an independent life. His first day in the land of wonder came to an end while Samuel, Sonia, and Bernard slept in one tiny room, and Reva and Schlamie lay tucked into their bed in a small alcove off the living room."

**Pan across apartment.**
**Schlomo in the dining room bed.**

*Narrator:* "The apartment grew quiet while Schlomo's head, resting against the pillow, began spinning from drink."

**A bare light bulb comes on and Schlomo rises to get a glass of water at the kitchen faucet, drinks, and then off goes the light.**

*Narrator:* "Schlamie must have felt the same, for after a few minutes he came from the tiny room to drink a glass of water. Hearing Schlamie fill his glass in the darkness of the apartment, Schlomo looked towards the shadow of his cousin with love and said,

"'Thank you, Schlamie.'

"Schlamie, surprised that his cousin was still awake, said kindly,

"You're welcome, Schlomo. Let this country bless us all.' And with that, headed back to bed, pausing at the last second to speak to his newly arrived cousin.

"'Schlomo?'

"'Yes, Schlamie?'

'Reva and I have been wanting to ask you, why did you arrive wearing a bathrobe?"

Jake Spinner, © 1976

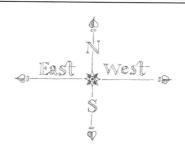

# SECTION 2

---

# The Joys Of Weightlessness

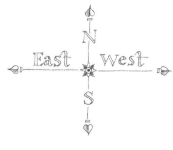

CHAPTER 9

# The East/West

In Which we meet two men -- one of the East/West whose mother had the devoted love of a painter, and the other a hobo in the world of modern locomotives.

It's summertime and I can't say why, but I'm thinking about rivers of ice and snow. At a gas station in Missoula I fill the tank and ask the attendant if there are any interesting roads leading north. Before I leave, I buy a copy of *The Daily Missoulian*, which advertises a "Full Roundup of All the New Films" in its entertainment pullout section. The attendant must have appreciated my request because the road he recommended quickly empties out to a meander of trees and wild Montana scenery. Montana is large enough to have places where trees, roads, and wildlife seem to coexist. The road is scattered with enough leaves and encroaching roadside plants to give it a softer feel than most. It makes me wonder how long it might last if people quit driving on it all together? Maybe it's because there aren't too many cars and the animals think of the road as their own, or maybe it's because I'm driving slow enough that there isn't that much noise produced from Zhitomir, but I've seen scores of squirrels, two porcupines, and even a small group of elk who slowly peered at Zhitomir as it drove past.

When I drive on roads like this, I actually have a chance to think. It's very relaxing, especially because I'm not going anywhere, and mainly, because I'm not going anywhere -- slowly. That seems odd, doesn't it, not to be going anywhere? Even in Larch, where I didn't lead a fast paced life, I still had a schedule and details that demanded attention. Life was like a series of connect-the-dot events, but the thing that was missing was it never connected enough to form a beautiful picture. Now, the dots are more random and I don't know what the picture's supposed to look like. I'm not sure why, but I think Fred would have called that freedom. Today, it looks like a gentle part of Montana filled with large trees, wildlife, and the verdant banks of a gentle river.

After a few hours of staring at the scenery I start thinking about what the evening holds and where I might stay tonight. It's a subtle shift from wandering to searching. Wandering is like how birds soar on thermals. Wandering is the joy of flight, but searching is that same flight only narrowing the pattern, taking aim on to something. Though I prefer the wandering, I have a good instinct for the search, so with the last light of the day guiding me, I pull into a vacant graveled lot in the town of Booker. Calling it a town is a stretch as I can see only four scabby buildings set against railroad tracks running to Canada on one side, the Swan River on the other. It's barely a town at all. There is a one-pump gas station with its electric Pepsi sign casting light against the adjacent and aging boards of Darryl's Feed and Farm with its two shaky stories. The gravel lot where I've parked Zhitomir belongs to an unlikely little restaurant identified by a gold leaf window sign forming the points of a compass and highlighting the East/West. The last of the four-building town is a small cottage attached and behind the East/West. That's all there is to Booker.

When he sees Zhitomir roll into his lot, the only person inside the East/West hauls his spry, seventy-year-old frame outside to stare at the side of the truck.

"I know I'm dreaming," he says, extending a welcoming hand and introducing himself as Vaughn Raker, the owner of the *East/West*. "What the hell is the Lost Sons of Zit Tummer? Is that how you say that?"

Two corrected pronunciations later I'm explaining what the truck and I are all about. Vaughn invites me to park in the lot for the night. He runs into the cottage behind the café, which he explains is his home, and brings out a heavy extension cord.

"I'll run back and get you a heater."

"No need," I tell him. "I've got one in the truck."

"That's good, you'll need it. We're sitting at 4000 feet here and mid-

August in Booker gets cold at night. You'll appreciate it later."

You can tell there aren't a lot of visitors to the East/West and Vaughn is thankful for someone to talk to. When I ask him why his place is named *East/West*, though the road it sits on runs north to south, he points to the adjacent Swan River.

"Has nothing to do with a road. The river turns from east to west here and that old river's been here longer than any road. None of these towns were ever road towns until about seventy-five years ago when they needed to bring equipment in for the copper mine in Fishkill. Even with the road, we still don't have much of a town here, do we?"

An hour later, Vaughn and I sit talking over a plate of gravy-smothered pork chops and rice in one of the *East/West's six* booths. Vaughn tells me, "The real town is up by the mine," then corrects himself. "Was up at the mine when they were running ore there. It's been over thirty years since the place closed down. There hasn't been a stitch of human activity since the late sixties but if you'd like we can take a visit up there sometime. You being a movie man of sorts, there's something there you might find interesting."

"I'd like to do that, Vaughn."

"So, tell me, Jake: it's not every day we get somebody here who drives around showing movies from a truck? What's your story?"

"Oh no, I never know how to answer that one."

"Come now," says Vaughn, "With the rig you drive I'm sure you have something to say."

"Well sure, I always have something to say, but I'm not sure it tells my story. What I do say is that fate seemed to pick me up by my ass and put me where I was supposed to be."

"You mean a woman, right?" Says Vaughn.

"No, I wish, but it wasn't. I kind of got a little kick in the behind from a few people who mattered to me and sent me out into a new orbit."

"And who were they?"

This is where it always gets a little weird. I'm not sure whether to tell people about the light, the visions, and the voices so I just say, "My uncle, Fred, for one. Fred raised me, and when he died he left me the truck, some money, and left me a note to get on with my life."

"What did the note say?"

"It wasn't so specific as much as it pointed me in a direction."

"And what direction was that?"

"Gee, Vaughn, I'll tell you, I still haven't figured that out exactly. I do know this truck, showing movies, meeting people, and hearing stories is a big part of it."

"So you're a wanderer then."

"It's a family trait, or so I've been told."

"Well good for you! At least you got a truck out of the deal. Hard to complain about that." Then Vaughn gets up and says, "Well, I gotta go tend to some things. I'll see you in the morning. Make yourself at home, but if you don't mind, shut the lights off before you turn in. Leave the one on in the window. It gives me a little comfort knowing there's a light shining out from this tiny little piece of the Earth for someone to see. "

With that, Vaughn walks out, leaving me alone.

When I finish my meal, pulling one last paper napkin from the tarnished metal dispenser on the table, I take a look around the East/West. You can see the imprint of new paint covering the space where jukebox cabinets hung some time ago. Even though the tables are empty, each one has topped off ketchup and mustard bottles, and there's a little glass with toothpicks set right between each one. The counter has six green swivel stools that look pale in the dim lights. Four hanging light fixtures dangle above the aisle between the booths and the swivel chairs, but two of them are missing bulbs. It's clean and serviceable, but if the East/West has ever been anything more than that, I'd be surprised.

Vaughn is right about the temperature too, because when I step into the truck, my bones start complaining about the cold. However, it doesn't take long to warm up a little less than 2000 cubic feet of air, and in fifteen minutes my little cargo cabin is toasty and I spend an hour reading an interview with director Howard Hawkes before falling off to sleep.

The next morning I wake up and make my way into the East/West. The place is empty except for Vaughn, and a young man sitting quietly in the corner with a knapsack and khaki jacket, reading a magazine entitled *Modern Locomotive.* Vaughn is cheerfully singing the Folgers jingle as he dumps a flask of steaming froth into a large daisy-covered pump pot. "The best part of waking up . . ."sings Vaughn, adding, "Yep, that oughta stay warm all day. Don't expect too many people today." Vaughn pumps out some Folgers and asks me if I take cream or sugar. I nod yes, and he reaches under the counter fetching a small wicker basket filled with wrinkled packets of saccharine and nondairy creamer. When I take my first mouthful, I can't help but think fondly of The Bakery Café. Clearly Vaughn is two cups up on me at this point -- his eyes are wide open and he's full of life.

"Hey, after you turned in last night I found something I want to show you." He hands me a tattered poster from the Fishkill Theater. The poster lists a program called "The Sunken Shaft Friday-Night-at-the-Movies" and it lists the month's offerings from February 1968. For seventy-five cents, or two dollars for miner families, you could have seen movies every Friday night in Fishkill.

"That's the place I want to show you. The movie house is still there, though there isn't much left of it. Last movie was in 1969. After that they tore up the floor and turned it into a roller-skating rink. That didn't last too long, as you can well imagine, but neither did the karate studio that came afterwards. Gee whiz, people do get some funny ideas. Hasn't been a thing in it forever, but I think the stage is still there and the screen too: place hasn't been used in decades. Thought you being a movie man and all you might get a kick out of seeing it. I can't go today, I got a bunch of things to do, but maybe you can stay around for an extra day or two. You won't be disappointed."

Then Vaughn gestures at the young man reading the magazine.

"This is Groat, my new helper here. He got tossed right off a train and they told him to start walking. What kind of heartless s-o-b does that to a kid?"

Groat sets aside *Modern Locomotive* long enough to shake my hand and when Vaughn leaves he starts telling me all about modern hobo life.

"I been tossed plenty, but it was a surprise check while the train was stopped for a stuck switch. Dangomatic, I was fooled by that. I never thought they'd open the car. Seventy-eight full tankers out of Alberta and they bother searching through the only six freight cars. They could have waited for the switching yard in Missoula but some of these new guys can get pretty particular about these things."

Groat's the torn-up type -- wiry, with ragged clothes and he probably hasn't had his scraggly brown hair cut in over a year. Still, he has radiant green eyes with the unwavering gaze of a survivor. When I lay down a couple of dollars for the coffee, Groat waves it away in a comfortable act of generosity.

"It's on me," then he tells me, "I saw you drive in yesterday. I live above

Darryl's." He points to the windows above the feed store. "It was kind of weird, because I actually heard of you from another hobo who was at a show you did a few years ago at a Wobbly gathering in Idaho."

"*Emperor of the North* in Sand Point?" I ask.

"That's the one."

Groat starts ticking off films he's seen about trains: *Runaway Train, Boxcar Bertha, The Grey Fox, Closely Watched Trains,* and *Avalanche Express.* Then, pulling one out of a hat he's too young to have worn, he says, "I loved *The General,* that Keaton classic filmed in Oregon. I been in that town. Cottage Grove: cute little town."

"How about *The Lady Vanishes* and *Strangers on a Train?*"

"I seen them all, even the ones that are set on trains but aren't about them."

Groat is another wanderer, but I get the feeling he didn't have the benefit of an Uncle Fred or Julian backing him. Despite all his rough edges, there's a soul in him that makes you care for him. Vaughn must have seen that too, otherwise he wouldn't have taken him in.

Booker turns out to be a fine place to stay for a while and settling in is easier thanks to Vaughn's hospitality. One morning we're sitting in the East/West talking when a car drives up and stops.

"That must be Betty on her way to Bison Creek. She's a feisty old hen, stops in every week on her way to visit her husband, Raymond. He's in the nursing home in Bison Creek."

In walks Betty Faraday, equal parts Sunday school teacher and ranch-hand.

"Well, hell does freeze over," shouts Betty, destroying her Sunday school teacher image right away. "You found an actual paying customer, Vaughn."

Betty says, "You're the guy with that truck. Of course. Heard a little about that two days ago."

"From who?" kids Vaughn.

"From nobody you need to know about, Mr. Raker," bellows Betty, and then says hello to Groat and asks if anybody needs anything from the civilized world.

"Bison Creek, the civilized world. Now that's a good one," says Vaughn.

"At least they got a real grocery store there," says Betty.

Groat asks her to pick up the latest *Locomotive Today* magazine if she sees it, and I, thinking for a second that "grocery store" might mean fresh coffee beans and even some half and half, am about to speak up, when Vaughn asks her to pick up a case of artificial sweetener and a case of creamer.

"Good to have the essentials, right Jake?"

So much for my dream. I let out an involuntary "I hate creamer'" groan.

When Betty leaves, Vaughn explains that Ray's been living in the nursing home for the past two years.

"It got too hard on both of them with him at home."

When I ask what Ray's illness is, he says, "Whatever all those old miners get. Tough old buggers, miners, but I'm sure glad I never worked a mine." Then he adds wistfully, "He was my best friend when we were kids." I sense that Vaughn has more to tell about this. "Betty was my high school sweetie. Not like we was engaged or nothing, but she was the same pistol then as she is now."

"So what happened?"

"Well, Ray was a good looking guy and he had some money from working in the mine. I went off to school for a year in Billings and when I got back they were married. No hard feelings. That's what happens and we'd never talked about marriage. Those two were meant for each other, but I suppose I kept a little torch alive for her."

That evening I'm sitting in Zhitomir taking the chance to write a note to Julian. He's been back from Rome for a while and I haven't dropped him a line. I finish the letter and walk it down to the East/West where Vaughn says he can drop it in his box for the postman tomorrow. Booker is too small to have a post office.

When I return, to Zhitomir, it's a little past six. I remember to turn on my phone in time to get a call from Eric. The connection is a little fuzzy so I walk out of Zhitomir towards the East/West. Eric sounds excited and I'm happy to hear his voice even if what he says is a little odd.

"I'd like to go to Canada."

"What's in Canada?"

"Bears."

"Bears?" I ask again and Eric says, "Listen, Jake, let me read you this article I read at Peggy's from the *Hudson Bay Sentinel* about Frost Cove's 'Grizzly Bear Invasion'."

"Wait a second, who is Peggy and what are you doing reading *The Hudson Bay Sentinel* in Driggs?"

"Peggy's one of the belly dancers, and we found *The Sentinel* on the Internet, but that's not the point, Jake, listen." Eric starts reading a familiar story about bears foraging at the town dump and developing a taste for garbage. They start annoying locals by knocking over garbage cans until one day a bear enters a house where an old trusty yapping dog alerts the sleeping napping owner, who flees in fear. Next thing you know, the bear is shot; there's resulting outrage over the bear being shot, then an environmental group organizes a protest; and now there's a big standoff and lots of publicity, which brings lots of people to Frost Cove, the town on Hudson's Bay where all of this is taking place and infusing the local economy with some sorely needed cash.

"So?" I say to Eric "What's the big deal?"

"It's the poem," says Eric. "Well, technically a micro-fiction piece that won first prize in a local contest about the bear thing. I'll read it to you."

### They Buried Browser Today

**Winning Entry to the Frost Cove Literary Group Short Fiction Contest
Stories had to be less than 100 words.**

They buried Browser today.
An affable fellow, picking garbage, sleeping in the occasional sun.

Stanley Pitinski, on his retirement cruise from 39 years in the Bronx Post Office,
heard there were bears at the dump.
When he tossed the blueberries, he didn't see Browser until the bear stood up
bothered by berries pelting his snout.

Bang! Stanley's never-used pistol dropped Browser.
Lucky shot for a retiree.

"I'm sorry I panicked," pleaded Stanley.

"It's okay," said the cops, "happens all the time.

"Too bad you broke the camcorder," they added.

"Yeah, too bad," said Stanley, " got it."

"It's too sweet, Jake, I should get some footage of this scene," says Eric

"It's a long way to drive for bears, Eric," I say, but by the time we're done talking, Eric says he's on his way to Booker.

"Less than a week, Jake. Hang tight, and you and I'll be on our way after that."

"Sounds good, but one more thing, Eric. There's a kid, well, a young man, here I think you'll enjoy. He's been a hobo of sorts and I think you'll enjoy getting to know him.

"I'll look forward to it, Jake. Isn't that kind of what we are, Jake?"

"What?"

"You know, hobos?"

"I guess so, Eric, but it's a little different.  In any case, don't shoot any bears before you get here."

When I hang up, Vaughn, who caught some of the exchange, says, "Somebody shoot a bear?"

"Something like that."

CHAPTER 10

# A Story Told
# With Pictures

**In Which** we tour the hidden world of Montana's Michelangelo and listen to a man speak of light in "Edison's day."

The next morning when I arrive at the East/West, Vaughn is excited about taking me up to the abandoned town.

"Groat here will watch the place and we can head up to Fishkill. We'll take my pick-up. I'm not sure about the roads out there. We had a lot of rain this summer and it can get pretty soft. No point running that big truck of yours. I have a little diesel that knocks like hell, but it gets me around."

Stepping outside before loading into the truck, Vaughn pauses like he's been hit by fairy dust as he takes a deep, audible breath. Exhaling, he says, "I love that smell, the rotting leaves and needles all melting into winter, ground covered everywhere with the compost of life."

Vaughn's clacking diesel is the quietest of the knocks between Booker and Fishkill. As Vaughn said, the road is soft and filled with holes, and we're lucky to make twenty miles per hour. There are places where Zhitomir would have been knocking branches off the low hanging trees on either side of the road, but what the road lacks in smoothness, the tree-lined river bank makes up for in beauty. Vaughn points out the old railroad grade, still visible through the trees sprouting up and lining the road between Booker and Fishkill and says, "They pulled a lot copper out of there."

We dodge holes and ruts in the gravel road and Vaughn's mug swivels and splashes, refreshing stain marks on his dash and floor. Vaughn knows the road, the trees, the bends in the river, where every turnout leads, and the history behind each discarded piece of equipment slowly melting into the brambles. He reminds me of Uncle Fred, and for a second a flush of sadness overcomes me. "The only reason they needed Booker at all was for the railroad junction. Train had to slow down and turn there. Helluva a reason for a town, don't you think? Truth is, my mother ran the East/West before I did. She was from Spokane, and when my Daddy courted her she didn't stand a chance. Nine months later, there I am, Vaughn Junior, but my Daddy wasn't exactly the stick-around type. The only thing I got from him was my name. My grandfather was a railroad guy who hooked Mom up with the place when the company needed someone to run the switching station at the junction in Booker. What a choice: stay home and listen to people talk behind your back about some Romeo who drops you once the baby comes, or move to Booker, Montana. That's how I got here. Don't suppose you can squeeze a movie out of that story and get me enough money to leave, do you?"

We share a laugh as he slurps down the last few sips of his coffee.

When he takes his eyes off the road for a second to place his cup into the swivel, a deer bounds across our path. Vaughn recovers in time to swerve and miss it, but there's a new splash of coffee on the floor.

"You know, as much coffee as I lose to splashes, I might as well drink decaf. Dang deer cut your path when you're not looking. I swear they wait for you to take your eyes off the road. You never hit the first one either, because while you're staring at it, the second one comes out, and bam!" Then he points to the front of his truck and boasts, "I lost two other trucks to deer before I got smart. I had a guy weld that little deer guard across the front. Pretty stout little grill, too. Costs me two hundred dollars, but it's cheaper than insurance. Finally figured out that if it worked for trains, it would work for my truck. They still get hit, but they don't destroy everything when they do. Still, I feel sorry for the poor things taking that hit and then running off to die alone. That's why I dim my lights the instant I see a deer. It gives them a chance to get away. You, too, for that matter."

Fifteen more minutes of bracing against bumps in the truck and we enter the now-defunct copper mining town of Fishkill.

"Why Fishkill?" I ask and Vaughn purses his lips and rolls his eyes.

"Figure it out. The mining company never liked that name. Bad publicity."

The town has the remnants of a once grand entrance: two of the largest lodgepole pine trees you'll ever see hold a sign stretched between them, forming an archway. For close to a hundred yards the road is lined with lesser, but still grand, pine trees. Except for the sign being covered with moss, and the neglected road, the entrance to Fishkill conveys a sense that something great beckons. That is, until the end of the trees, where the ruins of an exhausted, abandoned village appear like the aftermath of a plague. Rows of metal-roofed shacks lead into the center of town, where many of the buildings have been dismantled.

The only thing left intact is the improbable Fishkill Theater, looming like a hallucination amidst the rubble around it. It has an ornate sculpted facade and a gilt-covered ticket booth, smack in the center of the entranceway, flanked by two sets of double doors. Covering the walls on either side of the doors are broken glass cases that once held promotional posters of coming attractions, and at the bottom of each case amongst the shattered glass, there are still little piles of the metal letters used for spelling out the names of the movies in neat signboard rows.

Vaughn and I step inside the lobby, which, though musty and dark, retains a high ceiling with an ornate trim around the edges. Even in this tattered state, aging and abandoned, the Fishkill Theater's dignity remains intact.

Vaughn runs out to his truck and brings back a flashlight so we can see as we enter the main hall. It's difficult in the dimness, but the seats are gone, as is the main stage curtain. Flashing the light to the ceiling, Vaughn points out the circular mural of a mining scene. "My mother took up with a man named Lucky Williams right before the war. Lucky, short for Lucien, was an artist who came through on the train and got stranded for a few weeks in Booker when the river flooded and took out the junction. He was making his way from Chicago to Seattle, but he stopped here in Booker and found my mom who hired him to do the East/West sign and, the rest, well, you know how that goes? A good thing too, 'cause there wasn't no personal ads back then, if you know what I mean. They loved each other, those two, and maybe he was too late to be a father to me, but he was a good friend and he adored my mom. Only problem was there wasn't much work for painters here. In fact, there wasn't much work for anyone unless you were a miner, but Mom convinced the head of the mine that Fishkill needed something to bring prestige to the town, to set it apart from the rest of Montana, so she got him to pay for a mural on the ceiling of the movie house. It was at that point that Mom started calling Lucky 'the Montana Michelangelo'."

Vaughn moves the flashlight from figure to figure and we strain our heads upwards to see. The light stops on the face of a woman standing in front of a pair of store windows. One of the windows has stock prices on it and the other is a picture.

"See Jake, that's my mom standing next to the East/West. The painting is copied from *Il Bacio* -- that means "the Kiss"-- and it was by an Italian painter, Francesco Hayez. Lucky did that special for Mom, because he told everyone that's how he saw her.

"Oh, Mom loved coming to the movies here. The Sunken Shaft Film Series was her favorite activity. I know she loved the pictures, but you know what? I think she loved sitting beneath that painting more than anything else in the world. And Lucky, he died on the same day Sputnik went up: October 4, 1957.

"I remember one time back in the late '60s when a bunch of high school kids snuck in here and painted the screen with a massive peace sign. Next night, they're sitting in the audience with their parents, the miners and miners' wives, waiting for the show to start. Kids are sitting there giddy, anticipating their contribution to world peace about to come up in light and startle everyone. See, Jake, even here in Fishkill, Montana, they knew how to start a movie proper-like. You know the way they used to do it; they start the film right on the curtain, drawing it back real slow as the film begins. So that curtain starts coming back and there, bigger'n life, is Paul Newman as *Cool Hand Luke* knocking heads off parking meters all framed by a gigantic hand-painted peace sign.

"Some of the crowd boos and hisses, others start to applaud and whistle, the handful of peace pranksters are enjoying the confusion, and in the majority is a large group of folks who have no idea whether the peace sign is an intended part of the movie. The projectionist doesn't know what to do, so he lets it run.

"You know what? The funny thing was that after a while you kind of ignored it and watched the movie.

"It wasn't long after that the mine closed for good. It was 1969 - January 20th, the same day Richard Nixon was sworn in as president. Funny how you remember dates." Vaughn turns his flashlight down to light our path out of the theater. Stepping from the darkened hall into the remnants of the once-flourishing town, we stop to let our eyes adjust to the light. Vaughn has the startled look of a man who took a trip to the past, and he says, "Mom came up here for years until she couldn't get around any more, and even then she kept a copy of that painting beside her bed. It's hanging behind the East/West counter now. I'll show it to you later."

Our drive back to Booker is oddly quiet. The bumps and ruts seem to have disappeared, the trees preside over the road in solemn silence, and the river flows by without a riffle. Entering the East/West Vaughn asks,

"You got copies of some good movies in that truck of yours?"

"You bet I do, Vaughn."

"You think we could show one here? I can pay for it."

"You don't need to pay for a thing. If you can get us an audience and make enough popcorn to keep everyone happy, I'll set it up."

"Well then, how about tomorrow? I'll make a few calls and put out the word. There aren't a whole lot of things in Booker that get people together: this could be a lot of fun."

"I don't suppose you have any special film in mind?"

"Oh, Mom liked Katharine Hepburn. You don't by any chance have something with her?"

"Nothing but a passable copy of *The African Queen*. How will that do?"

~

The next night people start coming into the East/West. Mostly gray-haired folks Vaughn calls his "neighbors," but there's a scattering of others including a few people with children. One of the older guys comes up to me as I'm going through my projector-cleaning routine.

"Still got cigarette burns on the reels?" he asks, referring to the marks used to measure time or mark reel changes for the projectionist.

"Yes," I answer, "same as ever. Nothing's changed in film for quite a while."

The man introduces himself as Glenn Forbert, and explains that he was in the army in Korea in the '50s.

"One of my jobs was running the movies. After the war I moved to Fishkill to work as the mine's electrician."

Glenn asks me what I'm showing and when I tell him it's *The African Queen*, he laughs.

"I probably showed that film twenty-five times." Drawing from some buried instinct he runs a finger across the projectors and checks for dust. Letting out a big exhale, he says, "Do you need any help running these things?"

"You help me? How about I help you? I get the feeling you know a lot about projectors."

A few minutes later in walks Betty Faraday with her son, Little Ray, his wife, Amalia and their two children, Greta and Luke. I say hello to Betty and ask her about her husband. She says, "Thank you for asking, Jake. Raymond is slowing down."

Thirty minutes later there are about twenty people facing one wall in the East/West and watching a scratchy but still entertaining copy of *The African Queen*. If I haven't met any of them, they certainly are familiar with me. Groat, when he's not bringing coffee or little dishes of popcorn to everyone, is enjoying the madness between the two leads and takes particular delight in Bogart's song "There Once Was a Fisherman . . . "

Former corporal Glenn Forbert handles two seamless reel changes and the normally far-flung community of Booker share a few hours beneath a painting of two lovers exchanging a tender, clandestine kiss.

When it's over, even the kids are slow to rise out of their seats. They stretch and yawn until Betty belts out, "How about some thanks for the guy whose truck you've all been wondering about?" The small crowd shouts out a hearty thanks and Betty laughs while taking a seat at one of the green stools. When I ask her if she's seen the movie before, Betty answers, "Oh yes, and many times. It's one of my favorites. They showed it years ago up in Fishkill and I went all three nights. We used to do that a lot, my sister Jane, and me. We loved the pictures."

Little Ray, holding a sleeping Greta, comes over with his family. Six-year-old Luke says, "That was a lot of fun, Grandma. Old Mr. Allnutt and his case of booze."

"Just like a woman to take away a man's whiskey," laments Little Ray.

Little Ray's wife, Amalia, hasn't said a word to this point but glares at him and says, "You got that right, Ray." Betty reaches around her daughter-in-law with a loving arm and says, "I do love this girl."

Vaughn joins the little crowd and gestures to a table where he's set out a thermos of hot cocoa and pretzels, saying to no one in particular, "There's danger when you get these people together." He winks at them and says with a wry smile, "No secrets here."

Betty adds, "Oh, I seriously doubt that," taking her granddaughter by the hand to fetch her a cup of cocoa.

The following morning I'm enjoying the swivel of the old green stools at the counter of the East/West while reading film reviews in *The Daily Missoulian*. In between spins I'm experimenting with the perfect combination of non-dairy creamer and bear-claw icing required to bring the Folgers into shape, when Glenn, the Army projectionist from last night, comes walking in with a small satchel. He has Vaughn pour him a cup of coffee, which I notice he mixes with three teaspoons of sugar and three packets of creamer. Then, taking a seat beside me, he opens the satchel and pulls out a framed picture of a handsome Corporal Glenn Forbert in uniform, smiling proudly in front of a rack of projectors, all beneath a banner reading "Hollywood Goes to Korea!" He's holding a film can with the title *The African Queen* written on it and flanking the soldier are Humphrey Bogart and Katharine Hepburn!

"They came through with the U.S.O.," says Glenn, pointing at his cheek in the photo. "See that lipstick? Katharine Hepburn kissed me there! I've seen everything they've ever done."

Glenn is still smiling over that photograph when he surprises me by saying, "You know, I was looking at your projectors, and I think they need some maintenance. When's the last time you oiled the gears and blew the dust out of them? You got to take care of those things you know, especially taking them on the road the way you do. It's one thing to leave a projector sitting all the time; it's another to jostle them all across the country, in and out of moisture. I'd be happy to go through them for you. That was part of my job in Korea. And one other thing: a little bit of rubbing alcohol would bring up the fidelity on those sound drums. Got to keep them clean. That print you have of *The African Queen* is not getting any younger and it can use all the TLC it can get."

It turns out that former Corporal Forbert knows of what he speaks, and he does speak, and speak and speak between enthusiastic cups of the Folgers, each one amended with three sugars and three non-dairy creamers!

"Whoa, I almost forgot the thing I brought to show you." It turns out that Glenn, who knows all about projectors, films, and electricity, knows even more about bulbs. He takes out a small wooden box. Inside the box is a crimson piece of velvet, and when he unfurls the velvet there is a vintage projection bulb glistening like the day it was made.

"You see this little thing? A bulb is a bulb, right? Well, nothing could be further from the truth, Jake. Too few people appreciate how a light bulb is the perfect culmination of theoretical physics and technological ingenuity."

Hearing the word physics, I am relieved to set aside *The Missoulian's* review of *Pulp Fiction* to listen to Glenn.

"Do you know that in Edison's day they hand-crafted every light bulb? Edison, Tesla, all the early electrics guys blew the tubes individually, and the filaments were placed on their bases by hand. Look at this thing: look closely."

Glenn hands me the bulb so I can hold it up to my eyes.

"Do you know how these bulbs work?"

"Not exactly."

"See the conductors? See how polished they are, and the tiny little strut supports holding the filaments? It's all suspended in a spatial vacuum, set in a transparent tube and hooked into electricity to produce light. Think of a filament like a kink is in a water hose. The kink is like a big resistor. Electricity is the water and when it can't get through the filament it gets backed up: that's called impedance. So, you have all that electricity trying to push into that little-bitty wire, but there isn't enough room and because there isn't any way to escape it keeps on pushing until the filament gets hot and starts to glow. If it gets too hot it melts, and poof, an audience of two hundred GI's starts hooting and hollering and wishing they were back home, away from a war they don't understand.

"But," says Glenn, growing more excited. "That's the beauty of it: most of the time it doesn't melt because it sits in a vacuum where the resulting glow is light. Projected light is controlled fire, and fire is one of the fundamental forces of nature. These little bulbs are modern cousins of the old hand-blown creatures Edison had to use.

"In 1951 we had such long, beautiful bulbs. But I can tell you, even the Army didn't like paying for those things. Every time I submitted a requisition for those I'd hear it from Colonel Mikkelson. 'There are a lot of things beside light bulbs we need to fight this war, Corporal Forbert.' Maybe that's true, but try and get a bunch of kids to risk their lives without a little Rita Hayworth and the war would end in a second. Well, each of those bulbs was good for about thirty hours unless you bumped them or dropped them, spilled water on them, or looked at them wrong."

Looking right at me now, Glenn asks, "You do this a lot: don't you think the bulbs know when the movie's a good one? Did you ever notice how the bulb never burns out during a slow, boring stinker when everyone would be happy to get back to the barracks? No, always in the good films and then, boy, do you ever hear it!

"One night we were showing *The Outlaw,* and fizzle, the bulb burns out in one of those scenes that make it clear what Howard Hughes saw in Jane Russell. First they all gasped, 'Oh, come on,' and then the entire battalion starts screaming, 'Light the film, Forbert. Light the film, Forbert.' I'd left the replacement bulbs in my office so I bolted out of the room, hearing the chant the whole way. Luckily, I got it going again before there was serious trouble. After that I carried a spare in my shirt pocket."

Glenn pauses only long enough to mix up another dose of his unholy brew.

"No, you start thinking about movies, you better have an appreciation for the creation of light and the technology for it. We didn't have those fancy halides you use now. You can just about play baseball with one of them. But this bulb: bump it wrong and poof, it's dead."

Glenn takes the bulb and wipes it clean with the cloth before nestling it back into the wooden box.

"I'm saving this bulb for my grandchildren, when they're old enough to appreciate it."

That morning I experienced a deep gratitude for two things to which I had routinely paid little attention: projection bulbs and decaffeinated coffee.

# CHAPTER 11

# Late Nights And Mercator Projections

**In Which** we learn about the Ahab of grizzly bears and are reminded of "our place in the world."

True to his word, Eric arrives with two things; a video copy of *Project Grizzly*, a Canadian documentary about a Quebec man who had a chance encounter with a grizzly bear years ago and lived to tell the tale, and a letter from Clara that arrived after I left Driggs. My instincts were right about Eric and Groat: they connect like brothers. After dinner, Groat, Eric, Vaughn and I watch the film on a small television in Vaughn's house and learn about a crazy man who is the "Ahab of Grizzly Bears." Ever since the attack, all the guy does is prepare for the day when he can have another encounter with a grizzly from the safety of a "grizzly-proof suit." It is a fantastic film and sponsored by the National Film Board of Canada.

"I wish I could get them to sponsor me," says Eric

"Are you Canadian?" asks Vaughn."

"No," says Eric.

"I am," says Groat.

"Sweet," says Eric.

It's been enough sterling dialogue for the night and it's time for me to turn in. As we leave Vaughn's and walk back toward Zhitomir, I ask Eric about the bumper sticker on his van that reads, "Belly Dancing is Exciting!"

"Something I got in Driggs," says Eric.

Seeing that Eric plans to sleep in his van, Groat offers to let him stay in the feed store apartment.

"I wish it wasn't true, but there's an extra bed."

Eric thanks him but declines. "You know, I've been sleeping in a bed for the last week or so and I kind of miss my van," says Eric," and plods his way in that general direction.

"Goodnight, Eric," I shout to him, "remind me to tell you my story about bumper stickers sometime, okay?"

Two days later it's our last night in Booker. The evening is cold and clear, and a full Montana moon is rising over the hills. After a satisfying steak dinner, Eric surprises us, unveiling a pound of fresh-roasted coffee he's been saving, a gift from Seraphina. We have a moment of panic when Vaughn doesn't have an electric grinder for the tasty little beans, but then he remembers an old hand grinder his mother had in the house and retrieves that. Vaughn watches as Eric prepares the coffee, telling him he doesn't need to boil the water on the stove.

"Run it through the machine," suggests Vaughn, but Eric boils his own water as Vaughn stares at him confused.

"Are you sure that's coffee? I never seen anyone fuss over coffee so much."

A few minutes later, when Eric hands him a cup and Vaughn takes a sip, he cries out, "Mother of God, that's good!" then adds the artificial sweetener and non-dairy creamer to "Make it right." Please, Vaughn, say it ain't so.

Once the coffee starts him going, Eric gets inspired and retrieves his camera from the van. The presence of the camera changes everyone at first until the coffee starts kicking in. After a while nobody takes much notice. Eric has the gift of being invisible even while he's sticking a Bolex right into your face.

Groat asks if anyone wants to play cards and runs back to his room above the feed store where he retrieves two heavily worn decks of cards. Fortunately, one thing the East/West has in strong supply is playing cards, and Vaughn unwraps a fresh deck. Groat has an exuberant way of dealing cards while happily tapping his foot and humming.

We down the first pot of coffee, and about ten o'clock the coffee has clearly overridden the internal shut-off switch. In between uninspired hands of gin rummy, Groat starts opening up about riding trains all around North America, telling us he left home when he was sixteen and has been training it ever since. He once had a girlfriend who rode with him for a few years before "she fell back to Earth," as Groat puts it.

"Yeah, she went home to get a job and stay with her parents. Can't blame her, but it was great having the company."

Groat is a man-child for sure; he speaks like some wizened old sage of the rails. He reminds me of Jimmy Cagney with longer hair and worry lines on his face. There's something both impressive and sad about Groat. You know he's got some awful, painful history, and you also know he's never going to reveal even a touch of it. He starts talking about trains and he's a walking encyclopedia. He knows the routes, the switching yards, the engines and car types, and even knows the manifests for most of the trains.

"You think about what's clacking through America and it makes you shudder," he says. "Most people don't know what all those numbers are on the sides of those tanker cars, and it's a good thing too or they'd be running for the hills. We've run on cars where we saw stuff dripping from tankers and putting off fumes that made you hack your guts up. I had to jump off this one train once when all the vibration caused something very strange and smelly to spill and there was a corrosive drip-trail for nearly ten miles. I never found out what was in that car and I hope I never do."

That was the first pot of coffee and what started as a short turned into a feature. A little after midnight, Groat reaches around his neck and pulls out two intertwined chains with heart shaped lockets. One is gold and the other is silver. He replaces the gold one under his shirt and then opens the silver one and shows us the old photo inside of it.

"That's my sister, there's me at eight, and those are my parents." Vaughn asks where everybody is now, and Groat stares at the picture and says, "Things got kind of complicated after that. Everybody's fine, but I don't keep in touch too much."

"What's in the gold one?" asks Eric.

"Sorry, but that one stays where it is."

Groat will not reveal his story tonight.

Vaughn suddenly jumps up from the table and says, "It's a good thing

I remembered. You got a postcard today. Vaughn fetches the card and returns. It's from Julian of course and I explain a little about my uncle. The photo on the front is a cheesecake photo of Sophia Loren. I read the message on the back to everyone.

*Dear Jake*                                                                    *Today*

  *I received your card. Great to hear you're doing well. Don't let the bears into your tent. Is Eric with you? He left me a phone message about going to Canada. What's that all about? Are you going as well? Rome was great. Met an amazing woman at the film event, an American who puts video in the hands of refugees. Calls it the VPP - Visible Past Project. I'm sending you some of her stuff to show. Mostly shorts, some pretty rough, but should hold audiences. Amazing stories. You'd enjoy meeting her. Let me know where to send things.*

               *Onward, Julian*

*PS - You can pin this photo up beside your bed. Met her at the retrospective thing. J.*

 Vaughn's jaw goes slack and he says, "Your uncle knows Sophia Loren?"
 Eric says, "Julian knows everybody."
 "Well, I don't," says Vaughn, "but with that picture as the last thing I see tonight, I might stand a chance of a good dream if I head to bed. I'll see you guys in the morning."
 After Vaughn leaves, Groat and Eric are talking about the best route to Canada.  With something nagging at me from Julian's card, I read it again.
 Julian loves playing Cupid, and though I'm not sure, I can feel the tiniest arrow piercing my heart. When Julian says, "you'd enjoy meeting her," it means he's probably got something planned. Julian loves probing the depths of your mind and he thinks I was damaged by how I grew up. He wants me to find a woman so bad and is unbridled in his enthusiasm if I ever mention one. When I told Julian about meeting Sophie, he bought me a ticket to France. No kidding. He held that ticket for six months until I told him that Sophie was involved with Fabian. "Not to worry," said Julian, "no one can stay with a French man for too long. I'll hold it for a while." A little piece of me is hoping Julian is up to something.
 While I'm heady with the blood from Cupid's arrow, Groat runs to his apartment and returns with a leather-bound atlas with gilt-edged pages-a gift, he explains, from his old girlfriend's mother. The atlas is a lot like

Groat, a fine piece of work, but tattered from constant use. They're looking at the page with Frost Cove.

"It's a long way from anything," says Groat. Which I take to mean it's too far from a train line.

"No lines running north?" asks Eric.

"There's tracks, sure, but they don't use them anymore. It's so much easier to use trucks."

Eric invites Groat to join him, but Groat says he's got other plans. The two men sit drawing lines from place to place, train junction to train junction, town to town, each one another journey, each one another possibility. The trouble is every line they draw indicates Frost Cove is a long way from the East/West. Groat says, "If we were birds seeking a summer nesting site and adequate food, Frost Cove is closer than you'd think, but we're not birds. It's about twelve hundred miles," or as Groat boasts, "a little under 2000 kilometers."

In the small pages of Groat's atlas, Frost Cove sits at 62 degrees north latitude, 90 degrees west longitude. Staring at the page I hear my voice meld into Fred's as I say, "That is on the standard longitude/latitude grid. You could as easily place it on an arc connecting Malaysia and Senegal."

Eric responds to that comment with a confused look.

"Jake, what are you talking about?"

There's no point trying to explain it to them that it's one of Fred's speeches coming through. Fred had this thing about the Mercator projection. In high school, with some prodding from Fred, I did a paper on Gerardus Mercator, b. 1512 in Flanders (now Belgium) and died in 1594 in what is now Germany. Mercator is one of history's most accomplished mapmakers. He was able to draw a map that included latitude and longitude, accounting for the spherical shape of the Earth. The word atlas, used to describe a collection of maps, owes its origins to Mercator who chose to honor Titan, Atlas, and the King of Mauritania who was reputed to be a learned philosopher, mathematician, and astronomer. Fred had tremendous respect for Mercator, who was almost burned as a heretic for some of his ideas, but Fred never accepted any notion of space and time that didn't include an utter and mystical randomness (should there be any wonder that I live the way I do?). No doubt that is more than you wanted to read about Gerardus Mercator.

Before the astronauts started snapping pictures of planet Earth from up in space, Fred had pictures on his walls of the Earth sitting amongst its planetary siblings. Beneath that picture was Fred's shrine. That's what anyone who had the privilege of entering Fred's world automatically called it. The Shrine. On the wall was a draftsman's drawing of the solar system with lines extending into space. Its unruliness made it look like the hair on a person who'd stuck their finger into an electrical socket, but it all meant something to Fred. Lying flat on a shelf beneath the picture was a copy of Einstein's theory of relativity (Fred was good at math) with a horseshoe magnet sitting atop it. Nothing ever changed in that shrine. Ask Fred what it was about and he shrugged his shoulders and said, "It's a little complicated, but basically it's about knowing where you are in the world." This is pretty strange stuff for a guy who lived the way he did, never leaving the end of his road, but I heard him say it exactly the same way on a few occasions. "It's about knowing where you are in the world." One time I asked him what he meant by that, and he said "Jake, this is something I'm not sure you'll understand, but all that stuff about the shortest distance between two points being a straight line is a lot of crap! Pure mathematical fiction."

After a few minutes of my trying to explain some of Fred's theories of space and time, the two young travelers leave for their beds. When I follow a few minutes later, I walk outside into the night where I stand on Zhitomir's steps inhaling invisible cold air, and exhaling warm, moist vapors. I see Eric's already asleep, his van tucked behind the East/West. I turn my head and see no light in Groat's window above the feed store. The coolness finally chases me inside with the passing thought, "Oh, tender circus painter, what would you paint of this scene?"

I make my first attempt to sleep but it's not happening. There's too much coffee in my veins and too much moon in the clear night sky. If the moon is going to have its way with me, I might as well sit on Zhitomir's stairs for a while and take in the night air. When I reach for my sweater, the letter Eric brought from Clara falls off the chair to the floor. I'd completely forgotten it in the activities of the past few days. Before heading outside, I open it.

*Dear Jake,*

*Thank you for the last letter. I have been meaning to write for a while, but get so busy with other things. I enjoyed the description of the ranch where you showed the movies. I am so happy you are well and that your dreams are all coming true, and though I miss seeing your face and hearing your voice, I take comfort knowing your life is full of wonder.*

*First things first: I have taken the liberty of letting a young family live in your house. They moved to Larch six months ago. The man, Jason, is a carpenter, and Marion a very sweet young woman has taken up your role at The Sonnet. They also have a young daughter named Betsy, who is two years old. Houses need life in them. It seemed a waste to let it sit empty and I know you do not plan on living there again. I am not getting any younger and it is easier to have someone living there than for me to find someone to look after the place.*

*Otherwise, all is well here. The Sonnet grows dustier by the day. Jason has built me new shelves, but the books keep piling up all over the floor. An exciting thing happened a few weeks ago when I acquired an original edition of Whitman's Leaves of Grass. Can you believe it? The seller did not have an inkling of the value and I could have had it for nothing. Of course, I could not have lived with myself if I did that and I paid handsomely for it. Can you imagine, an original Whitman sitting here at The Sonnet? I should not go on about it, but it was very exciting.*

*Now, see, I have almost forgotten to ask how about you. I feel it in my heart that you are thriving. It must be wonderful to travel freely. Fred knew exactly what he was doing when he gave you that truck. Speaking of Fred, it appears you are not the only one to have visions, as your uncle is still quite present. I talk to him more often than some of the people around here might think is healthy. At least I can tell you without worrying about some silly person telling me I should consider seeing a doctor.*

*That will have to do for now. Rosalyn is on her way over and I promised to have tea for her. You remain in my prayers.*

*With great fondness, Clara*

Setting down the letter, an uncomfortable wave of emotion overtakes me. The thought of Clara growing older is discomforting. It was Clara who helped me leave Larch and it was Clara, when I handed my house keys to her on the morning I drove from town, who gave me a warm embrace and suggested I stop at the cemetery before leaving. When I asked her why, she said there were people who needed me to say goodbye to them. I told her I wasn't going to be gone that long, but Clara knew better, and she made me promise I would visit the cemetery. Once there, I walked amongst the Tollivers and the modest headstones of my great grandparents, Jeannine and Samuel, then my grandparents, Samuel Junior and Ariella. Finally, and this was hardest, of course, my mother, Eva, whose headstone was still absent of the weathered aging of moss and time. Her headstone was engraved with these words, *Gentle and Kind Soul.* It made me uncomfortable to see that with the exception of Fred, whose ashes had been scattered into Hiko Creek beside his property, Tollivers didn't get very old. I set Clara's letter down on my bed when a shudder of cold runs through me and ends the torrent of memory. I put on the sweater and, stepping out of Zhitomir, I have a chance to stare at the toy town in front of me.

Towns are like people and they shouldn't sleep with their lights on. Too many towns, and all big cities, live with an insomnia of signs and streetlights that only succeed in chasing away the mysteries of the night. Not so in Booker, where the only light is coming from the moon. Booker still sleeps at night. No streetlights, no burglar lights, no hums and flickers from transformers, or stores cursed by perpetual advertising lights. Except for one Hopperesque Pepsi glow, Booker renews itself with full and restful sleep.

It's cold tonight, and the air feels good as it runs through the weave of my sweater, raising goose bumps on my arms and neck. The coffee has finally departed, and when I step back into Zhitomir, the sheets are clean. My breathing slows and I'm hoping for kind dreams as I fall off listening to the Swan, flowing eastward, singing a gentle river ballad to the night.

The following morning Vaughn and Groat bid us farewell. Vaughn, feeling the need to send us off with something, stuffs packets of creamer into our hands and wraps each of us a bear claw. Eric asks Groat how long he plans to stay in Booker. Groat says, "No plans, but I got your number. I'll catch up to you sometime. You can count on it." I hop into Zhitomir, Eric into his van, and off we go, with Vaughn waving and shouting a farewell.

"I wish I were young enough to join you fellas. Come back anytime. It was sure a good couple of weeks."

CHAPTER 12

# The Best Pakoras In Primrose, North Dakota

In Which worn rotors lead us to the town of Primrose, fine women, three large elm trees, two kittens, one mechanic, and a quartet of fine singers.

Everyone has read *Alice in Wonderland*, but have you ever fallen through the looking glass? Eric and I did, landing in Primrose, North Dakota, my favorite town in North America.

Thanks to an early snow on Hudson's Bay, and neglected maintenance on Eric's van, we never made it to Frost Cove. With our sights set on garbage dump polar bears, while winding eastward through hundreds of miles of wheat, sunflowers, and corn, Eric's van starts squealing as we enter the little North Dakota town of Primrose. Primrose has a hand carved, wooden welcome sign that greets you on either end and states -- "Primrose: 614 Friendly People!" The town sits two miles south of the Canadian border on a well-used north/south trucking route to Winnipeg.

The Toyota's plaintive squealing escalates into an urgent grinding as I pull behind Eric at the first traffic light we've seen in two days. I'm not sure if Eric is ignoring it or can't hear it over the music to which his arms are flailing. Three bursts of Zhitomir's proud horn gets Eric to turn down the music and hopefully take notice of what his brakes are doing.

When the light changes to green, Eric pulls off to the side where I join him.

"I heard it, Jake. There's got to be a shop here. Follow me down the main drag and we'll have a look."

Fortunately, Primrose has a variety of main-street businesses belying the town's modest population and it doesn't take long for us to find a two-bay garage where the lone mechanic, hearing the sound coming from Eric's van, waves him into a vacant bay. The second bay of Tom's White Pelican Farm and Auto Repair has a large, green machine with mysterious implements attached to it.

The lone mechanic is Tom, a handsome and lanky man of about thirty-five who looks like a slightly greased-up Robert Redford. Tom wastes no time raising Eric's van to a working height with the hydraulic lifters. Then, from beneath his University of North Dakota baseball cap, he begins his inspection, then says, "Toyota brakes, at least they give you a loud warning."

Tom turns to me and says, "That was your horn up the street, wasn't it? Heck of a blast you got there. It's funny, but when I woke up this morning I knew something odd was headed my way. Ever get one of those feelings?"

"As a matter of fact, I'm getting that feeling right now," I say, though I can tell by the look on Tom's face that he wasn't looking for a reply.

As he unzips the bolts off the Toyota's wheels, Tom looks to Zhitomir and says, "Nice paint job: you show movies for a circus or something? We get the Shriners and the Gatti, but I haven't ever seen the Zeetoemeer before. Is that Italian?"

After removing all the wheels on the Toyota and carefully inspecting each one, Tom tells Eric, "You need new brakes and the rotors are iffy. I suspect this thing's been singing to you for longer than you've been listening. My parts supplier is closed on the weekend, but if I call it in now they should be here early Monday morning. I need to take a closer look at the rotors. If they're shot it could be Tuesday before I can finish and that's assuming I get that old thresher done tomorrow."

"How many cans of film will that cost?" Eric asks Tom, who is confused.

"That's money to him," I explain to Tom. "Each film can is a twenty-dollar bill."

"Without rotors, it'll be between seven and eight film cans. With rotors, double it."

Eric exhales deeply at the price.

"Are there any horse arenas nearby?" provoking a perplexed look by Tom until Eric explains his sideline profession while Tom replaces the van's wheels.

"There are plenty of horses. But arenas? No. Most of the money's across the border in Crystal Falls."

Ever the filmmaker, Eric has already switched gears from the cost of the job and asks Tom why the garage is called the White Pelican. As Tom lowers the van with the hydraulic hoist, he explains, "There's an isolated lake up on the border where I camp in the summer and there's a bunch of white pelicans living there. I love to watch them glide above the water when they're fishing. If I could be any other animal, I'd be a white pelican, so when I took over the shop and it needed a name, I called it the White Pelican."

Then Tom, realizing we're not going anywhere until the van is fixed, says, "You guys are going to need a place to stay. My sister Rachel has a camper park on the edge of town: you drove past it on the way in."

Tom walks to the edge of the street and points. "Straight down the road: nine-hundred-seventy-five yards to the front door. It's a big round lot with a chain link fence around it and three of the biggest elm trees you'll ever see. It's way nicer once you're inside than what you see from the road. Nothing fancy, but it's clean and she's got showers and all of that stuff. Tell Rachel I'm working on your van and she won't charge you much."

Then, while wiping his hands with a rag, Tom walks over to Zhitomir. "You must get a lot of strange looks with this rig."

He pokes his head under the chassis and says, "Be careful entering the camper park. You have enough clearance, no problem, but drive in slowly because there's a big pot hole in the driveway that can rattle your teeth loose if you hit it wrong."

Eric, more concerned with getting something to eat, asks Tom about restaurants in Primrose.

"There you're in luck. Ever since they built the hydro plant in Crystal Falls we get lots of folks through here: tourists, hunters, even Canadians jumping across the border to live the tax-free life in Primrose. There's a bunch of restaurants. My favorite is the Bombay. You'll be able to walk there from Rachel's. You can't miss it -- The Bombay Palace," says Tom with an ironic laugh. "Sign out front says 'The Best Pakoras in Primrose'."

Before hopping into Zhitomir for the drive to the camper park, Eric grabs his camcorder from the van, saying, "I think I may be needing this."

There is something exotic about this town for sure and Eric smells it. Eric has a nose for people's stories and the film possibilities in them. He mines community calendars, personal ads, bulletin boards, obituaries, and local papers. It's like he picks up where others leave off. He has the gift of seeing a blur and bringing it into focus.

To name a few blurs Eric has focused: he found Bootsy Gluck, a welder/sculptor responsible for building the welcome sign to Hickham, Nebraska: Home of the Hickham High School "Ever-Watchful Terriers." The dangling sign is suspended across the road, held between the mouths of two massive iron dogs. Lots of people have seen that, but beneath it is a much smaller sign, which reads "Hickham Nebraska. Population 435. The Only Crime Free Town In Nebraska." Eric has fifteen minutes of Bootsy on film welding projector brackets to the outside of Zhitomir while explaining why Hickham needs no police force. "It's not that everyone is so decent, but we're all working too hard to break the law. Besides, even if you commit a crime, there's only one policeman to catch you. The smaller the police force, the smaller the crime rate," says Bootsy before flipping down his welding mask and igniting the blue flame of his torch.

Eric found and filmed Lotte Policeno in Cusco, Indiana, a master's division discus thrower fresh from her triumph in the Masters World Championships in Istanbul, Turkey. Lotte had run a personal ad in the Cusco, Indiana, weekly paper *The Ideal,* which read as follows: "Elite athlete seeks companionship with available gentleman for fitness, fun, and whatever. No softies or shot-putters, please!" I swear every word of that ad is true. Lotte was disappointed when the spidery Eric answered the ad, thinking he was too skinny if not too young for her. To his and her relief she was thrilled when he only wanted to film her. Eric thinks *How to Throw a Discus After Fifty* is the film that will make him famous someday.

Which is all a way to bring us back to Primrose.

From the vantage point of Zhitomir's cab, I'm not sure campground is the right word for Rachel's place. It's a large circular piece of hard-packed ground about two hundred feet in diameter with grass that struggles to grow. The ground is a moonscape of chuckholes filled with muddy water. There's a tall chain link fence in modest repair with weeds and grass growing into it. Three huge elm trees sit on the perimeter of the lot providing a comforting blanket to the large patches of ground marked for about fifteen vehicles. The spaces are delineated by tire marks and electrical and plumbing hook-ups and there's a small flat-roofed building marked "Showers and Bathrooms."

Hearing us enter the lot, Rachel runs out from her house that sits inside the wide opening from the main road to the campground. The house, though small, is stout and well maintained and gives the impression that it's been around for some time. It's painted a bright yellow and is set off from the rest of the lot by a hip-high picket fence enclosing a small garden and a large, impeccably stacked firewood pile. Even though it's only September a plume of smoke rises from the chimney, giving the air a sweet, smoky taste. There's a hand painted wooden arrow on the fence corner pointing to the door of the house that reads "Office."

Coming from the house, Rachel slips on a pair of shoes and her eyes expand when she sees Zhitomir. With her hands, she carefully guides us across the bumps Tom warned us about.

"Careful, whoa, easy, that hole is way deeper than you think. You can lose an axle there."

Rachel is tall like Tom, but with attractive thick brown hair pulled back in a tight, single braid. Though she's probably in her late thirties, the deep lines in her ruddy face make her look ten years older. Inside the cab, Eric says to me, "Do you think she's pretty?" It's a funny question coming from Eric. When I don't answer, Eric pushes, "I'm not asking for me, Jake: you're the one who hasn't had a girlfriend in how long -- forever! Well, do you think she's pretty?"

"Eric, I'm shy but I'm not blind. Yes, she's pretty."

"Good. Maybe you'll bust out of that shell you like to wear and have some fun."

When I step out of Zhitomir, Rachel greets me with an unexpected hug.

"Tom called to warn me you were coming. He wasn't kidding about that truck being some kind of a sight! It kind of reminds me of Willie Nelson's tour bus that blew through here a few years ago. The sides of that were painted with a cattle stampede. They got stopped at the red light long enough for me to appreciate it. Some piece of work that was. Did you paint this one yourself?" asks Rachel.

"No, an old friend did it for me."

"Must have been a good old friend," she says. "That is impressive work."

Rachel helps back me into one of the spaces, all of which are vacant except for one with an Airstream trailer propped up on cinder blocks and attached to six concrete footings with chains attached to the trailer. Tom was right: from the inside the campground has a cozy feel owing mainly to three enormous elm trees giving cover to the place while framing the expansive view of the rising grasslands to the north. My eyes squint at that blank and steely vastness, and the air is so dry that with each breath my lips and throat feel like brittle windowpanes. The last sun of the day filters into the lot and there's a cool bite to the wind as we step from Zhitomir's cab.

"If you all don't mind coming over to the office I can get you registered," says Rachel. A welcome blast of warm air greets us as we step inside where Rachel gives us towels and soap, before she walks us out to the showers while explaining why the place is so empty.

"After Labor Day things slow down. It'll pick up again in a few weeks when hunting season starts. We have a pretty good whitetail season here. Mule deer too." Then, looking at me, she says with a hint of satire, "I don't get the feeling you guys are here to shoot deer."

"No, not this year."

"Well, not with guns at least," says Eric.

"What are you, some kind of scouts from Hollywood?" asks Rachel.

"No, nothing like that. We roam about showing movies," I say.

"Oh come on, and I'm home on leave from NASA. No one roams about showing movies. Look, I don't need any problems around here. No drug dealers, no freaks, and no trouble! You understand? Any man driving around in this rig better have a better cover than showing movies. So, what's your story?"

When Rachel talks like that I get a little excited and say, "Yes, madam, how foolish of me to think we could conceal ourselves from a woman of your stature. I'm Don Quixote, a Knight Errant, and this is my servant, Sancho Panza." Eric's eyes grow wide and he cannot believe what he's hearing as I continue. "We're on a noble quest to bring virtue, honor, and dignity to the world. You pray tell must be our fair maiden. If you will allow me to kiss your hand."

Hearing this, Rachel shakes her head and says, "Dulcinea, fair maiden, nuts, nuts, nuts. Now I know you're from Hollywood now with all that Man of La Mancha crap! Nice try. We have movies here too, you know?"

"Pray forgive me Madam if I have given you cause for offense."

"Look, you can stay, okay, but quit with the fair maiden stuff already."

Rachel's snappy, but she's pleasant and playful and she tells Eric he's welcome to stay in an Airstream trailer that she keeps for family visitors. "No charge, I have to keep heat in that thing anyway or it gets all moldy. Might as well have someone in there. You'll still need to use the camp showers because the plumbing's not connected in the Airstream, but it's cozy inside." This is a welcome relief to both of us because Zhitomir, though comfortable for one, gets cramped with someone stretched out on the floor in a sleeping bag.

When I ask Rachel about the chains on the Airstream she explains, "Tornadoes. We're past the prime season now, but I don't let anyone in there from June to August." Then she adds a perplexing "You being a movie guy should know that."

"What do you mean by that, fair lady?"

"Oh, please stop with that voice, will you? It wasn't so cute the first time either.

"You better have my brother check your exhaust pipe because I think you're taking in fumes. Tornadoes? Dorothy? Wizard of Oz?" Then she adds as an afterthought, "Hey, I hope Tom told you about the Bombay. Best place in town and The Cordials are singing there tonight. Local group: going to be some fun there. I might come down myself."

When Rachel walks back to her house, Eric says to me, "Where the hell did that come from, Jake? Man, you should trot that out more often." Then he heads over to the Airstream and I have a chance to sit with Zhitomir.

Zhitomir has a way of settling in, kind of sings a little as the engine and the body creak and moan until the heat dissipates. After a little while it all gets quiet, like the whole truck has fallen off to sleep. Fred had a different view of cars and trucks. Fred said that machines are cold pieces of steel and he laughed at people who gave their vehicles names and imbued them with personalities. "Would you name your toaster Kathy, or your chainsaw Melvin? Would you say good night to it?" But Fred never lived in the truck the way I do, and if only because I've spent so much time with it, Zhitomir has a personality. It's comforting to spread things out a little when freed from the constant rattle of the road. It's nice to lay open a book or not put away a pair of sneakers, leave the chair unfolded, and it's a treat to plug in the heater. Normally, I don't bother with the heater if I'm parked for the night. If it's cold I'll climb into my bed and dive into the covers waiting to get warm. But when things are settled for a few days, it feels nice to take the cool out of the truck, warm the wood and fluff things up some.

As the heater starts to work, I take a few minutes to write a short letter to Julian. I doubt Julian even knows there's a state called North Dakota, but I tell him where we are nonetheless, and let him know he can send something to Primrose. Something tells me we'll be here long enough for him to reply.

After finishing the letter, I shower, then stop by Rachel's office to ask where the post office is. Rachel says, "It's on the other side of town, not far, but not on your way to the restaurant. I'm running down that way in a few minutes and I can drop it there for you."

Walking back to get Eric, I glance back at Rachel's place and I get the feeling of having seen it before, but it's not real, it's a feeling.

When I walk into the Airstream, Eric has his video gear scattered on the bed. He is, literally, lying amidst it and reading a magazine called *Northern Heritage Farm Implements*. Then he says to me, "Jake, she digs you."

"You think? You liked the Don Quixote bit?"

"Yeah, sure, keep doing that and you'll end up in the Great Plains Nut-house, but no, she's got those eyes for you. You know, Donny Q, it wouldn't hurt for you to let people see that award winning personality you keep so bottled up. Besides, she's hot!" Before I have a chance to get Eric's defini-tion of hot, he shows me a picture from the magazine and reads out loud, "Today's northern farmer can work over a thousand acres with nothing but the assistance of modern machinery." Then he adds, "You know, Jake, that's a lot of space to work by yourself."

A few minutes later Eric and I eagerly step inside the Bombay Palace, where we're greeted by the sweet smell of anise. There are a few people wait-ing ahead of us so we take a seat on a comfortable bench beside the cashier. Across from where we sit is a glass-covered black frame with an old news-paper clipping from the *San Francisco Chronicle*. Above it is a hand written note, which reads:  Restaurant Owner's First Date! Eric goes over to read it and then gestures me over to do likewise.

## Cupid Uses Bison to Unite Couple

(A.P.) San Francisco, California.
The article is dated, February 14, 1978.

Mr. Matthew Harrington, a 36-year-old merchant mariner aboard the container vessel Royal Granada, is no newcomer to danger. But even this able-bodied seaman was surprised by events last week in Golden Gate Park.

Enjoying leave before his ship sailed for Singapore, Harrington spent the day in the park, observing a popular attraction, San Francisco's majestic bison herd. While watching them feed, he noticed something odd. "The herd suddenly turned and formed a semi-circle facing toward the corner of the pasture." Harrington and others were surprised to see a small group of people walking towards the massive animals. "I assumed they must be the zoo keepers, but when I saw they were all women wearing traditional Indian saris, I figured something was a bit daff." Harrington sprang into action as he saw the herd's massive patriarch lower his head and begin pawing the ground. Having worked on cattle farms as a child in Ireland, he instantly recognized the threatening posture of a bull ready to charge. Quickly scaling the twelve-foot cyclone fence into the pasture, he drew the bull's attention away from the group of women. "There wasn't a lot of time for thinking," he reported. "I was waving me hands and yelling at the ladies to get out, but they kept advancing. I knew I had to run towards them and shout at them to get out of there." Sprinting across the field, Harrington outran the bull and directed the women into a hay shed.

"Biggest problem was, one of the women had on a red sari. I had to lead the beast away from them by getting in his eyes. I couldn't take cover me self, but then he finally made his charge. I didn't have me cursed legs strong enough to outrun the big beast" Harrington said later from his bed in San Francisco's Sacred Mother Hospital where he is being treated for a concussion, broken ribs and various abrasions.

Eyewitnesses say Harrington sustained his injuries as the charging bull threw him twenty feet into the air and then calmly walked back to his herd to resume feeding. "I don't know if twas me bum or me teakettle that got the worst of it, but they are both a bit tender at the moment. I don't hold any hard feelings toward the beast. He was only protecting his lovely wives. I'd do the same if someone came into me own house unannounced."

Investigators discovered that the group of Indian women had been touring the park and entered the restricted bison compound through a normally padlocked gate. "We saw a strange man waving his arms at us as though he was going to attack us," said Rashmi Singh of the red sari. Fortunately, the women quickly grasped the threat to themselves when Harrington made his momentous sprint and they saw the bison in hot pursuit. "We were deeply concerned about the man's welfare when we saw him lifted into the air," added group member, Jasminda Panni.

After the incident, Ms. Singh, who was born in Bombay India but resides in Wyoming, visited the injured mariner at the hospital to thank him for his bravery. A friendship developed. "He saved our lives and now he has no one to take care of him. I wanted to stay to help him in kind. After only a few days, we both knew we were in love. It isn't every day that a man risks his life for you, you know."

Harrington is expected to make a full recovery and the newlyweds plan a celebration as soon as Ms. Singh's family arrives from India.

When he finishes reading the piece, Eric lets out a two syllable "swee--eeet," and then says slowly, "Jake, do you get the same feeling I do that everything in Primrose is like its own little movie." With the smell of the anise filling my nostrils, I answer,

"Maybe, but you know the thing that I'm wondering about?"

"What's that?"

"Why would a guy know it's exactly nine hundred and seventy five yards from his shop to the front door of a house?" Eric is not so concerned with that as I am and continues speaking about his movie idea.

"Who knows Jake, probably a joke. But I don't mean the place as a whole, well, not exactly." Eric is struggling to express himself. His hands grasp for the right words and he says, "It's not like one big movie with all these places and people in it. It's like discrete stories. First there's the town, then there's Tom and the White Pelican, then Rachel and the Campground, The Airstream, now this place. I mean, Jake, we're in North Dakota in an East Indian Restaurant named the Bombay Palace and the owners met when a buffalo almost killed them. They all have a story, a set, and a plot."

As he finishes speaking, a woman comes up to us and says, "Good evening, I'm Rashmi Harrington. Welcome to my restaurant. We have a table for you now."

Since we haven't sampled any other pakoras in Primrose, it's hard to compare, but the deep-fried pastries in the Bombay Palace, especially the

savory potato and onion ones, are delicious. It's a welcome change from the past few weeks of road food. Midway through the meal, a group of four women come into the room and make their way to the front. Each woman carries a tall stool, which they set side by side in front of a wall fountain of bead strands with flowing water. There's a little more fussing as the women remove their coats to reveal their matching powder blue satin jackets with fire-red silk embroidery across the backs:  The Cordial Voices. Across the front of each woman's jacket are their names:  Jane, Patty, Anne, and Rashmi, the same Rashmi from the article in the foyer. The women stand up, let their arms fall to their sides, and then Patsy reaches into her pocket and places a small pitch tuner to her mouth. A very impressive wall of sound emanates from the four women, who start singing "The Joint Is Jumping." If we're surprised, the rest of the crowd is not, and it explains why the place is packed. The sound of Primrose's own Cordial Voices fills the busy restaurant. Between songs, The Cordials explain that they're trying to raise money for their first trip to the Sweet Adelines Convention and Competition, to be held in Nashville later that fall.

Eric, who has been joyously sitting on the edge of his seat up until now, bolts from his seat "Need to get my camera, Jake. Man this is too good."

He returns a few minutes later with his camcorder and starts shooting The Cordial Voices in the restaurant. At first, people are annoyed with Eric dancing around the room with a camera. But soon enough, in that way that he can, Eric becomes invisible. For their part, The Cordial Voices are exactly as their name implies. Rashmi explains that the Sweet Adelines is an organization for promoting women's barbershop singing groups that's been around since the 1940s.

"Every year they have a big convention and competition somewhere. It's huge," Jane says. "We've been singing together for years, but we finally decided to take a shot at it. If we raise enough money we'll leave in early November for Nashville. Music City, USA! Grand Ole' Opry, Bell Meade Plantation." Then from the back of the room a man with a deep Irish accent shouts,

"Don't forget the Jack Daniel's Distillery!"

This comment meets with much laughter and the considerable approval of a table of men who we figure must be the husbands of the four singers. Eight songs later the women sign off with "I Didn't Want To Fall in Love" after enlisting the table of husbands to pass the hat. The Cordial Voices receive enthusiastic applause and I'm certain a few tanks of gasoline money for their trip to Nashville.

Returning to the campground, there's a television glow coming out of Rachel's window, and a plume of smoke rising from the chimney of her house. The curtains are open and we can see her inside, sitting with her legs up on a table, watching the television and knitting. She's also smoking a cigarette. She must hear us return because she jumps up and opens the door.

"Hey, glad I caught you. You'll need this," says Rachel, handing Eric a jug of bottled water. "The kitchen plumbing in that thing isn't hooked up. I've been working on it but haven't got it finished. Oh, I mailed your letter, too." Then, Rachel, self-conscious of the cigarette in her hand says, "Oh, sorry about the smoke. I don't use them a lot, but I sure do enjoy one from time to time." We all say goodnight, and start walking away when Rachel's door opens again and she shouts across the lot, "Do you guys drink coffee? Stop by in the morning and I'll put the pot on. I'm up early." Then she shouts again, "Hey, how'd you like the Cordials?"

CHAPTER 13

# Rose Tattoos, Ruby Sauce, And Rashmi

In Which we learn of the life of a decent woman who keeps her knitting close at hand, are warned about "testifying," and witness another film by Eric.

On the second morning in Primrose, before daylight, I'm sleeping a heavy, settled sleep in Zhitomir, when the unmistakable, sputtering explosions that is a semi truck air braking to a halt wakes me. There is a bit of irony in this, because for those of you unfamiliar with trucker's lingo, these brakes are better known as "Jake Brakes," and they can wake the dead. I'm not dead, but I am awake as the intrusion finally fades, but when I roll over I feel to go back to sleep, I feel a cold, wet spot against my cheek. Looking up to the ceiling, I see a drip coming from the window seal of Zhitomir's skylight where the condensation gathers. That's it for sleep -- my truck needs me.

When I step outside to head to the shower, I'm surprised to see Rachel awake and loading wood from the pile. "Do you need some help," I ask her.

"Damn Jake brakes woke you too?" asks Rachel, then, tells me to grab a load of firewood and come over for coffee.

"How about I grab a shower, wake up, and then I'll be right over?"

"Good, but don't forget the wood."

A few minutes later, cleaner, if still a bit groggy, I step into Rachel's house and deposit my wood beside the fireplace. The entry is a cluttered makeshift registration counter with a linoleum floor. Once you get beyond the counter it's a cozy place with balls of yarn strewn about and baskets with balls of yarn, and more baskets with needles sticking out of partially finished knitting projects - everywhere! There are sweaters, scarves, and knitted blankets in various stages of completion. On the long table sitting between her couch and television are numerous containers of beads and embroidery supplies. The living room has an overstuffed blue velour couch, two easy chairs, a table covered with more yarn, stacks of knitting magazines and also piles of mystery paperbacks filling it to the brim. There's also a roaring hot fire coming from the stone fireplace that dominates the room.

"I guess you can tell I like to knit?" says Rachel.

"Either that or you're some kind of yarn freak."

"I like to have something within hand's reach at all times. I get bored working on one thing, so I kind of stack up the projects. If I'm watching TV, I can work on those socks, or if I'm making toast in the kitchen, I can work a little on that sweater. Okay, it's a little nutty, but I like it, and what's the rush. You finish when you finish. We have long winters in North Dakota."

"It's fine by me. I tried knitting once but stabbed myself with the needles." Rachel laughs at that. Inside one of the baskets of yarn are two tiny kittens. One is a charcoal gray and the other is a calico. Rachel sees me looking at them and says, "Cute, don't you think? I got them the day before yesterday. My old cat, Angie died last year. There were a couple of kids in front of the grocery store the other day with a sign that said "Kittens." I knew I was toast the moment I saw it. I love cats. Haven't named them yet. Got any ideas?"

"How about Sancho and Donny?" I say, but Rachel gives me a look that says she's had enough of that bit.

The kitchen has a two-burner gas stove and oven, and a small rack of pots and pans that are too shiny to indicate they get much use. What at first appears to be clutter soon reveals its order, especially when Rachel sets one of the mewing kittens down on the floor and prepares the coffee. Everything she uses is within an arm's grasp. She fills an electric teakettle with water, opens the small cupboard and takes out two cups, then a third, and then a fourth saying, "I'm sure Tom's coming by this morning. He usually does." Then she fills a cream pitcher and sets that and the matching white porcelain sugar bowl onto the small wooden table that serves to form the boundary between the kitchen and the living room. "Hmm," she says, "a little bit for the kitties," and she pours a tiny bit of cream into a saucer and sets it down, to the joy of the tiny cats as they awaken. After reaching into her cupboard and taking out a hand grinder, she dumps fresh beans into it and begins to grind the coffee. As the aroma of the fresh coffee wafts through the kitchen, the brittle cloud from my rude airbrake awakening subsides.

Rachel does not miss this and teases, "Tell me the truth; you expected it to be horrible."

"Well . . ." is all I can get out before she says,

"That's reasonable. There isn't any good coffee for three hundred miles. This is, after all, North Dakota, part of the longest unfortified border in the world. That's a little North Dakota thing about the US and Canada. Maybe you've heard it. They don't tell you it's unguarded because there isn't anything to look after." Rachel laughs at that then goes on, "I have a friend who drives from New Orleans to Winnipeg every month who stays here. Can you imagine driving that all the time, New Orleans to Winnipeg? Hauls seafood and coffee up and hauls beef back down. You have got to love commerce."

"If it's commerce that brought you this coffee, then let's drink to commerce."

Rachel sits across the table from me and reaches for one of the baskets of knitting. She pulls out a project that looks like the start of a sweater. She sips on her unaltered coffee and starts knitting mindlessly as I put sugar and cream in mine. After a few silent moments she speaks.

"I'm making a sweater for my daughter, Becky. That's her on the refrigerator," she says pointing to a photo of a younger woman with a large parrot on her shoulder. "She's in Grand Forks at the college. She wants to be a meteorologist. Can you imagine that, a North Dakotan who wants to predict the weather? It's pretty simple I think -- summer: too darn hot; winter: too darn cold; spring: too darn windy; and fall; like you've been dropped into heaven."

Then she remembers she was telling me about the sweater.

"Becky's favorite color is teal." Rachel takes a long sip of her coffee then says, "You have any children?"

"None. The only relative I have is my uncle, Julian. He lives in New York."

"You don't sound like a New Yorker."

"I'm not. I have an Uncle who lives there. My father's brother."

"Where are you from then?"

"Larch, a little town in Washington not a whole lot bigger than Primrose."

"I guess that's no surprise. Small-towners get the urge to get out. No wife, no ex-wife?" Rachel continues while tugging free some more yarn from the basket. Her hands are a blur. Seeing me nod no she presses on, "Come on, every man and woman I know has one or the other." Punctuating this statement with a dramatic pull of the string of yarn she continues, "Me, I have two ex-husbands. Becky lives with her Dad. He was my first. I'm heading there next week and I want to finish this for her. I started it in June, but I kind of set it aside over the summer. As soon as I start making fires, though, I start knitting more. Look, it's silk." As she holds it up for me to have a look, it hits me that Rachel reminds me of the widow in the movie The Rose Tattoo. Before I have a chance to indulge this, Rachel asks me one last time if I don't have an ex-wife or two, then asks me to tell her about the Lost Sons of Zhitomir.

"Do you want the long or the short version?"

"As we say in the knitting world, it all depends on the quality of the yarn."

Two cups of coffee later, Rachel says, "It never crossed your mind to follow that woman to Paris?"

"Sure, it crossed my mind and I wrote her a few times, even thought about flying over but I was too slow and she got involved with her boss at the circus."

"Slow, yes, that I can see in you." Then Rachel blurts boldly, "But there's more to life than chasing romance. Trust me; I know. And, you still have the truck and something useful to do with it besides hauling coffee from New Orleans."

"There's nothing wrong with hauling coffee."

"I'm not saying there is, but movies, gee, everyone loves movies. That's why I didn't make it to The Cordials last night. I was watching Hidalgo. Have you seen it?"

"No, is it good?"

"I don't know whether it's good or not, but I can tell you for two hours last night I was somewhere else. Sure took me away. I won't spoil it for you, but you ought to watch it. It will bring tears to your eyes for sure. Do you have a DVD player in that turtleback of yours? If you do I can lend it to you. I get them in the mail, no late fees. I might even watch it again. I love looking at that cowboy. I read all about him in People Magazine."

I promise Rachel I'll watch the movie and then tell her about The Rose Tattoo.

"I think you'll like it. Order it and we can watch it together."

"It's a deal: you watch Hidalgo, I'll watch the Rose Tattoo."

A few minutes later Tom and Eric show up at the same time. Tom walks over to the stove and pours a cup of coffee for Eric and then himself.

"I couldn't survive without my sister's coffee." Tom drinks his black. "Did she tell you about the New Orleans guy?" Then Rachel tells the story again for Eric before changing the topic.

"Did you guys stay long enough at the Bombay to hear The Cordials last night?"

"Did we ever!" says Eric, "They're great. I'm going over to the Harrington's today to take some footage." Tom and Rachel exchange a playful look between them, which Eric sees and says, "Is there something I should know about?"

Rachel says, "No, but I sure hope you can handle your whiskey." Tom and Rachel laugh again and Tom continues, "Don't worry, it's nothing strange. Matthew has one of the only whiskey distilleries in North Dakota, and no one goes over there without sampling his stuff."

Eric genuinely surprises me by letting out a gleeful, "I can't wait." Then, as Rachel sets the copy of Hidalgo on the table, Eric sees it and says, "Hidalgo, I loved that film." Rachel and Eric start talking about the movie, while Tom wants to know about Zhitomir.

"What kind of mileage do you get in that thing?"

"It does pretty good for a five-speed. I get around seven if I don't push it." Tom is impressed.

"Seven, that's pretty good, but still a lot of diesel to burn if you're driving around a lot."

"Cheaper than a mortgage," I answer, eliciting an approving smile from Tom.

"How about the box? You have it all tricked out like a camper inside?"

"No, not. It's like a furniture showroom, but it's plusher inside than you might think. The walls and floor are cherry wood, a loft bed, desk, shelves and cabinets all mounted solid. But, there's no kitchen, no bathroom, and no shower."

Rachel smiles and says, "That's what we call full-service in North Dakota. Campgrounds rely on it to stay in business." After looking at his watch, Tom continues, "Listen, the great state of North Dakota has less than four people per square mile. I'm counting on a few of those square miles needing something fixed today, but I've got a few minutes before I open up. You think I can have a look at the inside of your rig?"

"You bet," I answer. Before leaving Tom stops and washes out his coffee cup and sets it in the drying rack. Then he gives Rachel a two-handed squeeze of her shoulders and says,

"I have a sweet sister, don't I?"

Rachel laughs and says, "That's the kind of treatment you get when you make good coffee."

Tom enjoys seeing Zhitomir and is impressed by the wood inside.

"I didn't expect this at all. You've got a regular little home in here. Did you do all this by yourself?" I tell him about the various things that have been done, about the loft and the skylight and the cabinets. Tom comments on how everything is fastened down. "Reminds me of a boat cabin." he says before heading out to his shop.

Rachel and Eric come by a few minutes later and Rachel hands me the movie. "You forgot this," says Rachel, and tells us she's off to do some errands. "If anyone pulls up, tell them to pick a spot and I'll take care of them as soon as I return." She asks Eric if he wants to hang out all day or run around town with her. "I can drop you up to the Harrington's later. Come on, it beats sitting around in a trailer all morning."

As Rachel and Eric climb into Rachel's car, she turns, as if embracing her campground in its entirety and says, "Maybe sometime you guys can come back when the weather is warm and show a movie here."

With all that coffee in me I'm anxious to weatherize Zhitomir. Fred would be intrigued to see a skylight cut into his truck's steel body, though

breeching the seamless steel might have upset him. It took me two years of staring at a blank cherry ceiling before performing the surgery. It was long overdue. The light made Zhitomir more comfortable. The sunlight and night sky are worth having to run a bead of silicon every now and then to keep things dry.

I keep a tube of silicon caulk under the driver's seat for that purpose, and when I open the cab door I'm hoping there's enough left to do the job. There is. Now, all I have to do is climb atop the box and run the silicon around the skylight seal. In a few minutes the caulking is finished and I stand on top of Zhitomir staring down at the little world in front of me. In this fleeting moment I appreciate the joy of this weightless travel around the country before descending from the top of Zhitomir to the cab and back to the ground where I turn my attention to the leaky door. I enjoy the little things of being on the road. I enjoy tending to the truck. Compared with taking care of a house and the ever-expanding things that go with it, taking care of a truck is simple. Besides, when your house falls into disrepair, you can still live in it. But your truck might stop running if you don't look after it.

When Fred first got the truck it had a large vertically sliding door, like most cargo trucks. Fred didn't like it: "too much rattle and bother." So, after the elephant remodel he welded the slider into the box making it a solid wall, and installed a wide side hinged steel door into the back. This did two things -- first, it limited the size of any cargo and, second with the height of the door over four feet off the ground, it caused Fred to build stairs to the door. Fred was very proud of the hinged set of steel steps that lifted and fastened out of the way when the truck was running. Unfortunately, most hung doors don't hold up to all the vibration of the road and the door has a tendency to work some air spaces around it. When I look at the cracks I realize the job is a little more involved than another tube of silicon will fix. It looks like I might need some welding done, so I decide to walk over to Tom's to see if he knows someone who can do the work.

Thanks to Tom's welder friend, Gary, by five-thirty Zhitomir is finally weather-tight again. I realize that with all the day's distractions, I never did eat anything. My stomach feels like a small fire; and I'm starving. I expected Eric to be back by now but with no sign of him I walk into town determined to get something to eat.

As I'm walking down the street I stop at an alley and looking to my right I see a glowing red neon sign, which says "Ruby's Creole Kitchen." I turn and walk until I'm standing in front of the unlikely restaurant. I read from a well-worn piece of cardboard suspended from a suction cup hook in the window, that says, "Rib Dinner Tonight."

Inside, Ruby's is like a hallway, with a skinny counter and skinny kitchen on one side and a wall on the other. I'm not sure two people can pass by in the aisle without some intimacy being exchanged. The counter has seven stools with salt, pepper, and a large stack of white paper napkins in front of each one. On the floor between the stools are three small enamel trashcans with the words "Napkins Here" on them. But, the most interesting thing is the rack of six small bottles of RUBY SAUCE with numbers on them sitting at each place. There's RUBY SAUCE #1, all the way to RUBY SAUCE #6. Lying against the side of the napkin stacks is a laminated sheet detailing the various sauces and the significance of their numbers.

RUBY SAUCE #1 will "wake you up with a mild slap to the face."
RUBY SAUCE #2 will "cleanse your tongue of any lies you've spoken."
RUBY SAUCE #3 will "let you experience first-hand the meaning of
     cauldron."
RUBY SAUCE #4 will "offer you ample reason to believe in
     reincarnation."
RUBY SAUCE #5 will "make you wish you had rattlesnakes for pets."
RUBY SAUCE #6 will "make you testify!

There are things worse than death. You can count on it . . . but you'd better count fast!

Opposite the counter is a wall of autographed posters and photos, ranging from a glamorous blonde in a satin dress to a skinny basketball player in his short shorts. I don't see anybody in the place, and stand staring at the pictures, until I finally read the lettering above it all, "Honor Wall of Famous North Dakotans." The pictures begin to make sense. One after another I find myself thinking, "I didn't know she comes from North Dakota." Then, like an apparition, an enormous black woman appears out of nowhere and is sitting at the end of the counter. I swear she wasn't there a second ago. The apparition speaks.

"Hi, I'm Ruby. Here for dinner?" Then she says, "You're not from

North Dakota are you? " Then she points to the picture of a hockey player that's signed, "To Ruby, from Cliff. Number Four hits harder than Gordie Howe. Thanks for the ribs!" I happen to know that Cliff died a few years ago. Then she directs me to look at the painted portrait of the Lewis and Clark party, "That's Sacagawea, she's from North Dakota, but she never ate here. Yessiree, Peggy Lee, Louis L'Amour, and quite a few others: they all ate here. I never was much of a Peggy Lee fan until she handled number RUBY SAUCE #6. A year later suddenly she's got a big hit named, Fever."

"You're a little early. Sign says we open at six," but then she ambles over to the window and finds the sign is lying face down. "Dang thing. Well, the sign is supposed to say we open at six. You're welcome to stay, but there won't be anything ready for awhile. I can give you some beans and rice to hold you until the ribs are ready. I hope you're hungry. I've got ribs, collard greens, candied yams, and corn bread for $8.95." Then flipping the sign back into place, Ruby lumbers behind the counter where she checks the ovens and pots. The smell of yams and pork fill the air as she closes the oven, taking a seat on her fortified stool at the end of the counter before demanding, "Who are you and what are you doing in Primrose?"

After the meal I walk back to the campground. Rachel pops her head out from her door to tell me she's leaving in the morning to see Becky in Grand Forks. She proudly shows me the finished sweater and then asks,

"If you're not running off, maybe you can watch the place for me. I'll be back early Wednesday afternoon and I don't expect you'll even have any one come in. "I tell her I'll be glad to look after things and then I ask her if she's ever eaten at Ruby's Creole Kitchen.

"Oh, my, I think the last time I ate there, Ruby was still skinny."

When I walk back to Zhitomir I'm surprised that there's no sign of Eric in the Airstream. Around 8:30 I hear a car pull into the campground and some loud, happy voices exchanging goodnights. Then, there's a knocking on Zhitomir's side and I hear Eric talking as he walks up, "Jake, Jake, Jake, are you there? Jake, I got to show you this stuff, it's amazing." When I open the door a blast of alcohol vapor blows in my face and Eric stands waiting with an excited, if somewhat rosy red, expression on his face. He is lit up. "Jake, I got to show you what I got." He comes in and fumbles around until he's assembled the right cords to attach his camcorder to the television. He's talking the whole time, "It's funny, Jake, they don't talk about themselves at all, but they tell each other's stories so well. I mean it's strange how well they do that. That must be love," he says. When the tape finally starts, the footage of Rashmi comes first. She's sitting in the garden behind her house and pruning rose bushes as she speaks. The footage switches between her hands and the flowers and thorns, and then from time to time, to her face as she speaks. Eric's questions prompt her replies.

"Look at her skin, Jake. Look at the brown against the red of the flower. Man, look at that, Jake. Nice, huh?" Then, you hear the first question from Eric, "Rashmi, can you tell me how you came here to live in Primrose?" "I'll edit myself out later," says Eric. I have this narration in mind, or else let it flow with silence and music. You don't need to hear the questions."

Rashmi begins speaking as we see her hands clipping roses off bushes.

"Matthew's last ship, the one he returned to after we met at the bison exhibit in San Francisco, well, the captain was ready to retire. He had bought a large farm near Primrose. Why is anybody's guess, especially for a seafaring man, but mainly he wanted to grow wheat and soybeans. After two years of losing money someone suggested barley, which made him think of Matthew."

Now we see all of Rashmi holding the long stems of roses in her leather-gloved hands.

"Matthew and I were living in California when his old captain called and invited us to visit. He mentioned something to Matthew about the barley and the two spoke for a long time about a voyage they'd had to Africa some years back."

Rashmi trims the rose stems with a small pruner, leaving little piles of discarded thorns on the table top, while arranging the roses into a crystal vase.

"You see Matthew grew up in a tiny town where there was a lot of poverty. His father was a carpenter but there wasn't a much work so he went to England. There are many sad stories about Irish leaving to work in England. Sometimes the money didn't come home; sometimes the men didn't come home. Matthew ran away when he was fourteen to find his father in London, but he never did. He stayed with Irish families, then lied about his age and got onto his first ship, a tanker going to Venezuela."

With a hand whisk Rashmi sweeps the rose clippings onto the floor.

"Matthew is a clever man, and he was given more responsibilities. Finally one of the captains paid for him to be trained as a proper seaman.

Soon he was traveling around the world on ships carrying logs, crude oil, automobiles, clothing, furniture, anything you can imagine. This he did for twenty years before I met him in 1975. His ship was on a food relief mission to Northern Africa, holding tons and tons of grain."

Rashmi dumps the clippings into a brush pile outside.

"The ship was impounded in port before they could unload the grain. Two rivals in the government were arguing over who got credit for distribution of the food. Can you imagine, people were starving and fools were arguing over who gets to give away the food? They were not allowed off the ship for a month. Matthew gets restless when he has nothing to do. He started puttering about the ship's machine shop and soon constructed a small still. He said that what the rats were eating every day exceeded what he needed to keep his little still going."

Inside the house now Rashmi stands at the faucet and draws cold water from the tap into the vase.

"That is how Matthew became a distiller and why we came to live here. Now he only uses the best North Dakota barley and makes the only organic whiskey in North America. This year he will uncask the first twenty-five year old batch. The governor of North Dakota will be coming for the tasting."

The last footage of Rashmi is a long zoom into an extreme close-up of her face. Eric stays on her face, and then once there is nothing left but her dark brown eyes, he dissolves into black.

Now Eric shifts to taping Matthew. He starts with an establishing shot of the steel Quonset building that serves as Matthew's distillery.

Matthew inside the building standing beside a gleaming copper and steel still.

"Rashmi probably told you she was born in Bombay and moved to America when she was ten - to Wyoming. Strange place for someone from Bombay to settle. From warm, humid, and Hindu to cold, dry, and American. The family came to run a hotel for her uncle, who was buying hotels in America. There are a lot of Indians running hotels these days."

Eric stops the tape here for a second. "Listen to this, Jake. I love what he says."

Matthew in front of grain storage barrels.

"In Wyoming they begin refurbishing a neglected but well built motor inn with 16 units, each with heated floors, tiled bathrooms, and wooden trimmed rooms. After a few months they got it all put back together and then when people start coming in, another Yank wanker from another motel down the street with an owner who writes "100% American Here" on his sign. His place is a dump, but it draws off customers for a while until Anshul, Rashmi's father, writes his own words on their sign, which says, "100% warm, clean, and comfortable, and $20 less/night." Anshul's smart. He says, "People love their country more when their wallet is full."

A large wooden table with a leather bound book inscribed "Distillery Journal.

Opens the page to Hungarian Rhapsody. Zoom in to see handwritten "Blend of Bartlett Pear Grappa with a Hint of Paprika."

"Yes, that is very subtle. Pour that over lemon ice and you think you're in heaven."

Matthew sitting at his desk.

"This is me special hobby. Because, you see, when I was a lad fruit was a special thing. If you ever got enough of it you didn't want to let a bit of it go to waste. Now here in America, you have a love affair with your apples. Oh, we'd heard that story about your Johnny Appleseed, and though I'll admit an Irishman likes his fruit as much anyone, I never did understand what all the fuss was about an apple. Well, come to read an article about this Mr. Appleseed and see that as your West was opened up, there weren't a whole lot of provisions around. Things like sugar and especially the spirits were quite hard to come by. Aah, but put in a few apple trees and wait a few years, then you have something. Can you imagine the anticipation of that flavor? And then wait a few more years until you have more fruit than you can eat fresh and you start mashing it up and well, you know the rest."

Matthew opening a door marked "Aging Room: Check Temperature Upon Entering."

We see a wall of numerous wooden casks on racks. The film then shows in close-up that the casks have names written on them: Essence 1988, Liar's Ascension 2000, Hard Winter 1997, Friend of the Poor 1992, Old German 2002, Hungarian Rhapsody 2001. There's also a table with identical glass decanters, each repeating the names on the casks.

"It wasn't easy for them. They were isolated in this country, but they worked hard. You have to work twice as hard to get a foot on solid ground here. I'm not sure they wanted to stay because when Rashmi was eighteen, they sent her to India for a few years. That wasn't going to work. One thing about America is she's seductive - once you get a taste of it you don't go back to the old rules. Of course, not every one got the taste that Rashmi did because when she left India this time, she moved in San Francisco. That's where we met when she had friends visiting her from Bombay."

We see a small oak cask used for aging a whiskey. It has a hand-scrawled marking on it, which identifies the contents, "Prabha's Beauty 1998."

"Named for me beautiful mother-in-law. In about twelve years, that's going to be very good. I have a buyer in St. Louis who has already paid for it. He gets the first two bottles. "Me mother, Irene, told me, 'You may not have shoes, or a house, or the warmth in your home that comes from the heating, but if you can but sing you'll never go hungry.' Me mother believed that no great singer should have to worry about paying for his or her supper. A lot is said about Irish women being long on suffering, but it can never be said they don't appreciate a good song."

Matthew fills two small glasses from Prabha's cask and raises his up.

"A small sample won't kill anyone. For, Prabha, who taught m' lovely Rashmi how to sing."

Matthew downs his glass, gives a little shimmy shake of his body, and exhales loudly.

"Amen, young man. If that's not Nirvana then what is? Now, put your camera away and let me show you about spirits."

As the video images end, Eric, perhaps feeling a bit loveless, himself, slumps into the chair with his eyes closed. He draws his hands to his face and pokes at his numb cheeks. Eyes still shut, he speaks softly, "The thing is, Jake: they tell each other's story. Man, it's like they don't even think of themselves at all." Then, he adds in a singsong voice, "That must be love." With that last gasp, Eric pulls himself up out of his chair, and once he has steadied himself again, walks out of Zhitomir to the Airstream, wondering out loud in the same sing-song mumble what time it is in Palau.

As I watch this talented young man walk away, I'm thinking Eric is going to make his place in a bigger world than the one in which I live.

*B*

# CHAPTER 14

# Bashkir Ponies And The Fiery Hooch Of The Steppes

*In Which* we learn the history of an amenable horse with good action that is suitable for general agricultural work, and how to retire a North Dakota farmer.

By Monday morning, coffee at Rachel's is a three-day tradition. Even with the plug-in heater, Zhitomir is cold in the morning. The temperature has dropped about ten degrees and the warmth of the wood fire in Rachel's home is welcome.

When Tom comes in about 7:45 this morning, he tells Eric the Toyota parts have come and that he will be doing the rotors on the van today. "I was hoping to get you off cheaper, but you need it done. If you come by later this afternoon I should be finished."

"I don't even know what a rotor is," says Eric but he thanks Tom for doing the work the same.

We all enjoy playing with the kittens, which seem to have grown in the past two days. Tom teases them with a string of yarn and says, "You going to give these guys names, Rachel?"

"When I have something picked out," she says. "And, by the way one of those guys is a girl, little brother."

"Hey, I want to tell you," Eric blurts "I reached my parents. They left the school in Senegal and they're headed to Palau."

"Where's Palau?" asks Tom, beating me to the question.

"It's in the South Seas," says Rachel.

"How do you know that?" Tom says with a little doubt in his voice.

"I just do," says Rachel, walking to a bookshelf where she finds an atlas and hands it to her brother.

"I got ten dollars says I'm right," says Rachel confidently. "Go ahead, little brother, buy me lunch." Tom reaches into his pocket, takes out his wallet, and drops a ten-dollar bill on the table.

"She can't bluff." Then he opens the atlas and flips through until he finds Palau and the look on his face tells us that Rachel is having a fine lunch today. Then Rachel says,

"He's always been a sucker,"

The conversation finally gets back to Eric's parents and after a few explanations, Rachel says,

"Man, I don't know what's going on, but everybody is moving around except us." Then she rises up with one last swallow of coffee and says, "I'm heading over to my friend Karen's, for knitting group this morning. If you want to borrow my car, you can scout around for some video work or do whatever you want; I won't need it."

Eric is happy to take Rachel up on the offer and after breakfast they head out for the day.

Around one o'clock in the afternoon, I'm writing at my desk in Zhitomir when I hear the deep bellowing rumble of a well-tuned truck pulling into Rachel's. Stepping outside, I see a shiny rig pulling a large horse trailer outside of the office. Coming from beside it is a loud string of strange words, which sound like cursing even if the words themselves are not clear. The trailer is boldly lettered with the following:

# Peter Alexander's Equines

### Specializing in Cold Weather Working Breeds

Spiti, Bashkir, Finnish, Gotland, Fjord, Hokkaido, Kiso, Jutland, North Swedish, Dole Gubrandsdal, Kazakh, Russian Heavy Draft, Icelandic, Konik, Murkozi, Vladimir, Hucul, Mongolian Stables in Lake Manitoba, Canada & Jakutsk, Russia.

After a few seconds the outburst subsides and from behind the truck comes a stocky, energetic man of about sixty with a thick gray mustache who walks towards me like a jubilant dog greeting its master. He waves his hand and smiles a gold-toothed smile, while shouting something that sounds like "Draz veet yee." And then follows it up with something a little more familiar, though in a thick and deliberate Russian accent, "Hey, you, Mister, you help me, please?" Before I have a chance to speak he says,

"Only for one night, one night only. How much?" Interrupting him to explain that I am not the campground proprietor, I tell him the owner will return later, but I can help settle him in the campground. Then the man reaches out his hand and introduces himself with a firm handshake

"Peter Alexander: Breeder of Cold Weather Equines."

I offer my hand and reply, "Jake Spinner, Director: Lost Sons of Zhitomir Film Society." Hearing this, Peter's expression changes at once to a curious look. His eyes flash back and forth from me to my truck. "That your truck?" I answer, yes, and then Peter gushes forth with a long string of Russian. He is disappointed by the uncomprehending look on my face before switching back into English and says,

"Why Zhitomir, if you not Ukrainian or Russian? Zhitomir in Ukraine. Explain, please," which I try to do, but Peter is still baffled. Hearing my explanation, he takes my hands into his firm grasp, and swelling with pride declares, "My name is Pyotr Alexander Poliakhov." He makes a point of enunciating his last name: "Pole yock off." He continues, "In Canada, I, Pete Alexander. Explain please, Zhitomir, why you not change business name? No one knows Zhitomir. This not Ukraine." It's not the first time I've been asked that question, but it is certainly the first time I've been asked it by someone who knows where and what Zhitomir is.

I help Pyotr get his rig settled in a slot in the campground and then ask him if he wants to walk into town and have lunch together.

"No, thank you, Zhitomir; have to feed and water horse." He walks off, then waves me over. "Come, Zhitomir, come see before you go."

Inside the trailer are six stout ponies with their heads facing into six separate stalls. Draped around the trailer is an elaborate and extremely tidy array of harnesses suspended on hooks and held in place by perfectly tied lengths of rope. There are some bales of hay, various tack, tools, and a boot and clothing rack. Set in a compartment are two large stainless steel jugs that seem out of place.

Pyotr, beaming with pride, explains he is on his way back from showing the team at an exhibition of working horse breeds in Minnesota.

"These ponies, Bashkir. Pound for pound, strongest animal on face of Earth." Pyotr walks over to each horse and throws his arms around their manes while breathing into their noses and speaking softly to each animal in Russian. "Maybe lady will let me take out horses. They tired from standing in trailer." Then he says, "Go, Zhitomir, go have lunch, then come back and I give you something special you never had before." He starts speaking to the horses in Russian again as I leave.

A short while later I return with two sandwiches, planning to share one with Pyotr, surprised to find Pyotr and his horses are outside surrounded by a small electric fence. Inside the makeshift corral sits Pyotr in a tee shirt, happily drinking from a steaming thermos even though it's hovering around fifty degrees. Seeing me, he yells,

"Zhitomir, come sit, talk for while. Bring cup, I have drink for you. Please. You like." Surrounded by the six ponies, Pyotr looks like a Cossack king on a redneck throne. When I join him he opens the thermos and pours out a strange smelling liquid, filling a cup for me. "This Kummis," says Pyotr. "Made from Bashkir milk. Bashkir have good milk for cheese, kefir, and Kummis, of course. Don't know, Kummis, Zhitomir? I read in Canadian book description of Kummis. -- Kummis called 'fiery hooch of the Steppes."

This pleases Pyotr and he laughs out loud while opening the thermos and taking my cup.

"First sip like fire, second sip like water, third sip like kiss of woman," says Pyotr with a mischievous giggle. Suddenly serious, he cautions me,

"Go slow, Zhitomir, but go. Good for soul." Seeing my hesitation, he says,

"No, listen, movie-man, listen Zhitomir: Siberia hard place. Kummis help. Trust me, Zhitomir, Russian know. Drink, Zhitomir."

The strange taste abates after a few minutes and soon the "fiery hooch of the Steppes" warms my throat. Pyotr signals that we have only begun by bringing another chair out and we sit talking, surrounded by the warmth and security of the six horses, which have their heads down eating hay.

"All living beings love Bashkirs," declares Pyotr reaching into his pocket for a stick of dry cheese, which he cuts into small slices with a knife. "Good with kummis, Zhitomir. Maybe your grandfather knew these tastes? Huh?" Then I reach into my pocket and produce the two forgotten sandwiches. The offering pleases Pyotr.

"Look, Zhitomir does magic, too."

Pyotr tells me he breeds horses at his stable on the north shore of Lake Manitoba where he has about five hundred acres devoted to preserving the heritage of the world's cold weather work horses. When I ask him how he started, he laughs and points to Zhitomir and says, "I wanted to drive around the world showing movies but job was already taken." Saying this, he steps over the electric fence and walks to the trailer where he proudly recites all the names on the trailer side. "All strong horses, but my favorite Bashkir."

"I was child in Siberia. My father sent for rehabilitation by Stalin." Then Pyotr, as if it is a reflex, spits on the ground and excuses himself. I ask him what the rehabilitation was for, and he says, "Who knows. Telling bad joke about Stalin, upsetting boss, not sharing vodka, who knows with Stalin? He was mechanical engineer before working fields of Siberia alongside pride of the Soviet Stud System. Soviets worked years to produce in a horse what they stole from men like my father. Soviets raised horses, produced famous Russian Heavy Draft Horse in Khrenul and Derkul. Soviets boasted horse was amenable. Horse had good action suitable for general agricultural work." Pyotr spits and apologizes again. "True, Zhitomir, all true. Sometime you laugh to stop crying. Siberians laugh lot. But what I learned then was what men lack, horse has in abundance. Never take away respect between man and beast. Have seen horse pull coal, and corn, and stone, and weak dying men, through snow so deep you cannot see heads as they work. Only see steam coming from gaping mouth and nose. No complaint, Zhitomir. Horse is remarkable. Honor to work with them."

An hour later, a car comes into the campground and drops off Rachel. A huge smile comes over her face, as if having a small corral of horses in her campground is the most normal thing in the world. She walks calmly over to the makeshift corral, stepping over the string of wire where she joins the horses with no hesitation. The horses must sense her warmth because they walk right over to her. After a moment with them she walks to where we're seated.

"I knew it, I knew it, I knew it! "shouts Rachel, "You're Cirque Du Soleil, right? Rumor has it there's a giant aquarium truck hauling a living blue whale on its way here."

Rachel laughs while tapping her head with two fingers and says, "How could I forget that it's National Weird Guys and Their Weird Trucks Month."

Pyotr and I rise to our feet.

"Rachel, this is Pyotr Alexander Poliakhov, also known as Pete Alexander."

Pyotr reaches out his hand.

"Right, of course, National Weird Guys With Their Weird Trucks Who are Russian Month. You know, the two of you could make up a great figure skating team."

"You are right, Zhitomir. She is remarkable woman."

While Rachel gets Pyotr taken care of, I decide a long hot shower is in order. With the kummis running through my body, I must be mid-song before I realize I'm singing 'Back in The USSR' by the Beatles in sufficient volume for the entire campground to hear.

A few hours later, Pyotr raps on my door.

"Say, Zhitomir, you inside?" When I open the door a cold blast of air greets me from behind Pyotr. When Pyotr steps inside I'm happy to close the door and keep the cold out.

"Look at this," says Pyotr. "Very nice. Yes. Maybe you smarter than you look, Zhitomir. I'm sleeping in bag on hay tonight. You have this." Then Pyotr chuckles playfully saying, "But not this," pulling the thermos of kummis from behind his back.

"Life is short, Zhitomir. Let's talk."

I set up my two folding chairs and Pyotr tells me all about his stud operation.

"My Bela, her brother Alexei, sends money from Russia. Yes, new Russia they call it. Lots of money," Pyotr laughs "Unless you don't have it." He laughs again, pleased with the remark. "Alexei has it and needs place to put it." He laughs again, "Horses in Manitoba better than banks in new Russia."

A little while later, Pyotr speaks. "I was eight years old when Stalin sent us to Siberia," Pyotr scoffs "Three years after Great Patriotic War. Maybe Comrade Stalin wanted more patriotism so he invites us to Siberia. Wonderful coincidence my father needing rehabilitation when Stalin need mechanical engineers for project in Siberia. Hello, Siberia.

"At least our village was small and you could wander freely. When I was ten I started going to the milking stables." Pausing for a second, Pyotr reflects, "You never know where life's passion will originate. Is true, huh, Zhitomir?

"When my father rehabilitated we return Moscow. I twenty-one and old enough begin working with horses. That, what I did thirty-five years until I left for Canada with family. One day, in Toronto, I hear, from other Russian, Canada giving people land in sparse areas. Bela thought it crazy, but I was curious. Good thing, curiosity. Received parcel in return for promise to work and improve land. Funny idea, improve what? Hard to improve tundra.

"Bela said me, 'Pyotr Alexander, what do you think you can do with that land, relive your childhood?' She was joking of course, but maybe she speaks with wisdom of woman. Soon, I start thinking only of horses. That was ten years ago, and now, many changes.

"Bela will only stay in summer. She likes Toronto better. She is closer to daughters, Katya, younger, is actress, and Lena, is like me, a horsewoman but now runs stable for English riding style. Not a lot to do in winter on Lake Manitoba. Maybe I'm crazy, but fifteen years in Siberia change my life. I lived in barrens, in snows, in silence, and now I don't like cities. I prefer company of animals.

"My father and mother stay in Toronto with Bela, but I do what I do. Now is very strange, people want horses again and pay lots of money for them. I sell a lot of kummis. Funny thing is I sell to so many who were in work camps. Funny how what was so awful then becomes precious now." Pyotr pauses, then adds, "Crazy world, yes, Zhitomir?"

Later that night I'm lying in bed looking through the skylight. By now Pyotr is probably sleeping soundly on a bed of hay beside his ponies. Eric I'm sure has returned and is asleep in the Airstream. The stars flicker through a high wisp of clouds drifting by, illuminated by moonlight. My bed is warm and dry, and I smell the moist odor of Bashkir horses mingled with the warm sweetness of cherry wood as I drift off to sleep.

The following morning when I step outside a chilling gust of air blasts my face and the elm trees are raining leaves. Eric's van is parked beside the Airstream and Eric and Pyotr have met and have evidently been talking for some time. When I look at my watch, I'm astounded that it is past ten o'clock. Greeting me, Pyotr says,

"Good sleep, yes, Zhitomir. Man sleep good after kummis." Then he turns his attention back to Eric.

"No, you come, make videotape, I send to Alexei. Good for him to see what we do with his money. He can show to friends, they give more money, he send some to me, and everyone happy."

Eric looks at me awkwardly. I think he's concerned about what I'll think of him leaving again.

"Don't look at me that way, Eric. I'm a big boy. I'll be fine."

Then addressing Pyotr, I say,

"Promise me you'll teach him about kummis. He's been showing some aptitude in that area lately."

"What's kummis?" asks Eric.

Pyotr waves off Eric's question.

"You'll know soon enough." Then Pyotr asks me sincerely, "He's a good boy, this one yes, Zhitomir?" I nod, yes. Pyotr turns back to Eric.

"Come, please. World needs to see my horses." Then Pyotr gives Eric a once over scan and says, "You have girlfriend?" To which Eric shrugs weakly, and Pyotr adds, "No? I call my daughter, Katya, to come and visit. I think you like her. Now, I go. They look at me funny at the border sometimes and I have long voyage today."

An hour later Pyotr hands Eric a map before he departs.

"Once you find lake, drive north." Then, taking my hands again as he did yesterday, Pyotr says, "Look, Zhitomir. You will come sometime to see world of horses. Maybe we show movie by Charlie Chaplin. That be fun, Zhitomir." Then, trying, but failing, to sound like an American, he says "See ya, par-den-ner," climbs into his truck and takes off.

As Pyotr exits the campground, Eric says, "Pinch me, Jake, so I know it's real."

A few hours later, Eric and I look at a map, musing about a possible rendezvous location. There's no need to make any decisions, especially with no screenings booked anywhere.

"I might even go see Julian if I can leave Zhitomir in Fargo and fly."

Before Eric left, we agreed to talk as plans changed and when he knew how long things would be with Pyotr. Eric and I have done this many times. Borrowing from movie language, "Good-byes are not a big scene."

"I was hoping to say good-bye to Rachel, but I guess she's already gone." In all the fuss of the morning I'd forgotten that she was going today, and when Eric finally leaves, the campground is lonely, until I remember I have to feed the two still nameless kittens.

Inside the kitchen on the refrigerator door is a note from Rachel.

*Jake,*

*Thanks for watching the kittens. There is canned food in the Tupperware and kibbles in the bag on the counter. Feel free to make yourself some coffee or hang out. You might enjoy watching a movie inside a house instead of a truck. Maybe we can watch the movie when I get back. If you need anything, call Tom. 743-6745.*

*Rachel*

On Tuesday evening, Eric's on his way to Lake Manitoba and Rachel's in Grand Forks. The road is quiet when I step out of Zhitomir into the night air and there's a crescent moon rising clear like an omen over the giant elm trees whose leaves steadily flutter down to the ground. The wind gains force and whistles around the campground. It's too cold to stand outside for long.

Stepping into Zhitomir, I pick up *Hidalgo* to watch at Rachel's.

When I get inside, the kitties are mewing, probably because the room is so cold. I start a fire and in a few minutes the room begins to warm and I put the disk on the player.

About ninety minutes later I'm crying over the love of a man and his horse with two kittens asleep on my lap. A hot fire, a comfortable sofa, no diesel fumes, and balls of yarn everywhere: a man could get used to having a home.

The next morning Tom comes by and we share a few minutes of coffee and conversation.

"Rachel called and said everything's fine. Becky loved the sweater, and Rachel's even getting along with Becky's Dad, her ex-husband, Christopher."

"Is that unusual?" I ask.

"No, not at all. They love each other, those two, but they're too stubborn to admit it. I think one of these days they'll get back together. Maybe not." Then Tom says, "Listen, Jake. I took a look at your tires and the insides of the rear axle are showing some age. How many miles are on them?"

"I'd have to check, but probably around fifty thousand."

"Well, keep an eye on them and replace them when you can. Some-times it's not the miles so much as the years that wears them out."

With my managerial responsibilities at the campground, I hung pretty close for the better part of the day, except for a quick walk to the post office where there still was nothing from Julian. In the late afternoon I started a fire in Rachel's house to welcome her when she returned. Around six, Ra-chel drives in with a quick horn blast to herald her return. When I open Zhitomir's door she shouts across the campground, "Hey, movie man, you like pizza? Come on over."

When I enter the house Rachel is unloading bags of groceries and other things from her trip.

"Becky gave me these earrings. She's got a friend who makes jewelry. Anything happen here while I was gone? Did the whale ever show up?" Then she reaches down and lifts the two kittens into her arms. "I sure missed you two. Mama's home."

It takes a few minutes for Rachel to settle in before we start eating the pizza. Rachel tells me the trip was good, repeating what Tom said about her ex. "I suppose I love the guy but do you know how embarrassing it is to admit it?" Then she laughs at herself.

"Listen, thanks for making the fire, that was very sweet. I hate coming home to a cold house, and it's only September. I might spend some time with Lola and Ben this winter." Then she jumps up and fumbles through a short stack of mail. "There it is," and she opens a DVD mailer and reads from the cover, "1955, *The Rose Tattoo*. 117 minutes. Anna Magnani and Burt Lancaster. Adapted for the screen by Tennessee Williams from his play of the same name. Academy Award to Magnani for best actress." Rachel sets the disk in the player and then says, "That doesn't say what it's about. How about you fill me in a little? Or are you one of those doesn't like to open his Christmas presents early kind of guys?"

"Alright, if you insist. Magnani plays a poor, rural, Italian widow who lives in America and sews for a living. Even though she's good looking, she's cranky all the time and is living the woe is me widow sort of thing, all the time thinking about her dead husband. She's got him so high up on a pedestal that she doesn't see what everyone else around her knows, that the guy was an unfaithful bum. Enter, Burt Lancaster, as a virile, Italian immigrant truck driver, even if he can't pull off the accent, who has the hots for the mom. Meanwhile, her teenage daughter, who's sweet but maybe a little tired of living with the old sourpuss of a mom, falls in love with an equally sweet American boy who loves her, but Mom is having no part of it."

"Wow, you do know movies, don't you. I thought you were going to say it's a mystery or a love story, or something like that. I tell you what, if you don't mind sitting tight for a few minutes, I'm going to make a bowl of popcorn and wash it down with a beer and then we can watch the film. Care to join me."

"Yes, Madam, I'd be happy to."

~

About fifteen minutes into the film, Rachel picks up the remote and pauses the disk, saying "Jake, it's not that I mind your eyes on me, but it's hard to watch a movie while someone's watching me all the time." I apologize and explain it's a casualty of showing movies all the time. "I tend to watch the people watch the movies."

"I suppose that makes sense, but how about you sit back and watch the movie? Okay?"

It's funny; because once I started watching the film what had reminded me of Rachel in the first place wasn't in it. The film is fun to watch, even with Burt Lancaster struggling to maintain a passable Italian accent, and we're both happy for the happy ending, which I'd forgotten is not a given in the earlier parts of the film.

When it ends, Rachel walks over to the two sleeping kittens and pets one with each hand until they roll over, their paws in the air, still sound asleep by the heat of the fireplace. Rachel then takes a cigarette from the same full pack that's been sitting on the mantle for days. She draws one out and lights it on an ember in the fireplace.

Exhaling the first draw from the cigarette, she speaks. "That's a lovely movie. It's touchy there for a while. I mean -- I wasn't sure how it would turn out. Do I remind you of her? Is that why you thought of it?"

"No, not really."

"Now, you're lying. I can see it on your face."

"Okay, maybe the setting, you know the house, the campground, you all by yourself and with your daughter, but that's before I spent enough time here to get a deeper impression. Forgive me, but sometimes I fall into a kind of movie trance where everything reminds me of something or someone from a movie." Rachel takes a deep drag on the cigarette and goes on,

"She's pretty wigged out there you know? There's a stretch where you think they might haul her off to the lulu bin. Oh, heck, maybe we've all had a few moments like that. I might have been a little like her fifteen years ago, but I'm not that Baronessa." Then, sitting down beside the fire Rachel reaches for one of her knitting baskets, begins knitting, and starts to speak very slowly while the kittens stretch and yawn, awakening from their sleep. "Do you have time for a story?"

"That's one thing I have in abundance, Rachel, and I like stories, so fire away."

"You know, Tom and I have different fathers, but oh lord, do we ever have the same mother. That's Annie, I mentioned her a few days ago. Annie lives in Bismarck with her latest boyfriend. She grew up in Minot but when she had me at seventeen she got out of there 'lickitty split.' That's what Annie said, 'lickitty split.' She moved to Bismarck, and when I was three, she had Tom.

'I never met my father. All I've ever heard Annie say about him is 'You're better off for it.' Tom didn't get off so lucky. He met his father after Annie slipped up one night when she was here ten years ago and mentioned his name and where he lived in Bismarck. Tom tracked him down and visited him without so much as a phone call in advance. The guy was about seventy-five and still working at the bar he owns, which is where he met Annie. When Tom came home after the visit, and I asked him what his father was like, all he could think to say was that 'he was nice enough to give me my drinks on the house.' He never even knew he had a son. That's tough to find out how anonymous your life can be." Rachel draws from the cigarette again and even though there is half of it remaining, she tosses it into the fireplace before continuing with her story.

When that cigarette flies out of Rachel's hand, I receive an unexpected jolt. It reminds me of my mother. I'd forgotten about her smoking cigarettes and the way the smoke would trail off around her while she sat in silence. Sometimes I'd watch that and wonder if she'd ever move again.

Before I can get too distracted by this, however, I receive a second jolt, this time in the form of two kittens simultaneously digging their piercing claws into my leg as they aim for my lap. That snaps me back to Rachel's story.

"Annie is fifty-four years old but she lies about her age. She can pull it off, too. She's got enough looks that in the dim lights of the places she lives nobody's going to doubt her.

"When I was fourteen Annie got hauled off to de-tox and Tom and I got taken away from her. We bounced around in and out of foster homes until a couple from Primrose took us in. That was Lola and Ben Gilbertson. This was their home, and at one time they had two thousand acres connected to it, which they farmed for nearly fifty years. They were very sweet to us, and if there was one thing being the child of Annie Dietering taught you, it was how to be sweet in return. Lola taught me how to knit and Ben taught Tom about mechanics and we learned to farm, we learned about hard work, and they kept being nice to us until one day I think both Tom and I realized we weren't doing the Annie act anymore but loved being here.

"Tom's shop, the White Pelican, was Ben's farm shop years ago. It's hard to believe now because Primrose has grown so much since then, but from the campground to the White Pelican was one edge of the old farm planted solid with sunflowers, wheat, or soy beans every year.

"Annie had good and bad stretches and she tried to be a good mother to us, but by the time the state gave Annie the okay to take us back, it was clear to everyone that we were better off with Lola and Ben. Annie tried to keep up with us, but eventually this boyfriend or that one got in the way and we saw her less and less. I shudder to think what Lola and Ben had to deal with in the days after an Annie visit." Rachel is scratching through the large wooden popcorn bowl now looking for suitable kernels amongst the old maids remaining.

The kittens are now curled up and asleep in my lap.

"Funny thing is for years I thought I was like Annie. I mean I got pregnant when I was 17, like her, and Becky's dad was too young to be a real father to her. But it was Lola who helped me see that I could do it. Lola said she wasn't going to stop loving me because I had a baby so young. She said she wasn't going to stop loving me if I didn't want to marry Christopher. Lola was the one who told me that things don't always work out the way everyone says they will. She told me once that had my mother's parents been able to love her instead of being ashamed of her, that Annie might have been able to blossom in the world, instead of shrivel and hide the way she does.

"Lola and Ben taught me about this place. I love the ground, the fields, the cranes; I love the grasses in the summer and the frozen lakes in the winters. I feel safer here than anyplace I can imagine, and even though he's a thick-skinned guy, like all of you guys, I know Tom feels the same." Rachel lets out a deep, and to me, very sexy exhale while pausing and relaxing into the chair. I know it's not kind, but for a second I wish things hadn't gone so well with her ex-husband.

"So, what happened to Lola and Ben?" With this question the somber tone of Rachel's story switched completely. Rachel sets the knitting down, as if she's surprised to find it in her hands and she stands up to add some wood to the fire.

"When Tom and I got to our early twenties, Lola told Ben she wanted to quit farming. Oh, that did not sit well with Ben. Ben did not like to be idle. When Lola said she wanted to move to someplace like Arizona or Florida, Ben got worried. The thought of playing golf or cards with a bunch of old folks did not appeal to him. Finally, Lola laid down the law and said it was her or the farm. For real: I remember the day she did it. Ben came over to where Becky and I were living and said that Lola was going to leave him if he didn't move away with her. That's something that breaks your heart, seeing an old North Dakota farmer cry. All Ben kept saying was "I don't know what to do, I don't know what to do."

"What did he do?" I ask.

"He didn't have to do anything. It got done for him. Now here's something they ought to make a movie about. The next day, June 8th, 1989, Lola and Ben were talking things over while Ben was fixing one of his tractors down at the shop. Out of nowhere the wind starts blowing pretty strong, but they're going at it pretty good and they don't notice until one of the windows shatters around them. Lola looks outside and sees a tornado swirling around the sky off to the north a little. She yells to Ben and they stare at the tornado and then it touches down as they dive for the back room of the shop for cover. It blows out the rest of the glass and a big part of the roof, before it rises up again and things get calmer for a minute. The house, my house, is where the storm shelter is and they have to get to it but when they step outside their car is turned over. They can still see the tornado moving off a little and they decide to make a dash for the house.

before they take off, Ben gives Lola a big hug and promises her if they make it to the house he'll do whatever she wants, sell the farm, move to Arizona, learn to play golf, whatever. So they tear out of the shop and start running towards the house. Lola says that when they were about two hundred yards from the house the tornado turned and came after them. She likes to say that she never understood why the good Lord starved farmers skinny until the day she outran a tornado. A minute later they're inside the house and down in the storm shelter. By the time they came out half an hour later, the house was still here, the shop's walls were intact, but there wasn't much else.

"The next day, Ben walked from the front door of this house to the front door of the shop with a tape measure wanting a hard calculation of the distance he refers to as 'The mad dash to Arizona.' That distance is nine hundred and seventy three yards, exactly.

"A few months later, they moved. Ben helped Tom rebuild the shop, helped get him set up. They gave me the house and when they sold off the land they helped me to set up the campground. All that land to the north was once part of this. The three elms here mark one of the corners and there are three more at each of the other corners. Ben's father planted those trees in 1922."

Rachel stops now and apologizes for the long story.

"There's no need to apologize, "I assure her. "I've got some stories of my own."

"Yes, I bet you do. It's the quiet ones who have the best stories. Maybe you'll tell your story someday."

I stay in Primrose long enough for Tom to find me some replacement tires and to learn that Eric is having a great time learning about cold weather equines and some of the by-products of their milk.

The last morning we spend drinking coffee together, Rachel tells us the names for the two kittens.

"What, Tootsie and Footsie?" says Tom.

"Brother, if you had half your looks in brains there might be some hope for you. No, their names are Baronessa and Burt."

*Jake Spinner*
*General Delivery*
*Primrose, North Dakota*

*Jake,*                                                    *Today*

*    You find some places to stay, don't you? Don't run over any Prairie Dogs with that big truck of yours. I'm sending three films from Nina Palliatti, the woman I told you about with The Visible Past Project. My favorite is the one by the Tibetan rug weavers in Nepal. The other two were done at a cooking school for displaced Cambodians. Let me know what you think. Next year their conference is in New York. I hope to see you before then, but if not you'll be sitting on one of their panels. Somehow, you must meet this woman. I'm off to Chicago for a National Endowment summit about the state of American independent film. Ask Eric to show you how to dial out on that phone of yours sometime.*

*                                              Onward, Julian*

*    PS. I'm forwarding a letter that came here for you. J*


The card from Julian shows a young and skinny Phil Jackson wearing his New York Knickerbockers uniform as he rebounds a basketball. Across the top of the glossy card it reads:

**1969:  New York Sports Memory -- Phil Jackson.**

As for Nina Palliatti, Cupid Spinner is drawing back his bowstring.


The letter is from Clara in Larch. I'm glad to hear from her.

If Julian's cards are telegraph efficient, Clara's are old world patient. The envelope is a delicate Robin's egg blue with an embossed return name and address. The letter is addressed to me care of Julian in New York, and the handwriting has a delicate style but firm ink hand. I use a clean knife to cut the envelope open carefully. There are two delicate sheets of matching blue paper inside with large, flowery, feminine handwriting filling the pages.

*Dear Jake,*                                              *28 August*

*    I hope this letter reaches you in good spirits and health. I trust that your Uncle Julian will pass it on to you. I have been thinking about you lately. While sorting through my belongings I found some things that Fred left in my care for you. There is a wooden chest with keepsakes from your family. You know Fred would not have saved them if he didn't think them important, so whenever you return to Larch they will be waiting for you.*

*    I keep up my subscription to The Tattered Edge and I have enjoyed your column. Don't stop writing. Whether you publish or not isn't so important, but it is healthy for the soul. Though I miss your visits and conversation, I hope the road is treating you well and you are engaged in work that has meaning for you. After*

*all, that is one of the few things we can control in life: our work. Forgive me for this, but I do hope you are keeping some account of your travels. That is vital. Yes, ever the English teacher.*

*As for Larch, our little town continues to change. I have a new neighbor adjacent to the Sonnet who sells "nutritional beverages." Most of the menu is gibberish to me, but he has wonderful fresh juices and it is so popular with the younger people. Also, I thought you might enjoy hearing that your old friend, the prosecutor, is running for congress. I'll keep you apprised of that as it develops, though I doubt she will have too much success if she continues with her uninspiring campaign slogan. It reads "Lating -- For a Change." I am still unclear what that means.*

*You will be pleased to know that Jason and Marion are using the Tolliver grounds and growing vegetables there. It is bright and colorful right now with sunflowers and vibrant rows of tomatoes, peppers, melons, and too many other flowers to mention. They're doing quite well and have asked about buying your house. Let me know what you think about that.*

*I hope when you have time you think of us here in Larch and know you are welcome anytime. Aging has its challenges, but I feel blessed to be alive and in command of my mental capacities. Life is ever graced by the creativity and kindness of others. I shall keep you in my prayers.*

*With great fondness,*
*Clara*

*PS. Thanks for the pelican feather and the jar of the "Ruby Sauce."*

CHAPTER 15

# Candelabras And Organs:
# A Seven-Day Fishing Trip

**In Which** we meet a mechanic/philosopher who speaks of computers and chess, the end of hippies, the great Garth Hudson, and things "gone," whose career was set in motion by an act of "incendiary malfeasance" and of the value of Lapsang Souchong tea, knowing twenty songs, and goodness that comes out of the dark.

*Day One*

After leaving Primrose, I continued a gentle meander eastward for a few weeks. Eric called to inform me he'd finished the work with Poliakhov. He's taking the money he earned and going to visit his parents in Palau. "I may stay for a while, Jake, you know, got to keep up with the folks." Then he asks me to do something, which I'd sworn I never would, "Jake, can you leave your phone on so I can call you without having to figure out time zones?" Before I can answer, Eric adds, "It's not like anyone is going to call and bother you. Heck, there's probably only four people who have your number." I have to admit that he's right, so I agree, and Eric says, "Sweet; I knew you would."

Since then I've been enjoying finding places where I can park Zhitomir for a night or two. Sometimes I stay in campgrounds or parks, and sometimes on pullouts beside rivers and lakes where I can sit for a few days, write, think, and watch birds migrating south as the days grow colder. As comfortable as a place is, however, after a few days that deep wanderer's gene of mine urges me to go -- somewhere.

One day, after the first hard ice of the season has melted from Zhitomir's windshield and I'm looking for a southward route, strange sounds start coming from Zhitomir's engine whenever I go up a hill. What started as a complaint has rapidly escalated into a loud warning and has me thinking of Tom in Primrose. Fortunately, over my years on the road I've found that every town that's too small to be big or too big to be small has a mechanic who can fix the truck. There are hundreds of thousands of trucks like Zhitomir carrying everything from potato chips and beer to furniture and lunchmeats. Someone has to keep them running. How you find that person is another matter.

All towns have a bulletin board -- somewhere. Whether it's the old-fashioned town square sort with a formal glass-covered case, or indoors in the grocery store, there's a place for people to post things. Flyers, photos, 3x5 cards, push pins, tacks and tape -- the modern-day equivalent of the town crier. If you read them frequently and have a good memory for telephone numbers, you can tell a lot about your neighbors. People love to post things, maybe even need to post things. It's a window on small town life: used cars for sale, birth announcements, craft club meetings, urgent gatherings about community events, things needed, items lost, possessions stolen, kittens, home-made cheese for sale, extra clothing and eyeglasses, warnings about unsavory characters unknown to most of the community. Bulletin boards are vital. It's how we check up on the herd. After all, don't we all want to know what our neighbors are up to? That, I swear, is as hard-wired in humans as fleeing fire or going to sleep when the sun goes down.

Presently, Zhitomir's engine health is counting on the existence of that bulletin board in Kelton Valley. Sensing perhaps that help is near, Zhitomir begins a loud knocking as I drive the long downhill stretch into the town of six thousand. Knocking down Main Street past Dairy Queen and Kelton Home Furnishings, I set my gaze on the parking lot of the Kelton Valley Food Cooperative and roll into it.

The very moment Zhitomir is safely parked, the engine quits. I remove the key and walk through the doors leading to the cooperative, and there in the entryway is the hoped-for mother lode, a large cork bulletin board including a small box of 3x5 cards and a few pencils for writing messages. Above the cardholder is this message: "Please date all postings. Postings will be removed after three weeks. Thanks." In a world filled with complex regulations this simple set of guidelines is welcome in its simplicity.

Someone has thoughtfully separated the board into a few sections:

Goods, Services, and Community Announcements. Under services I spy the business card of one Giuseppe S. Boccacio, whose hand-lettered card says

## Giuseppe S. Boccacio

Mobile Auto Repair & Philosopher
No Job Too Big or Small
No Thought Too Deep or Insignificant.
24 Hours. 794-5656

Of course it reminds me of Fred, although Fred never called himself a philosopher.

Giuseppe Boccacio surprises me when he answers his phone with these words: "I hope you're not in a hurry because it sounds like you threw a connecting rod." Puzzled by his knowledge of the predicament, I ask him how he knows who I am.

"I assume you're the fella driving that International with the wacky paint job who drove into town. I heard you comin' a mile away. I can meet you in the co-op café in a few minutes. I'm gonna need a cup of coffee before I can look at that mess." Hanging up, I'm left wondering if all mechanics hear so well.

With a few minutes to kill, I'm tantalized by the aromas wafting through the air. The shelves of the co-op grocery section open to a large and comfortable café that is equal parts tofu, macramé, and oil paint. The ceilings are high and the room needs four circulating fans to keep it warm, and to send the smells coming from the kitchen down over the counter. The counter sits atop a glass display case filled with things called Tonka Cakes, Nanaimo Bars, Fudge Swirls, and a scary looking collection of brown bars called Vegan Carob Fingers that seem to be ceramic models of the goods for sale.

After placing my order at the counter, and sitting down at a table, I'm struck by the café's huge white wall space on which hang twelve large, well-painted canvases, and a small banner advertising "Twelve Scenes of Embrace." Maybe I'll see them differently after my coffee, but it looks like the twelve scenes recount the progression of foreplay to consummation, although they are sufficiently abstract to allow for artistic doubt or interpretation. Imagining the large walls without canvases, I see that this room has theater written all over it. It has twelve-foot-high ceilings and adequate length for a large unobstructed projection.

The most intriguing feature of the Kelton Valley Co-op Café is how the tables radiate around a large Lowery Organ in the middle of the room. Atop the impressive instrument, sitting on a white linen cloth, is a large silver candelabra. While staring around the room looking for clues to why the organ is there, a loud burst of steam comes from behind the counter, followed by the cry, "Jake, your latté is ready!"

A few minutes later a scraggly-looking bearded codger of impressive size wearing mechanic's coveralls ambles into the café. The man has a mysterious aura about him that hints of the smell of diesel oil and he has a ceramic cup in his left hand. With his other hand extended, he introduces himself with a voice that pours out of him like rock from a dump truck, "I'm Boccacio, but call me Fish. Only people around here who ever bothered saying my full name was the police, and that's a story I'll save for another time." If Eric were here, the camera would be rolling. Fish is an enormous man. His hands are huge and his long, graying hair flows wide from his head in a way that makes me think he's the kind of guy you want on your side in a bar fight. Something about his polished marble-brown eyes make you think he may have some history with that experience. He's both tough and soft and I like him at once.

Greetings over, Fish rises and walks back to the counter to have his mug filled with coffee. Returning, he sits again and, without looking at what he's doing, he spoons and swizzles fully three heaping tablespoons of sugar into the brew, adding in an ominous baritone rasp "You know, black coffee is a drug." He pauses there and continues to stir the coffee before adding, "But, if you add sugar and cream, it's three drugs."

Fish laughs a satisfied laugh at his well-used joke and starts sipping at his brew.

"I heard you roll into town. I know the song of about every car in this little town and I knew I hadn't heard that truck of yours before. The sound of an engine crying is an old familiar tune to these ears. I'm guessing you got a bit of rev-up going on the way into town. That last downhill is hard on trucks when their brakes don't hold'em back. That's why I looked out the window in the first place. That's some rig you got. Is that all a joke?" Then he asks sarcastically, "You have some middle-of-your-life crisis after the little lady walked out on you, or do you show movies?"

I assure Fish that I do show movies and he asks, "Do you make them too? Because I'm long overdue to be discovered."

Behind the counter, the teenage cook says, "Oh, no, we're doomed. Fish has an audience. Everybody take cover, Maestro Boccacio is in the house."

The companion of the young man behind the counter who looks to be about fifty, beneath his yellow bandanna, urges Fish on "Go ahead, Fish, tell him about being an old hippie."

Fish starts laughing, stands up, walks to the counter and scowls while he receives a refill. Again, he adds three more heaping tablespoons of sugar and a generous amount of cream to prepare his elixir, while staring directly at me and occasionally removing the spoon to point at the teenager.

"One thing I will never figure out is what draws young miscreants to good coffee. Before I die, I'd like to find one good cup of coffee without it being served by some sassy squirt."

This is all said loudly enough for this specific sassy squirt to hear, provoking more playful exhortation.

"You tell him, Fish!"

Fish is now fully baited and hooked, if you can forgive the expression, though with his voice rising in volume, it's clear he's not going to be landed without a struggle. Speaking, so all in the café can hear, he says:

"All right, first, let me set a few things straight. There are no more hippies! There are only impostors and poorly attired chemical dependents seeking refuge under the banner of hippie. But the 'Hippie thang' is dead. '*Dudes*,' '*old ladies*,' and '*The Movement*' are gone. If you hear anyone using these terms, be on alert! They are smoke screens for that greater depravity of social intercourse commonly found advertised in *The New York Times*, *Cosmopolitan*, and Calvin Klein commercials. Abbie Hoffman is dead, Jerry Rubin became a bond trader and Dennis Hopper: all I need to say is, *Waterworld*. As for Hunter S. Thompson, he's lucky if he can remember his own name. Navel-meditating airheads who study Chiron and Homeopathy are not hippies. Yuppies who drive old Volvos or vans with Free Tibet stickers are not hippies! Stoners who smoke pot and sing, 'If I get home before daylight...' are not hippies! Smoking pot is not revolutionary! We're in a new millennium and shit has changed! As for the children of hippies -- they are not hippies. They may look like hippies and talk like hippies, they may listen to the music hippies listened to, but they are not hippies! These kids are living in their own generation and need to create their own Woodstock and Summer of Love. Is that clear enough?"

Satisfied he has set the world straight on this important point of history, Fish sets his coffee mug down, places his palms flat on the table, and lifts himself out of his seat.

"Now, let's go have a look at your rig!" While I walk outside to Zhitomir to lift the hood, Fish retrieves his tools and then joins me.

Fifteen minutes later, after silently staring, listening, probing, and then repeating the whole procedure a few times, with occasional trips to his repair van for one tool or another, Fish makes his pronouncement.

"Momma here was screaming and you didn't listen. When Momma screams you gotta listen 'cause your Momma don't scream unless she's in trouble."

It's uncanny how mechanics speak the same language. I'm thinking back to Tom, but I cringe with the knowing realization that, unlike Eric's brake job, horse show videos are not going to pay for this repair. Fish continues.

"Here're the rules. You pay for the coffee, the parts, and my labor. I get half up front, the balance when the job is done and you're satisfied, and I assure you, you will be satisfied! I ain't ever met a machine that was smarter than a smart man and I take it very seriously when one tries to break my rules. The day I work for a machine instead of the other way around is the day Giuseppe Boccacio takes leave of this planet. I have no plans to yield dominance to any machine. You can park your rig in my yard and stay there as long as you need to, but, Mister, your engine is gonna have to move inside for a while. It's gettin' too cold for me to work outside."

As he meticulously returns his tools to various pouches and boxes, Fish continues with the theme of man-over-machine dominance. He launches into an explanation of the chess match between the super-computer, "Big Blue," and the chess master, Gary Kasparov.

"Wasn't no chip that beat that little borscht-guzzling Russki. They wore down that little cabbage-lover with sustained human input and computing capacity. They claimed that computer was smarter than Kasparov -- I say pull the plug and see how smart it is now! You can call that the Boccacio Defense! There ain't nothin' in that hurtin' old engine of yours that some human being didn't invent. It's like digging through the layers of the earth. When you know how to read it, there's a hell of a story down there, and when the story is told it will be told that Fish prevailed."

Then, on a deep exhale, satisfied with his speech, Fish adds, "Good, first things first. We're gonna have to get you down to my place. I think you got enough engine left to drive down a few more blocks, and one last thing. When Momma here is healthy again, we put you to work showing a movie. Deal?"

"Deal."

Fish's shop sits behind his house, like the office of a wrecking yard. Stacks of cinder blocks, welded chain links, and used snow skis enclose his yard. There are towers of old wheels, piles of scrap iron, brittle white plastic buckets of bolts, hoses, and fittings, all forming a fortress around the large concrete pad where he does his work.

"This is your little homestead for a while so you best get used to it. Unless you're one of them can't-stand-a-little-clutter types, I think it's kind of cozy, don't you think?"

A few hours later, after setting up a large rolling tripod, Fish pulls the engine out of the truck. He lifts the hulking assemblage of iron from the truck and once he has it suspended, he stops to admire it dangling in the air. "There's your Momma. She's of a good breed. She's made to run forever and constructed with parts so finely machined as to be able to propel something over twenty times her own mass. Nowadays, everything's disposable, including the user. Not this old Momma here, she's made to work hard and with a little care she'll work hard again. Not the standard engine for this truck you know. Whoever put this in had a plan."

When Fish says this, I swear I see Fred above me dealing an ace from a set of cards.

Once he has the engine inside, Fish wastes no time getting to work. Every part, every bolt, every washer, every piece that comes out of it is laid on a cloth-covered table with accompanying meticulous notes about placement and sequence. Fish isn't a mechanic, he's a surgeon, but I discover that he's a surgeon who likes to work alone.

"Nothing personal, Zoom Lens, but I don't get paid to explain stuff. You best find some other thing to do while I get on this."

*Day Two.* Kelton Valley Co-op Café.

This morning Fish is telling me about his first ex-wife who left him for a toy inventor in San Francisco.

"Believe it, Zoom Lens, she left me for the man who invented the first *Transformer*. Remember those fidgety pieces of plastic crap that cost arm-loads of money and turned little boys into zoo-zoo warriors? Well, one day the first ex and I were sitting over a bottle of tequila in the Mission district, talking about which song is San Francisco's best. She says, 'Tony Bennett, I Left My Heart.' I say, 'Otis Redding, Dock of the Bay.' We're at a standoff when this dippy guy who's been eavesdropping at the next table, slides his chair over and chimes in, 'How about, "*Lights?*" I say something like "You gotta be kidding; the song by that singer with the ball-bearing voice from *Journey?*" And my first ex says, 'I forgot about that one. I agree.' The next thing I know I'm headed back to Kelton Valley all alone, and my ex-wife is married to The King of Transformational Plastics. And where do you think he got his idea? Funny thing, though, I heard that song the other day and I kind of like it." I know there's got to be some point when Fish will stop, but it won't be soon. I get another cup of coffee.

*Day Three.* Café again.

Fish produces, and proudly reads, a letter he received that morning from an engineer at the Jet Propulsion Laboratories.

*Dear Mr. Boccacio,*

*Thank you for your recent letter concerning the solar deflector system for the Galaxy VI Explorer Probe. I assure you, the modifications proposed will be given proper consideration. We, too, share your concerns that space explo-ration must not be limited by material inadequacies or engineering over-sight. We at J.P.L. pride ourselves in careful evaluation and development of alternative designs and materials and welcome input by those who share our vision of an expanded universe.*

*Sincerely yours,*
*Jasper Krenveld, Galaxy VI Project Engineer*
*Jet Propulsion Laboratory*

"This is what I'm talking about. I read about their deflectors failing and sent them an idea to fix it: hybridized titanium, Zoom Lens. Hybridized titanium, it's so obvious."

Not to me. I have no idea what Fish is talking about, but I wouldn't bet against him being right.

When you think there is no more reserve for Fish to draw from, another reservoir appears. There's no point in saying anything until he exhausts himself and arrives in the "mechanicking zone," as he puts it. Today I get to hear the story of his mentor.

"Yep, the first guy who taught me about mechanics was my best friend's father, Lem S.T.Y. Fuller."

"What does the S.T.Y. stand for?"

"Hah, you're too easy, Zoom Lens. S for smarter, T for than, and Y for Y-O-U. It's true too. Lem was one of them guys who ran on an even keel and had the knowing smile of a Buddhist monk. Not any ordinary grease-monkey and not like those high-tech computer operators who call themselves mechanics nowadays, but a real industrial revolutionary mechanic from the old school. Lem was one of those philosopher mechanics who roamed the world until their swift-decline-approaching-extinction in the twentieth century: a regular Archimedes.

"As a boy, he was part of the Okie migration whose family made their way to California in the thirties. One day at his high school they gave some kind of experimental intelligence test and Lem blew it off the charts. The next thing he knew, Cal Tech had invited him into the place. Full ride: tuition, residence, books, food, probably beer too and all the plastic pocket protectors you can use. Imagine that young son of a red-necked hillbilly at Cal Tech. He told me how much he loved physics and that math was a breeze, but he couldn't stand all the chalk dust and inside work.

"After two degrees, and forsaking some big time government support, he had to get back to the sanity, that's what he called wherever he lived. But there wasn't a whole lot of opportunity in the outside world for anyone in those days. Lem said, 'Too early for the bomb, too early for Sputnik. Sure would've loved building them rockets.' Those were tough times.

"Good thing it was also an era when cars were on the rise. Lem understood automobiles better than anyone I've ever met. Said machines and people were co-evolving and in another hundred years you wouldn't be able to tell which is man and which is machine. He once told me he had a calling for cars. You gotta understand this, Zoom Lens; this is a guy who could've been as easily drinking beer with Bobby F'n Oppenheimer at Los Alamos as running a pickle barrel machine shop in Modesto. He was part physicist, part machinist, part poet, and part clown, topped off with a heck of a lot of IQ and common damn sense!

"I know you're wondering where I'm going with all this about Lem.

Well, when I was sixteen I got arrested for, and I quote, 'an incendiary act of malfeasance,' unquote. That is exactly how they wrote it in the local paper. Fortunately for me, the judge knew my family, and at my sentencing he said that I was too young for the army and too smart to waste away in jail, so he was setting me up with a 'supervised' internship with Lem.

"My first few weeks, I swept the floors and cleaned grease off anything that needed it. After three weeks of that, I was thinking jail might have been the better sentence, when one day Lem finally calls me into the shop and shows me a metal lathe. 'See that,' he says. 'You can make a square chunk of steel into a supersonic airplane with that. You can make cars run faster, rivers run slower, and the universe bigger with it, but only if you learn the trade.

"Well, that was the last of 'incendiary malfeasance' for me. I had found my talent in the back of a pickle barrel machine shop. Inside of a few months I was turning out small pieces and after a few months I was doing most of the machining for him."

Fish rises from the table and fills his coffee cup. The sugar bowl is empty. He scrapes at it but only a few crystals come forth. Instead of taking it to the counter for a refill, he picks up the thumb-pour container of maple syrup from the counter tray and pours that into the cup. Looks like he's not done with me this morning. Have mercy, Fish.

"Yep, I was the poster boy for the juvenile justice system. The first time I saw that lathe I felt the call. Folks have this noble, romantic notion about their calling. Well, that's fine for them, but there's no guarantee a calling is going to make everyone happy. Darn things so often do the reverse. You can try doing other stuff, you can try to live a different life, earn your money at any old job, but there's this nagging tug at your soul all the time. You can try to sleep if you haven't answered the call that day, try to appreciate the things around you the way most people do, drink a beer and waste the day whittling on a stick or staring off into space, but still there's this nagging reminder dogging you: your calling.

"You could rightly say that a calling is a life sentence because everyone who gets the call can tell you there's no escape. Forget about sleep, forget about food, forget about peace of mind, until you answer that call. Best thing you can do is give yourself over to it and find some way to make it work.

"That's why I line up smaller projects: tune-ups, mufflers, brake jobs, timing belts and the like. You need little moneymakers to stay fit, to be ready, have your edge waiting for the Big Job. Kind of like those shorts you movie fellas show before the feature. You got to be ready to embrace the job that engages your mind, pushes your skill and satisfies your calling.

"You know what? I felt you coming weeks before you arrived. I was getting way too hungry. Not for money, not for food, but hungry, kind of spiritually hungry. I dread engine overhauls, they're so damn precise and you have to keep everything ultra-clean. But once you get into it, it's a pretty deep meditation. Step by step, you're bringing steel and iron to life. Pretty amazing stuff when you think about it. Not the same as buying a brand new engine made at the factory. No, sir. Not the same at all. While you're breaking it down, every piece talks to you like you're chipping away at some archaeological site. Then, putting it back together it's like giving birth . . . Okay, maybe not exactly the same, but you get the idea."

The cup of coffee is empty, and for a minute it looks like Giuseppe the "Fish" Boccacio is prepared to fill it again and drink and talk all day. Instead, he rises and walks over to one of the paintings, a dark and brooding canvas of two lovers in a desperate embrace. He stares at the painting for a silent moment until his eyes glaze over. His gaze shifts away from the painting, and, like a bolt of lightening, thirty-six ounces of coffee and twelve teaspoons of sugar ignite his metabolic starter as he explodes out of the café presumably drawn by his calling "to master the world of the inanimate."

*Day Four.* Café. Where else?

Fish and I are sitting at the Co-op doing the morning ritual, when someone walks over to the organ, removes the cover, carefully places candles in each arm of the candelabra, lights them, finally sitting down to play the organ. I ask Fish why she lit the candles and he says, "Ain't nobody told you about this thing yet? Come on over here." We walk to the organ and stand behind the woman. Flanking both sides of the original gold lettering are the sculpted initials G.H.

G. H.     𝕷𝖔𝖜𝖊𝖗𝖞 𝕺𝖗𝖌𝖆𝖓 𝕮𝖔𝖒𝖕𝖆𝖓𝖞     G. H.

"Tell me, Zoom Lens, you're old enough to know. Do you know who those initials belong to?"

"I don't know, George Harrison?"

"Duh, that ain't no sitar, Zoom Lens. G.H. stands for Garth Hudson, the one and only organ player for the Band. Please, please, please do not tell me you don't know about The Band. The Band who played with Bob Dylan, the Band -- Music from Big Pink, Stage Fright, Up On Cripple Creek, The Night They Drove Old Dixie Down, *The Last Waltz?*"

Seeing that Fish is about to walk away in disgust, I placate him by saying, "King Harvest."

"There you go, Zoom Lens. I knew you had it in you. You're quiet, but you got some depth."

Then Fish pauses, 5 . . . Fish sips, 4 . . . Fish swallows, 3 . . . Fish inhales, 2 . . . Fish exhales, 1 and . . . 0 . . . Fish blasts off!

"Well, Garth and The Band came through Kelton Valley thirty years ago on their way to a show in Chicago. It wasn't like today with million-dollar buses and private jets with all the comforts. They stopped here like y'all did when your truck broke down, only they had a busted rear axle, because their driver wasn't paying attention to the 'Rough Road' signs that used to line the entrance to town. Imagine that, The Band staying right here in little old Kelton. We had to unload all their equipment to get that axle off. Tofu Nirvana here wasn't a food co-op back then either, it was a vacant seed warehouse, and we moved their stuff inside here while I repaired their rig."

"No way! You fixed The Band's truck?"

"More F'n way than a cheese factory, Zoom Lens! You can imagine those boys was pretty used to keeping busy, being from small towns themselves, so one night they up and invited everybody down to the warehouse for a little concert. Some of the old folks were a little worried about having a rock-and-roll concert right here in Kelton, but everyone liked the boys, especially Garth, whom everyone started calling 'The Preacher' cause how he was all minister-like. That night there was a fright of a rainstorm, and the warehouse was packed. A few hundred people were sitting on makeshift benches, folding chairs, and wherever they could find a spot on the floor, and, damn, if about twenty minutes before the show was set to start, the power didn't go out. It wasn't that big a deal, because one thing we have a lot of in the Great White North is generators, so it was a matter of rigging one up to power all their amplifiers and instruments.

"After a few minutes, we had it all set up, but it was still pretty dark inside because we didn't bother to hook in the warehouse lights. That's when Garth came walking out with this candelabra, all fired up with twelve flaming candles, set it down on the organ and started to play. Man, you cannot begin to imagine what that was like. It was like some force was running through him and making its way straight into your core. I can't even remember how long he played before the others joined him, but it was a while. And I'll tell you something else: you can't get anybody in this town to agree on but one thing, and that is that the greatest musician in history is Garth Hudson.

"And if Garth is the greatest, the others aren't far behind. Levon starts kicking it up, and Robbie, and Rick and Richard; you can't help but love them when they sing. Soon, the audience takes to these boys like they was the local high school football players. You could tell they liked it too, because they were kids themselves. It was music like it's supposed to be. They enjoy the crowd and the crowd starts calling out for certain songs. They start playing 'Cripple Creek' and the first time through they sing it straight, but then Robbie nods over to Levon and the second time he sings Kelton Creek and by then, well, by then, The Band was certifiably favorite sons of Kelton Valley.

"It was a few days later when I finally got their rig put back together. The last afternoon, all the boys was in the warehouse loading up. The organ was strapped to a dolly and they were trying to roll it into the truck, when Garth holds up his hands like Moses and stops them, saying in that gentle, unassuming voice of his, 'Leave the organ here.' No one knew why until he explained that he thought the organ ought to stay here because he had a new one waiting in Chicago, and that things belonged where they had a purpose. Then he disappeared inside the truck and a few seconds later reappeared with the lit candelabra. With a whimsical smile, he set it on the organ and said to Tofu Senior behind the counter there, 'I've always thought this instrument sounded best with this on top of it.'"

Fish heaves a giant exhale, but he's not finished.

"Since then it's been a tradition that no one ever plays the organ without lighting the candles. Those guys could have pulled into any old town, or it could have been any old band or some other thing that landed here, but it wasn't."

Then, slowing his breathing, Fish goes into his deep meditative voice.

"This is the thing, you see. You don't choose your generation. You don't choose how other people will live or what their choices are gonna be. But you're all in it together, and you know the people of your generation better than any others -- the songs, the books, the follies, and today even all them celebrities are regarded like your own damn family. That's what media does, it takes all these people and events, and moves them into our minds as if they are real, and so we care about them. It wasn't like that before the last century. I mean, sure, you had your famous people who lived in little clusters of celebrity, like Mozart and Shakespeare and Vivaldi and Abe Lincoln and Dolly Madison, but for the most part they weren't known around the world like they are today. Stuff moved slower, and mostly people didn't care about people from far off. When news traveled in a saddlebag it couldn't have the same urgency. By the time something got to you the whole world could have shifted. But today, man, it's like the speed of light ain't fast enough, and you're reacting to the bombardment of things coming at you. Lord knows, you can watch this stuff on television and half the time they're givin' you ticker tape accounts of people's lives like stock-market quotes. Soon you'll be able to hook into some camera somewhere and get the play-by-play. Why not franchise your whole life? Imagine it! It'll happen, you watch. But hey! There's no point in pissin' and moanin' about it. That's the thing about generations. You move through yours and do the best you can with what you've got. When they die, you die, when they live, you live, and that's the way it is."

Fish stops for a second. He is slowing to a stop.

"Now, I got a little favor to ask you, Zoom Lens," says Fish as the woman at the organ begins to draw sound out of the majestic instrument.

"What might that be, Fish?"

"Can you get your paws on a copy of *The Last Waltz*? I know plenty of the folks here have seen it, but not together, not like that night. That would be something, a little town reunion. Shut the town down for the night and have a movie night together."

"I think I know where to get it, Fish."

Julian comes through.

*Dear Jake,*                                                        *Today*

*Scorsese lent me a copy of the film. Marty has to have 16 and 35 mm versions of everything. Look on the inside of the can: it's signed by everyone. The line drawing portrait on the can is by Joni Mitchell. Marty thinks it's great that someone wants to see it, and he went nuts when I told him the Garth Hudson story. You may want to send a note to Hudson and tell him about it. I think he'd be touched.*

*Where next? Don't you get tired of the road? I'm sending the VPP conference preliminaries to you. I know it's seven months away, but I don't want you to forget about taking part in the VPP panel discussion. No trips to Tierra Del Fuego, Jake!*

*Onward, Julian*


Me tired of the road? What's to be tired of? It's a gentle life. No schedule, no big responsibilities, no lawns to mow or wood to cut. Okay, no shower, no laundry, and no kitchen. But if I had Julian's schedule to keep, I would be tired. When Fred met Julian he said he finally believed the laws of thermodynamics. You know, that thing about how energy can neither be created nor destroyed but only transformed from one type into another. Well, Julian moves through the world like electricity. You can almost hear the crackles.


*Day Five.*

Fish tells me he's close to done with the truck. "Trust me, Zoom Lens, start setting things up for the show because I'll be done soon." While Fish plies his trade I spend my time setting up things with the Co-op staff, who have planned a community talent show to accompany the screening. They've dubbed it "A Chance to Step In Front" and there's now a short list of people who have been signing up to perform. As I said earlier, the room is perfect for a film. We remove a few paintings, project high on a wall, and once the perimeter of the projection is set, the Co-op staff paint on a set of curtains to flank the screen. Nice. The entire show can be set up in about twenty minutes, which impresses Richard, a.k.a. Tofu Senior, the co-op manager, who starts asking questions about renting films and running a little theater from time to time.

The following Saturday night the room is filled with borrowed chairs from a local church. People come. There are at least three hundred people fitted nicely into the space. The film is supposed to start at seven-thirty, but things go slowly due to the talent show and a few opportunistic "community" announcements. One little girl sings that song "Memory" from *Cats* while her older sister follows her on the flute. There's a fine three minute song by a gospel singer named Gina, who renders "Precious Lord" after a brief introduction about meeting with its composer, Thomas (not the big

band guy) Dorsey, and having her life changed to a righteous path. As she leaves the stage area, an intriguing young woman is standing off to the side. She opens her guitar case, sets her strap in place, and tunes her instrument. Unlike everyone who has come before her, this late-twenties woman shows no nervousness and her preparations have the routine of a well-practiced religious ritual. Fish is standing beside me.

"Pay attention, Zoom Lens. This girl can sing."

She has to wait out two more acts: one a six-year-old fiddler named Jacob, who unknowingly changes key a few times before finishing with a strong flourish, and then a sixteen-year-old tenor saxophone player named Ted, who delivers an occasionally squawking version of some song only young people seem to recognize.

Before taking to the stage, the guitarist takes a roll of blue masking tape and tapes a small card to the top of her guitar. With one last adjustment to her tuning, she takes her place at the front of the room.

"Good evening, Kelton. My name is Rosie, and I'd like to sing you two songs."

When Rosie starts singing "Down to You" by Joni Mitchell, the chatter in the room ceases. Out of her tiny body comes a sound that stops time and if the Kelton Valley Co-op Café had a personalized coaster, I'd keep one. Her voice captivates us with the song's precocious voyage, and when she finishes no one is sure whether to applaud or cry. Fish understands that applause is needed and initiates the well-deserved clapping.

Rosie's second song is a lovely ballad sung by a man to a woman about not having anything but his love to give to her on Valentine's Day. I haven't heard the song before and make a mental note to ask her about it after the show.

When Rosie walks off to warm and enthusiastic applause, a few awkward moments ensue as the young man who was to follow her to sing about his pet pigs decides not to go on. His parents are encouraging him, but no singer wants to follow someone who's reached deep into an audience. Fortunately, this is not a problem for an imposing man of words and up to the microphone strides Fish. No longer the soiled mechanic, Fish is clean and groomed, with his hair tied back into a thick ponytail. Barely noticeable (except up close), the ponytail is tied with a short length of fuel hose. His beard is combed and he's wearing a finely tailored dark suit, in which he resembles a rustic Luciano Pavarotti.

Fish's arrival at the front is my cue to be ready in the back. Standing at the microphone, he clasps his hands together in front of his heart, inhales once to steady himself, and introduces himself as if no one in the room knew who he was.

"I am the right honorable Giuseppe Salvatore Boccacio and being of sound mind and body" the audience laughs out loud but Fish ignores them and repeats the last line, "being of sound mind and body present for your consideration the following creation, entitled, *Looking For That Little Stream Where You Caught Your First Trout.*" Fish takes one visible inhale and his massive chest rises accentuating the formality of his attire, then bellows

"It's gone, man, long gone.

"So far gone you even gotta hurry to find someone with a memory of it."

Fish's deep-voiced recitation begins like a soulful epoch elegy, and by the time the first two lines are finished everyone is locked onto this timeless messenger.

Gone like big trees, wooden boats and large salmon.
Gone like the groups of Indians used to hang around Fourth Street sell
 ing trinkets.
It's gone like Model A's and Maxwells, hand cranks and fifteen-cent gaso
 line.
It's gone like the Good War, and 'Give Us Your Tired, Your Poor,
Your Huddled Masses Yearning to Breathe Free'.
It's gone like the Ten Commandments and 'Brother Can You Spare A
Dime'.
Gone like cold winters and teenage love and sleepless nights
Or hikes into nowhere, with crazy friends.
Gone like Lindbergh.
Like the Nobel Peace Prize and the Olympic Movement.
Gone like black-and-white photographs of grandparents on their wed
 ding day.
Gone like heroes and patriotism and truth
And little salutes by Cub Scouts.
Gone like safety and the boundless potential.
Gone like tireless muscles and an unbroken heart.
Gone like Jackie Robinson and the 'suicide squeeze'.
 It's gone like you can change the world,
Like rock-and-roll without fame.

Gone like Impressionism and poetry with a lunatic structure.
Gone like falling off to sleep easily.
Gone like silent movies of little blind girls and noble tramps on the
 streets of Paris
Gone like pole sitting and
Gone like prayers with simple requests and simpler answers.
It's gone, like caring about art, and belief in words.
Gone like faith, hope, and charity."

Fish drops his hands and the audience is silent and not sure whether he's finished. Before a few in the audience are about to applaud, Fish takes one last deep breath, re-clasps his hands and finishes:

"You looking for that little stream where you caught your first trout?"

With that, Mr. Giuseppe Salvatore Boccacio makes a deep bow to the audience, leaves the microphone and walks towards me. I switch on the first projector as the café lights dim to blackness in an orchestrated punctuation to Fish's recitation. Amidst the applause that follows Fish's poem, some five seconds later the following image begins the screening of *The Last Waltz*:

---

### This Film Should Be Played Loud!

For the next one hundred and seventeen minutes, it is played loud, bathing the audience in Fish's generation. Fish takes his place beside me and stands stout and tall the entire film. The audience sings to the songs making occasional comments like, "They all look so young . . . Look at Danko, he looks like an impish balladeer trying to find his lost love. Man, I was sad when he died."

Fish keeps bumping me in the side with comments like "Man, they sure do make some music." For nearly two hours the obligations of modern life and its primal gravity are suspended. We're all weightless together in an illuminated fantasy as The Band, Bob Dylan, Michael McClure, Eric Clapton, Paul Butterfield, Joni Mitchell, Ringo Starr, Dr. John, The Staple Singers, Ron Wood, Neil Young, Lawrence Ferlinghetti, Van Morrison, Muddy Waters, Ronnie Hawkins, Neil Diamond, gather on the stage and sing the film's thematic exclamation point: Dylan's, "I Shall Be Released."

As the Band plays the commemorative Last Waltz and the film's credits roll by, we look at the favorite sons of Kelton Valley one last time -- Levon, Richard, Rick, Robbie, and Garth. No one present wishes to awaken from this dream. Fish jabs at my ribs with one last comment.

"Man, if they ever need something to shoot into space in one of them time capsule deals, I sure hope they choose this."

*Day Seven.*

When I get to the Co-op, it's unusually somber. Even the espresso machine is sedate. There's no music coming from the kitchen, and only the sounds of rhythmic chopping as the staff prepare food for the day. I spy Rosie alone at a table writing quietly in a notebook with her guitar strapped over her shoulder. On her table is a pot of tea and a half filled cup, while beside her on the floor sits her guitar case. Rosie is striking today as her sleeveless shirt exposes arms covered with tattoos, including a large green parrot with a cigarette in its mouth on one forearm and a colorful replica of her guitar on the other. When I compliment her on the song from last night she graciously asks me if I'd like to join her.

"You're the film guy. Wow, that was so cool." Rosie gestures to the notebook, which is a heavily inked blur of words and chord notations. I can see that the card taped to her guitar is a listing that reads, 'Gandhi's Seven Deadly Sins'.

1) Wealth without work.

2) Pleasure without conscience.

3) Science without humanity.

4) Knowledge without character.

5) Politics without principle.

6) Commerce without morality.

7) Worship without sacrifice.

"I'm finishing up a few things on this lyric. Do you want some tea? I've got a whole pot. Lapsang Souchong. It's good."

I've been missing Eric's youthful company because Rosie's openness and her aura of simple ambition make her conversation welcome. I don't have the heart to decline the offer.

"Grab a cup, there's plenty. Better than coffee for you. I can't drink coffee; it makes me insane." Rosie sees me looking at her guitar case, which is covered with an array of decals. "Troubadour's badges of honor. Lots of miles." Then, getting excited, she touches one.

"This one here: Ireland. All singers have to go to Ireland. It's kind of like Mecca to Muslims. It's a funny thing, because the place can be so dark, dank, depressed, and talk about a history of being beaten down; but they're amazingly open to life and if you can sing, well, at least if you can throw your soul into a song, you won't lack for beer or food there. I tell people: you want to be a singer, get yourself twenty songs and head to any pub in Ireland. It won't take long for you to find out what you've got." Then Rosie apologizes, aware that she's been talking rapidly. "I guess I'm up on you, this is my second pot this morning. But, duh, here I am talking about miles. I guess you do some traveling too."

"Yes, but my miles are limited by the wheels on a truck," I say, to which Rosie says, "I doubt that. I saw that truck of yours down at Fish's place. Looks like someone's done some traveling."

I ask Rosie where she's from and she says, "Short answer: I was born in Columbus, Ohio and I grew up in New York City, but I've spent the last ten years knocking around wherever the wind blows me. I like to say I was born in the Delta Guitar Shop in Mobile, Alabama." Rosie doesn't need much of a confused look from me to initiate an explanation.

"I was going to music school in Indianapolis and I had a boyfriend named Slater. Slater Ray Williams, son of Henry Ray Williams, grandson of Donald Hercules Williams who was better known in Mobile as the 'Strongest Picker in the South'. Slater was the black sheep of the family because he took up the violin, not the fiddle, you understand?

"Henry Ray owned the Delta Guitar Shop, the center of the music scene in Mobile. You know, people would come in and play and talk and play and talk and sometimes talk, and sometimes play."

It was at this point that I stop Rosie only long enough to get a large cup of coffee. "Sorry, but I'm finding it hard to wake up this morning." When I come back with the coffee, Rosie continues without missing a beat.

"So, Christmas time ten years ago brings me home to Mobile. We're visiting the family and one night we take off to grab some privacy down at the closed guitar shop, thanks to a key from Slater's grandfather. It's a pretty amazing place, the walls are lined with guitars, mandolins, dobros, steel guitars, banjos, and we're messing around in the back when I must've said something that got Slater mad. I don't remember what it was, but you know how it is when you spend the holidays with family. Slater was pretty touchy. Next thing I know, he storms out of the place throwing the security door closed which automatically shuts the lights off and I'm stuck. I mean the place is dark and the doors are locked. I can't open them from the inside and the only telephone is in the locked office. Imagine that, pitch dark and locked in a room full of guitars.

I sat tight for an hour thinking Slater would cool down and come after me, but he didn't. After a while I began to get the idea that I might be stuck for a little longer than I expected. The good thing was that in the back of the store was a player's room, you know, a place with cozy chairs to hang out for a little secluded playing time, or to get away from the noise if you're trying out an instrument you're thinking about buying. I felt my way back there, thinking I might as well make the most of things. There was enough light that I could see the outline of the instruments on the walls and I started playing them one after another. The great thing was, I couldn't see the maker's names, the price tags, or any of the frills put on an instrument like inlay. All I had was the feel and the sound of the guitars. That's where I found Liza Mae here."

Rosie points to her guitar.

"That's what I named her. I had a lot of guitars in my hands that night and each one played its own song, but Liza Mae played the sweetest."

"How did you get out?"

"I ended up sleeping there that night. It wasn't until the next morning at breakfast when Slater's mother asks him where I am and he explains what happened. Oh, that did not go over well with the folks who came and got me. They were apologetic, begging for forgiveness, and not showing a lot of love for Slater at the time. They were surprised that I wasn't upset, until I explained about playing the guitars. Grandpa Henry was so moved by the whole episode that he gave me Liza Mae."

"And Slater?"

"Still the black sheep in the family, but he's concertmaster in the Atlanta Symphony now. We didn't last too long after that. Great guy, but his bow was a little tightly strung for me."

Thankfully, about the time Rosie finishes her story, my coffee kicks in -- in time for Fish's arrival. Fish, unlike most everyone else in the Co-op this morning, glides in like a man walking joyfully on a cloud. Even before concocting his sugar, coffee, and cream slurry, he chatters away.

"Well, I see you two have met." Then he takes Rosie's hand in his and does a polite bow, bestowing a kiss on the singer's hand. "This one is special, Zoom Lens. Catch her now before she's famous, because she will be famous." He sits down and starts preparing his brew. When it's right, he takes a deep sip, heaves deeply, and says, "Don't you love it: Bars, Dives, and Dance-Halls! Don't tell me it wasn't a great generation. That was a movie last night. I might buy me a jar of furniture polish and spend the day buffing up that old Lowery." Then, raising his voice loud enough for the counter and kitchen staff to hear, he bellows, "'Cause nobody else around here ever does a stitch of work!"

Before leaving, I ask Rosie who wrote the second of her two songs last night.

"That's by Steve Earle," Rosie says proudly "He's awesome."

Later that day, sitting in the café after a fifty-mile test drive in which Zhitomir is put through a few paces, Fish pronounces the job done. He gives me a list of procedures for breaking in the new engine.

"Go easy on her for a while, Zoom Lens. Momma is healthy again, but she's still Momma, and you know the saying: you got to take care of your Momma." Then he changes to a more serious tone than usual and says,

"You take care of yourself, now. It's a fine thing you're doing and I'm glad you broke down here. I'm waving a portion of the labor."

When I try to convince Fish that I have the money to pay him, he won't allow it.

"No, can't soak you for what I was born to do, Zoom Lens. That's final."

"Okay, but I have something for you then."

"What's that?"

"I'll be right back." I went out to Zhitomir and pulled a little souvenir that was given me years ago. I brought it inside and presented it to Fish.

"Well, lookee here, an old projector." Fish, takes a handkerchief from his pants pocket and exhales onto his fingers as he wipes them clean. An appreciative, satisfied smile forms on his face as he probes, spins, and toggles the old Bell and Howell "They for sure do not make these anymore. Look at this," Fish says, holding the little can of machine oil that was issued with the projector. The can, with the letters B&H written on it, embodies everything elegant about the projector's design. Fish says "Don't you need this projector, Zoom Lens?"

"No, I wish I did, but it's not grounded and the audio buzzes when you feed it into modern speakers. Besides, I think it belongs here."

"Well, damn, Zoom Lens, this is righteous. I got an idea." Says Fish, rising with the projector that he sets on top of Garth Hudson's Lowery Organ. "We got ourselves a new memento here, don't we?"

Then with a smile peeking from his beard and his big brown, grease monkey's angelic eyes moist with emotion, Fish says, "Zoom Lens, you'll always have a home here in Kelton. Promise me now, when you're out this way again you'll stop."

"Mr. *Giuseppe S. Boccacio*, I do so solemnly swear I will."

And I'm gone.

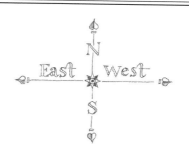

# SECTION 3

---

# There Is A Reason
# Movies Have
# Happy Endings

Fade Out essay from the *Tattered Edge*, Volume 15 # 3

# Happy Endings And The Reptilian Brain, by A.L. Janus

There is a reason movies have happy endings. People want the afflicted healed and they want David to slay Goliath. They want a two-hour escape in which obstacles are overcome, bravery is rewarded, and love is triumphant. Some people believe we've transcended these basic urges, and we can exist on a higher spiritual plane where our instincts are no longer driving our actions. We haven't. Human beings are complex in many ways, but not when it comes to plots for popular movies.

My uncle Fred, with his poetic utilization of science, said all humans are driven by that tiny little part of our brain, the first brain, the little mass of cells that simply says "fight or flight," "yes or no," "eat or starve," "mate or die." Fred was the first one I ever heard who called that using the "Reptilian Brain." Fred said there's a little dinosaur brain in all of us handed down from the jumble of contingencies that confronted us when we crawled out of the primordial soup. Movies follow the same rules as the rest of human nature. Stories with happy endings please us better than ones that leave us desperate or confused. We prefer to believe the world is full of happy endings. When all is said and done, what we seek in movies is what we seek in life:  contentment and simplicity. After we've picked the film, bought the ticket, gotten the popcorn, and found our seat, we want the guy and the girl, or the alien and the invaded, to figure it out, get together and live happily ever after.

Year after year after year, the films that sell the most tickets are the ones that don't confuse the audience. That's not to say you can't take a walk on the dark side from time to time. You can, but if you do (and any movie producer will confirm this), you better have some incredible hunk or babe to keep everybody watching (preferably you'll have both a babe and a hunk who look good in tight clothes and can kiss like nobody's business). There's too much reality in most people's lives to pay good money for what they can get free of charge out in the world.

If you don't believe it, flip open any popular movie guide to the pages listing the top grossing films by year; *Aladdin (1993), Crocodile Dundee (1986), Back to the Future (1985), Beverly Hills Cop (1984), ET (1982), American Graffiti (1973), Butch Cassidy and The Sundance Kid (1969), Bonnie and Clyde (1967), Ben Hur (1959, Cinderella (1950), Auntie Mame (1958), Going My Way (1944), Bambi (1942), Gone With the Wind (1939).* There's not a lot of meaning of life confusion on this list. To be fair, there have been a few films that crossed the line and were enormously popular. *Deliverance* was the highest grossing film in 1972, and *Dog Day Afternoon* (1975) followed suit. But *Dog Day* had Al Pacino riding the post-*Godfather* luster, and *Deliverance* had a great song and the best archer since William Tell, played by a hunk, Burt Reynolds. Okay. There's also *The Best Years of Our Lives* (1946) and *From Here to Eternity (1953)*, both war films with deeper underlying themes, but neither one leaves you confused about the meaning of life in general or of your own life in particular. As long as we know who is good and who is bad, we can handle it.

Even during the 60's, when the country was engaged in a struggle for its cultural and social identity, most of the big films were likely to leave you happy and without too much confusion. I'm sure you remember the Sixties, when it simply was un-cool to feel good. How could you with the Vietnam War and the rising tide against social injustice? If you weren't upset you weren't paying attention. But, even then, for all those who saw *Easy Rider, Midnight Cowboy, Who's Afraid of Virginia Woolf,* or *2001 A Space Odyssey*, there were more who saw *The Alamo, The Absent Minded Professor, How The West Was Won, Cleopatra, The Carpetbaggers* and *The Bible*. Here's a fact for you:  in 1970, even with the war in Vietnam still raging away, *Airport* was the top grossing film. *Airport*?!@@#$#%$^&

To be clear:  I'm not complaining about this. I am an escapist. Films that take me out of reality for two hours and leave me feeling good are welcome in my world. I loved *Gladiator* and *Flubber*! I've spent a lot of my life looking at movies and I've shown hundreds of films to audiences over the years. I've shown *The Burmese Harp* about World War Two Japanese war survivors, *Mindwalk*, about . . . well, I'm still trying to figure out what it's about, and I've shown *Elmer Gantry*, about the inner world of American tent show evangelism in the first half of the 20th century. I love *Elmer Gantry*, but the audience didn't. They started coughing, clanking their chairs, and before too long more than a few called it a night before I'd even cued up the last reel. Who doesn't want to escape for a few hours these days?

When you produce a film series, as I have in the past, there are a lot of requests that come to you. People have a favorite film, or what I call a memory film, a film that made a huge impact on them years ago, and they will twist your arm to show something like *A Clockwork Orange* or *The Tin Drum*. If you're smart, and I wasn't always smart, you'll watch it at home and let your gut (there's that lizard again) tell you whether it will be well received. When you're not smart, you'll find yourself at the back of the room squirming behind your vintage projectors as people march out of the room or sneeze, cough, clatter their chairs, or in a myriad of other ways show you they aren't happy. And then it gets worse, because, while the person who asked you to show the film is having a grand time, twenty others are not, and many of them are going to let you know as soon as the lights come on, or worse still, they won't say anything but won't show up to your next show. That's when you have to decide what you're all about:  are you about ART, or entertainment?

There are scores of great films that tear your heart out or push you deeply into uncomfortable areas. I have and I will show them. Maybe, at its best, a film can do both, make you think, feel, and even care about something in ways you never thought possible. But with years of experience watching that little reptile do his thing, I think it can be safely said that people want Dorothy to make it back to Kansas, if for no other reason than it makes the drive home from the theater a little more sweet.

There's a reason movies have happy endings.

# CHAPTER 16

# What Is Theater? And The Great Benny Goodman

**In Which** we take musical tours of "Benny World" and the Budapest Opera House, and we learn that "Theater is the suspension of space and time in which the audience experiences the eternal."

*Don Q,*                                                                          *Today*

   *Seen any Windmills lately? I spoke with Dulcinea a few days ago and am eager to get you two acquainted. Heard anything from Sancho, or is he still learning to Scuba dive? As for serious matters, I enjoyed the Happy Endings piece but I thought it needed more work. As long as you're on the road, why not bear down and give your loyal Tattered Edge readers a taste of your life?*

                                     *Onward, your fellow Knight Errant*

The card that accompanied this letter was a *Man of La Mancha* promotional photo showing Don Quixote, played by Peter O'Toole, and Sancho Panza, played by James Coco, together with Rosinante, Don Quixote's horse, and Sancho's nameless donkey.

One time, I asked Julian if he'd like to join me for a few weeks and he asked me if I had stopped taking my medication. When I told him I don't take any medication, he suggested I start. Julian's idea of travel is taking the elevator to the lobby, hailing a cab for Kennedy airport, and flying to Europe. Despite his thinking I'm nuts, I know he appreciates the stories.

Julian grew up when the world wasn't so open, and he's made a very interesting life for himself, but one thing I know Julian likes is stories. He's not going to smell diesel fumes to get them and maybe he likes them once they've been ironed out and put onto film, but he likes stories, and I'm happy to share mine with him.

This week I'm working with Osvaldo Latrobe, preparing the Booneville Woodsman's Ballroom for his Fourth Annual Benny Goodman Festival. My job is to screen *The Benny Goodman Story.*

The "Booney Wood," as the locals call the hall, was built by the W.P.A. and it exudes Depression-era grandeur. Tucked inland from the foggy pacific coast, it sits proudly atop a rock outcropping forming the vee between two roads, one that leads directly to the ocean, and the other into a fine stand of redwood trees. Originally built as a social gathering place for loggers, it had existed in a state of disrepair for some time before being purchased and renovated by the non-profit community group which manages it. The rent is reasonable, and the building is very successful because it has, grandfathered into its title, an alcohol permit. When you rent the Booney, you get the permit to use its bar. The rumor about the Booney Wood is that the right key can lead you to some very good whiskey.

As for the building, it is testimony to what can happen when you place extraordinary amounts of quality redwood in the hands of skilled craftsmen and hordes of other men eager to work, the same men who would a few years later be fed to the fate of even greater events. The Booney Wood, like many older community halls, has the timeless classical architecture of redwood paneled walls and plank ceilings attached to stout redwood beams. It has a fairly large stage with thick royal blue curtains and valence. It also has enough room to have a Steinway grand piano that is kept in fine condition thanks to the generous donation of "An Anonymous Patron"(or so it says on the small brass plaque attached above the Steinway name). On the hefty arching redwood beam twelve feet overhead and paralleling the stage hangs a well-outfitted lighting rail which is operated from an unusually well-crafted production booth cut out ten feet above the back of the hall into attic space that otherwise would be wasted. The booth allows us to project over the heads of an audience, and also to exchange some conversation without annoying anyone. The Booney Wood, save for a few modern conveniences, is a throwback to a different age when "it was a lot quieter," as Fred used to say.

January is not a big month for events at the Booney Wood, especially for midweek ones, so even though the Benny Goodman Festival is four days away, the setup has begun. All alone in the hall, I'm placing the film reels into their cans, when through the booth window I see Osvaldo walking in with another man. Both are carrying small instrument cases. They walk over to the piano, set the cases on its bench, and as their chatter stops they open the cases and assemble two clarinets, placing the mouthpieces in their mouths to soften the reeds. A moment later some duck-like squawking yields to a flurry of sounds, filling the wood-beamed hall, and then Osvaldo's friend gestures with his instrument, counting down to an exuberant explosion of music.

I stand motionless and hypnotized in my elevated perch, listening until the two joyful musicians complete the piece. Only when I come down the stairs to the main hall do they realize I've been watching all the time.

"That's 'Buckle Down,'" says Osvaldo. "Do you like it?"

"Like it? You guys sound sweet," I say, as if Eric were speaking for me, and then Osvaldo sets his clarinet down and introduces me to Charlie Clarke, who I learn is the leader of the "Swinging Tuxedos." Osvaldo explains his presence. "Charlie is the head of the National Society for the Preservation of the Music of Benny Goodman and his band will be featured during the movie."

"You mean before the movie?" I ask, confused.

"No, during the movie," says Osvaldo. "The best thing about that film is the music so we thought whenever they play a piece in the film, we'd have you turn the sound down and the Swinging Tuxedoes or some of the other musicians can play the pieces live. They all have the score for the film."

Before I have a chance to say that I think it's a great idea, Osvaldo chuckles, declaring, "It's like I say all the time: never let good sense get in the way of a bad decision."

A few years ago we were hired to show movies for the First Annual Boonevlle Benny Goodman Festival. Rumor had it that Benny Goodman once played his clarinet in Booneville while on his now-famous 1935 tour of the West Coast. So every year on the weekend closest to January 16th, the date in 1938 when Benny Goodman played his world-changing concert at Carnegie Hall, Osvaldo Latrobe holds his festival.

Last year's Third Annual Benny Goodman Festival drew thirty-seven participants for the Benny Picnic and Swing Band Barbecue. The turnout was a little disappointing, prompting Osvaldo to think all year of ways to increase attendance. In the end (but probably not while filling prescriptions to control delusional thinking), Osvaldo arrived at this conclusion: movies are popular, and even if people don't know the music of Benny Goodman they might nevertheless enjoy taking in a picture. It's this kind of thinking that keeps fuel in Zhitomir's tank, but even I understood that it was unlikely that Steve Allen's sincerity and Donna Reed's good looks would drive the economic engine of the Benny Goodman Festival.

It's hard to believe how many festivals there are in this country. *The Ginetti Guide to Fairs and Festivals in North America* claims there are almost 1,200,000 fairs and festivals in the United States and Canada. You can do your own math; but that's a lot of get-togethers, and they can't all be successful. There are festivals for foods, motorcycles, relatives of Mark Twain and Thomas Jefferson, lovers of the crawdad, or survivors of one or another great battle; festivals for illnesses, plants, religion, astronomical and geothermal events, chess; festivals to celebrate fish, birds, dinosaurs, quilting, music, model trains, canoes, war gatherings, peace assemblies, women, men . . . I'd like to include them all, but there isn't enough ink. It comes down to this, there's a festival for any two people who share anything in common.

In the world of festivals, the Benny Goodman Festival is as good a reason to get together as any other, and to the local committee's way of thinking, if it gets blended with a Goodman Family Reunion and the North American Festival of People Named Benny, it might draw a crowd and give a boost to the local economy. If it doesn't, at least it adds some excitement to the small town.

Osvaldo finances most of the festival out of his own pocket. He's a full-time pharmacist and part-time clarinet player who knows the life of Benny Goodman better than the side effects to most medications. Thanks to the card from Julian, I've got Don Quixote on the brain, and Osvaldo reminds me of Don Quixote as he supports his festival by "seeing in his imagination what did not exist . . ." Tayla Quimby, whose ailments and pharmaceutical needs underwrite much of Osvaldo's life, says holding a Benny Goodman Festival in Booneville has as much a chance of success as holding a sunbathing contest at the North Pole. "God love him," says Tayla, "if even one person has a good time, he'll do it again."

Osvaldo believes that hearing Benny, whom he refers to as "The Great

One," can instantly shift a person's destiny. Osvaldo maintains that music heals, art is pure, people have open minds, and that in living and learning the lessons of life, change is possible and people strive to be noble. It's hard not to love this guy or to embrace his philosophy.

Each morning over the next few days we run the film to a growing number of clarinetists who've come rolling into Booneville to practice the pieces. Apparently, Charlie Clarke and the National Society for the Preservation of the Music of Benny Goodman have a long and influential reach. It's a little weird, twenty-five clarinets playing in unison, but by the third morning rehearsal they sound pretty good. Most of them, especially Charlie Clarke, are as delightfully nutty as Osvaldo and they have an endless swell of stories and obscure musical references about their idol. Their conversations usually start with something like this: "How about Jack Teagarden and Billie Holiday?" "No, Winsocki, 1941 in Chicago."

"No way, Body and Soul, 1942 in the Palladium with Duke Ellington."

But they always end with someone lifting their instrument and playing.

Each night at bedtime when I climb into Zhitomir, which is conveniently parked to the side of the Booneville Woodsman's Ballroom, I lie down to the enthusiastic sounds of musicians who don't ever seem to grow tired. There are clarinetists aimlessly wandering the streets of Booneville and I'm left wondering how so many of them are able to escape their lives and travel to Booneville in the middle of January.

At last it's the evening of the show. It's obvious that this year's Benny Bash will set records for attendance. There are at least seventy-one people in the room, which is a fine turnout considering it includes me, two lighting technicians, and a bartender named Sprinkle, who works the "Benny Bar" mixing drinks which remind me of the menu at the Fritz Lang, only named after famous tunes by the Great One like:

"One O'Clock Jump": Bourbon and water.

"Let's Dance": Gin and tonic.

"Make Believe": Whiskey sour with no whiskey.

"Swing Swing Swing": Spanish coffee.

"The Scotch": Straight single shot, no rocks.

"Jersey Bounce": Vodka with a whisper of habañero sauce.

"Zagging With The Zig": Tequila with lime and bitters.

"Softly As a Morning Sunrise Charlie": Coffee with cream and sugar.

The Swinging Tuxedoes are setup on the floor in front of the stage and they begin playing while the rest of the Goodman devotees are milling around, talking, drinking, or fussing with their instruments, awaiting things to come in the dimmed lighting of the Booney Wood's splendor. About ten minutes before film time, the Swinging Tuxedoes stop playing. A local television crew sweeps into the hall and quickly begins videotaping interviews with participants. After the television crew leaves, Osvaldo comes to the stage and thanks "anyone who appreciates that obsession with great things is good for the soul."

Then Osvaldo introduces Charlie, who comes onto the stage and takes the microphone in his hands as Osvaldo walks off. Even though he's clad in a well-worn tuxedo, his tie is cocked to one side, giving him the appearance of a homeless man who scored big behind a dry cleaning shop. He looks the way you would expect a man who hasn't slept in three days to look, but as he speaks you notice his clarinet tucked under his arm, and the love that comes out of his mouth is enchanting. He has a gentle, melodic voice, and even the few kids who were forced by their teachers (and/or parents) to come to the show are now rapt with Charlie's words.

"My name is Charlie Clarke. I was born in 1938 on the day the one and only Benny Goodman played his monumental concert at Carnegie Hall. Tonight I'd like to tell you a story about my twin, not my twin brother, but a man I met a few years ago when I was traveling in Europe, and whose life and story will hold special significance for many of you here tonight.

"Some years ago, I was touring Europe with a small group of jazz musician friends, stopping here and there, setting up to play when we could. Sometimes we'd trade for drinks, a few times we actually got a paid gig, but mainly we got conversation and local color out of it all. Best time of my life," says Charlie.

"One day we're in Prague, and the place is kind of blowing our minds. I mean it's like you took everything inside of a museum and put it outside. That's how beautiful the place is. There's a castle, a real castle, and bridges across the river, and festive squares, and the place boils with life. The main bridge is the Charles -- 'Karlov Most' is how they say it in Czech and it's a wide, stone-arched, pedestrian bridge built six hundred years ago. That bridge attracts more life than you can imagine. It's filled with artists, musicians, photographers, jewelers, magicians, puppeteers, dog walkers, tourists, and whatever! So, we're strolling across the bridge our first night there checking out the sights, when we hear music coming from ahead. I mean music, well played and kicking, jazz! There's this sextet on the bridge with a big crowd around them and they are blowing."

"Blowing their noses, Charlie?" someone shouts.

"No, blowing some great music. And naturally, we stay and listen, and after a few minutes we take out our instruments and join in. At first they're annoyed, until they realize we can play, and of course we stayed off to the side so as not to cut into their scene. That's what it was; we played for an hour or more before we ever said a word, exchanged names, or anything. Pretty magical stuff, what took place beneath the glowing castle of Prague.

"As we finish, another group is waiting for the space, and the leader of the band, the clarinet player, Thomas, tells us in perfect English that Karlov Most is where half the musicians in Prague earn their living. 'We've got a little agreement about the space and not getting into each other's audiences,' he says.

"A few minutes later we're across the bridge drinking full liters of Pilsner in a sweet place called the Three Storks, and Thomas tells us his story..."

I was born the day the great Benny Goodman made his first concert in Prague. My mother and father were students in the music academy, and they both swear that somehow my mother suspended the labor of which I was the product for three hours, long enough so they could attend the concert. Back then, they didn't put the time of birth on the certificates, but it is no coincidence that my birth announcement has a ticket stub included in it. I keep it in my clarinet case.

From the time I was old enough to walk I had a clarinet in my hands. My father says the only argument he ever had with my mother was when she claimed that his giving me a mouthpiece to chew on caused me to stop drinking at her bosom. She says it took her a week of hot baths and compresses to ease her unplanned suffering. He jokes that it was a very exciting time to be a man. I guess it's fair to say I was never going to be anything but a clarinet player. Benny Goodman was a god in our family. Our Holy Family was an odd mix: The Pope, Dubcek, Dizzy Gillespie, Duke Ellington, and Mr. Benny Goodman. Even my reluctant grandparents had little to say against Mr. Benny Goodman because they knew he was an accomplished player. I don't think they made the stretch all the way from Mozart to Bee Bop, but they did enjoy Swing.

When the tanks rolled in on August 21, 1968 everything changed. I left with some of my friends. We were on a circuit, playing clubs in Berlin, and we quickly decided to go on to New York. It was a rich time and we took our music very seriously. Everything was serious then; poetry, folk music, and movies: why would jazz have been different? It was a profound period of history, but Swing doesn't thrive in somber moods and many of us became too intellectual in our playing. You're old enough to remember, we called our music experimental. If you blended a sonorous tone in a sustained minor key crescendo it was experimental. It's funny now, and also makes you want to cry.

I came home when Vaclav Havel spoke in 1989. Twenty-one years away from home. All Czechs missed being home. We put this group together to celebrate the Velvet Revolution, and we're still together. There's a core that shows up every day in the spring and summer, but we can't all make it every day. Playing Karlov Most is a fine gig. People are wonderful, everyone is happy; the tourists are all looking for a good time, and who better to welcome them? The pay isn't bad either. A tourist told me once that he felt bad that I had to play on the street, after so many years of hard work to become a musician. I told him to turn and look at the river. I love the swans, I love the sounds, I love the people, and I get paid fine. Like Strauss had his river, I have mine. Each day the river is a little different, but each day the music sings to an audience who loves it. Our banjo player, he's about your age, raised on that droning stuff they call Euro-pop. Listen to him now, he's like a cabaret player in a Brecht/Weill play. And Stephen, the singer, he's one part Satchmo, one part Harpo Marx; he's the best. When he's here, we draw the biggest crowds and sell a lot of CDs. This is what I was born to do, and this is where I'm happiest doing it. What more can I ask for?'

Finishing this story, Charlie Clarke calls for someone to hand him a glass of wine. He holds the glass aloft and speaks clearly into the microphone. "I raise my glass to the Great Benny Goodman and to all of you who have ever wished only to be a clarinet player. Three cheers for all of you!" All seventy-one people present raise their glasses, while Charlie returns to his place in his band and counts down a kick-off to "Sing Sing Sing."

Fifteen minutes later, a clatter goes up before we start the film as the musicians reach beneath their seats and set their music stands in place, each one holding a full score to the songs of Benny Goodman that are in the film. I've shown a lot of movies in my life, but this is a first. The anxious musicians in the audience all have their clarinets ready and their reeds soaked right. When Benny gets his first gig (aboard the river boat with the Murph Podolski Band), the musicians begin playing "By the Sea" with him. Ten minutes later, as the irrepressible talent of the Great One surges forward, Osvaldo plays along with the film version of "Waiting for Katie." If the film doesn't match the greatness of its subject, the colorful gowns of a vivacious Donna Reed, playing Benny's future wife, Alice, do. Every time Alice appears in a scene the crowd shouts out: "Blue Dress! Green Dress!" Even I join the shouting for the best of them all, the "Pink Dress!" Sixty-five minutes into *The Benny Goodman Story* a raucous roomful of clarinetists are playing "One O'Clock Jump" together, while scads of on-film dancers draw closer to the stage and musicians, to bear witness that The Benny Goodman Orchestra is about to take their rightful place atop the world of American music.

After setting the third reel in place, I run quickly to the bar and order a drink. Normally my work is done when the third reel is running, but not tonight. Song after song, I lower the volume in the Fisherman's Hall to allow the joyful attendees of the Benny Goodman Festival the chance to synchronize their playing with that of their idol as we get to rain down the finale of the annual Benny Goodman Festival, the dream child of a man who otherwise spends his days filling vials and bottles with caplets, pills, tinctures, and salves. Osvaldo's clarinet is the happiest of them all with the light from the projection reflecting in circles and whirls to the beat as he plays music with his idol. Swept up in the moment I only wish I could play the clarinet. Oh, yeah! Amen, daddy-o!

The day after any show is slow and even a little sad, but last night was an explosion that erased any opportunity for sadness. I didn't get to bed until three in the morning, infused as I was with the adrenaline of the Benny Bacchanal. I slept until noon, and I would have slept longer, but I heard an annoying drip outside of Zhitomir coming from the light rain falling today, breaking what was a somber quietness. I merged the drip into a pleasing drift between sleep and wakefulness for hours, not wanting to leave my down cocoon and the smell of the cherry wood mixed ever so lightly with a pleasing hint of diesel. I felt safe, warm, and content to close my eyes and dream of a melodic ocean of clarinets.

When at last I got out of bed, I took some time and put Zhitomir in order. I folded clothes, stacked books, and tidied up. While I was securing film cans on their shelves, I noticed one of my most prized possessions, a Hungarian documentary entitled *What Is Theater?* Inspired by Charlie's story about Prague last night, I pulled it out.

I don't know about you, but I get Prague and Budapest mixed up. No matter, it's a charming little film done in honor of Ferenc Lukacs, the former director of the Budapest Opera House. When Lukacs died in 1999, there was a massive outpouring of mourning for this tyrant of a man who had guided the opera for close to four decades. The film is a partly dramatized memoir (narrated by the deceased director's son, Pa'l,) showing what it was like to apply for a job at the Opera House years ago, while also taking us on a tour of the famous building. The version I have is subtitled. I set it on my bed thinking it might be fun to watch it later.

I have to head inside the hall to clean up the projection equipment. There's a crew of volunteers coming tomorrow to put the hall back together. That's good; I can work without any distractions. Setups and breakdowns go better with fewer distractions. By the time I get to the Booney Wood, it's almost sundown and the room is empty except for the scattered remains of the festival. It feels like the still warm ashes of a glorious bonfire. It doesn't take me long to wrap cords and pull tape. All that remains is the screen and a single projector when I hear the door open and in walk Osvaldo and Charlie. If I'm sapped, I can't imagine what they must feel like, and I don't have to:  their eyes are weary although there is a luminescent aura hanging over their heads as they stare at the empty music stands filling the hall.

Charlie says, "Hey, Jake, glad you're here. What a night that was. Thanks again."

"My pleasure, Charlie. There's nothing like the sound of happy clarinets."

"Best Benny Festival so far," says Osvaldo. "Next year will even be better."

"Can we do anything to help you?" asks Charlie.

"Sure, how about taking these cords out to my truck and setting them inside by the large gear box."

Charlie takes the bundle of cords and leaves for Zhitomir, but when he returns he's got a huge smile on his face and he's holding the Ferenc Lukacs film.

"I can't believe you have this. I swear, there can't be twenty people in the world outside of Hungary who even know about this guy."

"Yes, that's true, but one of the twenty is my Uncle Julian. How do you know about him?"

"I met him when I played with the Wisconsin State Teen Symphony in Budapest. The guy was a crimson prince. He greeted each and every one of us like we were the London Philharmonic and told us how proud he was to host us at the Budapest Opera House. Can you imagine how that made a group of cheese head kids from Racine, Wisconsin, feel?

Charlie picks up the can and opens it carefully, handling the reels as if he's had some experience doing so before. On the inside of the lid is a taped sleeve and Charlie takes out the note inside. It's from Julian, the note he included when he sent the film to me.

Charlie reads the note out loud. "As long as you're showing movies, you may as well create theater. Life is in the magic. Onward, Julian."

"Smart man, your uncle" says Osvaldo, and then he says, "How about you set that film up on this projector, and Charlie, you set us up a few of the comfortable chairs from the back of the room?"

"What are you going to do?" says Charlie to Osvaldo.

"I've got my own little setup to attend to."

Five minutes later, while I'm putting the film on the projector, Osvaldo is pouring aged Lagavulin Scotch from a bottle he took from a locked cabinet beneath the famous Booney Wood Bar. He also sets out a small plate of smoked oysters, crackers, and slices of aged Gouda cheese. The smoky vapors of the whiskey, oysters, and cheese fill my nostrils and the entire Booney Wood Hall seems to breathe its approval.

"So, it's true?"

"What's true?" says Osvaldo.

"About things hidden away in this place."

"Oh, yeah, you better believe it's true. There are special things hidden away in a lot of places if know where to look for them. Now, raise your glass, hit the switch and let's go to Budapest."

**The film begins with an establishing daytime shot of the outside of the Budapest Opera House. The building is gray, solid stone, heavy and a little oppressive. The film then cuts inside to a full shot of a well-dressed young man, sitting nervously in a stout wooden chair outside a large oak door. The young man fumbles in his pocket and draws out**

an envelope. We see his shaking hands unfolding a letter, as the voiced-over narration begins.

Narrator:  Can you imagine? You're eighteen years old and want to be an usher at the Budapest Opera House. Maybe you're a young musician and an acquaintance has encouraged you to apply. Perhaps you can't pay your rent and you need the job, so you apply at the Opera House. It's the perfect job. You can go to school during the day, practice, and then work at night in the world of the composers and performers you admire. You go to the office of the Opera one day and find that there's no application. No, instead, they ask you for your letter of referral. Yes, you must have a letter written in support of your application detailing who you are and why you should be considered for work at the Opera House.

 **Next we see the Opera house auditorium from the perspective of the first balcony center aisle.**

Narrator:  In a few days, if you are chosen, you are called in for an interview. Before meeting my Papa, the head usher takes you on an orientation tour of the theater and gives you a dossier detailing the history and particulars of the building, beginning with its construction.

**Now we see the hall and its deep burgundy chairs and lavish stage curtain, the ornate painted ceiling and crystal chandeliers, before cutting backstage to the fly system with its elaborate ropes and pulleys. A series of cuts shows the dressing rooms, property warehouses, coat checkroom, champagne vault, and ticket office.**

Narrator:  Nothing is left out:  dates of construction, costs, materials, dimensions, technical details such as the distances from stage to seats, even a detailed list of the seats in the balcony which have obscured views. Then, the most important information of all:  a detailed history of all the productions and players who have graced the stage at the Opera House.

**Now we see a wall of framed portrait photos and brass plaques with the names of the performers in the photos.**

Narrator:  After the orientation, you were brought to my Papa's office. Of course, you already had the job or you would not be getting all the attention, but you didn't know that.

**We return to the same door as in the earlier scene. The Director's office door opens. In the office are a sofa and set of plush chairs beside a table with a cut glass carafe and set of glasses.**

Narrator:  You would take your seat and my Papa would offer you a drink. Then he would ask you a simple question: "What is theater?" which you think of as a conversation starter, so you would answer casually: "Theater is performance, entertainment, a group of people out for an evening," confident that is the answer Papa wanted. But it wasn't, and in a professorial voice both romantic and imposing, my Papa gave you your first lesson in how to work at the Budapest Opera House.

**Here the film inserts text like the narration of the old silent movies**.

Narrator: Theater is a suspension of space and time in which the audience experiences the eternal . . .

**Next we see the *Staff Requirements and Procedures* notebook. Close-ups of pages titled "Hallway Lighting," Portrait Gallery," "Serving Alcohol," "Carpets," "Seat Cleaning," "Drapery," interspersed with brief cuts of staff dressing, greeting patrons, serving drinks, guiding people to their seats, checking coats, pouring champagne, holding umbrellas over the heads of visitors who arrive in cars on rainy nights.**

Narrator: When you work here, you learn how to transform an empty space into a theater, mold the special geometry of the room, its temperature, its color, and its taste to elevate an audience into a dream state. A big room with a stage is not a theater. An auditorium is a skeleton, but the muscle and the nerves are composed of the details of everything else: the lights, the sound, the seats, the curtains, the program, the soap in the bathrooms, the quality of the champagne, and the glasses into which it is poured during intermission, the polished brass of the handrails on the steps, well-vacuumed carpets, hot coffee and tea, ushers who are well-dressed and courteous, a ticket booth that is efficient and always offers you the best seat no matter what the price. Without a doubt -- it's unachievable perfection, but what is always available is the goal of achieving it. Because when you do, you allow the last part of the theater to come to life, and that is the blood, which is the work of the artists responsible for creating and delivering the performance to the audience. If any of it is missing, no matter how strong the talent, the show will fail. Sadly, the audience may not even understand the failure, but we do. When you work here at the Budapest Opera House, you must never allow that to happen. Here we always do our best.

**Next we see staff arriving in a snowstorm at the rear entrance of the Opera House, where they file in energetically and are greeted by a doorman who gently welcomes them by name.**

Narrator: Over the next fifteen minutes, Papa will inform you that the suspension of space and time does not apply to the staff. That you show up on time or you lose your job; that you wear the uniform pressed and fitted neatly to your body or you lose your job; that you address patrons clearly and assist them in any way they need, or you lose your job. All staff at the Opera House have the joint responsibility to become an invisible guiding hand which surrounds all patrons with elegance and serenity . . . or you lose your job.

**Now we see a wall of vintage theater posters with subtitles inform-ing us of the names of the operas. Boris Goudunov, Aida, Tosca, The Magic Flute.**

Narrator:  You see, we could do all of this in the old days. Oh my, people got fired for having a dangling shirt tail, or being rude to a patron, or talking amongst each other and keeping a guest waiting. Papa hired every employee himself:  ushers, coat attendants, bartenders, stagehands; and each one of them endured his office ritual. While Papa sat and chat-ted with them, he looked at their dress, listened to their speech, before giving his lecture. Anyone who remained in the Budapest Opera for any length of time came to admire the speech like the lecture of a great physi-cist or philosopher.

**Next we see a brief segment of newsreel footage of Lukacs beside Imŕe Nagy, the former President of Hungary, greeting an elderly patron in formal attire who is stepping from a horse-drawn carriage at the side entrance of the building. This is followed by another round of portraits of composers who've performed, or had their works performed, at the theater."**

Narrator:  Papa always said, "A composer studied and worked for years to achieve his or her genius. The musicians, singers, dancers, set designers, and costumers all honed their craft to deliver genius, and so too shall any-one who works in this crimson and golden hall. Whether selling a ticket or checking a coat:  You are part of The Theater.

The first few months you work as an usher you hate it. The veterans cor-rect you at the weekly staff meeting, which is short, and to the point about your shortcomings. If it weren't for the small paycheck you need so badly, you'd quit. But then, if your skin is thick, a few months pass and . . .

**Patrons leaving the show. Cut back into the hall where final clean-up is taking place. Eight staff, two crews like mirror images on either side of the central aisle, sweep the floors and whisk chairs to even**

**the nap of the fabric before lifting up the seats in the dimmed amber light of the now empty hall.**

Narrator:  One evening after a Saturday night show, after the musicians have gone and you're cleaning the aisles and putting up the chairs, Papa walks in unexpectedly and strides down the aisle. You think:  "What now? What have I done wrong this time?" But Papa comes to you and puts his arm over your shoulder, and though you haven't spoken to him since that first day, he addresses you by your name and tells you, "You did a good job tonight. That was a great show." And he helps put up the chairs, brushing the fabric with a brass-handled whisk he carries in his pocket, exactly as he did for the ten years that he was an aspiring musician working the same job. All the while he's talking about the show and describing the patrons -- how they walked in and who coughed when and who stood up in the middle of an act. As he speaks, you realize that you too noticed those same things during the show. While you stood to the side in the dark and the finest music in the world was played, you were unconsciously watching the audience. All those dreams that brought you to the opera in the first place are now rekindled. And the next day, when you come to work, you don't think about Papa or the endless annoying details, but only of guiding the patrons into that suspension of space and time in which the audience experiences the eternal. A few months pass, and suddenly it's your turn to break in the new usher.

As I said, you can no longer do that today. No, that great time in history has passed. I think if Papa were alive today he would lament the fact that management has replaced vision. There are no more impresarios today, managers and promoters and distributors. It isn't the same. My Papa lived in an era that for all of its flaws, still allowed an individual to create greatness.

**The final shot follows a lone usher walking up the center aisle to the hall's lighted exit where she departs. The doors close in perfect slow symmetry behind her. Then the lights of the auditorium dissolve into the signature of Ferenc Lukacs.**

The next day, on the way out of Booneville, I drop an autographed photo of Benny Goodman in the mail for Julian. He will cherish it. In the envelope is also a postcard of Winnie the Pooh with his head stuck in a honey jar.

*Dear Julian,*

> *I know you'll like this photo. You never know who*
> *You find on the trail to the North Pole.*

> *Yours in Honey, Winnie*

> *PS. Have you ever tried Lagavulin Scotch?*

CHAPTER 17

# The Sub-Committee On Community Morals: Four Rivers

**In Which** we meet the editor of The Four Rivers Conscience, and we witness the rise and fall of a small town controversy, played to a flamenco soundtrack.

After I left Booneville, it took a while for things to get going again. One month seemed to melt into another and though I did a lot of traveling, I also did a lot of sitting. Without Eric around to keep things from getting a little dull, things got a little dull. Well, dull maybe is too harsh, but every day can't be an epiphany, and maybe that's what winters are good for. Even nomads need a little down time, and I like down time. I like to read, do the crossword puzzle, drink coffee, and sleep while listening to the wind or the rain talk to Zhitomir. If I'd been born a hundred years earlier I would have made a great cowboy. Not the bang'em up shoot'em up type; I think you know by now that's not me, but I could have been the kind who sits by the fire, all alone on the range with his horse, with a tin cup filled with scalding hot coffee and playing "Down In The Valley" on his harmonica to the owls. Okay, I admit it: I've watched too many movies!

Even with the harmonica, the loyal horse, and the tin cup, eventually every cowboy needs someone to talk to. Enter Wesley Raymond Jackson, friend and editor of a weekly Idaho newspaper *The Four Rivers Conscience*.

Ten years ago the Smithsonian Museum funded a history project entitled "The Fabric of America: Elders Weave the Landscape." The project's goals were to identify and create video portraits of living people making significant cultural contributions to America. (Self-nomination was not permitted.) From some three thousand submissions, the Smithsonian selected one from each of the fifty United States and then dispatched a team to research and film a video portrait of each person for an exhibition at the museum, held in 1995.

Wes Jackson was one of the fifty who made the cut, and it was Wes Jackson who found me when I stopped here for the night on my way to nowhere in the first year I left Larch. Being a newspaperman, he smelled a story, and what started as a small feature about the Lost Sons of Zhitomir Rolling Film Society has developed into an easy friendship.

I arrived in Four Corners yesterday, Wednesday evening, and Wes told me there's a big stink going on in the town. Four Corners has an annual Cultural Celebration and they like to show a movie each year that celebrates the cultural heritage of its different people. The big stink has to do with this year's film, *Carmen*, Carlos Saura's 1984 flamenco interpretation of the Merimée story and famous opera.

Wes always gives you some history before getting to the point, so he told me, how over the years they've shown *Seven Samurai, Sounder, The Black Robe, Cimarron*, and the less thematic *Singin' In The Rain* that was also shown to get away from the obligation of having a purpose. "The first few years it was simple. We had Grant Daley, a rancher who lives up in the hills a ways who was a wrangler on two films they made here in the fifties. Those Hollywood folks used to love to come here to get away from the studio. Grant was a guy who needed some money, so he took care of the horses for all the pictures made around these parts. Grant's a big tall drink of water and the next thing you know he's standing in for Gary Cooper even if he does have a distinctive triangular face and doesn't look a thing like Cooper. As Grant says, 'You can cover a lot of flaws with a cowboy hat.'

"So, we showed the Cooper films and Grant's family all turned out, everyone was happy, and the festival was a success. Then we had Liona Gingold and all the films she worked on, and her family turned out and everyone was happy and the festival was a success. Well, then what? Now we're out of local tie-ins, so we started looking deeper into the history of all the people from around here. Big surprise -- it isn't all about European Caucasians and Indians. Come to find out that this region has been holding people from all over the world for a long time:  Indians for sure, then whites, Basques and their sheep, Japanese who settled here after the internment, black cowboys.

"One year when we featured Japanese food, a bunch of the former internees told stories, and their grandchildren did an exhibition of their parents' and grandparents' history here. That mightily upset most of that whole ranch crowd who would rather not talk about their own history or what happened to Japanese Americans in that time. You see, it comes down to this: some of them hired out the internees and believe you me, they didn't pay them anywhere near close to what they were worth. It's one thing to say you built something with your own two hands, but it's another thing completely when those hands were basically forced labor. That's a history people don't know what to do with, and they'd as soon leave it untold."

The next morning, I joined Wesley and his weekly Thursday gathering of friends for breakfast in the Pronghorn Restaurant, a refurbished hunting lodge of the same name. In a word, the motif of the Pronghorn is taxidermy. The restaurant boasts trophy mounts of more animals than most zoologists can identify. It's strangely cozy once you get used to all the glass-eyed critters staring down at you as you eat. Above the counter on the wall of the Pronghorn are two flanking antelope heads with splendid racks. Between the two heads are two original photographs; the first is a local historical image of Teddy Roosevelt holding up the head of two trophy antelopes. The other photo is an incongruous image of Dean Martin, Raquel Welch, and Jimmy Stewart, all on horseback receiving instructions from director Andrew V. McLaglen.

The waitress/owner of this photo, and of the Pronghorn, is another vestige of the heyday of western films, the aforementioned Liona Gingold. The well-proportioned Liona was a stand-in for Ms. Welch in the movie *Bandolero* when it was filmed some thirty-four years earlier in her hometown of Brackettville, Texas. Liona retains both her ability to ride a horse and her looks, which made her a valuable stand-in for the voluptuous, but non-equine, Welch. Liona used all of her assets for four more westerns filmed in the areas around Four Rivers, earning her enough money to buy a place and settle down.

Like Raquel Welch, Liona's seductive form makes watching her set out place mats very pleasing. The mats are intriguing, portraying North American game animals in wilderness settings enhanced by some visible human presence: smoke from a campfire, a hunting cabin, a rifle set against a tree.

Scattered around the café the usual gathering of friends and regulars talk beneath hewn lodgepole timbers and the cool smoke essence of seventy-five years of fires in the massive stone hearth. If it weren't for the current controversy, talk would be about politics, hot summer droughts, the death of an old-timer, a car accident, or great moments when someone from the community makes a splash out in the world beyond the four surrounding rivers. The topic doesn't matter a bit. Small towns do their business face-to-face in casual conversations: at the post office, spaghetti feed, 4-H picnic, or local café.

At the table this morning is the six-foot, six-inch former basketball player, Chester Danko, drinker of pure hot water and still the only physician in the community, even though he had supposedly retired to write poetry and tinker with tractors manufactured in the year he was born. Joining him are Ray and Susan Howley, who grow sugar beets on the land her grandparents homesteaded in 1889 and to which Ray and Susan returned after taking early retirement from non-diplomatic State Department positions overseas. Unlike Chester, both Susan and Ray drink their coffee with cream and sugar, and they wear matching denim jackets over white T-shirts. In between them sits Brenda Garcia, the vibrant manager of the Four Rivers Electrical District, who drinks decaf with cream, saving the caffeine buzz she'll need later to deal with staff at the office. Rounding out the group is Wesley Jackson who, as a concession to the medical advice he receives free of charge from his friend across the table, reluctantly makes do with herb tea.

When Liona asks, "What'll it be?" Chester says, "What I want, or what you're willing to serve?"

"All I'm willing to serve you is on that there menu, so maybe you ought to get some toast and jam and consider yourself lucky."

Winking at Liona, Doc Chester continues, "I was hoping for something I could get my teeth into."

"With your teeth that's simple," says Liona as she scribbles and speaks, "One bowl of oatmeal."

Everyone busts out laughing at that, even Doc, who no doubt is unfazed. Susan and Ray stop laughing long enough to order eggs and toast. Wes orders an omelet, then says, "You better go easy on Liona here, Chester, don't forget she can shoot, ride, cook, and probably wrestle better than you, and one of these days she's going to kick your . . ."

"Thank you, Mr. Jackson, but I'll fight my own battles and one foul mouth per table is enough," says Liona before asking Doc, "A little more hot water for you?"

Chester is well prepared to answer.

"No, I'm in enough hot water already. I would like some French toast. You know toast from France?"

"Are you finished Moan Surr Danko?" says Liona in Texas-drawled French that catches the Doc off guard, adding, "That's the only French you're getting out of me."

"What a waste of a fine foreign tongue; that's not exactly what I had in mind," says Doc, recovering.

"Danko, one more comment out of you and I'll teach you how the French use a stethoscope."

And so it goes back and forth until Liona returns to the kitchen with the breakfast orders and conversation shifts to the editorial and letters that appeared in *The Four Rivers Conscience* yesterday, all of which were written by those at the table, and all of whom make up the FRCCFC: Four Rivers Cultural Celebration Film Committee. In a small town, people wear lots of hats.

Wes Jackson wrote this editorial.

---

### Protesters Denounce Lust and Debauchery

An uncertain chapter in the history of this proud county was written last night when a small group of belligerent people disrupted the planning meeting of the Four Rivers Cultural Celebration. The protesters are seeking to halt the scheduled presentation of the award-winning 1984 Spanish film, Carmen that transposes a novella by Prosper Mérimée novella to a modern setting in a Flamenco dance troupe that is certainly charged with erotic and sensual themes. The nine protesters held signs reading, "No porno," "Lust is the Devil's Tonic" and "What's Wrong with John Wayne?" Group spokesman, Miller Felk, a local poultry farmer, claims the film portrays "immoral and gratuitous acts of lust and debauchery." The film has been screened and selected by the Four Rivers Celebration as part of this year's program honoring Spanish cultural influences in the region.

Celebration planners were meeting when the noisy protesters stormed the room. Felk made his way to the front of the room and read a statement detailing the group's intention to prevent any screening of the chosen film, saying, "We will do what we must." When asked by planner Brenda Garcia whether he had seen the film, Felk replied that he had not, but that his wife, fellow protester, Tessie Felk, had it on good authority that the film was pornographic in content and an affront to all decent values held in common by the Four Rivers Community. Asked by Committee member Garcia why he was protesting now instead of during six months of public planning meetings in which he might have voiced an opinion, Felk said, "I didn't know the film was a porno until recently." Pressed to explain what he meant by "We will do what we must," Felk said, "You'll see!" as he and the rest of the protesters stormed out of the meeting.

*The Conscience* believes that those who participate in public life should not yield to those who do not, and that the film should go on as planned. Make your voices and opinions heard, Mr. Felk, but not after the fact, and not under a loosely veiled threat of some unspecified action.

In response to these events, Chester Danko wrote this letter.

*To the Editor,*

*I submit a brief poem in response to the protesters who seek to censor the screening of the film Carmen at this year's Four Rivers Cultural Celebration*

*Neighbors?*
*There are people right beside you sharing common air and space*
*who cordially pat you on the back with a smile upon their face.*
*They greet you with "Hey, neighbor," exclaim they wish you well*
*while hiding darker thoughts inside, condemning you to hell.*
*They trust you not and fear you, and think you are possessed*
*believing you don't read the Book that makes them feel so blessed.*
*They'll never speak the truth out loud or tell you to your face*
*for that is what the frightened do and for this we are disgraced.*
*They'll snipe and snip and cite the rules claiming all is well intended*
*their strategies all justified as long as "Right's" defended*
*They never meet you on the street and say, "I challenge your opinion"*
*rather secretly amass and plan to rule the small dominion.*

*So take your righteous claim to good, and that smirk upon your face,*
*and stick both where the sun don't shine and choke on your disgrace.*

> *Sincerely, Chester Danko, Medical Doctor and Veteran*
> *of the United States Army (6 years), aged 79.*

Ray and Susan Howley wrote this letter.

*To the Editor,*

*Kind residents of Four Rivers can rest well today knowing that nine of its citizens want to shield us all from the scourges of modern immorality. Yes, a crusading army of righteousness swept in from the Heavens to uphold and defend all that is decent and noble in Four Rivers. Faced with the prospect of sordid, foreign pornography winnowing its way into the consciences of local citizens, a brave band of warriors seek to prevent the Devil from flamenco-dancing his naked way into our lives. What possible way can we thank these warriors for defending us from this invasion of diabolical smut so we may thus rest calmly within the fortress of our eternal values?*

> *Sincerely, Ray and Susan Howley, Four Rivers.*

Brenda Garcia wrote this letter.

*To the Editor,*

*No one is forcing anyone to attend the film Carmen. It is available for previewing in the Four Rivers Cultural Celebration office, and those of you who find it offensive or ill suited for your children may simply choose not to attend.*

*I grew up to the rhythms and energy of Flamenco music. My mother was a dancer and she taught all of her children how to sing and dance to the music she so loved. Carmen is not a great movie, but the extraordinary dance, flamenco music, and the sexual and emotional tension it has are what makes life worth living. The first bullfight scene that gets played out by the cast of the dance troupe at the birthday party is very entertaining. Everyone who watches Carmen wants to be at that party.*

*Don't miss it!*

> *Sincerely, Brenda Garcia*

Their letters, and all the commotion caused by the film is what the friends discuss this morning at the Pronghorn.

Chester Danko starts.

"Lord in heaven, what will they come up with next? They're a bunch of unthinking fundamentalists. One time it's nudity, the next time insurance liability, or the septic system is too small, you used too much sugar at the community hall, it's not suitable for children, blah, blah, blah. It's always about something, but you know what? It's about them. They're a mean spirited bunch of narrow-minds who can't handle change. They dislike everything they don't understand or can't control."

Wesley is next.

"I went to high school with Miller Felk and I knew Tessie Felk when she was Tessie Bricklehunt. I even took her to a school dance once and tried to kiss her -- she gave me a slap I'll never forget. If you think she's stern now, you should've known her then, but I'll be damned if we're going to let her and her friends destroy something most of the people in this town want."

"What the hell are they so darn agitated about? It's a movie," says Ray.

Wes answers, "A week ago, Tessie calls to tell me there is going to be a special meeting of the SCCM: Sub-Committee for Community Morals to 'discuss' the content of the film chosen for the celebration. I asked her if I could sit in on this 'special meeting,' but you know what she told me? She says it was 'closed to the press.' I asked her why she was even bothering to call to let me know, and she blasted back, 'Cause you're the one who writes that paper and maybe you'll think about writing something decent for a change!' After she hung up I was a little confused. I understood a group of citizens getting together, but what was this 'sub-committee' thing? If there's a sub-committee there's got to be a full blown committee somewhere. Oh well, no big deal, I thought, it must be the same old yahoos blowing off steam about the upcoming program. They do have a right to their opinions. I thought Tessie would provoke old Miller to beat on his chest like he always does and that would be the end of it. Honestly, I'm surprised by their stamina."

Ray responds, "As far as I'm concerned, they can kiss my petooty."

That draws a good laugh and then Brenda, who has been pretty quiet, speaks. "My grandmother, you know, she used to have a lot of chickens, and she told me over and over again that life comes down to chickens."

"This should be good," says Susan, and Brenda continues.

"My grandmother always said, 'When everyone knows their place, it's all calm, and everyone's content. The funny thing is if you look at the flock, you have some tough-feathered old daddy who thinks he runs the show. He's got great tail feathers so he gets all the hens, but he's also got responsibilities. He has to watch over everybody, protect the flock, and he's got to be ready to meet any surprise attacks that come from the flank.'

"I remember her saying it like it was yesterday," says Brenda. "Some kind of attack always comes from the flank, whether it's a dog, or a coyote, a hawk or a weasel occasionally, when you come out in the morning to see your birds, guess who's nowhere to be seen? That's right: Big Daddy's done his job and is sitting in the stomach of some much-contented predator. All the hens wake up confused -- where do we go, what do we do, is it safe -- until the next Big Daddy steps forward. Hens will stay around for years, but in the same time one Big Daddy after another will come and go."

Brenda concludes her grandmother's allegory with, "If you ask me, I think Felk is another Big Daddy fluffing his feathers for the flock. Don't pay them any mind. They'll be gone soon."

For a moment the table grows quiet as if everyone is imagining Miller Felk in feathers. Chester finally breaks the spell, and he's quite thoughtful now.

"You all know I started my practice over in Pinkston. Well, for years they had a 'Cross' in the town square and for years there was a crowd of people clamoring to tear it down, saying it violated the Constitution. Who knows, maybe it did, but I loved it. Because every year before Christmas this thing would get all heated up. There'd be letters and talk on the radio and all kinds of debate about it, and if you only half-listened to both sides there was a kind of current in the air. That, my friends, was the sound of passionate opinion."

Wes interrupts.

"Is it still there?"

"Which one, the cross or passionate public opinion?"

"The cross."

"Heck, no, they finally moved that old cross to some church yard and there she sits. But when they removed the cross they also cut out something of the town's life and spirit. I missed that when it went away."

"So, what are you saying, Doc? I'm confused" says, Ray.

"Stay with me for a moment or two. What I'm saying, the truly sad thing about it all is the people who used to thrash it out with such enthusiasm don't have anywhere to vent their passion anymore, and if you all remember your history, you'll know that always leads to trouble. Try to suppress true passion and what you end up with is some ill-begotten form of it. About the only things I personally take as truth are the things I can verify. For example, I know when I jump up in the air that I always come down because in all my born days I have never seen one single thing fall up. Therefore I trust the law of gravity. What's more I have never failed to see the sun come up on any one of those days; I've even noticed that it gets colder in the winter and warmer in the summer, which gives me a lot of respect for astronomers. But the big bang? The speed of light? Why dinosaurs disappeared, whether plants are as smart as animals, and any number of reasons about why the world is or is not in danger: those kinds of things are beyond my grasp . . ."

"Danko, what's beyond my grasp is how you can talk so long without taking a breath," says Ray, and Wes adds to his slightly older counterpart, "Or at his age, at least a piss."

"Show the movie or not, Doc?" asks Susan.

"Come on guys: you all know what I'm going to say. As far as the Felk mob is concerned, if they can't handle seeing private parts I don't give a steaming cow pie about them. The worst thing you can ever do with a bully is to let him have his own way. But we may be able to outmaneuver them. The only official complaint they've made is that the showing is scheduled for a public building. They've got whiff enough of some claim there to make a big fuss. But I've got another idea," says Chester, as Liona, who has been listening in at the counter returns to the table to refresh the cups.

"What's that, Danko, add a second film like *How Green Was My Valley?*

"Not exactly what I had in mind."

Chester Danko's idea spoke directly to another history lesson. Chester suggested reviving a part of the town's past. Four Rivers once had twelve hundred people and two movie theaters -- The Forum with three hundred seats, and the Flood Waters Drive-In. Fortunately the Forum still operates, but the Flood Waters sits like many fading ruins invisible except for its screen, which stands like the unfurled sail of an abandoned sailboat heading aimlessly towards the rocks of some barren shore.

"Let's show the movie at the Flood Waters."

All eyes at the table sparkle. One hour later, after a telephone call to the Flood Waters' current owner, Garby Clifton, whose three grown children were all delivered by Chester Danko at no cost, the floodgates open, so to speak.

In its current existence, the site that was the parking area for the Flood Waters Drive-in, is being used as a log deck for the ever-smaller pine trees going to the mill. The screen is made of perforated metal panels that are shedding rust flakes like an elderly actress wearing too much face powder. A lot of drive-in screens were made of metal, sometimes they were corrugated, sometimes perforated sheets like this one, and up close, you can imagine the images might be distorted, but when you project on them you get a perfect image to fill the night sky. A number of the panels on the Flood Waters' screen are loose and the paint is peeling. That's not surprising if you consider that the screen has stood like an enormous sail in the wind for fifty years, but it's nothing that a few screws, pressure washing, and a couple of gallons of paint can't fix.

Soon enough, the high school kids Brenda has enlisted to help do the work are blasting away at the screen and I turn to the sound and projection. The old projection building is a dump -- literally. The space is strewn with mountains of junk and the smell inside is a blend of mouse nest, mildew, and rot. It is intolerable. Incredibly, though, while looking around inside I stumble on four boxes of chrome-plated window speakers. These are the speakers all drive-ins had that were hung on poles from which they could be secured to the car's window for sound. They are completely unusable after years of rodents having gnashed away at their wire insulation. (I do set them aside, however, and will make a point of asking Garby Clifton if he might let me take them. It would be fun to pull off the road some winter month and start soldering away at them. Who knows?) We'll have to set up front speakers, but that's easy and the sound is better.

Before the morning is over the remaining logs are cleared away out of the main area and the high school kids have removed all the junk. In the parking area, a bulldozer is smoothing fresh gravel into place and Brenda starts setting up tables and chairs for dining.

By the next morning the Flood Waters has undergone a restoration that Wes says would have made old Bill Johnson proud. There are hay bale bleachers, picnic tables to hold a Spanish feast and, freed from being inside, there's an area for barbecues and tables of fresh fruit. There's even a makeshift stage for musicians and plenty of room to dance. What started as a polite party is turning into something so much more. I dig into my collection and pull out one of my favorite films, *Garlic Is As Good As Ten Mothers*, a succulent documentary about food and history by Les Blank. The sun reflects a sparkle on the river flowing past the revitalized theater and the protest that sparked this activity is only a remote memory now.

About two o'clock in the afternoon a large pickup truck pulls into the Flood Waters, followed by a car full of men. In the back of the pickup is a large object covered with a blue tarp. The men stop their vehicles and with some frantic hand gesturing finally pull to the side of the old drive-in projection building. Within minutes they erect two collapsible tents, the kind you see artisans beneath at every fair, flea market, and festival around the country; except these have sides to them, which prevent anyone from seeing what they unload from the back of the truck. By four o'clock, that tented area is a busy gathering place for most of the people around. Curious, I walk over and one of the men flashes a pleased, conspiratorial smile while he shows me what's inside. It's a large cask filled with a special "cider."

"Is it anything like kummis?" I ask, but the man looks at me as if the spaceship dropped me off.

"This is the cider of Asturias. Come see me during the film and you'll be happy."

The colorful hand-painted signs that were scattered around the county redirecting everyone to the Flood Waters have done their job, and at five o'clock, with film time scheduled for eight-thirty, the party is on. Visitors to the celebration mingle around the grounds of the Flood Waters and when they're not eating bacalao a la Vizcaina (codfish stew with peppers), Basque lamb stew, garlic soup, tongue in tomato sauce, or Basque potatoes, all of which are ladled generously from large pots, manned, not staffed, in the Basque Men's Cooking Club tradition. People can bid at the silent auction fundraiser for the Four Rivers Basque community which has items such as "One Load Of Crushed Rock," "One Hour Reiki Massage," "Two Tons of Alfalfa," "One Men's Haircut," "Two Dozen Baby Chicks," "One Bone-In Ham," and the much coveted "Ten Lines of Bowling, shoes included," at the Deer Crossing Lanes in Gossage (a mere seventy-five miles away), all available at the right bid. There are two live bands, one playing Basque folk music and the other Flamenco, as children, and a few daring adults, borrow steel-toed boots and shoes to see what sounds they can bring out of the plywood floor set up for the occasion. Also, freed from the restrictions of public oversight, there are abundant bottles of red wine for all to enjoy.

As film time approaches, the crowd is a testimony to what can happen when people live with the throttle wide open. When Brenda finally gives me the nod to start *Carmen*, it takes a few minutes for the audience to shift their focus from what's alive to what's on the screen. But film images cast against a large screen in the middle of the night are powerful, as is the compelling staccato of Flamenco dancer's steps, and slowly the film seduces every one. Saura's *Carmen* is like a sharp steel knife piercing your own flesh and you smell the blood. Add the wine, the "cider," the air, and the darkness to the fire of Paco De Lucia's guitar, and the eroticism is strong. The film takes you to another place.

Brenda, Susan, Ray, and Wes are standing not far from me looking proudly over the scene they have created. They're drinking Asturian cider when Susan asks no one in particular whether they should be concerned about the underage drinking.

"Can you imagine what the Felks would say? I mean it's illegal, right?"

Taking a deep sip, Brenda Garcia raises her glass in the direction of three-term County Sheriff Javier Zorilla, sitting with his arms around his two teenaged children watching the movie with bottles of wine sitting on the table in front of them.

"I don't think it's going to be a problem," says Brenda, raising her glass to the reflected light of the movie softly floating into the heavens. She offers this toast: "The rooster is dead. Long live the rooster!"

———————◆———————

**Wesley Raymond Jackson's Smithsonian portrait begins with a silent sepia toned project title.**

*The Smithsonian Presents*
## The Fabric of America: Elders Weave the Landscape

**As the title fades we see nothing but a blurry golden screen. We hear the rushing sound of a forceful wind for about twenty seconds before any clear image appears on the screen.**

**As the wind roars, the golden blur before us slowly comes into focus showing golden, flowing grass hills, and a confluence of four fingers of water. Over that image comes:**

Wesley Raymond Jackson
b. 1926  Newspaper Editor. Four Rivers, Idaho.

Another fade and we see a more expansive view of a mountain valley floor covered with golden fields, we see that the fingers of water are rivers coming together.

The next image is a handsome, white-haired man in his sixties speaking from a jutting panoramic hilltop with the confluence of four rivers below him.

"I was born in Four Rivers fourteen years before the Wold War II began to rage. My father, who was from Illinois, was the first postmaster in Four Rivers. It was an interesting perspective from which to observe the life and unfolding history of a town rich with ranching, timber, and farming thanks to the abundantly fertile ground watered by the wealth of the nearby rivers."

Wes Jackson points to each of the rivers.

"What you see beneath us here is the confluence of the Little Hoochie, the Elk, the China, and the Tamarack. Every spring as long as I've been alive, the snow has melted, causing them to flood in this spot. The soil is fertile, and its fertility has created a home for human beings for thousands of years. It's kind of a little Nile, if you will. Measured by any primitive standard, Four Rivers is an area of great abundance."

The face of Wes Jackson dissolves into a herd of elk resting in a grassy thicket, cutting to a large field of round hay bales, cutting to a vast spray of water emanating from rolling irrigation pipe across rich green fields, cutting to a large herd of horses grazing in a verdant pasture.

"Nothing is truer than the saying that 'water is life' and when life is made easier the mind turns to other things. Enough water means food is seldom scarce, and when people have time to do other things besides fend for their basic needs, well, some say what results is art, some call it creativity or philosophy, while most don't call it anything but whittle sticks, throw pots, write poetry, paint, dance, or stare at the clouds floating by. For hundreds of years the people in this area had time to watch the clouds float by."

Next we see a vintage western two-story red brick building with a sign above its arching entrance that reads,

**Now we see Wes Jackson wheeling stacks of newspapers in a hand-cart and loading them into the back of a Jeep Cherokee.**

"Every Wednesday night I pick up 2,000 copies of my paper, *The Four Rivers Conscience*, the only paper that covers this area. It's a 24 page tabloid with news, photos, editorials, high school sports, letters to the editor, wildlife features, regional history, cooking, birth announcements, obituaries, community calendars, and anything else I can find to stick in there that might be interesting to someone. Occasionally, when things are good, there might even be some advertising.

"Now, I have to distribute them. It's going to be a long night."

**Now we see Wes inside his vehicle and some footage of the rolling hills and pastures he drives through in the fading light as he drops short stacks of twenty-five to fifty papers on the doorsteps of businesses. Most are closed. We see him make drops at Harnish Gas Station, Valley Health Clinic, Straight Arrow Café, Rapid River Drugstore, Keedle's Farm and Ranch Supply, Schroeder's Grocery.**

"I'll deliver papers anywhere they have a counter. Each week about 1800 people gladly plunk down fifty cents to read what's going on in the Four Rivers region. By tomorrow morning, less than ten hours from now, people will be reading this paper and, like the subtle changes in an aroused beehive, a low buzz and hum will run through the region for a few days."

**Next we see a small street with a handful of business storefronts. The camera zooms into one small windowpane with gold-leaf lettering that reads:**

THE
## FOUR RIVERS CONSCIENCE
### Giving Voice to Those With No Voice
SINCE 1923

**The camera shifts inside where Wes thumbs through neatly shelved archives of the Four Rivers Conscience.**

"As money piled up beyond the post-depression expectations of the residents, a town grew up to meet the expanding commercial and social demands. You certainly wouldn't know it now, but Four Rivers Junction once had a mercantile, a drug store and soda fountain, even a clothing store unusual for such vast expanses of land. After the war, a new prosperity swept through the country and Four Rivers found a market eager for its wheat and potatoes, its straight pine logs and beef cattle. Every drop of water that came from the four generous rivers returned in the form of dollars."

**We see Wes sitting at his desk with his feet up as he lights a pipe and smokes.**

"Well, as we all know, dollars can translate into folly, my friends, and folly may not endure, but it sure makes things fun for a while. Every person should have at least one folly in his or her life. My current and biggest folly is this newspaper. I'll tell you now, if you'd asked me in my twenties what I'd end up doing, publishing *The Four Rivers Conscience* would not have been my prediction. I wanted out of this place. Didn't ever want to farm or ranch or work in a sawmill. No, sir. I was one of those bookworm kids, and though my contribution was fairly small, once Mr. Hitler and his thugs were dispatched, all I wanted to do was see the world I had read about.

"My insightful mother and father sent me packing to college in Milwaukee, where I thrived in a setting far different from Four Rivers."

**Shot of Wes Jackson's College Diploma from Marquette University; pan to Wes picking books from his shelves.**

"I loved every minute of it -- I loved Twain and Chaucer and Cervantes and Faulkner, even Tolstoy and Brecht. Literature made my blood run hot. In those wonderful times, if you knew books, you could get a job for that. The world was awash with enthusiasm for ideas. You could write and read and tell others about history. That era was a golden, halcyon wave and for nearly thirty-five years I traveled the world and nothing slowed down.

"Each time I came back, unbelievably, somehow this laconic little town had changed. In 1955, William Johnson, for years the only black man in Four Rivers, opened the Flood Waters Drive-In and what a change that was for the town. If ever a world was turned on its ear, that's what happened then. This is a pretty isolated place, but if you started sticking pins in a map for every farm, ranch, mill family, and everyone else who lives around here you'll see you have a lot of pins up there."

**We see a tall fence surrounding an enclosed lot of junked cars, trailers, boats, and various piles. Then a pan to the arched and gated entrance to the fenced lot with a barely perceptible sign, "Welcome to the Flood Waters."**

"In the summer everybody came to the Drive-In: Saturday Night

Drive-In Movies. By then my mom and pop had their big sedan and they'd sit in that car with the speaker suspended from the half-open window. After a while Mom would stroll back to the concession stand and buy her popcorn -- once the first short began so the line was shorter -- and she'd wave at all her friends as she walked back to her car. Then silence struck the suddenly hypnotized crowd as the movie began.

"There I was living the most modern of lifestyles, while my parents were simply watching movies. On one of their visits to me in New York, I threw a dinner party in their honor. People started talking movies, and the next thing you know they're all gathered around Mom and Pop, who are actually leading the conversation. Postmaster Jackson of Four Rivers and his bride: erudite film critics! Long ago, my parents fell in love with the movies and they had never once missed a show in thirty years. Every Friday night, after my pop had cleaned up from work, they'd share a glass of brandy, and head off to the Shanghai Restaurant, gone now, and then to the Forum or the Flood Waters for whatever was showing. If you add it up over the years, that's a lot of pictures and a lot of chop suey."

**Wes Jackson scribbles a calculation on a small pad.**

"Thirty years times one movie a week, sometimes two if there was a double feature, I give up, it probably totals somewhere around two thousand. While I was reading books from the past, Mom and Pop were soaking up movies of the time, and there was a point at which they seemed to have become the modernists and I, the relic. It was odd, hearing them tell stories about this or that movie star and how the films had been made, even details of intrigues between the actors and actresses. They could tick off Oscar winners like multiplication tables.

"It wasn't long after that I started thinking about Four Rivers. As the seventies came and went -- you remember -- ideas were not so welcome anymore. The reception for them became noticeably smaller."

**Now we see a closeup shot of a bold, large type, *Four Rivers Conscience* headline:  REAGAN LANDSLIDE!**

"In 1980, when I came back to visit, my mother wanted to know what I planned to do with the rest of my life. 'You've got no family, Wesley, and all your friends seem to be scattering.' I was fifty-three and I'd never stopped to consider the rest of my life before. I swear. I lived. Mother had a point when she said things were changing. She's the one who told me about the newspaper being for sale. It must have been pretty obvious to her that I had a bad case of ants in my pants. She said, 'If nothing else, you can always buy *The Conscience*. You know what they always say: the last refuge of un-bridled opinion is a small town newspaper. The press is only free when you have your own.' And she went on. She said that buying a newspaper was like paying for a headache, but she winked at me when she said it, knowing that wink might hold all the temptation necessary to get me to consider the whole crazy proposition."

**Next we see a closeup shot of a legal document.**

CONTRACT OF SALE FOR THE FOUR RIVERS CONSCIENCE:

a Newspaper, including but not limited to, its name, privileges, and responsibilities. Sale price: $6,100.

SELLER:

Jerome Gaylord Evans. Buyer: Wesley Raymond Jackson. November 24th, 1980.

"So, I sold off most of my stuff, came back to Four Rivers, and bought this tiny little newspaper. Had I thought about it, I never would have done it. Today, when anyone asks me how I came to run this paper, all I say is, 'I experienced a momentary lapse of judgment.' You see, the name of this paper is not the *Observer*, not the *Sentinel*, the *Guardian* or the *Times* or the *Dispatch* or the *Courier* or the *News*; no, it's *The Conscience*. It felt as though the paper was alive with the purpose of its own name and that pur-pose started flowing through me like a wild obsession. There's absolutely no money in it. Heavens, no, you couldn't draw enough advertising out of this area even if you stuck pins into a voodoo doll of J. Paul Getty.

"And I can tell you this, when the world finally started catching up to Four Rivers, it caught up fast."

**Next a series of cuts show *Four Rivers Conscience'* headlines: Feds to Regulate Water Allocations . . . Power Generation Given Priority over Irrigation . . . Army Corps Hearing to Discuss Dam Feasibility . . . Army Corps Plan Would Flood Sixteen Ranches: 12,000 Acres!**

"Change gives you something to write about: desperation and con-troversy and scandal all sell papers. For years the paper had been a simple sounding board for good ideas, but it now slowly evolved into battles over water rights, government control, land scandals, all the things that tear like angry hands at the heart of anything decent. I found myself sitting at *The*

*Conscience*, and for the first time in my life, my books weren't so helpful to me, because as the pie got smaller the fighting over crumbs got bigger. I found that when you leave a place and come back, people are suspicious of you. Everyone knows that you had left your clan and some part of them wants you to pay your dues for a while before they're willing to let you back in. They know things you don't and they aren't sure you can be trusted with, or even appreciate, the truth. They're not sure you're going to stay around when the going gets tough. So it took some time before people opened up to the paper, and me, but eventually they came around. With all the change, the very people who once mistrusted me now looked to the paper to make some sense out of the world."

**Wes fumbles through a stack of old papers until he finds the one he's been looking for. He holds it up to the camera. The headline reads:**

Army Corps Nixes Dam Project. Now What?

**Next we see semi-trucks lined up at a weigh station with closeup shots of their license plates: Kansas, Tennessee, New York, Florida, California, Washington.**

"They didn't build the dam, but Four Rivers was now solidly connected to a world it hid from for so long. I suppose it was inevitable. Happened to thousands of places across the country."

**Wes tamps out his pipe into a large ashtray, reloads it with tobacco, and lights it. He exhales a deep train of bluish smoke and sighs.**

"I believe I used to write about events more often than I do now. Those times were filled with events. Lately the stories are more intimate, more personal. It's hard to explain, but I intend to keep doing what I do. I remember the day *The Conscience* officially transferred ownership from Jerry to me. After it was all signed, sealed and notarized at the old stone County Courthouse in Harnish, I took Mom and Dad out for a celebration lunch at the Roundhouse Steakhouse across the street from the courthouse. That sounds funny, doesn't it? The Roundhouse Steakhouse across the street from the Courthouse. We got our menus and ordered, and when the food came, Mom took our hands and spoke, 'Our Father who art in heaven, hallowed be thy name. Thy kingdom come thy will be done on Earth as it is in heaven. Give us this day our daily bread and forgive us our trespasses as we forgive those who may trespass against us. And, lead us not into temptation but deliver us from evil. Amen.' My mother often spoke the Lord's Prayer.

When the check came, I took it and boasted that it was on me. But my

Pop took it quickly as my Mom gave me one of those looks that said, 'Let your father have his way.' Then he said, 'If you intend to spend the rest of your life giving voice to the silent and looking out for the common good, you're going to need every last dime.'"

Three weeks later I received a copy of the *Four Rivers Conscience* in the mail. Inside the paper was a follow up piece by Wes Jackson explaining the sub-committee intrigue. As it turned out, Millers' crusade was a front for a larger organization. For years the Felks had been selling their chickens to a company owned by Frederick Huffman, a retired poultry tycoon with a deep checkbook and even deeper beliefs about the state of the world. After making his fortune in California, Huffman chose to retire to Four Rivers "to escape the deepening cesspool of moral decline rampant in California and live in the purity of original virtue." He was the man behind the Felks's sub-committee, quietly exhorting and funding them. As Wes Jackson noted, "There are, indeed, other committees and other sub-committees and no doubt we have not heard the last of them."

Reading from *The Conscience* I find myself smiling once again. I can conjure the fresh memory of Four Rivers, *Carmen*, the cider, Liona, the Flood Waters, Wes, Doc, Brenda, Susan and Ray, and two antelope heads perpetually watching me drink coffee. For one night beneath the stars of the pristine sky in a place called Four Rivers, we did indeed find another way home to Kansas: only this time, it was Idaho.

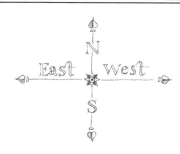

SECTION 4

# Pictures At An Exhibition

Fade Out essay from the *Tattered Edge*, Volume 16 # 1

# On Bedtime Stories, by A.L. Janus

Nostalgia can be deceptive, and memory is a selective filter. Closing my eyes, I remember a time of matinees, when any time of the day was right for a story. Is my memory accurate? Where has the matinee gone? Does it matter? Where has the warm sun on an upturned face mindlessly staring at the movement of clouds gone? Where has playing hooky for a chance to spend an idle day gone? Where has wistful, timeless contemplation gone?

There seems to be no time to be purposeless anymore, and only scorn for those who dare engage in this deepest privilege of human nature. Those who drift or float may meet with a rude reception for their unwillingness to be part of The Machine. We've become willing participants in our ever-expanding industriousness. We are working . . . working . . . working . . . Was it ever not so? Does it matter? Nostalgia can be deceptive, and memory is a selective filter.

But all days must end, and once the belly is full and the dishes are cleared, the kids asleep, facts checked, bills paid, news consumed, and the endless responsibilities of upholding the imperative of our epoch's obligations finished, then with what remains, we allow ourselves to be idle before we sleep and renew ourselves for another rotation in the engine.

And then there are bedtime stories: once we were children and our parents read them to us, repeating again and again the tales of Pooh and Piglet, Sal and her dad, Bartholomew and his hats, Suzuki Bean, or a mother duckling braving the streets of Boston in search of a home for her brood. Once we were children, our minds free from numbing chatter, worry, and responsibility, our dreams vapors of innocence.

Is my memory accurate? Does it matter now?

Once we were children and we'd roam the streets looking for Coke bottles, saving pennies to see the new picture, in a time when pennies were precious and movies were escapes. Once we were children and Saturday afternoons we watched Stan and Ollie, Charlie and Buster, elephants were exotic, and carpets could fly. In careless nights our imaginations filled in the blanks, painting pictures to complete fantasies richer than any reality. Once we were children, sheltered from the world, believing in our heroes, believing in a tomorrow without limitations.

Is that possibly so? Does it matter?

Now we are adults. Many of us watch movies before we sleep, merging our lives with people real or imagined, characters in a world of dreams. There are Stanley and Blanche, Babette, angels who seek to be human, ships at sea in faraway water, travelers riding camels beneath the radiant blanket of a sheltering sky. Stories disturbing to our dreams slowly displacing the vapors of innocence we floated in when we were children, and our parents read stories to us, repeating again and again the movements of Pooh and Piglet, Sal and her dad, Bartholomew and his hats, Suzuki Bean, or a mother duckling braving the streets of Boston in search of a home for her brood.

Once, we were children...


A.L. Janus has submitted a short list of his favorite Bedtime Stories. *The Secret of Roan Innish, Car Wash, Babette's Feast, Broadway Danny Rose, Ninotchka, Black Orpheus, In America, Trouble In Paradise.*

# CHAPTER 18

# Pictures Before An Exhibition- Lighthouse Island

**In Which** we meet Dr. Antonina Palliatti, who believes that stories heal better than medicine, and we watch freighters go by while becoming the central figure in a global conspiracy plot.

*Jake Spinner*
*General Postal Delivery*
*Lighthouse Island, British Columbia*

*Jake,*                                                                              *Today*

*It is twenty-four degrees and snowing here today. February in New York!@#$. I'm sending you a little package. Found this one-reeler on "eBay" and got it cheap. Date says 1924. Look closely and you'll see Betty Boop's grandmother (well, sort of). Worth running through the editor one frame at a time . . . not quite Snow White, is it? Pretty racy stuff for those days. A lot of innovative things were done before Hayes and his censorship thugs got their claws sharpened. Heard an interview with Chuck Jones the other day, said he liked to slip in single frames of Bugs or Daffy naked. I always liked Chuck. Let me know how it comes off. Also, spoke with Nina Palliatti again in New York. Am enclosing a piece from the Washington Post and some clippings you'll find interesting. As I've said before, you two ought to meet. Mark this date on your calendar:  May 21, 2004:  New York City. Three months should be enough time for you to drive to New York.*

*Onward, Julian*

## *Visible Past Project Turns Camera Around, from The Christian Science Monitor. West Timor*

Antonina Palliatti washes the tiny mangled arm of a four-year-old girl, injured by a mortar explosion two hours earlier. The slender, dust covered doctor politely asks the only translator in the compound to "Tell her that she's beautiful and her pain will fly away soon." Dr. Palliatti sets aside a syringe and warmly grasps the young child's arm. Holding it, she places her own forehead against the small one before her. Standing nearby, the girl's mother welds one of her hands to the doctor's and the other to her daughter's neck as the women stand, calm and silent. The little girl asks her mother the name of the panther-like dark-eyed woman with long black hair who has been working on her. Before the translator can pass through the question, the young doctor, says "Nina, my name is Nina."

A roving camera crew from Global Communications Link captures the work on tape, and six hours later Nina sees the scene replayed on a television in her hotel room with a voice-over that makes her blood boil. "International medical volunteers attend to the innocent victims of tribal conflicts raging in this region." There are fifteen carefully edited seconds of Nina working on the little girl, making certain there is no closeup of the missing arm Nina had to remove. Then the images shift to scenes of the Red Cross unloading pallets of food and medical supplies from a large helicopter. A handsome, well-spoken "Foreign Relief Worker" speaks authoritatively about the vital work of his agency, and international condemnation of the violence in the region. Back in the hospital, another story is shown. Crude, but compelling, and with no narration, it is the videotape taken by the sister of the injured girl capturing the scene of the three women together.

Nina Palliatti speaks passionately about the events that inspired the Visible Past Project. "In my first years as a relief doctor, I was struck by the heartlessness of news coverage. Everything was framed large in terms of governments, economics, or religious turmoil, while I was working with people on a closely personal and very often tragic level. No one was recording their unique and poignant stories. After watching one too many television journalists point their camera at suffering children to acquire thirty-second sympathy spots, it came to me: 'Turn the camera around.' I asked my father to send two camcorders to a refugee camp in Tanzania where I taught anyone who wanted to use them how to capture these stories on film."

Dr. Palliatti continues "After injecting and feeding, sewing and salving too many people in too many situations where lives had been torn apart for any number of mindless reasons, I came to believe my medical practice had to answer a deeper cry. At that time I could not articulate what I was see-ing or why it shifted my work. All I knew was what I saw in the eyes of the people with whom I worked: that although medicine could sustain life, it could not sustain hope."

The Mission Statement for the grant proposal Nina had filed with UNI-CEF read: "The Visible Past Project will give voice to the deep cry shared by all homeless and displaced persons. Common to every refugee, exile, orphan, discarded conscript, or innocent victim of social turmoil is a story filled with fear and longing." As she continues to speak, Dr. Palliatti does not hold back her judgment. "Most journalists are constrained, either by their organiza-tions or else their own lack of depth, from telling the stories I hear from mothers, fathers and children -- too many wounded and dying people." This fueled her decision to put the camera in their hands and offer them a chance to tell their own stories.

"If you want to find out what someone sees, put a camera in their hands. Amazing things can happen. Grandmothers stooped from years of harvest-ing rice, young people with missing limbs, or scars from bullets or land mines in their backs, parents of lost children, and famine survivors will tell their stories with no filter, and if the stories they tell are raw and technically flawed, at least they'll be honest, unlike news stories manipulated by charity agencies, television networks, governments or anyone else with a profit-mo-tivated agenda."

Over the years, Visible Past had produced stories from children as young as three, to a piece by a one-hundred-and-one year old woman from Somalia who walked around a camp asking everyone, "Who have you lost?" Her film was more powerful than any proclamation from the United Nations. "Who have you lost?" Chinese adoptees in Sacramento, Palestinians, Rwandans, Kosovars, Serbs, Cambodians, Tibetans, Albanians, Moroccans, Irish nurses working in London, Senegalese Christians living in South Dakota, Afghanis in Pakistan, Guatemalans in Los Angeles, Russian Jews living in the West Bank, Africans in Paris, reservation Indians in Oklahoma. Nina Palliatti's Visible Past Project captures the personal dimension of the twentieth cen-tury's very own global transmigration and Diaspora. Nina Palliatti had seen and understood that the value of a story is in its telling, not in its reception, and she most definitely did not believe in the self-serving pity bestowed on the have-nots by the haves.

Ask Nina Palliatti what fuels her work and she answers thoughtfully, "In my life and work I have seen many children with hunger in their bellies or pain in their bodies put to sleep with little but the comforting words of a parent or sibling holding them in their arms. I have seen firsthand the supplicating effect of bedtime stories. Our work is often criticized for being political because we capture and present the real stories of afflicted people. Our work is to help people tell their stories to a wider audience, to assist them in their struggle to be heard, their struggle for representation."

When asked how she perseveres in the face of so much suffering, Dr. Palliatti responds philosophically, "I travel between the darkness and the light. I'm uncomfortable if I stay too long in either world, but I can walk the tightrope, the taut cable binding the two together. Perhaps that is my freedom: to move freely between them. More important, this is my work," says Nina Palliatti, daughter of an Italian immigrant father who gave his daughter a love of life and healing. "My father was a doctor in Italy, but his profession was stripped from him when he came to America. He was an amazing man who taught me to appreciate the daily needs of those whose lives seldom receive the attention they deserve. My father taught me there are many ways to heal. I became a doctor because of his example."

Dr. Palliatti will be present at the Visible Past Project's annual symposium/fundraiser. There, she hopes to share the stories and storytellers, and draw attention to the Project's work. The symposium will take place in New York City at the Eli Horton Hotel, on May, 21, 2004.

Lighthouse Island forms a small community surrounded by saltwater. I've been holed up here for the better part of a month in a Provincial Park campground with a view fit for a king. From the steps on the back of Zhitomir, I can gaze out upon a wide expanse of water and watch boats and whales come and go. I particularly enjoy watching smaller freighters that are my truck's nautical counterparts. They remind me of little Sicilian donkeys steadfastly chugging past with impossible burdens on their backs. Every day the water changes, the sky changes, and so do my moods. Islands seem to have that effect on people, if the ones who come and go here are any indication.

The campground is quiet, except on weekends when people flock to the island by ferry to breathe in some salt air and wander the beaches. There's a small town five miles away, and it has a few stores, a post office, and a clean laundry. I've taken fondly to having fresh, clean clothes, especially because there are two hang-outs with good coffee, a few restaurants, and even a small movie theater called the Foggy Beacon Cinema where I go each Wednesday when they change the picture. So far I haven't seen anything worth a mention, though it doesn't matter so much what they show. I enjoy going. I've also acquired something, which may change my life for the better:  a rather nifty ten-speed bicycle that someone left at the campground with this note. "Free! It's done good service for me, but I'm ready for something better. Give to good home, please." The campground host and hostess, Merle and Louisa Trager, thought I might enjoy riding it into town instead of hitch-hiking. That was very thoughtful, and I do enjoy riding it a lot.

I rode it into town yesterday, stopping at the post office where I was pleased to receive a letter from Clara forwarded by Julian.

*Dear Jake,*          *March 12*

*I send my fondest greetings to you, dear boy. I am moved to write to you after reading the Bedtime Stories piece in the Tattered Edge.*

*It is a lovely piece, but I hope the loneliness that underlies it is not what you feel personally, but rather something you have only observed. I know from our conversations over the years, that growing up without parents allowed you to develop a unique compassion. I suspect there was some event that inspired you to write the Bedtime Stories piece. Don't be afraid to give the details, Jake. I have often wondered what your life on the road must be like. Perhaps you will tell us all someday?*

*That said, I will not bother giving you a boring list of details from Larch. The Sonnet is doing well, though it is getting difficult for me to keep on top of all the things necessary to keep it as I like. Fortunately, my niece Rosalyn has been help-ing me a few days a week since Marion left to work the farm. I'm not sure I could do it without her. My Juice Bar neighbor had to shut down. Sadly there was not enough business and an Internet Café that serves coffee drinks has replaced it. It certainly is popular, always full of people who seem to do little but stare at com-puter screens and make odd noises. Occasionally one or two of them will drift into the Sonnet and once they stop making those sounds they are quite pleasant.*

*I do hope to see you before I'm too old to remember your kind face. I think of you often and keep you in my prayers.*

*With great care, Clara*

Since reading Clara's letter I've been moody and, unusual for me, sad. I spent the day cleaning Zhitomir, even going so far as to borrow a vacuum cleaner from the Tragers and then proceeded to clean and reorganize my little world. I even bought new sheets for my bed in town when the elastic corners of the ones I've had fell apart when they did battle with a proper washing machine. If I'm moody, at least I'm moody in clean surroundings.

Julian has enjoyed having me in one place long enough to keep feeding me information and videotapes of the Visible Past Project's work. Until I read the article about Palliatti I hadn't thought much about meeting her, but now I'm surprised to find myself feeling curious about her. I am captivated by what she said about walking between worlds. I often feel suspended between worlds myself, and I'll be interested to find out what she means by that. I've highlighted it and taped the article with her picture near my desk. I find myself glancing at it when I'm inside. Soon enough I'll have to leave for New York, but for now I'm in no hurry.

This morning I got the crazy notion to do something I don't do often. Eric would be proud to watch me call Julian to ask for details about the symposium. I think he'd be shocked that I know how to use the phone. I never expect Julian to be in, but after two rings he answers the phone with these words:

"Well miracle of miracles, the nomadic Spinner actually calls. Still on the island?"

"Yes."

"Me, too. Mine has two million crazy people? Yours?"

"A few less. How did you know it was me?"

"Jake, there is this thing called the modern world and when you live in it they give you a little device called 'caller identification,'" Julian says sarcastically.

"Sure, Julian, but it would have killed films like, *Sorry, Wrong Number*."

"Good point." Then, he says, "I'm glad you called. What's new? Did you get the letter?" Then he tells me he'll be the host of the *VPP*'s banquet and moderator of a panel discussion:  Film As a Consciousness-Raising Device."

I don't say anything, but inside I'm groaning as Julian continues.

"I've assigned you to that one. You're expected to deliver a brief talk and then answer questions. Most of the audience will be college kids, some press and the usual film types."

When I can no longer withhold my displeasure at the notion of consciousness-raising, Julian gets a little agitated.

"Palliatti made the same sort of noises, so I'll tell you what I told her. You may not believe you can change the world through ideas alone. So what? Not everyone has the capacity for action and many of the people coming to the symposium genuinely care about things, even if they don't know how to change them. When they see the films, or hear you speak, or meet someone whose life has been touched by the work, they do what they can. What they can do is write a check and they trust you to use it well and do what needs to be done. Consciousness-raising, fundraising, pity, sympathy, the words don't matter. show up and tell people what you've seen and what you do."

Julian finishes his speech with no indication that he wants a rebuttal, adding, "The other thing is, you need to send the organizers a list of your ten favorite films."

This time I groan out loud.

"Come on, Julian, what for?"

"Jake, they have this idea for raising money by posting the lists anonymously and have people buy an entry form allowing them to try and match the list to its author. The winner is the person who matches the most lists correctly. There're going to be some heavy hitters posting lists too. Kofi Annan, Paul Newman, even some of the New York Yankees. That'll be fun, trying to guess Annan's list from some baseball player. There are three prizes, including two lifetime passes to twelve of New York's best theaters. Not bad; I might enter myself."

When I balk at the request, Julian asks,

"Have you and Nina been talking? She said she didn't want to do it, either, said it was frivolous. But I convinced her."

"How'd you do that?" To which Julian responds in a very solid impression of Vito Corleone in *The Godfather*,

"I made her an offer she couldn't refuse. Listen, Jake, it's all for fun, right? The world won't lose much sleep over this. Trust me, Jake, if I were you I would be thinking more about meeting this fantastic woman and less of your attitude about lists of favorite films. Copy something out of *a Facets' Catalog,* if you like."

Then, his tone softens again, and even on the phone, I can feel Julian looking directly into my eyes like he used to years ago. There had always been times when Julian, not the fatherly type, would sense he was my father's brother and something stirred, some family responsibility, some connection to the things of his family, things unavailable to me, and in those moments, time would slow.

"Jake, this is how we have to do things in the real world. You learn to roll with it and occasionally something wonderful happens because of it." Then he sighed and added, "It's a list, Jake. It won't hurt you to do it."

Then, as if there were a starter's pistol going off, Julian says, "Listen, Jake, I have to go. There's this waitress at the Chinese restaurant . . ."

As Fred once said about Julian, "He'll pick your pocket but leave a piece of candy to let you know he's been there."

Before hanging up, he offers to fly me to New York. "It's cheaper and faster than driving that truck of yours."

"That's true, but no thanks, I'm looking forward to the drive."

After speaking with Julian, I spent the rest of the day washing Zhitomir's exterior from top to bottom. It is safe to say I now have the cleanest rolling film society in the world. At eight o'clock I'm fresh out of procrastination. I've got some work to do and I summon my alter ego, A.L. Janus.

A.L. Janus can be fickle. I don't always know when he's going to show up, and I can't summon him. As the Visible Past Project conference draws closer I've felt his presence more. Someone once addressed a  letter to "*Tattered Edge* Movie Critic, A.L. Janus." I don't think of myself as a movie critic. A.L. Janus was conceived to let me comment on how audiences watch movies, and I'm pretty darn good at describing that. If I stray from that sometimes, it's only because I have a lot of time to think and I can run down some strange alleys. I hope I don't go down one of those alleys tonight, because I feel like working on the *VPP* talk.

I sit down at my desk and pour the last coffee from my thermos. For twenty minutes I sip and stare at my desk until the coffee kicks in. After one long exhale,  I stand and stretch my arms, like the slow moving wheels of a great steam locomotive screeching into motion. One minute later the top ten list is complete. That was simple. I simply added *The Burmese Harp* and *Children of Paridise* to the films heading the *Bedtime Stories* piece. To refresh your memory they are:  *The Secret of Roan Innish, Car Wash, Babette's Feast, Broadway Danny Rose, Ninotchka, Black Orpheus, In America,* and *Trouble In Paradise.*

Now I'm on a roll and wonder what Kofi Annan will have on his list. I press my fingers into the tiny keyboard, and the coffee and the moon begin their flirtation. If Jake Spinner moves gently through life, A.L. Janus is restless. Jake Spinner yearns for sleep while A.L. Janus wants to ride with Icarus. Jake wants to meet Nina, who wants to meet A.L. Janus? Does she want to meet Jake? A.L. Janus  is supposed to deliver a talk about something he knows nothing about to a crowd of people who know everything. My gray matter is congested tonight. At last something releases, and words begin flowing from the inner river. Tonight's writing will have to yield to impulse. Thank you Clara Spengler for this bit of advise, "When writing, always leave yourself tomorrow to see things clearly."

---

### First Draft of Talk for the Visible Past Project Screenings

*I want to thank all of you here today, especially Dr. Palliatti and the Visible Past Project, those in attendance and also, Julian Spinner, for the invitation to this year's symposium.*

*I'd like to speak for a few moments about film from the perspective of one who stands behind the projectors. That's what I do: I watch people watch movies, and I've been doing it for over fifteen years. I hope there're a few of you here who have had this experience.*

*When I watch movies that I'm not showing, I watch them like everyone else. If a film moves me, I disappear until it's over and I come out and slowly grope my way back to reality. Sometimes that takes a few seconds and sometimes it takes months. But when I show films in makeshift theaters created in horse arenas, Grange Halls, farms, community centers, schools, armories, or any place spacious enough to cast images against a painted wall or a portable movie screen, it's different. When I show films, I hear audiences gasp, cry, go silent, cough uncomfortably, grow calm or become agitated. And what I've observed over these many years is that you can't throw technique at an audience. Unless there is something in the story to which they connect, nothing can move them.*

I stop here, confused by the point of my talk. I'm not sure what I'm saying to them, or even if I'm speaking to them. I remind myself that Julian has repeatedly said, the purpose of the conference is to raise funds for the Visible Past Project, not to become some de-facto film summit. My speech isn't working. It's a jumble. Jake Spinner wants to bail out and go listen to the sound of the ocean, but A.L. Janus presses on.

*Most of you, especially those of you over forty, have had the experience of sitting in a dark room with a projector ticking away while it casts light onto a blank screen. How many of you here have sneaked into the light column and done finger puppets and shadow play? Once there's one set of hands doing shadows, soon more join in and now there're lots of hands and someone starts adding dialogue to the movements of the animated shadows. Slowly a movie unfolds, primitive yes, but still a movie. The need to tell stories goes very deep, doesn't it? It goes to caves and rock walls. While the first films ever made are credited to Edison and Lumiere, perhaps cave people made movies with shadows cast onto rock walls illuminated by fire.*

*It isn't about movies. It's about the basic human need to give and receive stories. We all need to share our stories, and while the participants in the Visible Past Project don't need film or videotape to tell their stories to each other, they do need film to tell their stories to the world, and they need the support of all of us if they are to continue to tell their stories in their own voices, from their own perspectives.*

When I stop writing, I look at the photo taped beside my desk and blush at the realization I've been writing to Nina Palliatti. I write the *Tattered Edge* pieces to Julian. That's natural. Julian has been the source and filter of most of my ideas about film. Now I'm struggling to keep Julian out of my head, guarding this conversation. I'm staring at the photo of this woman, knowing I will meet her, surprised by excitement. Eric says I am a fool when it comes to women. He says I hide, play Mr. Nice Guy, Mr. I can listen to your story and never say boo about anything that shows I'm flesh and blood. Okay, Eric, I'm looking at this photo and I'm feeling things! I'm feeling that I live in a truck and haven't felt the touch of a woman for a long time. Geez, I don't even have a pet!

I witness the sunrise from the wrong side of time. That's what Fred called "all nighters." Dawn breaks a diffuse gray morning sky, the steel sea broken by spitting whitecaps extending for miles in every direction.

Then my cell phone rings!

"Jake, are you up?"

"Eric, is that you? Where are you?"

"Palau, where else would I be?"

"Cleveland, maybe. Who knows? How are your parents?"

"They're nuts. Teachers, you know. They're always working, but we're having a good time. I learned to dive; there are these amazing caves here, and I'm filming some fishermen, Jake. It's totally awesome; these guys know more about fish than you can believe. And the color, man, swee----eee---eeet. I'm all rigged up to shoot underwater. Call me Eric Cousteau! I've got some great footage, but I need to edit it. I think it's going to be a good film.

What about you? You sound a little fuzzy."

"Fuzzy, maybe. I stayed up last night working on something."

"What's her name?"

"Nina." This throws Eric who is used to getting the better of this kind of exchange.

"Jake, man, are you serious?"

"No, I stayed up working."

"All night? You stayed up all night? Oh, man; you've got some good coffee, don't you?" Eric says with a hint of envy in his voice. "Not me, I've been drinking Nescafé and Kava. It's kind of like coffee, but its zing is different from coffee. It can make you a little zoo zoo. I'll bring you some when I come home."

"When's that?"

"Soon, I hope. I need to edit this footage and get it out, and I want to go to New York for that conference, if you don't mind."

"Why would I mind?"

" Just checking. Listen, I think we should show a film in New York."

"What do you mean? New Yorkers won't go for that."

"Sure they will. New Yorkers go for anything. I've got something in mind and I'll tell you about it when I see you. Any chance you can pick me up? I had to sell the van."

"You sold your van? Why?"

"Needed the money for something else. I'll tell you about that, too, later."

"How'd you sell it from Palau?"

"I sold it to Peggy"

"Who's that?"

"Peggy, 16mm film Peggy, the belly dancer in Driggs."

Suddenly, it dawns on Eric that he's not sure where I am, about the same time it dawns on me that I have no idea how Peggy in Driggs got Eric's van which, the last time I saw it, was heading to Manitoba. I'm too tired to ask him about it.

"Jake, where are you?" When I tell him, Eric says,

"Wow, must be pretty cool. I figured you'd be on the east coast by now."

Then the realization of what time it is comes clear to him.

"Man, Jake, I'm sorry. I thought it was east coast time. It's way too early for this call."

"Don't worry about it. I'm awake. I told you, I was writing my talk for the conference."

"Right, Big Time Jake in New York City! What's it about?"

"I have no idea. Any suggestions?"

"Not unless you want to speak about cleaner wrasses and scarlet finned tangs."

"What are you talking about, Eric?"

"Fish, Jake. Cool, colorful fish."

Eric tells me all about the reef fish of Palau. We make plans for him to call me when he's ready to leave. I suggest he fly directly to New York, but he says that would be too big a change. He'll land somewhere along my route to New York.

"Got to have a little road time to break back into things, Jake."

By the time Eric and I finish speaking, I am ready to climb into bed. The last thing I'm thinking about as I fall off to sleep is, "Get it out? Who's going to buy a documentary on fishermen in Palau?"

A few days later, when I ride into town, there's a letter from New York waiting for me at the post office. I stuff it in my pocket and open it when I sit down for coffee at a wobbly table in the Bottom Feeder's Café. There is a distinct spice smell mingling with the coffee. It's got me baffled. When I hold my nose to the cup, there's nothing but coffee, but when I put the cup down it returns again. It's familiar, but I can't identify it. Then, as I open the salmon-colored envelope with "A. Palliatti" in the upper left corner, the spice scent becomes even stronger. It's cardamom, and it's coming from the handwritten letter from Antonina Palliatti written on an olive colored leaf of rustic paper. The cardamom evokes a Bedouin caravan bathing in the low angled light of a radiant desert of golden brown. Talk about enchanting!

*Dear Jake,*                                        *February 7, 2004*

*I'm writing this letter to you to express my appreciation for the simplicity and tenderness of your piece, 'Bedtime Stories', which your uncle Julian passed on to me. I especially enjoyed the sentiment you expressed about having "time clear of the numbing chatter of worry and responsibility." It reminded me of my father.*

*When I was a child, my father would send me off to sleep with his original tales of Jocco the monkey. Jocco was his childhood pet, a rhesus monkey given him by a friend who ran a small traveling circus. My father brought him back to life, relating to me the joint travels and camaraderie of the two of them as they traveled the world. Jocco was many things, including the Italian Emissary to the Syrian Council of Magic Carpets, a world class bicycle racer, and of course, an excellent chef of desert cuisine. There were nights when my father was too tired, but he told me Jocco stories more nights than not. Sometimes, when I view the films, the stories told by participants in the Visible Past Project, I find myself reminded of the comfort that my father's stories brought to me and allowed me to fall off to sleep.*

*I'm not sure why I write this to you. Julian has been very supportive of our work and of me personally as well. He speaks of you often with a deep love and admiration, but I believe he thinks you might enjoy a correspondence. He tells me stories of your childhood visits to New York and the life the two of you shared. How fortunate you were to have such a man in your life.*

*I look forward to meeting you at the Symposium. Though it will, no doubt, be busy, I hope we can spend some time together.*

*Yours, Nina Palliatti*

Nina, she signed it Nina, I thought, as I finished reading the letter. Not Dr. Palliatti or Antonina Palliatti, but Nina. Why that should matter to me is silly, and I'm also curious why it took so long to get here.

I'm not sure how long I've been staring at her letter or inhaling, but when I look up, there's a decidedly atypical resident of the island, about ten years my senior, wearing a charcoal tweed driving cap, a matching woolen sports jacket with a lighter gray shirt and tie, sitting at my table. He introduces himself.

"Hello, young man. May I introduce myself? I am Theodore Barker. I hope I'm not interrupting your meditation, but I believe you are the gentleman with the movie truck, yes?"

I nod yes, while shaking Theodore Barker's extended hand. He continues speaking in a delightful, jolly old fellow sort of pip-pip British accent.

"I own the Foggy Beacon, do you know it? The movie house?" Your hosts Merle and Louise Trager are good friends of mine. They said you are quite the interesting fellow. If you don't mind, what exactly is it you do with that truck?"

"I travel around the country showing movies."

"That is marvelous, a cinematic Gypsy. Splendid," says Barker, then quickly, "I say, forgive me, but your cup is empty. Let me get you another."

Theodore Barker, who extends no offer of being called either Ted or

Theo, goes to the counter and returns with two full cups.

"I hope you have some time for a chat." Then he trails off, "Though I suppose you must. You're on Lighthouse Island, after all, and if there is one thing we have in abundance on this fair little rock, it is time for conversation."

Theodore asks enough questions about Zhitomir to satisfy him that I'm not completely out of my mind, before shifting to his own story. He explains how he landed on the island twenty years ago when the sailboat on which he was cruising tied up for the night.

"Two bloody months of waves and wind and a relationship that was anything but satisfying yes, I was glad to get off. When things go bad on a boat they go very bad, indeed. Not that I minded, my companion and I were not that serious, but well, you know, there isn't any place to hide from someone on a small boat."

Theodore retreated from the sailboat with his belongings, took a room in a local hotel, and a day later the forty-two foot schooner, Sudden Impulse, raised its sails and cast off with her six remaining crew members on board.

"To my way of thinking, I was not stranded, but rather freed from my obligations. I thought, 'why not spend a little time here?' Little did I know I would still be here twenty years later.

"I suppose it was destiny. Once a movie man you know, always a movie man. Before leaving England, I owned a small movie theater, The Majesty, in Hullavington, a township some ninety miles west of London. It's an odd little village, but with the Royal Air Force base close, we made a rather decent go of it until, even with the vigorous protestation of none other than Prince Charles himself, nothing could spare us from the inevitable. I like to say that Her Majesty was defeated honorably in battle by a 'sterile quadraplex' that opened outside of town."

Then, satirizing his English accent in a voice worthy of Winston Churchill, Theodore adds, 'The Majesty is now a tea and sweater shop called The Cup and Woolens, catering to Yanks who want a taste of our enduring English traditions."

An hour later, Theodore and I are wrapping up our conversation when I tell him about the films I carry with me and about the Visible Past Project shorts.

"Can't possibly show any of the features; I'm simply booked solid with new releases. One has to commit months in advance to the releases and the distributors button you down pretty tightly. It is all about marketing, they like to say. But the shorts, please drop them by. I would be happy to give them a look. Perhaps we can make something out of them and give this little island a sample of something unique."

The following morning I learn a lesson about island life when I ride my bicycle to a small park strategically positioned for whale watching. By the time I arrive, the sky is threatening to let loose a heavy rain, but there's an undaunted group of about ten eager mainlanders decked out in glowing outdoor attire colorful enough to scare away any creature wary of humans. Scattered like pepperoni slices on a pizza, they stand on the rocky bluff with binoculars poised at the ready. The ten have come from a van marked "Whale Encounter," and the two guides in charge of the group sit with their backs to the ocean smoking cigarettes. Clearly, the thrill of whales has worn thin for them. One guide says,

"He's some CIA bigwig who did propaganda for NATO -- supposed to be amazing stuff, Chechnya, Bosnia, Poland. Stuff THEY don't let the public see, you know: the real stuff," says Guide One, to which Guide Two responds skeptically,

"What would a CIA guy be doing in Chechnya or Poland, and why is the guy here now?"

"Think about it, man. Russia, Chechnya, Poland, conflict. Who cares, dude? The thing is that he's got the stuff THEY don't want YOU to KNOW about. And the reason he's here? Duh; it's safe here, man. Think about it. He's got to get the films out somewhere off the radar screen. If he drops this stuff in Los Angeles or New York, they can trace it back to him. But, if he shows it here, gets a little word of mouth thing going, you know . . ."

It's a very entertaining conversation, and it goes on like this for a few minutes. It's the most extraordinary weave of ideas I've heard in some time, and I'm trying to follow the plot of the big conspiracy until I hear this:

"Yeah, go out to the campground. He's parked out there. Look at the truck. It's got some funny pictures on it and some name like, Lost Souls of Zarathustra on it. Check that out if you think I'm making it up. What's that all about? It's real, man, and that's the guy, but don't get too close, he's dangerous. You'd be dangerous, too, if THEY were after YOU."

It's me! They're talking about me! In less than twenty-four hours, five short films about cooking classes in Thailand, concrete block houses in Nepal, young sisters learning to ride a bicycle after losing their feet to land mines in Sierra Leone, Grandma Chicha teaching her family how to clean a chicken during a hurricane, and a weaving collective of widows from the Guatemalan civil war, have somehow turned into a global conspiracy bigger than anything the world has ever known--and I'm in the center of it! Now I'm listening, because the underlying rationale for the conspiracy is about to be revealed by Guide One to Guide Two. The moment is at hand when I can find out what I'm up to and the "powerful secrets" I possess, when one of the pepperoni slices yells, "Thar she blows!" and both guides jump up to join the rest of the pizza. So much for getting the rest of my role in global domination.

Later that afternoon when I meet Theodore at the second of Foggy island's great hangouts, The Viceroy Donut Shop, he can explain why, if not what, I overheard.

The Viceroy Donut Shop has room for ten people to sit at its pink Formica counter on which are painted lifelike renditions of donuts. The counter rests over a full glass display case filled with actual donuts, which are prepared fresh every day in the back. Other donut paraphernalia in The Viceroy includes porcelain donut napkin rings, donut-shaped steel tables glazed with painted-to-look-like-chocolate icing, a plaque bearing "The Donut Lovers Manifesto," and walls covered with brightly colored donut wallpaper. From the ceiling are suspended various plastic donut models ranging in size from a realistic donut to three large jelly donut models, resembling together a model of the solar system. It's a very strange place, but they don't mind if you nurse your donuts and coffee all day long. The Viceroy is always full, but never crowded; as if there is some unspoken understanding that it's not worth waiting to sit down. Lastly, a pungent smell of grease in the air greets you on the street before you enter, thanks to an exhaust vent over the door.

"Welcome to island life, Jake. There is a great deal of time between ferryboats and people pass the time by talking. Gossip has been elevated to a fine art. The only thing this island has more of than gossip is rumors."

Theodore gestures for me to look around the tiny donut shop, which I do, and in a surreal moment I see two people at each of the other four tables actively chattering away in secret tones.

"Thanks, now I'm going to be checking the donuts for microphones."

"No need for paranoia, old boy. Consider yourself honored. When I bought the Foggy Beacon, rumors spread that I was fronting for Rupert

Murdoch, who was secretly buying up the island to turn it into his private retreat. Stick around here and quite possibly you will become apprised of more about yourself than you dare to imagine. Now, about the films, I would like to show them on Sunday. You were right about the technical particulars, but they are lovely and deserve an audience. I shall need to find a video projector, unless you have one, but that is all it should take. I have a feature at eight so I will post it on the marquee, along with some entice-ment, to begin at six. Sunday is actually busy because many people are waiting for the ferry to the mainland."

"What are you going to call it: The CIA Film Festival?"

"Yes, that is not such a bad idea, but I was thinking something a bit catchier like James Bondage! That would certainly get the buzz going, wouldn't it?" Then he points to the kitchen and whispers, "By the way, they hide the microphones in the crullers."

As Theodore stands up to leave, a truly rumbling thunderclap jolts ev-eryone in the Viceroy and within minutes it starts raining hard. I'm tempt-ed to stay put and ride the day out doing crossword puzzles, eating donuts, and reading magazines, but my body lets out a huge groaning reminder at the thought of a few nights ago and the still lingering effects of that all-nighter. Another day of caffeine is not what I need. Instead, I scamper through the rain to the little bookstore called The Raven's Nest, and I go in-side to kill some time while the storm passes. The store reminds me of Clara and The Sonnet with its mix of old and new books arranged into sections titled Women and Maritime Achievements, Gardening in the Rain, and recommendations by local citizens like Keeper Finney's Favorite, which is an interesting little book titled *Adrift* by Tristan Jones, a current-day Welsh sailor/adventurer who describes his thoughts when he finds himself land-bound in New York City. Keeper Finney is Archibald Finney, Lighthouse Island's last surviving man to actually staff the beacon for which the island was named. An automated light replaced Finney over twenty years ago.

I'm drawn next to a large section of photo books, including a remark-able book that reminds me of Larch, about the logging communities of the Northwest. The photographer's name is Darius Kinsey, who was born in the same year as my Grandfather Tolliver.

Reading the loving memoir in the preface by Kinsey's daughter, I think of Sophie's Circus of the Lost Worlds' in Paris, and then, Nina Palliatti jumps into my thoughts. Either the memory of Sophie shifted to the only woman I've allowed myself to think about for some time, or else Julian is floating about with his quiver. I'm jolted back to reality when I place the two Kinsey books alongside *Adrift* on the counter, and the clerk says,

"Those two are going to set you back some, but they're worth every dollar." I concur, saying,

"Yes, they're amazing photos, aren't they?"

"Without a doubt," says the woman, who introduces herself as Mae Cowan, the owner of the store. "That book is getting hard to find. I buy them whenever I can, and they fly out of here."

"My name is Jake Spinner," I say offering my hand, which Mae shakes across the counter. "I have a friend who loves vintage books. She'll love this."

"Well, Jake," says Mae, "I put them out this morning. They must have been meant for you."

When Sunday evening finally comes, I feel the pre-show jitters when I arrive at the Foggy Beacon. I'm not used to being in the audience and I wish I had a projector to clean or some chairs to set up, or even some popcorn to pop.

At a quarter to six, the theater is close to filling two thirds of its one hundred and twenty seats. More people come in every minute, including the two guides from the whale park. By six, when Theodore walks down the aisle to the front of the screen, the theater is full.

"Good evening friends. Thank you for coming. I know a few of you came expecting naked spies and James Bond, but I think most of you know that is not what we have for you tonight. What we do have are some very personal and unique films. A visitor to our little island brought them here and I would like him to tell you about them and the people responsible for them."

Zing! I wasn't expecting that. Speaking in public does not frighten me, but it's not as if I'd been planning anything or that I thought about the films enough to say anything terribly intelligent. When I walk to the front of the theater, Theodore introduces me and the two whale guides lean over and start whispering to each other.

"Good evening everyone. I wasn't expecting to say anything tonight so I'll be brief and say how much I've been enjoying your lovely island. Some of you may know my truck, the *Lost Sons of Zhitomir*."

I overhear a few people whisper, "That's how you say that."

"These films were sent to me recently. They're short films, documentaries, if you will, about people all over the world who have been [I'm about to say afflicted but something stops me] cast into difficult situations. They were given cameras and enough assistance to tell the stories of their lives as seen through their own eyes and in their own words. The organization that helps them do this is called the Visible Past Project, and my next stop after I leave here is their annual conference in New York City.

"I hope you find something in the films and that you can see past their technical deficiencies. I hope that you appreciate these stories. Thank you for coming and also, thank you, Theodore Barker, for opening up the Foggy Beacon to show them."

I'd like to say that everyone is eager to see the films, but about a third of the people in the theater drift out as the films are shown. Those who stay grow quiet and thoughtful, and after years of reading audiences I can tell you that when the sisters from Sierra Leone start laughing as they take turns trying to fit their footless legs into special bike pedals fashioned for them, something snaps in the audience. They see the two sisters laughing, and though it's uncomfortable to do so at first, they too begin to laugh. I remember reading once that laughter is another way to cry. So, on one Sunday night in a secluded island off the beaten path, we cry together in a tiny little movie theater, our hearts touched by some unusual bedtime stories.

On Monday morning I meet Theodore at the Viceroy Donut Shop where Theodore is already dipping a donut. He takes out an envelope and hands it to me.

"Do you mind, Jake? Please send this on to the Visible Past Project for me." Inside is a check for five hundred dollars.

"That's very generous."

"No, not really, I'm sure they can use a helping hand. We took in quite a bit of it at the door. I wish it were more." Then Theodore lifts his donut from the coffee where it hangs suspended and dripping while he asks me, "How much longer do you expect to be around?"

"A few more days. It's a big continent and a long drive."

"Have you figured your route yet? Canada might be lovely this time of year. Things are pretty well thawed by now."

"I'll consider it. I have a month. I'll let the wind take me."

"Spoken like the true nomad. Too bad you have to go. You're fun to have around. Have you ever considered settling in somewhere? It is a good place to live, this island, even with all of its gossip. We sure could use a film man."

"I don't think so. There's already a film man here."

"Not for much longer. I'm thinking about getting out of the old Foggy Beacon soon enough. Time to move on to something new. I could make you a very decent proposal. You might like a theater that doesn't need new tires every fifty thousand miles."

We both laugh at that.

"No, thank you, Theodore, but I'm not there yet."

"Of course you're not. Who would be, what with the thrill of the road, something new each day, the endless peregrinations of a free spirit?"

"Something like that."

"Oh, well, it was worth a try. However, I'm not giving up on you, Jake. I shall keep you apprised of my intentions and give you the right of first refusal."

Three days later I drove Zhitomir on to the early morning ferry and after four hours of watching seagulls, cormorants, and sea lions, I set my sights east.

CHAPTER 19

# Three Tuxedoes

**In Which** we learn about tuxedoes and the legacy of
"The Wailing O."

I received this note from Julian in my last days on Lighthouse Island and I'm starting to wonder if all Spinners are clotheshorses. The card is Elmer Fudd dressed in white tie holding a shotgun across his chest at the ready. In the cartoon caption, Elmer says, "One must dwess pwoperly to hunt for wabbit."

*Jake,*                                                                                              *Today*

*Thanks for the call, how's life on the rock? A few more things about the up-coming VPP event -- the banquet is formal, but the other sessions you can get by with a suit. I have a spare suit if you need it. I'm looking forward to seeing you dressed in one of your tuxedoes. I hope you'll enjoy the Saturday panel. There's going to be a fair amount of hot air, but not much more than normal. Call when you get close; I've arranged a garage for your set up. I'm looking forward to seeing you, Jake.*

*Onward, Julian*

*PS. Nina P. is extraordinary. Be prepared, J.*

It is fair to wonder why a man who lives in a truck has three tuxedoes. I'll explain. Many fabulous things are brought to me after showing movies.

I'm not sure why, but people often give me souvenirs related to films, actors, or people who have had some connection to the movie. For some reason, they think I have some deeper connection to the films.

I am the proud owner of three suits of formal wear: one set of tails and two tuxedoes. I acquired and wear them in strange places. Each one has its own story.

I like to go "black tie" when showing *Tuxedo and Fur* films. *Tuxedo and Fur* films are movies where sophisticated people do sophisticated things such as drinking martinis, smoking cigarettes in holders, and commenting on everything from yachts to hairpieces. In *Tuxedo and Fur* films the women wear jewels provided by *Tiffany* and the hairdressers, gown makers, and makeup artists get special recognition in the pre-film credits. *All About Eve* and *Trouble in Paradise* by Ernst Lubitsch are my favorite *Tuxedo and Fur* films. Films from the thirties, where cocktail glasses tinkle as wealthy people are attended by nameless servants to the strains of a piano, are *Tuxedo and Fur* films. Any film with a dead fox dangling from a woman's neck is a *Tuxedo and Fur* film. Any film with a line item in the budget for mothballs and mustache wax is a *Tuxedo and Fur* film. Films made with pelts of mink, chinchilla, or sable before there were warning labels on cigarette packs or disclaimers certifying that "no animals were hurt in the making of this picture" are *Tuxedo and Fur* films. If Marlene Dietrich sings slow cabaret from a seductive androgynous stage, it is a *Tuxedo and Fur* film. Most films with Fred Astaire or Cary Grant are *Tuxedo and Fur* films. The tuxedo may not originally have been designed for Fred Astaire but it certainly never looked better on anyone.

The tuxedo is a strange thing. The garment originated in the late eighteen hundreds when a rambunctious gang of blue-blooded New York kids hanging out for the summer took scissors to their formal tails, creating the first dinner jacket. The impulsive creation was later named for the town in which the dandy boys did their cutting: Tuxedo Park. Due to their destructive whimsy (albeit a whimsy allowed only to those who can afford to destroy something expensive), they succeeded in both mocking their elders and creating a fashion that survives to this day. In this time of comfort and informality, it is baffling why the tuxedo still has a function, unless the flair, character, drama, pizzazz, panache, excitement, or leadership of the wearer is revealed in contrast with others similarly attired.

Enough of that, I can get carried away. Maybe it's this simple, people like to dress up. Different clothes make you feel different and we all need to feel different from time to time. I love to dress thematically for a film when I can. If I'm showing *On the Waterfront* -- I dress like a stevedore; if I show a Western -- I dress like a cowboy; I show *The Women* . . . it's tricky, but I dress like a woman. Yes, I did it once, never again, my profound apologies to all women.

I once wore a tuxedo at a livestock auction. The auctioneer, Riley "No Thumbs" Stokes, had wanted to attract attention to his business and hired me to show a film the night before his weekly auction. Why not? After browsing the livestock, you could watch a movie and eat. Not one to lose money on the deal, "No Thumbs" told me he'd start each bid five dollars higher than normal to make up the lost revenue. Of course, you won't be surprised that we showed a young John Wayne in *The Big Stampede.*

"No Thumbs" invited the local television stations and told me I'd stand out better in a room full of cowboys if I wore formal attire. "In a room full of horses the lone monkey stands out!" said "No Thumbs." It worked, too. No one will ever know how many people came to buy cows, how many to see the movie, or how many wanted to see a guy standing in a cow-pie wearing a monkey suit.

Tuxedo One. In Butte, Montana, in a thrift store frequented mainly by unemployed miners, I found an impeccable set of tails. Of how it came to be there the clerks had no memory, for it had hung unsold for many years. Someone said, to the sound of some amused laughter, that it belonged to the mine's chief financial officer, Roland K. Henry, who was often summoned to New York for meetings with "The Brass." The clerks laughed. I didn't get the joke until one of them, seeing my mysti-fied look, explained that in a copper mining town the clever working of brass into a sentence was considered worthy of a laugh. The two clerks then started a slightly impish discussion about whether the man needed the tails for financial meetings or, exchanging a not so subtle wink, wink, "because he liked opera." When the wink-winking subsided and the clerk removed the garment from its aging plastic bag, we found the suit had been made in Dublin, Ireland by *O'Sullivan and Sons: Tailors of Distinc-tion.* The tails fit as if they'd been tailored for me personally and I bought them for thirty-five dollars. Alas, a search of the premises failed to turn up a box of accessories the store manager swore he'd seen "recently" and which was meant to be included. As I was leaving, one of the clerks said to the others: "It would take brass balls for a man to wear such a suit in the Big Sky State."

Tuxedo Two was a gift from Caitlin Josephine Dwyer, the granddaughter of Bryan Connolly, who was once summer valet to William Waldorf Astor when he took up summer residence in the suit's original birthplace: Tuxedo Park, New York. The lovely Mrs. Dwyer told me the story of her grandfather, the tycoon's able and astute valet, and a former copper miner from the town of Castletowne Beare in southwest Ireland.

"It's very strange if you think about it. My grandfather had run from home to escape the mines and two years later he finds himself in the service of one of the wealthiest men in the world. Let me tell you, Jake, 'in the service of' is a far cry from being well paid by. It was my grandfather's job to make sure Mr. Waldorf Astor should never appear in anything less than a perfect wardrobe. He did his job well by making sure that any worn or unstylish garments were removed from his master's wardrobe. True, it is likely the removal of some of those garments was a wee bit hasty and the sale of those very same garments provided a welcome supplement to his wages. Further, it was that supplement which accelerated the reunification of his family, most of whom were still shoeless back in Ireland. And that, as we like to say, is simply what we call the luck of the Irish!"

Apparently, the family has an inclination towards clothing, because Mrs. Dwyer is the owner of Caitlin's Attire, a formal rental shop in Mitchell, South Dakota. Caitlin's Attire sits two blocks from the world famous Corn Palace" and has provided wardrobe to celebrities such as Bob Hope, Rosemary Clooney, Count Basie, and Joey Heatherton, all drawn to the unique Corn Palace, which the lovely owner is known to boast is "The Northern Tier's Greatest."

I did a showing there one winter, not in the main hall, mind you, which was equipped with a glorious projection booth and a magnificent 35mm projector, but in one of the side conference rooms. It was a benefit for Hilde Lund, a local resident who had lost her home to a flash flood during the previous summer. In the middle of the third-reel of *North by Northwest*, the real Maguffin hit us, a power outage (The Maguffin is what Alfred Hitchcock described as the unlikely event setting in motion an entire plot, e.g. a mistaken identity, etc. etc.) The darkened hall was evacuated and a small crowd was standing on the street in front of the Corn Palace surveying the scene. Minutes before, a large truck had skidded on the icy street and plowed into the main power pole causing the power outage. The darkened cold and icy street at once became very, very dusty when the truck's tarp blew off in a gust of wind, sending ten tons of corn meal flying in every direction. If you wanted to dust pastries you couldn't have done a better job than that gust of wind. Fortunately, the power was soon restored and we resumed the show.

Imagine a flour-coated assemblage of people, including me in my O'Sullivan tails. That is how I met Caitlin, who introduced herself by saying, "If you bring that suit to m'shop I can put the order back in it."

The next day, when I took the suit in, Mrs. Dwyer was dumbstruck at the suit's origins. She said that she had something that might interest me in her back room, and there she revealed a stunning tuxedo complete with shirt, cummerbund, sleeve pins, a tiepin, a black silk bow tie, and even a pair of shiny patent-leather shoes.

"Now, that's a worthy tuxedo," said Caitlin, "and I'd be surprised if you'll find anything like this in your average formal shop." Then, with a mischievous smile on her face, she laid open the jacket, exposing no label, but only the silk embroidered initials *W.W.A.* She told me the story of her grandfather and said she was tired of seeing the old suit hang all alone in the back of her store and would be honored if I would accept it as a gift. Of course, I begged to decline until Caitlin made her feelings clear.

"Look, I've been hanging onto this suit for decades now. Every three or four years I take it out and tell this story. Nobody around here cares and the suit does no one any good hanging in a closet. I want you to take it, wear it, and if you have a chance from time to time to tell how you got it, all the better. My grandfather was the first one of us to make any headway in this country, and it's a doozy of a tale if you ponder it. But the Irish in me holds that rags to riches might go back to rags if I hold on to this thing any longer. My girl is coming in here tomorrow morning and if you come back, she'll fit this thing to you better than your own skin." Then Caitlin Josephine Dwyer rocked back on her heels and, bringing forth her best Irish brogue said, "And that will be done for the pleasure that's in it."

Tuxedo Three is the one I will wear at the Visible Past Project banquet. It came to me one evening after a screening of *Woman of the Year* for the annual banquet of the American Association of University Women in Jefferson

City, Missouri. That evening I wore the Butte tails to lend "the proper air of
sophistication," as Lucille DeLorme, graduate of Smith College, 1912, had
requested. The Missouri Historical Society had recently acclaimed Lucille
as "the oldest living university woman west of the Mississippi River." Seeing
me in the suit, Mrs. Bernard DeLorme slowly but expertly adjusted my col-
lar and refolded my silk pocket square. "A proper Beau Brummell requires
attention to detail," she said with the right air of haughtiness. Ten minutes
later when I walked into the kitchen for a cup of coffee, a young woman in
her twenties admonished me that "wait-staff need not be in attendance any
longer." It took me a moment to convince her I was not one of the caterer's
waiters. Such can be the confusions with formal attire:  in a room full of
lionesses, a monkey can look like a monkey.

After the film (the most silent and reserved showing I'd ever done)
was over, I was putting away my equipment when a gentle old woman of
about ninety approached me. As the room cleared, she introduced herself as
Vitella Malcolm Brathwaite and began telling me about her husband who
had died six years earlier. She had a younger, very attentive but oddly silent,
companion at her side who I thought must be her caretaker. She told me
her husband had been a man about my size, a comment that seemed strange
at first, adding that in the Swing Era he had been a musician who traveled
the country playing trumpet with Artie Shaw. They later lived around Hollywood, where he worked in various bands. I sense this story is beginning so
I set my work down and bring over some chairs for the two women.

Then Vitella continues.

"My husband appeared in *A Star is Born*, the version with Judy Garland. It's the scene where Norman Maine finds Esther singing in the late
hours' nightclub. You are too young to remember this era, but as the popu-
larity of the bands gave out, it was harder for my husband to get work and
we returned here to our hometown where my husband taught music at
the high school until his retirement. They named the auditorium for him.
Orestes Dunbar Malcolm Brathwaite Auditorium, and they have his two
favorite trumpets in a case by the stage."

She goes on to tell me how after his death, she faced the hardship of living with, and finally sorting through, his things. "You see, I have a tuxedo
which my husband wore for many years. I'm a strong woman, Mr. Spinner,
but when I saw you in that suit, it reminded me of when Orestes was so
young and handsome and it made me cry. I couldn't bring myself to part

with it and I've always felt someone would come along who might appreciate it. I hope you don't think it strange."

Far from strange, it brought tears to my eyes and I gladly accepted the
gift the next day over chicken soup and fresh-baked rolls. Vitella's companion, who I learned was her and Orestes' mute daughter, Cornetta Lilybet
Brathwaite, served us lunch. Cornetta had baked the rolls that morning and
she took great pleasure as we ate them with butter and French apricot jam.
After eating, we looked through photo albums of the Malcolm family, including collections of the young "Wailing O," as he was known in his touring days. There were endless pictures of the teacher Orestes Malcolm working with students or standing proudly in front of a well-attired ensemble
bearing names such as "The Young Duke Ellingtons" or "The River Flood
Jazz Ensemble." When I said the "Wailing O" had left quite a legacy, a tear
fell from his daughter's eye and she embraced her old mother.

The silent daughter takes the photo album from her mother and flips
the pages, then points to a large black-and-white photo of the "Wailing O"
playing his trumpet on the set of *A Star Is Born* with a soulful Judy Garland
looking on.

"Orestes said he enjoyed working on that film. I even met Mr. George
Cukor at the production party when they finished shooting the picture."

Such is the unexpected kindness that brings us rare gifts.

I was pleased to respond to Julian's offer with this reply.

*Dear Julian,*

*Tuesday? Wednesday?*
*I'll take you up on the suit.*

*Love, Jake*

CHAPTER 20

# 5000 Kilometers As The Crow Flies

**In Which** we experience the Paprika Plains and shift transmissions into another gear.

I see a lot of truckers while driving and they see me, too. Sometimes they wave a hello, or from time to time they'll give a quick blast of the horn, but for the most part even with the fancy paintings on the sides of Zhitomir, it's another truck rolling down the road. Truckers see all the other trucks, and in a world filled with everything from circus rides to nuclear waste, The Lost Sons of Zhitomir is another teamster putting in a day's work.

I've been looking at the road atlas for weeks, thinking over a route between Lighthouse Island and New York City. It's a big continent and I've been pondering whether to opt for miles or kilometers. Of course, it's the same distance, but there's something intriguing about kilometers. It's a bigger number. I figure it's about 5,000 kilometers. I've got 31 days and I need to get there a few days ahead. If I can average one hundred seventy-eight kilometers each day, that's about one hundred twelve miles each day, I'll be there in time to get settled for the Symposium.

Nowadays, one hundred twelve miles, or one hundred seventy-eight kilometers, hardly seems like much of a drive, does it? I've known people who drive that back and forth to work every day. I bet they get numb after a while. But I'll venture a guess that before the twentieth century most people who ever lived on the planet Earth didn't travel one hundred seventy-eight kilometers from where they born in their entire lives. In less than a month I will roll across a vast concrete and asphalt pathway and I want to remind myself to see the rivers, mountains, prairies, and sky before me. This is to be the sixth such traverse of my life. Someday, maybe, I'll write another book and call it '*The Six Traverses of Jake Spinner.*' Probably not.

Even as I roll off the ferry I haven't marked out a definite route. Eric called the other night and he can fly into Toronto. I'll pick him up five days before the symposium begins and we can coast downhill all the way into New York City. I set my course eastward and start rolling.

For three days I've been letting go of the island. I miss the wind and staring at the water everyday, and the mountain air is different from the salt air, but I've found some comfortable places to stay and each day has a different sky, a different smell, and changed colors. My first night, I stayed at the Chinook Dreams Campground, where they smoke fish all winter in an old wooden smokehouse surrounded by huge furry cedar trees. When I woke up all I could think about was eating smoked salmon. The second day I had driven quite a bit further than my required increment when I found myself staring towards the foothills of the Rockies and found a little pullout where I could stare at the snow covered peaks. Normally, I get up early and drive until I find a place to eat breakfast and drink coffee. Some nights I eat out and others I take out my stove and make some quick soup while thumbing through the Kinsey photos. I've also read the article about Nina Palliatti a few times. I enjoy staring at her picture.

In a few days I enter Saskatchewan, near Dunsmuir, under a radiant colorful sky. It's not red or orange or gold but a dynamic chromatic canvas extending for hundreds of miles. I can't help but be affected by it. Part of me wants to pray, but instead I roll down the window and begin howling like a wolf. When I stop for breakfast that morning, I strike up a conversation about the color of the sky with a man from Saskatoon who tells me, "That's what Joni calls 'Paprika Plains.'" When I ask him, "Who's Joni?" he fires back a look that's equal parts contempt and dismay. "Why, Saskatchewan's own, Joni Mitchell, of course. She wrote a song called 'Paprika Plains.' Who else would it be?" Then he tells me what record it's on and later that day I detour into Regina and buy it on CD so I can listen to it while I'm driving. You can get it yourself and imagine what a few hundred kilometers of driving through Saskatchewan feels like.

Continuing eastward, I stop one afternoon in Manitoba near Dog Lake and try to phone Poliakhov, hoping I can detour north to see his place and enjoy another bout of kumis. But the person who answers the phone tells me, "Boss in Russia buying horses." Too bad, that would have been worth the drive!

By the time I get to Lake Huron, the days are noticeably longer. Despite the sunshine, the wind is still biting. It's the first time I've been "on top" of the Great Lakes which strikes me as odd. Canadians think of the Great Lakes as "down there" while most Americans think of them as "up there." Eighteen days on the road and I'm thinking about "up there versus down there." As I said, I cannot imagine what it's like to be a trucker. I'll bet some truckers have deep philosophical thoughts, at least the ones who don't listen to the radio constantly.

Then, slowly and steadily, the surrounding world changes. I sense the pace picking up as I head toward southern Ontario. It may even have been the change in the song Zhitomir sings as it rolls over roads. Smooth roads hum and all that rolling metal enjoys the harmony. But rough roads, roads filled with asphalt patches and the deterioration of thousands upon thousands of cars and trucks pressing into them every day, do not have harmony. Fred would not appreciate this next statement, but Zhitomir does not like all the holes in the road. Fred would say, "Buy a new set of leaf springs and quit complaining." In any case, the road has a different sound to it. The cafés are busier, and though the people are still friendly, they are more cautious. It starts getting even faster as I draw towards Toronto.

Welcome to the hum and buzz of more people.

The thing about hum and buzz is it feeds on more hum and buzz. This morning, when I stopped for breakfast, a trucker sitting next to me was talking about witnessing an accident in Quebec three days ago involving two chemical haulers. Before he could even describe what he had seen, another guy started telling about an explosion he saw once at a refinery in Louisiana, and before he could get his story out, yet another guy starts talking about a gas explosion he saw outside of Yellowknife. It was like watching a poker game with everyone holding good cards and no one knowing how to bluff. No one finished telling his story. They were on the go, and so was I. By the time I left that place I was hell bent for Toronto with Zhitomir reaching the rarified speed of sixty-seven miles per hour before I caught my breath again and backed it down to fifty. Eric's plane is scheduled to arrive at four o'clock this afternoon and I'm only forty miles away with eight hours to go. What's the rush?

The rush turned out to be three hours to find a place to park Zhitomir when an airport security patrol stopped me even before I reached the entrance. I finally convinced the officer that I wasn't crazy, and that he should at least let me go even if he would not allow me to enter the airport. At last, after inspecting the inside of Zhitomir, he escorted me to a motor hotel with a large parking lot and van service to the airport.

Precisely on time, Eric strides into the waiting area looking great. He has the refreshing demeanor of a young man coming into himself. He is tanned, stronger, and taller, with a short beard and recent haircut, although he's wearing a torn tee shirt with "There's No Reefer, like a Coral Reefer" written on it. That's Eric. When I ask him where the hair went, he says,

"Too hot in Palau to have all that mess and it got in the way of my scuba mask, Jake. No big deal, it's hair. It grows back."

Unlike myself, Eric hasn't had a gradual transition into things and as he puts it, he's "freaked out." "Man, Jake," he adds, "we have to get out of this mess."

"Eric, we're going to an even busier place."

"Yes, I know that, but at least I can get a day or two to adjust."

Then, shaking his head in dismay, Eric says, "What do you think all these people do?"

Our conversation over the next two days ranges from the fish in Palau to Fish in Kelton, Minnesota. Eric gets excited when I tell him about the life and times of Salvatore Boccacio.

"You're kidding me. The guy put the projector on Garth Hudson's organ? That is too much. Man, I missed some stuff."

Eric tells me about his parents and their plans to move to Thailand, about the film he mentioned on the phone and life in the South Seas.

"It's a different world, Jake. It's like when you first get there you've been dropped into some cheesy adventure film. You know, tropical breezes, fresh fruit, fish, sailboats, lovely tanned women, and it doesn't seem real. I spent my first month there waiting for the shoe to drop, but then it doesn't, and after a while you start taking on another sense of time and things don't seem so pressing."

"Did you like it?"

"Parts of it, for sure, but I'm not wired for it. I got tired of hanging out all the time. That's when I started the film. That kept me going."

Then Eric tells me why he needed to sell his van.

"I'm going to NYU Film School. I think I'm ready to take the plunge. Besides, Julian says he can help me get a scholarship and that I can live at his place. I'll need to talk to him about that." Then, out of the blue, Eric asks me if it's okay?

"If what's okay?"

"Staying with Julian." And before I have a chance to ask him why it wouldn't be, Eric explains. "You know, Jake, I mean he's your uncle and, well, I've always thought Julian was kind of yours, you know, kind of special, and I don't want to step out of bounds with you, Jake."

"That's thoughtful of you Eric, but you don't need my approval and you're not stepping on my toes. Julian is great for me and he'll be great for you."

If Toronto's hum and buzz was strong, New York is like a billion times Toronto. As we draw closer to the city, cars and trucks blow by us like we're standing still. As we get closer I get the feeling that if I let go of the wheel, some purposeful magnetic force will carry us into Manhattan. New Yorkers take for granted the power of their city. I remember the first time I came to visit Julian in New York three years after my mother died. I arrived by plane at night. I had the chance to look down on the illuminated pointillist mosaic that is New York. It scared and excited me then and it still does.

As Eric and I cross over the Tappan Zee Bridge, we get a distant look at the New York City skyline to the south. If I'm excited, I can only imagine what Eric must feel as he leans to the edge of his seat. He has become very quiet, but his eyes are bugging out of his head.

Thirty minutes later we're circling around a bizarre set of ramps leading to the Westside Highway beneath the George Washington Bridge when Eric quickly reaches into his bag and takes out his video camera.

"Man, I have to record this, Jake; first time in the center of the world for this boy from Oregon." Then Eric let's out some multisyllabic sound that is completely unintelligible.

"What does that mean, Eric?"

"That's Polynesian for 'It's good to be home!'"

It takes us a while to wind our way to the Eli Horton Hotel, especially as Eric insists we divert through the Tribeca neighborhood because he has an overpowering feeling we're going to run into Robert DeNiro. When we don't spot DeNiro, Eric says, "Well, Bobby must be out of town." So much for any small town shyness on Eric's part.

Julian has arranged for us to stay in the same hotel where the conference is taking place. The other night on the telephone he said, "I want to give you guys a taste of Hotel Life. It's on me. Also, they have a service garage here where you can park your truck. You owe me one; it costs more to park it than for you guys to stay at the hotel."

As for the Eli Horton Hotel, the entrance spills warm crimson light out to the street, reflecting from the mirror-walled lobby. Two doormen greet visitors as they step from their cars into the Circus of the Lost World's opulence that is the Eli Horton Hotel. There's enough gold leaf, carved marble, beveled mirrors, and polished brass to fill a theater. In fact, Zhitomir with its elegant theater fits in better at the Eli Horton than Eric and I do. The parking valet, Roberto, is apologetic when he greets us in a deep burgundy and black suit, the top hat on his head embossed with *E.H.* on it.

"It's a lovely truck, Mr. Spinner, and I would feel terrible if I did anything to hurt it."

The valet's supervisor, sensing a problem, comes over at once. After a brief consultation with Roberto, he says, "Mr. Spinner, we're terribly sorry, but our valet is unable to park your vehicle for you. We take great pride in our service, and we apologize for this inconvenience. If you don't mind driving your vehicle to the hotel's parking garage, the Eli Horton will gladly supply you and your companion with a complimentary dinner this evening."

"Oh, yeah!" exclaims Eric. "We're in New York!"

# CHAPTER 21

# The Definition Of Symposium

**In Which** we experience hotel life and listen to a man who takes seriously the definition of symposium.

Saturday, symposium day, I awaken to a dark room on the twelfth floor in the middle of a big city. It must be morning, but I can't tell because the thick curtains blocking out the windows in my room are closed. At last the clock on the room's dresser comes into focus. It's 10:30 a.m.! I can't remember the last time I slept this late. I'm groggy, grumpy, and my nose is dry from breathing circulated air. Even a shower doesn't wake me. I need a cup of coffee.

The elevator to the lobby opens onto a shimmering hallway replete with ruby-colored crystal chandeliers and polished marble floors, stout mahogany tables, velvet furniture, and more mirrors than you might find in the home of Narcissus himself. The Eli Horton lives up to its advertised "old world grandeur." The grand lobby of the Eli Horton Hotel is the embodiment of a *Tuxedo and Fur* film. I think the marble may owe its luster to years of fur being draped across it and I would not be surprised if the revolving door delivered Greta Garbo herself at any moment. The Eli Horton lobby shimmers with a euphoric and carefree gemstone light. Who wouldn't want to stay here?

Sean Penn, John Sayles, and Howard Dean walk by immersed in conversation, and a huge cluster of bright lights encircle a striking woman who moves through the commotion surrounding her as if she were alone on a beach. The other guests who have been making fast work of pastries, artistic plates of fruit, croissants and loaves of Italian bread, sculpted butter and silver bowls of various jams, hard-boiled eggs, thick slices of bacon, and pitchers of fruit juice: orange, grapefruit, mango, and black cherry, suddenly stop with their mouths agape as Sharon Stone and her entourage pass by.

After Ms. Stone passes, I need coffee fast, and soon pour it into a lovely china cup from a silver urn. As the thin liquid fills the cup and a weak acrid aroma rises to my nostrils, I am reminded that, "New York, the greatest city in the world and it has lousy coffee!" As I sip the weak coffee, I think fondly of Vaughn Raker and his concoction at the East/West. Sadly, I accept what is available and walk with the cup to join the lobby full of symposium visitors congregating in front of a phalanx of easels with poster boards holding the Top-Ten Film Lists.

There are thirty-one lists beside my own. You can purchase your ballot at a table off to the side where there is a large poster listing the names of those who are represented. The ballots cost not ten dollars as Julian had said before, but a more philanthropic fifty ("Tax Deductible," the poster reminds all). There's a line forming to purchase them! I am clearly not in Kansas anymore! My Top Ten list is in good company with those of Kofi Annan, Paul Newman, Maureen Dowd, Tom Hanks, James Gandolfino, Bernie Williams, Chick Corea, and Martin Scorsese, to name a few. However, there is one thing that sets my top ten apart from all the others: it's the only one people have to ask, "Who's that?" when they read my name on top of it.

With the coffee finally doing its job, I wander amongst the posted lists and notice two things. First, most of the lists resemble each other, and second, most resemble The American Film Academy's "Top 100 Films Of All Time." There are some exceptions, and I'm surprised to find another list which I think is mine because the first five films are *Babette's Feast, La Strada, Black Orpheus, In America*, and *The Secret of Roan Innish*, but the other five are not. They are *Two Women, Nights of Cabiria, City Lights, Madame Rosa*, and *Lone Star*.

The other three sides of the spacious lobby perimeter are lined with small three-sided booths in which the Visible Past Project's films can be viewed. Each booth is equipped with a DVD player, television, and headsets so visitors can watch the films and meet the filmmakers. One booth has a fourteen-year-old Tibetan girl named Sonam, who speaks perfect English and patiently answers questions about her film entitled *"How To Prepare Tibetan Momos."* Sonam is drawing quite a crowd, especially since she offers samples of the delicious momo, a tasty dumpling. Another booth has an elderly woman clad in a multicolored dress, who's from Turkey. Her film "Block by Block" shows how her family rebuilt their home after a devastating earthquake destroyed most of her village. Another booth has an enormous Russian woman named Olga, who speaks a few words of English while showing her film "The Oldest and the Fattest" which captures her life sorting fish on what she proudly claims is the largest fishing boat in the world. The film tells the surprising story of a culture of elderly women, usually grandmothers, who go to sea for long stretches of time to raise money for their families. Olga stands beside the monitor, proclaiming proudly in her thick Russian accent,

"That me: oldest and fattest person on ship."

Another booth has a small, dark, olive-skinned man who speaks softly. His film is entitled "Amazon Butterflies." It shows the world of the indigenous people of the Amazon River system who earn their living retrieving exotic specimens of the colorful insects for tourists or collectors. The booth draws a large crowd of people, and when I get close enough to see some of the footage I understand why. The color and setting are truly beyond any possible fantasy, and yet it is a real world, though one which the translator explains "is endangered by government restrictions on collectors seeking to protect the populations of the wild butterflies."

Sitting now, I'm off to the side watching, when through the revolving door comes Eric, wearing red canvas sneakers, blue jeans, and a T-shirt with "PALAU" written across the front. He's carrying a brown paper bag and has his camcorder slung over his shoulder. Spying me, he wends his way through the crowd and then reaches into the bag.

"Here, Jake, or do I need to call you A.L.?"

"Jake's fine."

"Well, Jake, I have something for you."

He takes out a tall paper coffee cup that says Café Borghese on it. Pointing at my cup, Eric says, "I can't drink that crap. No way. Do you know I had to walk six blocks to find this, and then, $3.75 each. But it was worth it." Eric hands me the cup.

"Eric, you have my undying gratitude."

"Pretty wild scene, heh, Jake? This is a blast. I like it! You know I saw Kurt Vonnegut in here this morning. I didn't know what to say. I love that guy. Then, I turned my head and it was Jennifer Connelly." I give Eric a blank stare that tells Eric I don't know who Jennifer Connelly is. "Jake, man, you have got to watch some new stuff. She's totally hot!"

When I ask him his plans for the day, he tells me he's going to wander around the panels, see if he can get some footage with the filmmakers or anyone else, and then he heads off. Eric can fit in anywhere.

Finishing my coffee, I finally fill a plate with food and spend some more time in the lobby looking at the lists. At 11:45 the crowd begins moving into the banquet room for the symposium's keynote address. Standing in the back, I'm distracted by doing a quick count of about six hundred chairs, set up in front of a stage and dais, behind which is suspended a large movie screen. I feel a tap on my shoulder. It's Julian, standing with Nina Palliatti and Senator Hilde Ghurkin.

"Jake, I'd like to introduce you to some people," says Julian, confidently directing each one of us together for the proper greetings. I know I shook the Senator's hand, I know I said something suitably polite like, "Pleased to meet you Senator," or "It's an honor, Senator." I know I made a witty remark about something, but I can't remember what, because most of the world, and certainly Senator Ghurkin, disappeared when I met the eyes of Nina Palliatti. I remember the touch of her cheek, how her skin was warm and smooth when she instinctively offered a polite, European two-cheek kiss instead of a handshake. I swear I smelled the cardamom that scented the first letter I received from her. I remember that Julian led us to the front of the room where we sat alongside the other invited guests, and listened to Senator Ghurkin welcome everyone to New York and speak about the importance of film and culture, and the evolution of a new world. I remember Senator Ghurkin introducing Nina Palliatti, who then spoke about the Visible Past Project. I remember vividly the warmth with which she presented the VPP filmmakers by name, with a short description of their films if they could not do it themselves in English. While Nina spoke, I forgot why I was in the room and I floated in an intoxicating vapor.

When the welcoming speeches came to an end, Julian came over to me and asked,

"What's up, Jake? Didn't I warn you? You better snap out of it because you're scheduled for the afternoon session at two-thirty."

As planned, Julian will host the panel for an audience of university film students. Besides Julian, Nina Palliatti, and myself, the panel includes Dr. Jesse Williams, Film and Society Professor at Missouri State University, Loki Nouveau, the editor of *Celluloid Nation,* an alternative film quarterly, a one-named artist, Folio, who works for The National Endowment for the Arts evaluating grant proposals for "New Media," and Victor S. Hayes, the Curator of Film for a New York organization called The Media Vault.

By the time Julian introduces the various panel members and I listen to their opening remarks, it is clear that I am out of my league. These people know film in ways I do not. They have a depth and range that is humbling and, unlike me, who knows little about films of the past ten years, they keep up.

In his opening remarks, Folio (who stands at least six feet six inches and has ears filled with dangling metal rings, dresses entirely in black including black nail polish on his thumbnails, and has two impressive scars flanking his navel resembling facing crescent moons, which he shows to the audience while explaining they are self-inflicted wounds to express solidarity with persecuted artists all over the world) speaks about film as "native intuition." Though there is nothing about Folio that gives a clear indication that he is native of anywhere, it doesn't matter. Watching Folio is like watching a tornado, and by the time Julian introduces me, I have tossed aside the much-revised speech from my all-nighter on Lighthouse Island. I simply introduce myself as A.L. Janus, explaining that my work and writings come from very personal experiences of watching audiences receive films.

After Julian finishes with the rest of the panel introductions he invites the audience to ask questions and we start with this.

"What do you consider the most important film ever made, and why?" To which Dr. Jesse Williams energetically responds, "D.W. Griffith's *Birth of A Nation* for its impact on the social fabric of a country struggling to come to grips with its racist heritage."

Loki Nouveau says, "J. Waters, *Pink Flamingos,*" which prompts a big laugh from the crowd and a few of the panelists, but Loki persists, "It broke open gender and shattered civility. No small accomplishment."

Then Victor Hayes jumps in with "Kubrick's *Dr. Strangelove,*" saying it pointed out the futility of the rational underlying the nuclear age. Discussion goes back and forth like this for some time with Julian deftly guiding things around the room and panel.

For the most part he keeps away from the exchanges but at one point says, "It should come as no surprise that we have different opinions about what is important."

A question gets shouted from the audience that turns things in another direction, "Is the notion of consciousness raising irrelevant if we consider the expanding role of the Internet?"

Folio is rabid with desire to take this question and he rises out of his chair with a persuasive argument that "consciousness and technology have become unified in an evolutionary process which has rendered indistinct the boundaries separating culture and art from machinery." Folio's physical presence embodies the "New Media" which he works with. He is otherworldly as he speaks of spontaneous fire ceremonies in the slums of Brazil, of neon tube launchings onto an auto dump in Seattle, of tire fires in Fresno, all presented as art, rage, or reflection on the world. I don't understand much of what Folio says, but when he gets excited his earrings start clanging against each other and when he stands up for effect, he looks like Dracula spreading his cape before draining another victim.

So it goes for another fifty minutes as I sit mute while listening to the panel discuss Eisenstein, Ray, Pialat, Wertmuller, Kurosawa, Oshima, Bergman, Mikhalkov, Riefenstahl, Costa Gavras, Szabo, Pasolini, Kubrick, Sissako, Fellini, Godard, Rivette, Buñuel, until Julian finally cuts us off to allow a few closing questions from the audience.

In my silence I've noticed that the audience are on average at least twenty years younger than most of the panel members. Finally, with time running out on the ninety-minute session, a small and compelling man confidently strides to the microphone and the room goes silent as people recognize Martin Scorsese. Scorsese looks over and flashes a knowing smile at Julian, then directs his question to the panel members.

"Would each of you please be so kind as to say what single film has made the greatest impact in your life, for any reason, personal or political, and how old you were when you saw it for the first time?"

Julian directs all of us to please answer the question with no qualification or discussion.

"*Shane*," answers Dr. Jesse Williams. "I was eight."

"*Pippi Longstocking*," answers Loki Nouveau. "I was nine."

"*The Man with the X-Ray Eyes*," answers Folio. "I was seven."

"*Cool Hand Luke*," answers Victor Hayes, "I was nine."

"*The Greatest Show On Earth*, I was seven," I answer.

"*Little Women*, I was seven," says Nina Palliatti.

Then Julian, looking at his watch, begins to thank the audience and the panelists and encourages everyone to attend the other panels and take part in the remaining activities in the lobby, but before he can close the session, Scorsese, still with the microphone says, "What about you, Julian? What's your answer?"

This stops the room as Julian turns around and smiles before answering,

"Laurel and Hardy, *Laughing Gravy*. I was about ten."

That brings to a close our discussion about "Film as a Consciousness Raising Tool" and starts an enthusiastic swarm of people around Martin Scorsese.

Much to my delight, before she is swept back into the whirlwind of the rest of her afternoon, Nina comes over to me and says, "You got that right, Mr. A.L. Janus."

I have no idea what Nina is talking about and I say so.

"Got what right? I had nothing to say."

"Not what you said; what you wrote." And she reminds me of 'Once we were children.' Each one of us was influenced by a film we saw as a child, Jake."

The rest of the day roars by. Julian stops me in the lobby during a break in one of the panels and says, "Everything's going well. I hope you're having fun. Are you in love yet?" Before I can even form a reply, he's off again.

When I get back to my room it's close to five o'clock. Now I get to take a long hot shower and use all the towels I want. One could get used to hotel life.

Before I take my shower, Eric knocks at my door with some news. "I told you we'd see him: DeNiro is here."

"Did you talk to him?"

"Are you kidding? I tried to get close to him but my mouth went dry? Maybe he'll be at the banquet?"

"I thought you weren't attending the banquet?"

"I wasn't," says Eric with a mischievous smile, "but what do you think about this, Jake? Julian got me into the banquet and I'm sitting with Jennifer Connelly!"

"Great, be sure to impress her with the Palau shirt!" I kid Eric, who kids right back.

"No, Jake, it's black tie," he says making a sizzling sound as he draws his fingers under his chin. "Style city, have to look pretty. I'm meeting Julian outside in a few minutes. He's said I can borrow one of his tuxedoes. I should have thought to bring one of yours."

Eric will look outstanding in a tuxedo.

At seven o'clock I am escorted to my table for six in the formal dining room of The Eli Horton Hotel. The room is filled with about fifty tables with place cards, and I'm the first to arrive at mine. I'm surprised to see the other names include Senator Ghurkin and her husband Michael, Julian, Nina, and Folio. Unfortunately, I saw Folio leaving the Horton with a young woman from the afternoon session who asked him about "state suppression of eroticism" so I'm not expecting him to be at dinner. Too bad, dinner with Folio would have been unpredictable and entertaining.

Expecting that Nina Palliatti will be making the rounds throughout the banquet, this is shaping up to be a rather lonely table. However, after a few minutes, a waiter removes the Ghurkin nametags, explaining they received word that the Senator had to return to Washington, D.C. unexpectedly. The waiter then sets a new tag in one of the places with none other than the name Tanner Scofield, which brings a huge smile to my face. Tanner is Julian's closest friend. Now I know the evening cannot be dull. Before Julian and Tanner arrive, I see Eric across the room engulfed by Julian's borrowed tuxedo, but speaking with a lovely young woman I assume is Jennifer Connelly. I wave in his direction, but Eric appears to be entranced and he isn't looking further than his own table.

Finally, Julian arrives with Tanner, and Nina comes by long enough for all of us to say how lovely she looks. She is tastefully elegant in a sleeveless black gown with an amber silk shawl draped over her shoulders. She doesn't get to sit down before she gets swept away again and moves table to table, her amber shawl reflecting like a flame of golden light. It's the final chance for the VPP's Director to connect with people, agree to radio interviews, arrange for articles in *Newsweek* and *Time*, and "raise a small blip on the radar screen of a world's conscience," as Nina said earlier today at the keynote session. She is too intelligent to believe all these people truly care about her work, but she cares about it, and her devotion doesn't allow her to dull her sincerity or conviction. All day I've observed her engaging one person after another with her ideas and the needs of the Visible Past Project. No matter how frivolously the conversation may have begun, Nina finds a connection and speaks with the other person as if nothing else matters but the shared moment. You cannot help but be moved by this woman, and if observing her work the banquet room is exhausting, watching her is not. Even as they begin dropping plates of food in front of us, Tanner, Julian, and I are content to enjoy our drinks and show little interest in the food.

Tanner has wasted no time getting revved up, no doubt availing himself liberally of the bar in the rear of the hall. His martini glass still half full, speaking a perceptible level or two above the room's din with a hint of his famous sarcasm, he pokes at his plate with a fork and says, "I never eat an animal I can't identify." Tanner Scofield, a.k.a. Oleg Padrewlski, is a small man in his mid-eighties who, defying his age, retains an impressive Einsteinian head of wiry black hair and a set of perfect teeth. He has the look of a well-tailored, bow-tie-wearing fox terrier. Tanner survived the Nazi occupation of Poland, then came to the United States where he changed his name but not his take-no prisoner's attitude. He is witty, irascible, and he loves to drink. Tanner is a semi-retired screenwriter whose credits spanned the forties to the eighties, and if there is one man with more energy than Julian, it's Tanner.

Julian, ever the catalyst, asks, "What do you think of the film lists, Tanner?"

Bang! Not that he needed the prompt, but Tanner is now unleashed and speaks in a voice that carries to the surrounding tables.

"Do we have any good reason to expect a decent, God-fearing United States Senator to have something subtle, foreign, or off-beat on her list? No, but it would be nice. my friends: *Field of Dreams, The Wizard of Oz, Casablanca, Steel Magnolias, Some Like It Hot . . .*" Tanner shakes his glass and takes another sip before continuing. "It's like a guest list by the *Great Gatsby*: even the good ones should be embarrassed. All the lists: they're all 'nice' in that 'turn this over to your press secretary' kind of way. I walked around and as I read them I started thinking of Nixon watching *Patton* all the time when he was president." Julian looks over at me and winks as Tanner heats up.

"Maybe that's all we can expect of a culture whose myths and lore are more concerned with profits than art. It's a fact, and it's not worth getting into a fuss about, but all the same, once I'd like to see Dassins' *Rififi* or *The Wages of Fear* on someone's all-time favorites list, even *Fritz the Goddamn*

*Cat*! Do you think any of them beside Scorsese, Sayles, and Penn even know who Godard is?"

It's Tanner's table and he's taking no prisoners. He barely notices when Nina returns to the table and takes her seat. She looks exhausted now, as she leans against her elbows on the table and rests her head on her hands.

"You know, all the newspapers list the top-grossing films as an item every week now. Not *Variety*, but every paper large enough to have an entertainment supplement. What damn difference does it matter to the public how much money a film makes? Are audiences supposed to feel a sense of accomplishment because they're making someone else rich?"

Nina smiles at Julian and me to let us know she's enjoying the tempest in which she has landed. That's good, because Tanner has more to say. "Then there's the army of film critics who aren't critics at all because being critical means thinking for yourself, and arriving at and stating opinions which may occasionally be negative; and negativity, why that's become as feared as polio was in my day. No, instead they blah blah blah about the 'feel good movie of the summer' or 'blah blah blah has more action than blah blah blah.' The truth is there simply aren't that many stories to be told once you get past Shakespeare and the Greeks, so who can blame movie makers for making the same thing over and over again? The beauty is in the retelling, in adapting a story to a fresh time or an unexpected context. How many Westerns were moral polemics during a time of political censorship? Today they call any modern day adaptation of *Romeo and Juliet* 'bold and controversial storytelling!' So, to answer your question about the lists: it would be nice to see that some of the prominent invitees had at some point in their lives been exposed to a mythology larger than *Some Like It Hot* and *Easy Rider*."

Now Tanner, barely out of breath, downs the remains of his drink, then holds the glass aloft until he gets a server's attention and tells her, "Listen, Sugar, there's fifty dollars in this for you if I get this back in the next five minutes." The waitress scampers off with every intention of collecting on the offer.

Now Tanner looks at me.

"Well, Jesus Christ, I've been talking so much I haven't even taken a minute to greet the rambling man himself. Look at you; you're a far cry from that skinny little kid Julian lugged around. How the hell are you? Julian tells me you're out chasing windmills? Is that back in vogue?"

"No, I found the windmills and I'm on to the North Pole."

"Oh, Christ, Julian, he can't be related to you. He's smarter than he looks."

"Thank you, Tanner. It's good to see you again. You're looking well."

"That's right, above ground and not dead."

Tanner's drink returns, a smile comes to his face and he hands the waitress the promised fifty dollars, saying, "You're doing great, Sugar. Keep it coming and there's another twenty in it."

Julian, perhaps feeling the need to point out to Tanner that our hostess has returned, says, "Tanner, do you think Ms. Palliatti needs to hear all of your oratorical repertoire in one night?"

To which Nina jumps right in and says, "No, please do continue, Mr. Scofield. After the day I've had this is delightful." Hearing this, Tanner looks at Julian and sticks his tongue out.

"Delightful, Spinner. Did you hear that?" Then pausing for a second, Tanner continues. "So, my friends, do you know what a 'symposium' is? Do you?" The question is directed at no one in particular but Tanner's eyes fall to me for a response.

"Yes, of course I do. A gathering to exchange ideas."

"Not bad," says Tanner to Julian. "He's a smart kid, your nephew, but that's not entirely correct." Then he turns to Nina, "And you Dr. Palliatti?"

"A festive summit of ideas? There's an Italian word I can't remember..."

"She's smart too," Tanner says, "but you're both wrong, and I dare not ask the elder Spinner here lest he give us some long reply which will also be wrong."

Tanner reaches into the breast pocket of his tuxedo and pulls out a slip of paper.

"I wrote this down a while back and I keep it here for these occasions." Then he reads.

"From the *Oxford English Dictionary*. Definition number one of the word symposium, its origin is Greek: A drinking party. A convivial meeting for drinking, conversation, and intellectual entertainment." He pushes the paper on the table. "Look, see if you want, but you know it's true, so I suggest you begin upholding your part of the deal."

A half-hour later, he's still going with only two more drinks in him. Slightly mellowed, he starts speaking about the movies he saw in the lobby this morning.

"Dr. Palliatti, storytelling isn't easy. It's not like we're huddled together by the fire on the prairies or stirring coals in the middle of a cold peasant winter in the old country. Finding an audience is hard enough. You can spend your entire life finding the words or the pictures to tell a story well, only to find out there's no one to tell it to.

"When I was starting out in Hollywood I knew this guy from the coffee shop I went to every morning. He claimed he'd written two thousand screenplays and hadn't had a single one made into a film, and he'd sit there ticking away on a typewriter making all the other writers envious of his ability to work amidst the hubbub. If you asked him about his stories, if you didn't believe he'd written them, you'd be in for quite a surprise because he could recite them scene by scene, over and over again, never getting them confused, whether telling it to the newest doubter or simply retelling to someone who enjoyed 'seeing the movie again over coffee. No doubt he spawned quite a few 'made' screenplays in that coffee shop, because there are only so many plots. It's like that great line spoken by desperate Joe Gillis, played by William Holden in *Sunset Boulevard* when his script gets trashed by Betty Schaeffer, played by Nancy Olsen: 'That's the problem with all you readers, you know all the plots.' Every trained screenwriter has etched the mantra of 'plot is everything' inside their heads, but every good producer knows that plot had better have color, taste, texture, and, better still, a come hither full-bosomed starlet in a revealing low-cut gown, or the movie won't work. Yes, even the simple pristine stories of your filmmakers, Dr. Palliatti. It isn't easy. I commend you."

Tanner finally exhales and rises to his feet.

"Julian, my friend, if you'll be so kind, I think I'd like an escort to the men's room."

Julian and Tanner walk off together, two old friends arm in arm.

At first, Nina and I sit quietly. We exchange simple questions about our work. She tells me about Africa and I tell her about Booker. The words don't matter so much as their tone and after a few moments we share stories of longing. "We are both motherless children," Nina says. "All motherless children feel alone." Nina tells me about growing up with her father. I tell her about Fred and Julian. "You would have liked my father, he sounds like your Uncle Fred."

When I tell her about Clara, Nina says, "You need to visit her. People don't stay young forever."

There is no reason why the two of us should be confiding in each other, needing each other, and drawing closer. In a crowded room of people, in the center of New York City, in an awkward, shared second, we reach our hands into an intimate weave of fingers.

By the time Tanner and Julian return, the banquet has lost much of its energy. Most of the tables are cleared and the staff scurry to and fro cleaning up. Tanner leans forward, resting his elbows on the table as Julian speaks. "This room reminds me of a politician's funeral."

"What the hell does that mean, Spinner?" asks Tanner.

"It means the only mourning is when the bar closes," says Julian.

"Who said the bar was closed? My girl is on the way with another round." Then, turning his gaze to Nina and exhaling deeply, Tanner says, "Julian, there are a few things I've been meaning to say."

"Oh no, we're in for it now." says Julian. "You know he gave a fifteen minute speech at The Academy Awards?"

"Sixteen, to be precise, but that was before it was televised, so let me say what I want to say. First, I've been meaning to thank you for bringing me here to meet this beautiful woman. Second, you understand, Dr. Palliatti, that your work will be best served if it never so much as touches a large screen or a Hollywood promotional campaign? It would be ruined. Don't you agree, Jake the Teamster Spinner?"

"Why should I agree with that?"

"Because you're an honest man, Jake. I read your stuff in that rag your uncle started and from what you describe, you've seen an America I've never seen. I'm an immigrant, you know, and there are only so many doors open to 'your huddled masses yearning to be free.' Don't get me wrong, America has been good to me, but I've only lived in New York and Los Angeles. I was seventy-five years old before I swam in the Pacific Ocean. You write from places I can hardly imagine, and you see things I wouldn't know exist if you didn't share them."

"Mr. Scofield," says Nina, "you're right. Jake's essays are not about the movie shows. They are about a seldom revealed world."

"Come on, I show movies in little towns and describe what happens."

"True, Jake," says Nina, "but you're the only one who sees what you do. It's unique, rare, and tender."

Then, in what may be the first time in my life I've actually said the right thing at the right time, I say, "Much like yourself, Miss Palliatti."

"See, he's a Spinner after all," says Julian flashing a proud grin.

It's 10:15 p.m. on a Saturday night in New York. There'll be no more money made, no more issues discussed, and the Visible Past Project can continue its mission for another year, having received the generous support of its admirers. Julian, ever onward Julian, shifts gears. "They say that all great cities have secret treasures, and I know where this city keeps one of hers. I'm hungry for some real food. My treat."

CHAPTER 22

# How To Write
# A Love Scene

**In Which** we receive two dissertations: one on an 18th century French painting and the second on hot dogs.

New York is a big city packed onto a small island. Like in all fabled places, if you are lucky, deserving, and diligent you will find buried treasures there.

Ten minutes after Julian, Tanner, Nina, and I pile into a taxicab in front of the Eli Horton Hotel, we find ourselves walking downstairs to the basement floor of a refurbished brownstone building that houses La Violette Restaurant. La Violette has six tables, no other patrons, and a massive fireplace offering a crackling fire that warms the room.

The restaurant is the passion of Julian's friend, Florian Chamberry, who, though born in France, now lives in New York and directs North American sales of French soaps for Savon. As Julian told us in the cab, selling soap is a job, but running a restaurant is a passion. La Violette is open only on Fridays and Saturdays, and until two a.m., so you can still have a meal after a show. Florian and his family live in the upper two floors.

The ambiance is Renaissance, but the music is cacophonous and loud when we enter the vacant room. Fortunately, a young man scurries into the kitchen and in a few seconds the room is silent except for the trickle of water in two crystal fountains. The same young man directs us to a table with stout, upholstered chairs and we take our seats beside one of the many replicas of French paintings that adorn the creamy plastered walls of the room. The painting is "L'union de l'Amour et de l'Amitie" (The Union of Love and Friendship), identified only because Julian's asks the young man who will be our waiter, and is pleased to provide the answer.

"Paul Prud'hon 1793; Monsieur Prud'hon lived and painted from 1758 to 1823."

Then, Julian, expecting Florian, asks where Monsieur Chamberry is and the polite young man explains to Julian,

"Monsieur Chamberry is in New Orleans for the weekend at a sales conference for soap importers."

Hearing this, Tanner cannot hold his tongue any longer. "Imagine that, a soap sellers' Mardi Gras. In a town like New Orleans I'll bet they can get themselves worked into quite a lather." Nina laughs and then reaches across the table to hold Tanner's hand. Tanner is very pleased by this. "You see, a real woman appreciates a bad joke." When the waiter asks us if we'd like anything to drink, Tanner says, "I'd like a double Scotch please, unless we're eating frog legs. I hate frog legs after Scotch." Julian and Tanner have raised enough trouble together that it doesn't take much of a look from Julian to indicate to Tanner that he needs to ease up.

Nina says, "That's all right, Tanner, I agree. Frog legs go so much better with gin. Please make mine a double."

"There," says Tanner. She can drink too."

Eating and drinking is a good way to finally let down from the frantic past week, and thankfully, the meal is not frog legs, but a hearty recipe of beef stew and potatoes from the Chamberry family farm in Bordeaux, topped off by a romaine salad and then fresh Camembert cheese.

In complete defiance of his age, Tanner has an impressive ability to shift mood and remain eloquent as his body metabolizes alcohol with impunity. Reaching a more reflective plateau, he raises his glass as if to offer a toast, but instead out comes a speech worthy of Albert Finney in *The Dresser*.

"I believe you've gotten me drunk," he admits languorously. "Not that I'm admonishing you for this; rather I thank you, as I dwell far too seldom in the realm of the spirits." I'm certain Tanner is aware he's doing Finney, and except for the occasional hint of a long suppressed Polish accent, his Shakespearean tone is perfect. "Now I cast my gaze upon this creation suspended before us."

Nina adds, "Yes, I've noticed you looking at that painting, Tanner. Does it mean something to you? I've never seen it before."

Tanner continues, though Finney begins to fade back into Tanner. "No, my dear, I have not, I've never seen it before, but it holds me. Is it too pretentious to say it is speaking?"

"What does it say?" presses Nina, and in this moment I can imagine what Nina is like when she is doing her work. She is very gentle with Tanner, and though I doubt he needs much prodding, Nina is coaxing him along in a way that would be impossible for either Julian or me. Tanner continues,

"It tells me Monsieur Prud'hon never had to please a producer."

Julian exhales audibly and playfully alerts us,

"I think we're about to become enlightened; we all better fill our glasses and get comfortable."

"Thank you, Julian, for that," continues Tanner pointing a finger at the painting. "Simple, innocent, mythic, the essential ingredients of any successful story, disregarded time and time again by people who should know better."

"The myth or the innocence?" asks Nina.

"The simplicity. What we call myth evolves out of the simplicity of something that repeats itself over and over in such a way that it is familiar to everyone. Tell me," Tanner presses us, "what do you see in the painting?"

"Cupid lurking behind the oblivious lovers," I say.

"A woman feigning disinterest," says Nina.

"A glowing torch and wings," I add.

"A red rose garland," says Nina.

Julian and Tanner exchange a satisfied glance as Tanner continues.

"Look closely: Love and Friendship are characters in this little drama. They are not *in love*; they are all lovers and all friends. He carries the fertile torch of desire while she, beneath a deep and beckoning blue velour cloth, conceals the vessel holding the eternal continuation of the species. Look at that mischievous Cupid doing his best to make sure that the cloth will be removed at some point."

At this point in Tanner's speech, Julian catches my eye and furtively points to the door leading to the kitchen. I see the door slightly ajar and the waiter peering at our table, listening to Tanner. As Tanner continues, I nod to Nina who is now part of the subplot in Tanner's story.

Tanner raises his hands, thumbs touching, index fingers pointing up to frame the scene like some cliché director. He speaks in a rapid-fire staccato. "She looks away . . . He gazes at her face . . . His confidence is buoyed by the warmth of his torch. He knows he will prevail, because a man with wings can fly . . . He is invincible . . . She is doomed to succumb to her desires. Fade and Wrap!"

Tanner holds his glass firmly and takes another sip.

"I'm a scriptwriter and it's my job to know human nature. My guess is that most women would be drawn to anyone who possessed both fire and flight."

"I told you to get comfortable," chortles Julian. "Tanner, you are the last of a dying breed."

Tanner finds Finney again and bellows, "You, Sir, please refrain from using that blasted death word around me. As I grow older that is an inevitability I am forced to come to peace with, but which I still seek to evade."

Tanner's bellowing alarms the waiter who betrays his listening when he lets go of the door that squeaks back and forth.

"What I mean by that," Julian replies, "is that you are one of the few remaining who understand the classical nature of storytelling."

To which Tanner replies, "That's a polite way of saying I've had dozens of stories rejected by producers who complained my work lacked immediate action or raw sex."

Tanner points to the painting again and Nina squeezes my leg under the table while nodding to the kitchen door which slowly opens again.

"You can see that our painter lived in a time when the world was still driven by a more natural sense of the inevitability of reproduction. You are all smart enough to know that's a fancy way of saying it was okay to be horny! There was still a lot of room on the planet. Not like today, when you can barely take a step without stepping on the toes of one of our brethren. The disposition of this painter was not one of haste and tension: Monsieur and Mademoiselle Amitie and Amour will be making babies, and you won't have to wait too long. Anyone of that time who viewed this painting knew exactly what was going on. Today, you'd have to strip away the cloth, enlarge the genitalia, and the torch would be a gun."

Our waiter, who has up to now been content to remain hidden, comes out from the door and takes a seat on his hands.

Now it's Tanner's turn to join the conspiracy and he waves the waiter over to the table and says, "I'm glad you finally decided to join us. Why don't you pour yourself a glass of wine and stay for a while?"

Nina, pointing an accusing finger at Tanner, says, "You knew he was there the whole time?"

"Of course, I did."

"But how?"

"By watching the three of you play 'let's make fun of the old drunk writer.' Now, if you can all settle down I can continue.

"Talk about storytelling:  a lot has changed in my lifetime. Look at Stanley and Stella Kowalski. Did Tennessee Williams need to reveal the consummation of the bestial attraction between those two? Did he have to take us behind the curtain so we can witness Blanche being taken to her inevitable fate? No, of course not, but if Kazan were making that film today it would be obligatory that he show Stella full bosomed and naked inside of the first fifteen minutes to get the rating. And that wouldn't be enough. The publicity department would launch a campaign all over the country to make sure you understood there was more to come, because Blanche is the star, not Stella. They'd launch a teaser, filling billboards and Sunday supplements, saying something like, 'You thought the first fifteen minutes were shocking! The ads would make sure we know that we get a peek at Blanche also. And you can forget Vivien Leigh, only one of the finest actresses ever to take script in hand. No, opposite some sculpted, modern-day Brando would be cast an Amazonian doll that could make normal women cry while their men chewed off their knuckles. My last years in Hollywood taught me to use terms like 'impactful, gripping, and passionate,' in place of 'lurid, graphic, or sexual.' The old standbys 'spine tingling, relentless, and compelling were no longer strong enough."

Looking directly in my eyes now, Tanner says, "Certainly, you, Abraham Lincoln Janus, have formed an opinion about this in that luxury of time afforded you while rolling around the world."

Now it is Nina's turn to coax a reply out of me, only this is done with a simple look while awaiting my reply.

"I'm speaking as Jake Spinner on this one, Tanner; but I've never thought of the scenes you described in *A Streetcar Named Desire* as love scenes. I think the only true love scene is the one between Mitch and Blanche."

Julian's head falls forward and then he blurts out, "Oh, and I thought we were winding down."  But Nina asks me to go on and I continue.

"I'm not saying anyone ever called those love scenes, but Mitch's fumbling, his embarrassment over his sweaty shirt and pride in his physique; I suppose, his genuine innocence contrasted against Blanche's need to find hers in the wreckage of her life; that's a love scene, though a complicated one for sure."

"You're on to something there, young Spinner, I'll give you that."

Then Nina asks, "Would you be so kind then, Tanner, to tell us some of your favorite love scenes?"

Tanner now shifts in his chair, and for the first time there is something revealed in him now that wasn't there earlier, as if the alcohol, the words, and the exchange of ideas have opened the gate to the fortress inside which lives Oleg Padrewlski, and from which he is happily sprung.

"First, you should know, Nina, that I've been asked and have answered this question many times. It was a standard question posed to lecturers at film schools. In fact, at one time Syd Field and I joked about adding a chapter to his book, *How to Write A Screenplay*. Syd said, 'No way' he'd do that. I asked him 'Why not?' and he said 'Why give it all away in one chapter when I could make a killing with a whole new book on the topic!'

"It's not easy to pick them out of a hat, but I have two favorites. Every time I've watched *A Star is Born* I get a pang when the Judy Garland character, Vicki Lester, tells the studio head over the phone that she can't make movies anymore . . ."  Hearing Tanner refer to the movie, I think of "The Wailing O" and the suit I'm wearing.

"Lester is a star at the top of her game and she is speaking of endearing affection and devotion -- to her fading husband, Norman Maine, the man who breathed life into dreams she didn't even know she had until she met him. She's willing to give it all up to save the hopeless man she loves. Is it real? Are they the two most sympathetic characters we've ever known? No, but it's incredible screenwriting to craft a love scene between two people and one of them isn't even in the room but sleeping off his final bender, dying in the shadows."

"And the second?" asks Nina.

"The second is far less serious and I love it. Lubitsch, the great Lubitsch, I wish I could have worked with him. *Trouble in Paradise*, 1932, a great movie year and there are two great love scenes in the film. I like the first one the best, when Lily and Gaston first meet and pickpocket each other while dining. The exhilaration each one feels when they find their thieving soul-mate is delightful. It's all capped off by the famous Lubitsch touch. In this case the first kiss of Lily and Gaston on the love seat followed by a fade to the now empty love seat. The rest, well, is as we say, the rest."

"There're a lot of different love scenes. A love scene can be a woman with a tumbler of gin in one hand and a telegram in the other, her face puffy from crying, as she reads her man isn't ever coming home from the war, like in *Summer of '42*. A love scene can be playful and comic, with a curtain dividing a bed, like in *It Happened One Night*; it can be complex and bestial on a beach like in *Swept Away*. You can have a love scene between two lunatics driven by the moon, like in *Night of the Iguana*, written by my old friend John Huston. Believe me, if he didn't get it right, Tennessee Williams would have let him know. You can have two septuagenarians reading Emily Dickinson aloud to each other if you know how to make it work.

"Love can have sadness, can result in redemption or failure, it can be one-sided, even unconsummated, and it isn't so easy to put all that complexity into a single scene. A love scene depends on everything before it."

Tanner says derisively, as if answering the same producers who have rejected his work over the years, "Love isn't lust, groping and disrobing before a flurry of close-shot bell-jar kisses, the kind Hollywood stars learn, and what publicity people sell as passion.

"Sex and love are different. It isn't what happens in the bedroom so much as what happens before. Today, those Hollywood hacks write love scenes with no soul. They throw two physical specimens together; strip the clothes off the women to get the 'R' rating, tease the audience with a few peek-a-boo shots, and it's all done in the first twenty minutes so they can get on with the film. To succeed as an actor today, you had better know how to take your clothes off. Not so in the thirties. There weren't going to be any clothes taken off in those times, so the challenge was to capture love before it was physical and allow the audience to fill in the missing parts."

Renewing his energy, Tanner takes a sip from his glass and continues.

"But, enough of me, let's play the game -- I ask, you answer. Don't think first. What is love, Jake?"

"Love can be a common focus and admiration. Love is how two people meet, what they see in each other."

"Your turn, Nina."

"Love is how they turn away to conceal their shyness, how they struggle with being close, how their lover's breathing is captivating."

"There you go. It's always the woman who gets it right," says Tanner, and then surprises Julian who has been quiet for a while.

"What about you, elder Spinner?"

"Love is Tracy Lord and Dexter Haven, Cary Grant and Katherine Hepburn in *A Philadelphia Story*. Two unyielding aristocrats vying for dominance like opposite poles of a magnet."

"Right, nice safe answer, Spinner," says Tanner, "but that was the thirties and the forties and the fifties. It all got opened up in that sweeping naturalism of the Vietnam era. We were allowed to be natural, no more Hays' office; we could show bodies and things never before seen. Have you ever read the Code? The Code was designed to uphold the morality of an entire country. Hah! Look at it sometime, and then examine what it did. Every single thing the Code sought to preserve it ended up destroying." Tanner exhales, but he's clearly not finished. "What is our favorite fruit?"

"Forbidden fruit," says Nina.

"Right, you're catching on. Thirty years of forbidden fruit let the apples ripen to an impossibly tempting sweetness. But we were forbidden to show the fruit. We understood its flavor and we wanted it as much as anyone today, but we had to be more clever.

"You see, that's love, and from the vantage point of someone who's beyond the draw of carnal love, that's a love scene I can write. What happens behind the closed doors, that's something else, and if you want to put it on screen, go ahead and get in line for mediocrity because there's lots of it being done."

"What was the first love scene you wrote?" I ask Tanner. "Oh, you'll love this. I was working on a nothing picture with Earl Cowell, one of the last giants of the early age. The picture has an eight-day filming schedule, still in the old system, mind you. Cowell didn't worry too much about scripts, he fired the original screenwriter and then they hired me to do any fill-ins. He called me the skinny Polish Kid. Cowell, he barked a lot and hoped things worked out like they did in the twenties.

'Get me lighting, get me wardrobe, get me make-up, and get me the skinny Polish kid! Write me a love scene and have it ready in two hours!' And he meant it. There's not a thing tying the two characters together and I have to write a love scene for them. I'm twenty-eight years old, my marriage is shot, my life is a mess, I haven't made love in over a year, and I have to write a love scene in two hours between two people who don't know each other and the same thing that is killing my marriage is dictating movies at that time: you can't reveal anything too truthful. She's a poor girl who got thrown out of her home, he's a rich guy off to prove to Daddy he's worth the inheritance. Pretty lightweight stuff, and, as I said, the Code may be a little looser in the post-war environment but still hovering like the rhythmic requirements of a sonnet."

"So, what did you write?" asks Nina.

"I'm getting there. When I leave the set I've got no idea what to write and I'm starving, so I walk to the commissary and there I see these two extras who don't have enough money so they're sharing a hot dog. They're sitting at a table and each one has half a hot dog on a lonely porcelain plate. They didn't even have money for coffee.

"As I'm watching them, I close my eyes and start dreaming everything I hadn't allowed myself to want or feel or demand or accept or believe was possible, and I had to do it quickly. I know you can appreciate the inspiration of a deadline. You can't write love scenes without knowing hunger. Love is the ideal; it's not the real. We feel love in Mother and Father, puppies, warmth and food, in shelter from the driving rain, in hot tea and strong coffee, in a cup of cocoa topped with little floating marshmallows in the hands of a frightened child, we feel love in sacrifice. Love is something sought after, seldom achieved, and despite all the Harlequins and the soap operas, love does not always conquer all. It is so rare and special that when I closed my eyes that day, all I could think of was everything I'd neglected to share with my wife, all the things I found fault with, and I wrote what I should have done in those times."

Nina says, "How did you bring them together?"

"Well, first things first, I gave them a couple of bucks to buy some food and then I stole their hot dog and topped it with everything.

"So, here's the scene. Trudy and Hank, the characters' names, are walking from different directions on the Coney Island boardwalk. It's dusk and they both spy the last hot dog stand with its lights on. They arrive there at the same time. It's the forties, mind you, so he stands off for her to go first, and in that moment they look and see there's only one hot dog left. She offers to give it up to him but he's a gentleman and demurs gracefully while walking off. He's got his back to her, when she yells for him, 'Hey, mister, wait,' and they end up sitting on a bench sharing the hot dog, watching the moon come up and the rest follows from there."

"And Cowell, what did he think?" I ask.

"He hated it! He went nuts, 'I ask for a love scene and you buy me a hot dog?' But, he was stuck for time and so he used it and then I was fired that afternoon."

Tanner slows his speaking now.

"We're all fumblers and stutterers and spillers, you know?" Now Tanner throws his hands forward and says directly to Nina and me, "I saw you two sitting on that stage across from each other. I watched and I listened, and I wrote the scene. I saw you both looking at each other for approval. I watched both of you flush red with blood when you spoke about something you believe in. Those other people up there, they were extras. I don't know if you are falling in love, but if I know anything about life, I know you should be. I was there. In a room filled with a hundred people you spoke only for each other." Then it stops as suddenly as it has started and Tanner exhales and speaks gently to Nina and me, "What good are all those bedtime stories you show and you collect if you have no one to comfort you?"

CHAPTER 23

# To Say We Did It

**In Which** we take a long walk, listen to a poet-in-the-wind who had a friend who walked across heaven, meet two of New York's Finest, share a slice with His Honor while listening to "Luck Be a Lady Tonight", and visit two stoops.

Someday I hope Eric writes his version of this story, because without him it would never have happened. He swears from the first time he heard about the conference and we made plans to attend, he's been planning to show a movie in New York. While I was sleeping off gin and stew, Eric was up early walking around Manhattan scouting locations. He tells me what he found later that evening in the bar of the Eli Horton.

"Do you realize how small Manhattan is, Jake? You can walk the length of it in a few hours."

"Yes, but that's not possible is it? I know what you're saying though, Eric. In the summers when I stayed with Julian, I never understood why people were always hailing cabs or dropping into the subway when they could walk as quickly for free. Julian thought I was nuts for wanting to walk places. He told me it was cheaper to take the subway than wearing out my shoes by walking."

"Especially the shoes they wear," says Eric. Then he begins telling me about the place he found. "It's a vacant furniture store with a big parking lot, and the cool thing is the parking lot is framed by the back sides of two other buildings with no windows. There were enough people walking the neighborhood today so I'm sure once we start projecting there will be plenty of people who come."

"What about the screen?"

"Don't need it, that's the beauty of it. There's a freshly painted brick wall that will be a perfect screen and we can get a nice throw if we park Zhitomir across the street. Might as well put it to use before they paint it with something else."

"And sound, what's your idea?"

"It's not perfect. We can't run cords across the streets, but we can set the speakers on top of Zhitomir and crank them up."

"What about the neighbors?"

"I don't know Jake, the whole block is dead and the adjoining buildings are offices, so I don't think it should be a problem, but I'm going tonight and check it out to be sure."

Eric's excited, and I don't have the heart to tell him I'm more concerned about meeting Nina later than I am about showing the movie. It's Eric's first splash in New York, and he's got the "Big Apple" buzz that only people who haven't grown up in New York get. New York can swallow people up like the Leviathan did Jonah without a burp. Eric, bless his inspired, intrepid heart, has instincts honed on Donkey Basketball, the Waffle Festival, and the Spring Tulip Parade and Community Barbecue and he has no doubt what he's doing will be great! If it worked in Noti, why won't it work in New York?

When I ask him, "What do you want to show?" he starts squirming.

"You're going to make fun of me."

"Spit it out, Eric. For once I have a date that means something to me and I've got to get ready."

"Okay, okay, Jake, it's a little traditional for me, but it would look pretty sweet up on that wall. It's got a great line about New York, big stars, and it, it's, it's . . ."

"Eric?"

"*Casablanca.*"

"It's perfect! I'm in!"

"Really?"

"One hundred percent!"

Then the wheels start turning in his head and he says, "Of course, we'll warm them up with some *Quasi at the Quackadero* to keep things a little balanced, and then as he rises to leave, he reaches into his pack and hands me a flyer:

## The Lost Sons Of Zhitomir proudly present
# Casablanca
*Featuring:*
Humphrey Bogart, Ingrid Bergman, Peter Lorre, Sydney Greenstreet, Claude Rains, Conrad Veidt, & Dooley Wilson
*Directed by*
Mihaly Kertész, better known as Michael Curtiz, in 1942.

*Plus a fine program of short features*

**Location:** **Time:** **FREE TO ALL!**

"You already printed a flyer?"

"Well, not … a … flyer."

"What do you mean?"

"I printed a thousand!"

Big Apple meet Eric Mariette.

At ten I meet Nina, who is sitting at a table, sipping club soda, and wearing jeans, a white pullover, black sneakers, and the same silk scarf she had on last night over her gown. When I tell her I recognize the scarf she tells me, "It's my lucky scarf; it was given to me by a woman in China who promised me it would always keep me safe. She's been right so far. Have you recovered from last night?"

"It's hard to tell. I'm starting to take on a different rhythm."

"What rhythm is that?"

"New York, big city, different than what I'm used to. I'm used to going to bed when it's dark and waking up when it gets light but I haven't heard a bird except for a few pigeons in front of the Horton all week, and I'm starting to miss the sound of the wind when it blows around Zhitomir."

"Zhitomir? That's your little truck?"

"Not so little, . Zhitomir is a big truck and it presents a big face to the wind. When I'm inside I can feel it rocking, or feel a gust and hear how it whistles across the cab, and there's a high-pitched song that the wind makes when it passes over the mirrors that's comforting."

"I'd like to meet this truck sometime."

"I'm not sure that's a good idea, Zhitomir can get pretty jealous."

"No woman can come between a man and his truck?"

"Then I'm doomed."

"Are you flirting with me, Spinner?"

"Well, I'm doing the best I can. How am I doing so far?"

"The night is young, maybe you can get better."

"They say danger lurks in the big city."

"Who says that?"

"They do."

"Who are they, truck man?"

"You know, they, they who say the things they say."

"It's scary you actually get paid to write things."

"I don't get paid much."

"Good, because they say words are cheap."

"Who are they?"

"The same they who say there's danger lurking in the big city."

"Are they right?"

"Let's find out."


Finally, after a week of talk, a week of too many words, and the numbing chatter of meaningful conversation, we fold our arms together and walk out into the cool of a May night in New York City.

When we leave the Horton we walk past closed shops and gated subway entrances that look like barbaric Roman passageways into the bowels of hell. The street vents blow foul air, and as we wait for lights to change on corners, rusted, acrid, metallic air rushes against our faces. We walk past the ornate windows of exotic rug shops with signs that inform, "To the Trade Only." A bicyclist rides by, but he seems so strange, small, and out of place in this gargantuan urban tarmac. If the street names and numbers are still familiar to me decades after summers with Julian, the city is not. No one owns New York except those who live in it, and if you leave, it doesn't await your return. New York moves steady and inexorably past you, and if little towns change slowly under the pace and obligation of twentieth century overhauling, New York is made over constantly. Even if I recognize the landmarks, the Empire State Building, the Chrysler Building, Madison Square Park, Gramercy Park, Third Avenue, Second Avenue, Twenty-Third Street, Fourteenth Street, I don't know the city and I probably never did; I was a visitor for a little while that happened to be during my childhood, and so like all childhood friends who became blood brothers during that age, we share a bond.

We turn a corner and find ourselves suddenly greeted by lights and activity. Trucks are unloading flowers and food, and there is a coffee shop called 'Muriel's Nighthawk' providing a sanctuary for the nocturnal to take their fifteen minute break. Inside the coffee shop, an elderly man looking like a mature Oliver Twist, blocks our path, holding out a sad remnant of long stemmed red roses that he'd gathered from the droppings on the street.

"Fresh red roses for a lovely woman," he says to me, though his eyes are locked onto Nina.

"Hard to resist that," I say. "What's the cost?"

"For all, or one?"

"How about for all?"

"Seeing as it's for such a lovely lady, how about five dollars?"

Nina takes the man by the arm and says, "Five dollars! What's your name, sir?"

"My name is Charlie."

"Well, Charlie, it's very kind of you to make us such a deal, but we'd be stealing from you? We'd be criminals if we gave you less than ten."

Charlie cannot believe what he's hearing.

"Jake, give this man ten dollars before he comes to his senses and charges us twenty."

Charlie is very excited to complete this transaction, and while we get two coffees to go, Charlie takes a seat at the counter and orders eggs, potatoes, and toast. Then, flashing the ten to the man working the counter, adds, "Yeah, and some bacon too!"

Exiting the Nighthawk, if we aren't silent the whole time, we don't talk about our work but only about what is passing in front of our faces. At least we have roses with us now because, charming as Muriel's Nighthawk was, its coffee only confirms again that New York is not a coffee town.

We walk insulated in a mysterious cloud until we reach the harbor. Though it doesn't smell sweet like it should, it is a blank black space in flickering landscape and we continue walking, drawn now to the edge of the great city. There stands Liberty with her torch lighting the harbor of a late Sunday night, early Monday morning in Manhattan. And now we're not alone. There are others, staring outward as we walk to the edge and find a bench on which to sit and stare. Suddenly, from the silence of our walking dream, words pierce the night. A poet is reciting his verse to no one.

So the night grew sweet and long and tired and I didn't want to leave
wanted to stay in the wind, the wind, the wind
wanted to stay in the wind, the wind, with you.

So warm and fatigued, my head on your soft stomach
Staring at your eyes so heavy but awake
Could have trailed off to sleep in so many a moonlit night
Could have trailed off to sleep
But wanted to stay in the wind, the wind, the wind
wanted to stay in the wind, the wind, with you.

Hearing the poem, Nina offers the roses to the poet, who embraces them like a newborn baby against his chest. When I reach into my pocket, the poet stops me.

"Don't need no money, brother; got plenty a that. Got more money than I'll ever need. But roses, now that's something I don't see everyday. Roses are food to a poet. Roses been feedin' poets for centuries." Then the poet points over our heads and says, 'Turn around, there's something I wanna show you that ain't there no more.'"

When we turn around, the poet points up to the sky and says, "See there, a friend of mine walked across heaven there thirty years ago. Walked right across heaven in front of every ones' naked eyes. Well, you know, the world don't like when you walk right across heaven in front of their naked eyes, so they arrested my friend and asked him what he thought he was up to walking right across heaven in front of their naked eyes. And my friend, he told everybody he didn't mean no harm, walkin' across heaven like that, he was walkin' on air, guided by angels and his own genius."

It wasn't until he said the last line that I remembered the morning at Julian's thirty years ago in August when I woke up to Philippe Petit, the French aerialist, walking across his high wire between the now departed

World Trade Center Towers.

"That was my friend," said the poet.

And with that, Nina and I thanked the poet and turned towards the Eli Horton Hotel to finish our walk through the layered passage of time.

Tuesday afternoon, Eric and I drive Zhitomir through midtown Manhattan. It takes us three hours to traverse the two miles from the Eli Horton garage to our destination. It's a little before three o'clock when we pull into the furniture store parking lot. Now the waiting begins until we can begin setting up for the show. We can't leave Zhitomir unattended and we can't start setting up for another two hours, so we sit. I've got my book of the Welsh sailor in New York to read and Eric has a film magazine entitled *Urban Documentarian* to keep him busy.

At five o'clock Eric starts setting up. The first thing he does is set the generator in place, but before he finishes stringing the power cord, a patrol car with two of New York's finest shows up, officers L. Kravitz and N. Benigni. Looking at Zhitomir, Zhitomir's out of state license plates, and then the two of us, they are very suspicious. After checking our identification and calling in Zhitomir's license plates, they get down to business and ask us what we're doing in this parking lot. The answer has them shaking their heads. Officer Kravitz tells us, "Look, fellas, there's no fuckin' way you two are going to show a movie here tonight. Got that?"

Officer Benigni looks at us like we stepped off the boat and says, "Are you nuts or something? You think you could get away with some shit like this?" Then says, "You could start a riot or something."

Kravitz then asks, "What was you gonna show?" To which Eric replies, "Casablanca." "Hmm, haven't seen that one. Is it a good picture?"

"Benigni cannot believe what he's hearing. "Lenny, you ain't seen Casa fuckin Blanca? What planet you been livin on?"

Officer Benigni's knowledge of film history gives us a moment's hope that the show might come off until he responds to his radio and then says, "No way. I spoke to the lieutenant. You fellas gotta clear out."

Then their radio sounds a command to their next assignment and they tell us they'll be back to be sure we're gone in thirty minutes, and they take off.

As they drive away, Eric says, "I have an idea. Call Julian and see if he can pull something with the city.  If not, we'll find another place and run the thing anyway."

Julian laughs when he gets the call. "I was worried somebody would muck things up for you. I'll call the Mayor, but don't count on anything. Even the Mayor can't get everything he wants."

Fifteen minutes later Julian calls with the reply.

"No, can't do it. The Mayor's assistant explained that a few years ago somebody started showing films from their apartment on the weekends and before too long there was a thriving scene there. Somebody complained about noise, congestion, drug dealers, whatever, and there was a big stink in the paper and they had to shut the thing down. But I have some good news. His Honor is a film lover and he has an idea. His brother, Jerry, has some buildings on the lower east side he's renovating, and there's a large courtyard entrance that can hold a few hundred people. Technically, that's what the Mayor said, technically, it's private property, and so if you call the showing a private party, it can fly. You can run off those flyers of Eric's and hand them out on the street, but don't let it get out of hand."

Eric is thrilled.

"It's like Ratso Rizzo getting the invitation to the Warhol Party in *Midnight Cowboy*. It's destiny, Jake. What's the address?"

Julian is still talking. "The Mayor's brother has a guy named Joey, who'll meet you there in an hour and help you set up. He's got keys to the buildings and can get you squared away with all the power you'll need."

With sunset coming and little time to spare, we drive Zhitomir crosstown in much lighter traffic to the lower east side where we meet the Mayor's-brother-Jerry's-guy-named Joey. "Joey Bop," that is, who far from the expected errand boy, is instead a dynamo who knows a little about promoting things in the city. After greeting us, Joey Bop tells us he loves the idea of showing movies on the city streets, and how a few years ago he had organized a rodeo in the Bronx.

"A guy I grew up with in the Bronx, Terry Fallon -- we graduated from DeWitt Clinton High School together -- get this, Terry's pop was from Oklahoma. He moved to New York when he married Terry's mom, Gail, who he met, get this, on the Staten Island Ferry when he was visiting. True story. Terry's pop was a ranch hand in Oklahoma, so he got a job working the stables in Van Cortland Park. Terry was always hanging out down there listening to all the guys talk about this and that, and his pop was always telling stories about bull riding back in Oklahoma. Terry was a good rider too, 'cause he spent summers back in Oklahoma with his pop's family, and when he gets out of high school he tells everyone he's headed to Texas to ride bulls and become a rodeo star. Get this, six years later; Terry Fallon finishes tops in the National Rodeo.

"So he's visiting the family and he's showing us all the rodeo champs' big belt, and we cook up this crazy idea to bring a rodeo to the Bronx. He pulls the strings with the rodeo guys, I pull some strings with the city." Now swelling with pride Joey Bop says, "I guess I'm the kind of guy everybody wants to help, and the next thing you know I'm getting my picture taken with Ty Murray and Cody Hart in Crotona Park. We sold twelve thousand tickets! That's a lot a Yippee Eye Oh Ty Yay, right?"

As Joey Bop speaks, I realize I left Zhitomir idling in front of the building and I interrupt him to tell him I have to run back to the truck. Joey Bop finds this funny and laughs, "Don't worry about your truck. Nobody messes with Joey Bop. It won't be a problem, trust me." Then he says, "Listen, I got one little favor to ask . . ." It turns out Joey Bop likes Bugs Bunny cartoons. Thankfully, this is not a problem because next to the Chuck Jones Estate, Warner Brothers, and Lumen Desire, Julian probably has the most intact collection of Bugs Bunny cartoons in the world. One phone call and Julian is all over it, saying only, "Be sure you introduce me to this Mr. Bop."

The courtyard is a cavernous quadrangle surrounded by four buildings, each with wide stone stairways leading up to majestic paired doors with glass panes leading inside. Above each doorway hang large brass lights which throw four amber circles of light onto each of the stairways. The central part of the courtyard is a freshly planted lawn that, while partially grown, could use another few weeks to fill out. The apartments in the complex are about to be put up for sale for a price Joey Bop says "will make a lotta people happy."

We can hang our screen over one stairway, project from the landing of another, and it should work fine. The sound will be a little harsh, with the brick walls rattling the noises, but Eric comes up with a great solution. He gets Joey Bop to open some of the courtyard-facing apartments and he sets speakers in four windows. Eric runs a sound check and incredibly, by seven-thirty, we're set up and ready to go except for two things: Joey Bops' Bugs

Bunny cartoons, and . . . yes, an audience.

Neither one would be a problem. I call Julian about Bugs Bunny and to make sure he doesn't forget to have his cab stop at the Eli Horton Hotel for Nina. Eric, a man on a mission, grabs his flyer and tears out of the place to find a copy shop where he can print flyers and hand them out on the streets, in restaurants, at newsstands, by subways, and to everyone he passes.

In less than an hour the place starts filling up. People come from the nearby hospital, neighborhood apartment buildings, a small residency shelter; even seven Tibetan monks from the Lower East Side Buddhism Center show up and take their seats cross-legged in a golden circle formed by their robes. A small group of Hell's Angels thunder up to park their bikes outside and are greeted by some of the shelter residents. "The Angels give the shelter people rides when they need to go somewhere," explains a young woman who lives in the neighborhood.

To the delight of all present, Tony's Napoli Pizza starts hauling boxes of pizzas in and giving them away. "Courtesy of the Mayor," Tony dutifully shouts as each slice is placed into the hands of a hungry voting citizen.

By the time Nina and Julian arrive, with the Mayor, everyone is having a good time. They're all caught up in the euphoria of something weird and unlikely, and they start sharing smiles and food, and stories, and we haven't even started the film.

At eight o'clock, Joey Bop is treated to the snide and familiar voice of Bugs Bunny booming out into the balmy Manhattan night as he eludes the ever-predacious Elmer Fudd.

"Run Bugs, run, that little fucker is after you," shouts someone in the crowd.

New Yorkers talk to their movies. It reminds me of the late director, Joseph Vasquez, whom I heard reminiscing about his childhood in the Bronx and how people always talked to the screen as they watched the movies. By the time *Quasi at the Quackadero* plays, we're having a full-blown party, as Quasi's allies in the crowd warn him of the perils he's facing.

"Watch out Quasi, she's going to mess you up, Bro'."

"Don't trust her, man, she's dangerous."

"I told you so! You didn't listen to me and now you gonna have to watch your ass forever!"

His Honor, with Joey Bop, Julian, and Nina, stands beside Eric, not far from the projectors. "Extra cheese, right?" says Joey Bop as he hands a slice of pizza to the Mayor. Everything is humming. It's Eric's show, and he was right about all of it. New York is a lot of small towns folded into a bigger town, and we have one of them watching our movie tonight.

In the pause between *Quasi* and *Casablanca*, the Hells Angels start chanting, "Bogey, Bogey, Bogey." Enlisting the help of the Buddhists, another group starts chanting even louder, Bergman, Bergman, Bergman! Now I'm worried, thinking we could have a repeat of Altamont on our hands, but once the film starts those worries evaporate. When *Casablanca* lights the courtyard, the crowd is transfixed. Julian slips away from the Mayor and tells me he had dinner with Ingrid Bergman once when he was working with her daughter, Pia, on a piece for CBS. Year after year *Casablanca* gets acclaim as one of, if not, the best film of all time. It's hard to argue with it. It has everything: a complex good guy Bogey; a gorgeous female lead, Bergman; brilliant, amusing and sympathetic side characters Lorre, Rains, Wilson, and Greenstreet, and it's set against the backdrop of a compelling and profound political setting. I've seen it twenty times and on this New York night, it's as fresh and entertaining as ever.

Before the first reel change, Julian slides over and says he wants to show me something. He asks Eric to mind the projectors for a while.

"I know you want to see the movie, but you won't mind; I promise." He asks Nina to join us, and the three of us slip out of the courtyard and walk arm-in-arm for a few blocks until we arrive at a block of remodeled five story buildings. Julian stops in front of one of them.

"Look closely, Jake. It may be familiar."

I stand staring at the familiar building in an odd way, looking, looking, and trying to understand what it is, until Julian can't wait any longer.

"This is the building where Schlamie lived; this is where Schlomo walked to in your film. It's not a family story; it's a real place. They lived here on the top floor. It does not look the same, for sure, but it's the same place, the same stoop, and the same walls. Your great Uncle Schlomo came here to live with his brother and he was the one who earned the money to bring my mother to America. I should have shown it to you years ago, but when you were young, it didn't seem important. Back then it was a tiny little apartment without heat or running water half the time. A person was better off on the street."

The hardest part of the moment is coming face to face with a tangible reality of my own father's history. For all my life, I never believed any of that was real. It had all been stories, even the imaginary memories. This was the first time in my life that anything connected to my father was real to me.

Thankfully, Julian wasn't about to let it get too serious. "You can figure it out some other time, but at least you have something to think about now. We had better get back to *Casablanca*."

By the time we get back to the courtyard, *Casablanca* is driving to its climax. With about twenty minutes left before Ilsa gets on the airplane with Victor Lazlo, Nina says she'd like to see Zhitomir, adding, "I've seen this one a few times. I know the ending." We walk out of the courtyard where Zhitomir sits in the shadows of a streetlight, making it hard to see the painted sides.

"Too bad you can't see it in the light, "I say, and Nina answers,

"There'll be other chances. It's what's behind the curtain I'm most interested in." When we enter, Nina quietly looks inside of Zhitomir. She sees the article about her taped to the wall beside my desk, and doesn't say anything for a moment. Then she touches her finger to the clipping and takes my hand, "I've kept your Bedtime Stories piece pretty close, too, Jake."

After another minute in which I find myself strangely self-conscious of the impression "my home" must make, Nina says, "The wood is lovely. It's warm, the loft, the desk, the walls and cabinets. I see why you like it. I lived in a van in Algeria once for three months before I went to medical school. It's a good feeling having everything you need at a minimum, isn't it?" Then, looking at the films in their cabinet, she says,

"It's perfect."

"Perfect.    You're the first to describe it that way."

"No, I'm serious, Jake. You've got it down to the essence. What's missing?"

"A shower would be nice and occasionally I wish I had another window and . . ."

"Okay, I see your point."

The next few minutes pass in an awkward silence. Nina looks around Zhitomir and I try not to think about what's happening between us. Stupid movie guy that I am, all I can think about is Bogey and Bergman. I didn't need to see the big scene at the end to know how that turned out.

Nina breaks the silence by asking me "What do you think of *Casablanca's* ending?"

"As a critic or as a person?"

"How about as a man?"

And for once in my dang life I got it right.

"I always wished she stayed with Rick. I know, I know, I know why she has to get on the plane; you know the good fight and all, the higher calling, and all that, but I've always wished she stayed with Rick."

"Me, too." says Nina.

Then we kiss.

We return to the courtyard in time to observe the contented faces in the crowd who are slowly rising to leave.

One of the Hells' Angels, whose leather jacket identifies him as 'Crusher,' complains to one of the Buddhists, "Man, she should have stayed with Rick. I mean, come on, that cat, he don't care about her. He's all in to the big bad war. Mr. Big Cause."

And the Buddhist says, "Yes, he does not appreciate the heart of his companion."

Slowly, the crowd stirs back to life with little comments as they walk off.

"See, I told you, Rick never says 'Play It Again.' That's going to cost you twenty dollars."

"That little cat, Lorre, he freaks me out. He's weirder than shit. You remember him in the *Maltese Falcon*? He's like Pee Wee Herman in lederhosen. You know what I mean?"

Thirty minutes later, the courtyard is empty except for a few of Joey Bop's guys cleaning up an impressive collection of pizza boxes. The Mayor, Joey Bop, and Julian are seated on the stoop below the projectors discussing New York films.

Joey Bop is making his case for *A Bronx Tale*, but the Mayor is having none of it.

"You Bronx guys are all the same. Now, *French Connection, Mean Streets*, both great," says the Mayor, "but I love *The Taking of Pelham 123.*"

"Yes, dude, that one is great!" says Eric as Julian laughs out loud, and then asks the Mayor, "When is the last time you were called dude, your Honor?"

To which Joey Bop responds,

"That is one of the kinder things his honor gets called."

Their conversation gets interrupted briefly when the Mayor yells across the courtyard.

"Yo, Bobby, good to see you." Bobby waves back, and Eric says, "Is that who I think it is?"

Then the Mayor, ignoring Eric's bugged out eyes, says to him,

"If I were you, I'd be very proud of this and if I may quote from another fine New York film: "We came, we saw, and we kicked its ass!" Eric, trying to guess the correct film reference, asks, *French Connection*?" And the Mayor answers, "No, *Ghostbusters*!"

I'm not Tanner Scofield. I don't know how to describe what happened this morning when Nina and I took another walk, but I can tell you the sun was out and it felt warm on our faces. We both enjoyed that. We spoke about what it must be like to be a chimpanzee living in the Central Park Zoo, and we rode the carousel together. Sitting on the steps of the Metropolitan Museum of Art was so entertaining that we didn't go inside. It was too much fun watching people outside. As we sat on the steps, Nina told me about Hindu gods who neither live nor die but transport others across the span from life to death, from earthly life to heavenly life. I told her about Fred and his theories about fire and space. We ate a hot dog together, one hot dog, and it wasn't because we couldn't afford one for each of us. Things are comfortable between us, and though neither one of us dares to mention anything about ways of seeing each other again, we both understand it will happen. Walking past the booksellers on southeast corner of Central Park, I find a book that I buy for Nina: '*To Reach The Clouds*' by Philippe Petit, our poet's friend, the eccentric French aerialist who dared to walk across heaven right in front of everyone's naked eyes. Tanner is right, "It's not easy to write a love scene," but you can if you quit worrying about what the director will think.

Later, Julian, Nina, Eric, and I are at Julian's, eating Chinese takeout food, and amidst the familiarity of Julian's cluttered apartment we eat and talk about everyone's plans. Julian is leaving in a few more days for Japan where he'll be a judge for this year's Tokyo Film Festival. Nina is off to Peru where she's starting a VPP having to do with traditional riverboat builders who are endangered by the importation of modern boats and engines into their once remote tributaries of the Amazon River. And me, tomorrow morning I'll begin another traverse of the continent with the only certain destination a return to Driggs for yet another go-around with Seraphina and her crew. I have a piece for the *Tattered Edge* due in three weeks that I haven't even begun. Eric, the only one remaining, will set up his room at Julian's and start editing his Palau fishing film. He also received some good news this morning; he got a personal call from the "dude" he befriended the other night asking him if he'd like to do "special projects" for the dude at the Mayor's Office of Film.

We're an odd room of four people in motion, like animals in migration, following the scent of water, the spring bloom of flowers, or the melting of ice and emergence of grass.

We are four people discomforted by the complicated emotions of saying goodbye. So we don't.

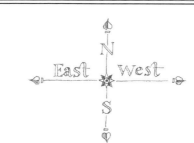

# SECTION 5

## The Pull Of Gravity

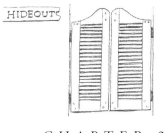
HIDEOUT

CHAPTER 24

# How Angels Die

In Which we meet the German "Villy the Kid," learn of the passing of an old friend and experience the force of attraction between objects.

Eventually, no matter how many times the road forks, how you direct yourself away from your past, or how many memories you place in the back of your mind, there is a road that leads you to the place you once called home. There is something in human beings drawing us to the place of our birth. Perhaps we are like salmon that live but a precious few months in their natal waters before heading out to the vastness of the oceans. If they survive the trials of pelagic life, they return to the pool of their birth to replace themselves. Ichthyologists explain this by saying the fish form an instinctual map guided by something they call "attraction water." Fred, suspending his scientific bent for a moment, probably would have branded this "hogwash," but it doesn't matter. Humans yearn for a homeward pilgrimage and seek their origins, whether it is to a street in New York City, a stream on the Olympic Peninsula, or a tiny village in the Ukraine.

Maybe we need to know the starting point of our journey, and perhaps we need to see the results of unmade choices -- roads not taken, partners not married, children not birthed, sentiments not felt, fruit trees not planted. I sometimes wonder if it's the opposite for those who remain in one place their entire lives. Are they consumed by a growing intensity to roam, to wander, to see the unseen, to break out of the shell and see the world?

The excitement of the week in New York City slowly subsided as I drove west again. Despite an unrelenting hundred and fifty years of new settlements, development, and change, the west retains its vastness, and occasionally you stumble upon a place where the capillaries of modern existence don't deliver much blood. Those outposts are disappearing rapidly. Roads have yielded the task of disseminating ideas and temptations to airwaves, but there remain a few pockets where even those currents don't flow strongly, and I find myself in one of them:  Cedar Monk.

I spoke with Nina the other night and explained to her that Cedar Monk is a remnant town. Like so many others across the country that once proudly laid claim to the title "inland empires," Cedar Monk has swollen and now receded with a bygone economic prosperity. Some empires had trees, some had water, others had mountains rich with ores of copper, bauxite and gold, and some had unique features where people sought communion with their gods. Not unlike Booker with its railroad, Cedar Monk owes its existence to a vast basin of lush pasture capable of supporting thousands of cattle that were food for an expanding nation in the early part of the 20th century.

Cattle, grazing beneath the snow-covered peak (resembling the head of a Franciscan friar from which legend holds the town derives its name), were herded and held before boarding trains for their last breaths in Chicago. By the middle of the 1960s, the rise of interstate highways, trucking, and electricity eliminated the need for places like Cedar Monk. The Santa Fe spur line that transported its riches was soon gone, and now all that remains is natural beauty, a street, a saloon, and a memory.

The saloon where I find myself is named the Rascal River Hideout. You enter the Rascal River by pushing aside two slatted saloon doors open to the air and sprung with squeaky hinges. The Hideout, as it is known to the locals, is a cluttered restaurant adorned with famous western figures: dusty oil paintings of Billy the Kid, Doc Holliday, Crazy Horse, Jesse and Otto James, and Buffalo Bill, among others. The place is like a gunslinger's antique shop, its crowded walls and ceilings jammed with holsters and pearl handled pistols, bandoleers, framed newspaper clippings recounting the great train robberies, stage coach holdups, and amid the clutter, a large sepia print of Sitting Bull. There's a sign above the bar that says, "No dusting under pain of asphyxiation!"

The unlikely museum is the collection of Otto Walter Guenther, born in Mannheim, Germany, in 1939. He owns the Hideout with his American wife, Juliette, who avoids the saloon as much as possible by working as a nurse in nearby Coronado. The main attraction is "Rustler Pete," a robotic carnival gunslinger. Pete is a menacing bad guy with a painted face bearing a slight resemblance to Lee Van Cleef in the famous spaghetti western *The Good, The Bad, and the Ugly*. The sign that came with Pete says, "Try your luck for only a quarter." Time has inflated that price to a still reasonable fifty cents for a chance to out-duel Pete. Two quarters in the slot and Pete begins snarling and taunting, "Well, pardner, you don't look fast enough to out-draw me, but you may be fast enough to die." Then his robotic arms start moving--ready, aim, and then fire! No matter how fast you are, Pete wins the first round, but if you're willing to spend another fifty cents Pete can be taken down. His dying words gurgle, "You got me. I guess my luck's run out. I never thought I'd end my days starin' up at the likes of you." Then his pistol-toting arm lowers and his eyes close, at least until the next wanna-be gunslinger empties his pockets of change.

Otto's German accent has been ironed out by forty years in the United States, but when he says 'yah' or the "W" sound he is revealed. "Yah, some people come in every day to draw on Pete," says Otto between sips of beer. And Otto drinks beer, not one beer, not some beer, but lots of beer and it doesn't look as if he has any plans to stop. "Unless you've ever shot a man, it's a lot of fun."

Two glasses ago Otto told me, "Yah, I got a story for you, film guy. Have I got a story for you! A real doozy, too!"

It appears I'm going to have to wait because Otto is telling other people other stories before he tells me the promised story and he roams, full beer glass in hand, doing that with the other patrons in the Hideout. Clearly, Otto enjoys telling stories, and he's a friendly guy with warm green eyes making him look twenty years younger than his sixty years. Finally, Otto returns, placing two fresh liter glasses of beer on the counter and sits down on a bar stool across from me.

"Yah, vee vill need these. I got a story for you. Yah, I do. Listen to this. My grandfather built the first movie theater in Mannheim in 1927. *Das Capitolium*, 1200 seats and as pretty a place as you'll ever see. Not like these

four-valled cracker boxes you go to now in shopping centers. Nope splendid crystal chandeliers, esplanades carpeted in royal velvet, and curtains like
you wouldn't believe. And the seats, you wouldn't think of spilling popcorn
on those seats. I grew up in that theater and my Aunt Ingrid, the old spin-
ster of the family, lived in an apartment above the lobby. Mr. Churchill
even dropped a bomb on the place in 1943, but it vas a dud. My grandfather said it had to be dud to match the German films he vas obligated to
show during the var ven ve vere cut off from American films. Auntie Ingrid
even played piano in the early days. Can you imagine a nice German girl
practiced on Beethoven and Mozart playing to all those movies? It drove
my grandmother nuts."

Otto reduces the liter of beer considerably and continues.

"I saw all the movies but my favorites vere always your Vesterns. The
pictures changed every Tuesday and Friday. I'm sure I spent more time
vatching movies than sleeping. Vesterns vere very popular in Germany. I vas
like a lot of German kids who knew all about the "Vild Vest." I'd race from
school to the movie theater and help Ingrid load the carbon rods. I loved
Glenn Ford, John Vayne, Gary Cooper, Alan Ladd, and Jimmy Stewart. I
alvays liked the outlaws--Die Bandits, Granny called them in German--but
they veren't bandits like she thought. She didn't understand the American
outlaws who bucked the railroads, robbed the banks, or resisted the large
cattle owners veren't the bad guys like vee thought of them in Germany.
And, yah, oh yah, I vanted to be one of them."

The rest of the liter goes down Otto's throat. It's impressive.

"Look at me. Who vould have thought I'd go from this to this?" Otto
points to a childhood picture of him and his brother standing in front of a
large Nazi flag, saying, "That's me vid my brother ven ve vas kids, and that's
me at tventy-seven in my U.S. Army uniform in Vietnam. I vas a soldier,
and not any of that made-for-TV stuff either. Vietnam vas a real var vid
bullets flying around, and svamps and fear."

Otto pauses long enough to appropriate my untouched beer.

"No point letting this go flat," says Otto. Rising to his feet takes the
steel-eyed stance of a gunslinger and speaks deliberately while flexing his
fingers against an imaginary pistol on his hip. "Are you sure you vant to
go for your gun now, Macintosh? You don't have your hired hands now.
It's you and me. Two men, two guns. All your money can't help you now.
Only one of us is going to valk away from this so you best prepare to meet

your maker." Then he draws his hand across his hip and guns down his imaginary adversary, spins again, shouting out, "Bang--the guy hiding in the stable! Bang--the guy on the hotel roof! Bang--the guy hiding behind vindow of barbershop! Bang bang bang--the guy shielding himself from danger behind the pretty voman in the general store!" Then he blows on the end of his invisible gun, spins it into its holster, and retakes his seat. "That vas me, Villy the Kid," says Otto, pausing long enough to reduce the contents of his beer glass before resuming his tale.

"After the var, during the occupation and vat they called 'De- Nazification', my grandfather vas denounced. Showing movies was a big deal during the var. They didn't let anyone have access to that stuff. If Grandpa vas going to stay in business he had no choice but to vear the little Nazi pin and show vat vas approved. Yah, trust me, you couldn't say, 'No thank-you, mein Fuhrer.' Think about it. And because vee Germans keep such good records about everything, there vas a paper trail of my grandfather to some meetings. The guy who snitched on my grandfather had been a Gestapo officer who needed some help to save his own ass. He produced a list of Nazi sympathizers vid my grandfather's name on it. They arrested him and brought him in for questioning, then he spent some time being de-Nazified. Yah, that's vat they called it.

"Vile he vas gone, Auntie Ingrid had to run the theater by herself. Finally, when they let him go he was ready to make changes. My grandfather vas alvays looking for a vay to make things better. I'll tell you, vid a theater in the family there's alvays something going on. He started having concerts for the Americans. Great shows, too. I saw Bill Haley play there in 1958. His good buddy was stationed nearby and came to listen. They didn't dare announce that Mr. Elvis Presley vas standing in the vings. Yes, sir, Elvis Presley.

"Yah, sir, right then and there I knew I vas going to America. Of course, my grandmother had other plans, and believe me little old Granny Ursula could freeze boiling vasser vid one of those Prussian looks of hers."

Otto finishes his beer and looks off into a silent space with a confused look in his eye and says wistfully, "You know, I always vondered how my grandfather ever landed her in bed. Maybe those old Prussians have a soft side?" Then he returns from his little daydream and continues with the story.

"Vell, my grandmother raised me and she vas from the old school. You know--I vas going to learn a trade. I'll give her that--diesel mechanics earns a steady paycheck. "But as soon as trade school vas done I vas gone. I joined the merchant marine on the first ship going to America. I vas an engineer working boats on the Great Lakes. In my time off I'd make my way down to Chicago, Milwaukee, anyvere they had beer and girls, and you know how that goes. One night I got into it vid this guy who starts calling me Adolph . . . next thing you know I'm in jail in Chicago and they're threatening to send me back to Germany. It's 1965 and things are heating up in Vietnam. The judge, Valter Knoblach, says, 'Otto, you haff two choices: go back to Germany and never come here again, or you can find a vay to make America think better of you.' My lawyer explained to me that meant I could join the U.S. Army or the Marines. I had two days to make my decision.

"The Marines said they vanted four years, the Army said three, and so I joined the Army. The next thing you know, I'm in Vietnam. Yah, I didn't ever imagine I'd have to spend three years in Vietnam to get here: some var that vas. You know vat the scheisse is, movie man? Too many guys didn't make it home from the scheisse. Yah, that's vat they say, isn't it? One man's scheisse is another man's gold. Vell, Vietnam vas my ticket to America. Fight in Vietnam and get citizenship."

Otto describes earning two Purple Hearts and then citizenship to the country he dreamed about his whole life. "A lot of the guys in the scheisse wrote nicknames on their helmets--Rebel, Loner, Vyatt, Slinger, Shooter. Mine said "Outlaw." The guys in my platoon called me Villy the Kid because I vas good vid my service revolver and always pretending to be a gunslinger. They'd line up light bulbs, canned rations, bags of rice, vatever they had, and I'd draw and spin like I learned in the movies from Glenn Ford."

Now Otto walks over to the wall and takes down another photo of him in Vietnam wearing his "Outlaw" helmet. He's holding an M16 in front of an attack helicopter with a bulldog painted on the nose. The bulldog is wearing a spiked chain that has "Tenacity!" in bold red letters on it.

At this point in the story Otto leaves for a few minutes to take care of some new customers. When he returns he's got two fresh liters of beer and hands me one.

"Listen, movie man, didn't anybody ever teach you how to drink beer? You better start catching up to me or you von't last the night." Then, drawing a sip from his new glass, he sighs in deep satisfaction as the beer settles in his stomach.

"Ven I got discharged they sent me to Fort Lee, New Jersey. I had a buddy there from Vietnam who offered to put me up vile I found vork. I can tell you, it took me exactly three days there to see it vasn't for me. I didn't vant any part of all that. I had my citizenship so I bought a car and I set out to find the vorld of the Vesterns I'd seen back in Mannheim. I didn't know vere all those movies came from and I didn't know vere people like that lived. Shit, I didn't know anything. I vas young and stupid, but off I vent and six days later I vas staring at a sign that said 'Indian Reservation.' I vas surprised ven there vere Indians, because you know, it vas New Mexico so I expected it to have Mexicans. That's how naive I vas, but at least it looked like vat I'd seen in all those movies as a kid. Vell, at least ven you closed your eyes to the wrecked cars and trailers. It vas as close as I ever found to the vide open spaces of the cowboys."

Three beers later we're not talking about movies anymore. Otto's green eyes are ablaze and mine are floating in my head, which I hope is still on my shoulders because I can't feel it when I poke it with a finger. Otto tells me the trade his Prussian grandmother insisted he learn has taken him all over the world.

"Mongolia, Australia, Siberia, China, Nicaragua, diesel engines don't have passports. Did I ever think I'd stop moving? God, no, but look at me now sitting in this place vid my third vife and all the time to do anything I want. And vouldn't you know? All I vant to do is stay put and drink beer. Yah, I get that urge sometime to take off, see an old friend, or drive, but mostly I stay put and drink beer with friends."

Then Otto asks me, "Vat about you? How long do you stay out on the road?"

"I've been out four years."

"No vay. Four years on the road. No house?"

I gesture to the outside, "That truck is my house."

"You live in that thing?"

"Yes, I do. Would you like to have a look?"

"You bet," says Otto, and he walks to one of the tables and asks a young woman named Kathy to watch the place for a few minutes. Kathy has obviously done this before because she stands up and walks to the bar where she reaches down for an apron. As we leave the saloon I notice I'm a bit unsteady on my feet.

It takes me a minute to get the stairs unlatched, but finally I do and I enter and turn on the light to welcome Otto inside. Otto's reaction is like

Nina's was. He didn't expect to see something so nice. Zhitomir never fails to surprise people.

"Pretty nice digs you have in there. Who vould ever think? Did you do all this vork?" he says while running his hands down the cherry walls.

"No, a lot was done by my uncle Fred. He gave me the truck. A lot of it has happened over the years."

"You know, it looks like a display room in a furniture store. Do you mind?" asks Otto, now scanning the shelves with the film cans." I guess you do have a lot of movies in here. They must be heavy."

"They sure are. That's why I only carry my favorites."

Now Otto is thumbing the film cans, looking at titles, browsing my film library.

"You got any Vesterns in here?" Then Otto stops and exclaims, "*Destry Rides Again*! I love this film! You know, for Germans this is one of the best. Dietrich and Stewart." He starts singing, "See vat the boys in the back room vill have . . .' She sure could sing, and that one raised a few eyebrows back home, but not for me."

Otto pauses again with a grimace like someone who bit down on a lemon and says, "She vas a little manly, don't you think? Germans love that bawdy stuff, you know?"

Then he asks, "You have projectors?"

I lift open the cushioned bench to reveal the four projectors neatly stowed. Otto is impressed.

"Mind if I look at one?"

"Not at all."

He lifts one out, sets it on the table, and traces his fingers through the film path, careful not to touch the lens or sound drums.

"Yah, 16 millimeter. Nice. Vee had thirty-five millimeter, you know. Different, of course, but vee also had two of these because during the var a lot of prints were sixteen." Now he opens the bulb housing and smiles at the halide bulbs. "Ours vere the old kind, beautiful, hand-made glass tubes. Oh, you didn't vant to touch one of them before they'd cool off, and they melted the film if you stopped the mechanism too soon vid the film in the track. Expensive, and they'd burn out. Ve vere very gentle vid them. My grandfather kept a small book vid all their serial numbers, dates of service, and their running hours. "You have screens too?"

I point overhead to a narrow elongated cabinet fastened to the ceiling.

"In there. A twelve-by-twelve freestanding and a twelve-by-sixteen fold-able with grommets I can fasten to hooks on the side of the truck for out-side shows."

"You know, ven I first saw that thing drive into town, I thought: vat sort of cuckoo is this? But, yah, this is some complete vorld you have."

Then he says, "You vant to see my collection? I got them all. It's inside. I got hundreds of Vestern videos."

When we return to the saloon, Otto refreshes our beers and we go to his office where, as promised, he has a wall filled with videocassettes, hundreds of cassettes, generations of films with handwritten labels on the outside of each tape.

"You can get three to a tape," he says. "Vid all the movie channels now you can get them all. Look, *Johnny Guitar, High Noon, The Vesterner, The Oxbow Incident, Man Vidout a Star, The Magnificent Seven, Sergeant Rout-ledge, The Man Vid the Gun.*" Then, to my delighted surprise, Otto says, "Do you know this vun, *Lonely Are The Brave*? Not a Vestern, but a good film anyway. Last cowboy kind of thing." Otto is excited and is on to the next film before I can answer. "Look at this one: *The Man from Laramie*. You remind me of him a little."

When we leave the office and enter the saloon, Otto goes behind the counter and pops the tape into his VCR and fast-forwards through *The Good The Bad and The Ugly*, which appears on the small television behind the bar, until he gets to *The Man from Laramie*.

A few other patrons gather around the bar as the film begins with one of the worst songs ever written. Fortunately things get better after that and by the time the handsome Will Lockhart, played by Jimmy Stewart, exam-ines the remains of the massacred troop holding Lockhart's hidden purpose, the song is forgotten. The man from Laramie has a score to settle, but with whom? Otto is locked to his seat now behind the bar, and the rest of us are dug in for the duration.

In the film we meet Barbara, the pretty young woman who asks the mysterious but sympathetic Will where his home is. He replies, "I can't rightly say anyplace is my home . . . I always feel I belong where I am."

Otto taps me on the leg and whispers, "That's you, yah?"

For the next ninety minutes we're all held by an unusually complex battle for justice with wide open spaces, mule trains, Apaches, Pueblos, half-breeds, gingham, ruthless men, pretty ladies, scorned women, law-

men, advancing civilization, a modified Cain and Abel, a psychotic drift-
er, animal abuse, and a few shifts in sympathy for several characters. It
is a fine and satisfying film, and fortunately, by the time I make my way
back to bed in Zhitomir, the world is put back together and a better place
to live.

The next morning comes abruptly in the form of an impressive thun-
derstorm before sunrise. Staring up through the skylight, pulses of light-
ning illuminate the inside of Zhitomir like intermittent flash bulbs and I
listen to loud thunder as I lie flat on my back. For a half an hour the storm
unleashes its rainy staccato on Zhitomir's metal top, making my bed feel
like the center of a snare drum. When it finally slows, I throw on some
clothes and grab the tiny excuse of an umbrella I keep in the netting on the
wall, where I have things like gloves and hats, and head outside to the first
light of morning.

I'm surprised when Otto is already in the Hideout amiably holding
court with a few coffee drinkers, some from the night before who obviously
enjoy Otto's stories better than what awaits them at home. Otto shows no
signs that the evening has sapped him of any energy while he explains his
"theory" about "Vesterns."

"Yah, old Alec Vaggoman, he's part snake and part hustler, and you respect him even if you don't like him. Poor sonofabitch is going blind, loses
his vorthless son, loses his vould-be son, then has to accept that neither one
of them had any honor. Of course, vee never take the Old Man to task for
his past, only his vorthless progeny who gets blamed on a soft mother . . .
Then, if the old sonofabitch isn't lucky enough, he gets his child sweetheart
back, the one he left at the altar to the conniving vomen from the east.
Now, that's a real Vestern."

Taking a breath from his film review, Otto sees me and says, "How's
your hand this morning, Lockhart," referring to last night's gunshot wound
in the film.

"Hand's doing fine, Waggoman," I reply, holding the incapacitated paw
in the air. "It'll heal better when I drink some coffee though. Two sugars
and some cream, please."

"Coming right up, soldier."

While Otto gets the coffee, I pick up *The Coronado Dispatch*, newspaper to the Jackson, Haines, and Kylee Tri-county region in which Cedar

Monk sits. When I start thumbing through the paper a strong wave comes over me and suddenly I feel like a cat that senses an earthquake before any human does and stands in the most solid part of a house in anticipation.

You never know when your orbit is going to shift. One second you're floating around the planet without a care in the world, the next you're crashing to earth and not sure if the heat shields are in place. Flipping the page I read this:

---

### Clara Miriam Spofford Spengler, 93.

Clara Miriam Spofford Spengler, born June 8, 1911 in Cedar Monk, Wyoming, died peacefully in her sleep on June 30, 2004 of age-related causes. The only daughter of Bertina and Joseph Spofford, she met and married Bernard Jules Spengler while a student at Wilson Education College. Alongside her husband, the two taught in Larch until his passing in 1960.

Known lovingly as Mrs. Shakespeare to five decades of students, she was named Larch High School's Teacher of the Year numerous times. She was a lover of words, and after leaving the teaching profession opened a bookstore, The Sonnet, in Larch, surrounding herself with the works of her favorite writers. She was the founder and enthusiastic supporter of the Young Western Authors Retreat (Y.W.A.R.).

She was a lover of animals and leaves behind her two miniature donkeys, Dylan Vonnegut Pasternak and Emily Sylvia Anais.

All who knew and loved her will remember her.

Clara is survived by her cousins, Miriam Hankins and Rosalyn Vazquez.

A memorial gathering will be held on July 6 at 7pm in The Sonnet, 1789 Main Street, Larch, to celebrate her full and wonderful life.

Remembrances to: Young Western Authors Retreat.

Clara's death overwhelms me. All I can think of is the day that my mother died. I was old enough to remember the events, but young enough not to understand them. The phone rang in the afternoon and when Fred took the call, it was like the world stopped. When he set the receiver down on the hook, he stood staring at the wall, his face empty and his eyes growing wet with tears. Fred was a tree, a tall tree, a solid vibrant life-giving tree, and seeing him standing like that I knew something awful had happened;

I felt it and it scared me. After a few minutes he made a phone call, and I heard him say softly, "I'm going to have to tell him and I'm not sure what to say." Then he said, "Yes, please come." When he hung the telephone up, Fred called me over and we sat down together. Fred held a picture of my mother in his hands and he put his arm over my shoulder and drew me close to him. Then he said that he had something very sad to tell me, and he told me that my mother had died a few hours ago. The funny thing was, I felt more concerned about Fred than myself. I don't know how long we sat together, but we were still there until Clara came a little while later. When she arrived, she huddled Fred and me together.  We stood there for what must have been ten minutes and Fred buried his head into Clara's shoulder. It was weird to see tall Fred stooped over like that while all cried. Clara made dinner and we ate together in a strange silence. I was the lucky one of the three. I didn't understand death.

After dinner, I took a bath. Before I went to sleep, Fred came in and sat on the bed and asked me if I needed anything. That had never happened before. Then he actually placed his hand over my heart and said to me, "Your mother was a very sweet person, Jake. I'm going to miss her terribly." Then Clara came in and sat with me, and read me Winnie the Pooh stories until I fell asleep.

I left my coffee on the counter and went out to Zhitomir, where it takes a few phone calls to reach Miriam Hankins, Clara's cousin, who had been thoughtful enough to run the obituary in her hometown in case there was anyone who might care to hear about her passing. Miriam speaks kindly of Clara and tells me Clara's will specified that her ashes be spread into the Caudell River where it intersects with Hiko Creek. (Hiko Creek runs through Fred's old property.)  With an oddly scandalous giggle for a woman in her sixties, Miriam says, "Clara said that was the only place she'd ever made love where she felt free and full as a woman, and that she wanted her ashes spread there. We'll be heading out there the day after the memorial service at The Sonnet and since you'll be coming after the chest anyway, you're welcome to join us at the ceremony."

"What are you talking about? What chest am I coming after?" I ask Miriam.

"The one Clara's been holding all these years from your Uncle Fred. No one around here was even sure we could track you down, so it's a good thing you called. There's also a letter for you."

That's the thing with death. All children are born free of secrets and mysteries and darkness and histories, everything at birth lies ahead and nothing is urgent. But in death there's revelation and the possibility of settling up, shedding light, or telling those mysterious little pieces of our lives we've concealed for so long that have meaning to us . . . and perhaps to others.

"Force of gravity," that's what Fred always called anything having to do with reality--and though it wasn't Fred himself, I can hear him inside my head as I hang up the phone with Miriam. "Force of gravity, Jake, can't ever escape the force of gravity. It's not a variable; it's a constant. You can shoot a space capsule out there--all it takes is a lot of fuel and a cylinder of metal, and you can float that thing around freely as long as you want. You can even stick a man in there if you got enough air, food, water, and courage. But you can never escape the pull, Jake. Something eventually brings you back, and then all that freedom can taunt you like a cruel joke because now you've got to make your way back home, and there aren't any soft landings, a lot of friction, a lot of heat, and a whole lot of hazards before you land."

Sitting on the edge of the bed, my body feels heavy and then my eyes fall upon the Darius Kinsey photography book I bought for Clara on Foggy but neglected to send. I feel an overwhelming sadness that I never found the ten minutes necessary to send that gift to Clara.

I feel the heat of reentry as I return to the Hideout and pick up my coffee. Otto, seeing my face, asks, "Vat happened to you, Lockhart, you look like you fell out of the sky?"

"Something pretty close to that, I'm afraid. I found out an old friend died."

"Here?" asks Otto, a little confused.

"No, she was born here, but she's from Larch, my hometown. Her obituary is in your paper. She was an old teacher of mine and a good friend of the uncle who helped raise me: a very special person."

Otto's still confused. "How old vas she?"

"She was 93, lived a great life, and died peacefully in her sleep."

Things settle as Otto dumps my cold coffee and pours me a fresh cup. He pulls over his stool, leans forward on the counter, and says, "There's no sadness at the end of a long life vell lived. That's a blessing, yah? I hope I'll go that way. Yah, your friend must have been an angel: that's how angels die."

CHAPTER 25

# Out Of The Fire
# Comes Goat Milk?

**In which** we experience the short, intense heat of reentry recalling
Uncle Fred's words the night of high school graduation, see a flag
at half-mast, and consider the changes brought by goats.

In the years before I left Larch nothing ever seemed to change. In the
years since I've left, nothing appears the same. When Larch was a wagon
station for North-South travelers, Lester Douglas, the county's first elected
representative after statehood, planted clusters of oak trees every five miles,
starting in Larch and heading to Zenith exactly one hundred miles away.
Entering or leaving, you always saw those five-mile clusters of trees with a
wooden arrow marked "5" "10" "15,". . . I remember watching them grow
larger the day I drove out of Larch. Now, both the signs and the trees are
gone and so is the winding two-lane road, replaced by a four-lane tongue
of asphalt, testimony to some engineer's ability to take a straight edge and
pencil to two points on a map without ever knowing the trees, streams,
hills, or pastures which lie between.

As I draw closer to Larch, I see signs for my old nemesis the prosecutor
who is now running for congress, and large stores around larger parking lots
with names like Mega Value and Digital Warehouse. It makes me wonder
why Clara never mentioned any of this in her letters, usually writing that
things were pretty much the same as they'd always been. But then, Clara
was old and didn't drive, and she lived in town. Most of these changes are

on new and outlying ground, and as I enter Larch itself and drive past the still active Regal Theater, I see that must have been true. Except for a few new buildings and a total turnover of the businesses, Larch is physically the same as when I left.

Continuing down Main Street, I drive beneath a banner spanning two light poles on opposite sides of the street thanking you for coming, or rewarding you for staying which says, "*Larch: Stay Tonight, Stay Forever.*"

The changes in Larch make me wonder if I was the finger in the dyke of progress, because Larch is not the same place I left.

Heading to the opposite side of town, I see the new Larch High School building. Sadly, its flag is at half-mast and the reader board beside the road says, "Farewell Mrs. Shakespeare, Clara Spengler: Larch's Greatest Teacher. We will miss you." The floodgates are opening now and when I drive on and see The Sonnet, my stomach can no longer hold the emotions I've been containing. My chest seizes as my body warms and tears begin streaming from my eyes.

I remember the evening of my high school graduation when Fred sat me down before we headed to the ceremony. I had my gown on, the tassel atop my head was like a loud fly buzzing around, and I was nervous about walking on stage to get my diploma. Fred, rising to the occasion (which he knew demanded something bigger than a congratulation), pulled out a dusty bottle of whiskey and set two glasses on the table. He poured one for himself, and then one for me, and said, "Jake, have you ever wondered why people celebrate with this stuff even though it tastes so bad?"

He saw I was cautious about taking the glass and said, "There, take a sip, I want you to have the taste of it in your mouth while I speak."

I did, wincing and choking it back as it burned my throat and seized my nostrils as Fred continued.

"Okay, here's the deal; sane men drink whiskey to remind them of the good things in life, Jake. It's not called 'spirits' for nothing. That sting and fire has a mystery which gets to your soul." Then Fred slowed his speech and spoke gentle and slow, very kind.

"So, listen, I'm not your Dad or your Mom, and I wish they were here to say what I probably can't, but here's a little something I been thinking about for your graduation."

Then Fred took another sip from his glass before continuing.

"Jake, when I was a kid I couldn't wait to get away from this podunk little town. My mother and father were like royalty in this town. Successful, respected, and decent, gosh they were decent, like you and like your mother. I had everything I needed, and your mother did too, we had a warm home and the devoted love of our parents. We didn't have a care in the world. And with all that, from the time I was ten I had my sights set on anyplace but here. You think I started fixing cars because I loved wrenches? Not at all: cars were the way out and the wheel is still the greatest invention of all time. Back then it wasn't like you could pull up and move; in order to get out I had to give Uncle Sam a few years of my life first. But at least I was out in the world. If that damned war did anything, it was to open the eyes of a lot of kids in towns like this who might not otherwise have gotten a taste of the world. I found new music, met lots of interesting people with new ideas, or at least ideas new to me, and I enjoyed the company of women in ways I never would have in Larch. I learned to dance, ate lots of different foods, drank wine, and it was all pretty good, swimming along in the world of new ideas. When I got home I got the GI Bill, and next thing you know I'm a hotshot preparing a lecture about Poor Old Jim."

I didn't want to interrupt Fred, who was rolling along differently than I'd ever heard him before, but I had no idea who Poor Old Jim was and said so.

"Poor old Jim is the name my cronies in the philosophy department gave to Nietzsche's guy on the tightrope. The great man, der ubermensch, the elevated man. Poor Old Jim is the one who takes leave of the herd to see the big wide world, risking the perils of standing alone. Nietzsche puts Poor Old Jim on a tightrope where he feels the sensations of being alive even as the herd is waiting for him to fall. One day, I have my notes all together, and I'm walking to my class to unleash 'God is Dead, now try this.' My lecture spins a few heads, but suddenly I did something unusual: I looked up and noticed there were more sleepy eyes staring at me than enlightened ones, and the words started failing. The truth was I didn't believe in those words; I'd learned them and it was easy for me to do. But about the time I was supposed to be fitted for a pipe and start wearing a beard to make me look older, it wasn't so easy anymore. Not the work, but the academia dance. Having opened the door to freedom, it became clear to me that I preferred the smell of grease and cars and dirt to the stifling air of lecture halls and teachers' lounges. I preferred a drizzly morning and the sound of water flowing through a stream to the narcissistic duels of academics. And the next thing you know, I'm working on cars again, and then, when my folks got killed I found myself back in Larch." I think it was at this point that Fred remembered we had to go to the school, and maybe,  maybe he saw the same look in my eyes as the ones which had transformed him years before, because he stopped quickly, then said,

"Oh yeah, you're wanting a point to all of this, aren't you? Fair enough. Here's the deal. You and me have a lot in common; our blood, some history, losing our parents too young, but you ain't me Jake, and that's the point. All young people are supposed to go out into the world, look for new things, tear down old things, and challenge everything you've ever been told and everything you've ever believed. What you do with it all, no one knows. You can spend your life like Poor Old Jim doing that balancing act, feeling the thrills, walking the edge of death and life, and damn if it probably don't feel good. Or you can come home and bury your head in grease and gears like I did. It's up to you, Jake, but you owe it to yourself to at least find out what you're meant to do.  Cause if you stick around this place too long, you'll rot like a stump. And if there's one thing I can tell you, Jake, it is that you're better than that."

I will leave to your imagination what we did after that, but arriving at the school auditorium that night for graduation, I can tell you I was a little looser than usual and some of my classmates asked me later why I danced across the stage to get my diploma.

Staring into the windows of The Sonnet with its Closed sign and darkened insides, I'm not certain whether I'm in pain or numb. After a few minutes I drive on, my mind spinning with memories as I near my old house. The house is no longer white, but a deep blue with gold trim around the new windows, there's a children's play-set in the front, a chain-link fence surrounding the backyard, and the trees are taller. There's smoke coming out of the chimney and fortunately a new roof, especially if the chimney is the same one I left behind. The old laurel hedge has been removed to make way for a well-kept vegetable garden and there's a row of blueberry bushes leading up to the front porch. About the only thing remaining is the little daphne I planted in the months after Fred's death. It is large and proud, though without flowers at this time of the year. Seeing the daphne restores my calm and after a few minutes I can look at the house, now appreciating that it looks better than when I left it. I'm tempted to knock on the door, explain who I am and ask if I can look around, but it feels awkward. I sit there for a while with Zhitomir idling, staring at the place, trying to feel something, wishing there was some music to tell me what I'm supposed to feel, but after a few minutes there I realize I'm not feeling much of anything except for being happy I left when I did.

I head down the road towards Fred's old property and if I didn't recognize the stream and the trees I easily could have driven past it. There's a new barn where the house used to stand and a beautiful orchard of young fruit trees surrounding it. The pastures are green and full, though grazed down, apparently by a large number of nubian goats I see off in the distance by the trees fronting Hiko Creek. A sign out front says "Jackie's Organic Produce and Goat Cheese. Sign Up Now!" And there, neatly tucked into a new shed, is Fred's McCormick tractor, easily fifty years older than the Volvo station wagon parked beside it with the bumper sticker that reads "Buy Local."

I think about driving down to David Hilger, Fred's old friend the veterinarian, to see if I might be able to park Zhitomir in his yard, but decide it would be awkward to knock without warning. I consider heading over to Clara's in case someone is there and I can take care of the business with Fred's cedar chest, but I need some time to let things settle. I know there is more to come but for now, I head out of town and drive to the County Park where I can stay for the night, living the way I live now. If Larch has changed, so have I.

Sitting in Zhitomir, I remember something Fred always said when we watched the early space flights come back to Earth. There'd always be that point when Walter Cronkite and Wally Shirra would explain the perilous forces confronted returning to the earth's atmosphere. They'd talk about insulation and extreme temperatures and communications blackouts while they sat and waited nervously through the most dramatic moment. Not Fred. Fred said about reentry, "You're either toast or you're not, but dead or alive, it's all over pretty quickly."

◁

CHAPTER 26

# "Stand Up; Speak Your Piece; And Don't Stop Until You're Done!!!"

**In Which** we honor an old friend in the words that she taught us to love.

"Stand up; speak your piece; and don't stop until you're done!"

If you had Clara Spengler as your English teacher, you had that command etched into your brain. In Clara's days, especially in a small town like Larch, you had a teacher for an entire year. You soon found out that, with Clara Spengler, that year could be long and miserable or it could be dedicated and productive. The choice was yours. She was one of those old-fashioned teachers who didn't crack a smile until Thanksgiving, not coincidentally, the same time your first paper was due. Every student had three required papers in English Literature: the first was due the Wednesday before Thanksgiving; the second on the closest school day to Abraham Lincoln's birthday; and the third on the day closest to Memorial Day.

There were few surprises in store for you with Mrs. Spengler. You either knew of her reputation or you had brothers and sisters or parents who had become capable readers and writers in her class. The first day of every new year she made things perfectly clear, "You may leave here and never read another book and you may leave here and never write another sentence, but you will leave here knowing how to do both!" It was equal parts boast, threat, and challenge.

Do something well for a long time and you make a lot of friends. On the night of Clara Spengler's memorial service her friends begin gathering a little before seven. Mingling in the crowd there are a few familiar people to say hello to while avoiding the repeated, "Where have you been, Spinner?" It's notable how many adults, most of whom must have developed later friendships with their former teacher, still refer to her respectfully as Mrs. Spengler. There are quite a few multigenerational groups: grandparents, parents, and children whose appreciation of literature was due to their teacher's passion for words. Each has come to pay one's respects." Clara Spengler has earned the respect of a lot of people in this town.

As people gather, they speak, they hug, or shake hands and "checkin" the way neighbors do. I find myself imagining what I would be saying had I remained in Larch. Most of the people gathered are familiar with each other as friends, neighbors, and rivals. The things they say, questions they ask about children, about meetings, about events shared and common everyday things hold something I don't experience. But tonight, they don't answer the "How are you" with "I'm fine" or "We're good" or "Things are going well." There's something about our shared purpose this evening that elicits more honesty.

I'm feeling a high school reunion kind of awkwardness when an old schoolmate, Frankie Hobart, spies me and says, "Look at what the dog brought in: Jake Spinner, the long lost son of Larch. I heard you roam the world now. Is that true, or have you been holed up somewhere storing food and waiting for the end to come?"

"You mean it hasn't ended yet, Frankie? But, no, I don't roam the world, only a small part of it and when I read about Clara--Mrs. Spengler's-- passing in the newspaper a few days ago, I thought I should come home to say goodbye." Speaking of coming home sticks in my throat a little as I haven't thought of anyplace as home in a long time. I'm uncomfortable calling Larch home and start thinking of Will Lockhart in *The Man from Laramie*. After all the times I've spoken of Zhitomir as my home, of traveling and having no need to be from somewhere, not needing roots as it were, it feels rehearsed and inauthentic.

Fortunately, Frankie Hobart, pharmacist and vice-chair of the Larch Chamber of Commerce, is better able to ease any rough spots in casual conversation and kindly lets me off the hook by telling me about his family and his work, and thanking me for coming to the memorial.

"Well, stop by if you have the chance, Jake. You probably haven't seen the new pharmacy. We're on the north side of town about five miles out. You can't miss the big sign, 'World of Drugs' in red neon. Lots of changes in our little town since Mrs. Spengler taught us about old Richard the Third, don't you think? I still remember you kneeling down in class that day screaming, 'My horse, my horse, my kingdom for a horse!' It's nice to see you," says Frankie as he starts walking off before turning back to ask, "Say, Jake, I'm curious:  what book did you bring?"

"What do you mean, Frankie, what book?"

Frankie explains, "I guess you didn't hear about this. Our beloved teacher left one last assignment. The memorial announcement asked everyone to bring a book with them, something special, or for those who were her students, something they may have read when Mrs. Spengler was our teacher. People have been bringing them in the past few days and I guess they're all laid out inside on the tables."

A few minutes later when the doors to The Sonnet are opened and we file in and fill the small store to the brim, the books are indeed all laid out, and included amid the book-filled tables and shelves are notes, letters, and small pieces Clara Spengler wrote over the years, including comments from report cards. I find one that could have been written to me.

"It's not enough to be a reader, you will do well to learn to write some things down." That comment was a standard for Clara Spengler when she saw people with their nose buried in a book.

Looking at the materials gathered in The Sonnet, I come across a short piece Clara wrote for the *Larch News*, a paper published locally until the mid-eighties when it merged with and became the *Valley News Statesman*. The *Larch News* was a weekly paper and had a collection of columnists who rotated pieces under the heading "Community Voices." Clara was one of the voices and this piece was entitled 'There Are No <u>Important</u> Books". It is the same point Julian made years ago at the film symposium. I guess it's true: great minds tend to think alike.

Clara's words state, "Books are written for people to enjoy, occasionally they inspire us and even may alter our lives, but we should be careful not to seduce ourselves with analysis to the point where we can no longer appreciate the song because we seek to know the singer. I have no purpose in reading or teaching literature other than to enjoy and respect the craft and occasional beauty with which writers tell their stories."

She goes on to say, "In my experience, if you want to flatter an author, don't ask him or her about their books' deeper symbolism,  read it, and if you meet them somewhere, offer to buy them a cup of coffee."

Fifty years. Clara Spengler taught from 1931 to 1981 and lying on the tables in The Sonnet are but a few of the books with which "she enjoyed and respected the craft through which writers tell their stories."

*Dr. Zhivago*, Hank Gooding, Class of 1959
*Ballad of the Sad Café,* Felicia Moffett, Class of 1969
*Moby Dick*--( Kidding) John Carrew, Class of 1971
*The Maltese Falcon*, Dexter Drake, Class of 1951
*The Bible*, Alice Paisley, Class of 1946
*Letters from the Earth*, Lester Pritt, Class of 1936
*A Coney Island of the Mind and Other Poems*, Sandy Kellog, Class of 1961
*Elmer Gantry*, Ted Maizel, Class of 1947
*The Flowers of Evil*, Abigail Frances, Class of 1973
*The Captain's Verses*, Francine Holland, Class of 1973
*Matthew 5:1, The Sermon on the Mount*, Patty Robeson, Class of 1942,
*Ariel*, Louisa Sanchez, Class of 1971
*The Poems of Emily Dickinson*, Dorothea Kinsey, Class of 1938
*Under Milkwood*, Keller Benko, Class of 1962
*Another Country*, Anders Pollard, Class of 1966
*A Midsummer Night's Dream*, Paula Gaylene Trebber, Class of 1951,
*Death Be Not Proud*, Jerome Daye, Class of 1969
*Slaughterhouse Five*, Ina Mae Gergen, Class of 1982,
*The World According to Garp*, Rick Montello, Class of 1980,
*A Streetcar Named Desire*, Lucy Samuels, Class of 1955.

Each book represents a harvest of sweet and precious fruits. Clara Spengler was the person who guided each of us to the fruit we needed. Clearly Otto Guenther was right about how angels die. In her career, Clara Spengler gave fruit to thousands. I'm looking down at the books, reading the cards, thinking of how much lies hidden in the lives of people and what influences them, about what they share and don't. I'm staring at a well-worn copy of *Catch 22*, when an old classmate approaches. I'm not certain I am any more composed now than when I went to school with Rosalyn Pelton.

"Say, Spinner, it's true. Someone told me they saw that circus wagon of yours drive into town. I should have known that Cousin Clara could reel you in. Where are you living?"

Eyeing Rosalyn, I am reminded of why I was so distracted during class in high school.

"Rosalyn Pelton. You still live here?"

"Yes, never left, but it's Rosalyn Pelton Vasquez, now," she says, waving her ringed finger at me. "You have one of these?" she asks and lifts my hand up to see. "No, I don't suppose you would. Are you still so shy?"

Rosalyn's interrogation is playful.

"Jake, how come you never asked me out? You wanted to, right?"

"Sure, Rosalyn, I always wanted to ask you out, but I never could figure where out was in Larch. And then, you scared me with your confidence and your beauty."

"Hah, beauty and confidence? I guess I had you fooled. So, Jake, still burning diesel fuel all over the country?"

By the look on her face, Rosalyn did not expect my answer to be yes.

"I can't even imagine what that would be like. I read your pieces and I thought you were living back east . . ."

"You read my pieces?"

"Sure, Clara posted them each month in the window. You think an old English teacher would let a success story go unnoticed? She kept track of everyone. Remember Jaycee Rae? You remember her, she sat in the back, had the weird hair and the long fingernails? She lived with her grandmother?"

"Who could forget Jaycee? She was cool."

"Well, she writes some scandalously saucy Harlequins now under the name Hallie Florabunda. Clara kept every one of them on a shelf along the back wall. Signed, too. You bet she didn't let anyone forget that A.L. Janus is none other than Larch's own Jake Spinner, class of 1970. Here, let me show you something. Rosalyn walks me to the back of The Sonnet where a few cozy chairs and a small table and lamp sit beneath a wall of shelves and a small bulletin board. The wall is pinned with clippings about young authors from the Western Writer's Conference, but there's a piece from the Washington Post under the headline Visible Past Gathering Sparks Film Discussion. There's a photo of the symposium panel with my head circled in red ink and a caption, in Clara's handwriting, which reads, "Local Boy

Makes Good. Larch High School graduate, Jake Spinner."

"How's it feel to be famous, Jake?" Then, before I can protest the comment, Rosalyn says, "Listen, you'd better grab a seat before this thing begins. I need to help Miriam. There are a lot of people here tonight and you know what that means."

This prompts us to speak simultaneously, "Stand up, speak your piece, and don't stop until you're done!"

There are no seats so I stand off to the side as Miriam Hankins, the woman I spoke with on the phone from Cedar Monk, moves to the front of The Sonnet. She resembles Clara. Her posture is perfect, making her look taller than she is, and her hands move with grace and assurance as she begins speaking.

"I'd like to welcome you all to this joyous celebration to honor the life of Clara Spengler. I know it would make Clara happy to see all of your lovely faces. You, her friends and former students, were her life's passion, at least one of them, and you know better than anyone that we are surrounded by her other passion:  these books and the words within them that she so cherished.

"Thank you also for bringing your books. You all know were she here, she would be excited. Clara would remember when you first read it, and she might even embarrass you with a story about you from one of your classes in high school. Clara was a woman of many gifts, and when Rosalyn and I were thinking about what to say tonight, the thing we admired most about Clara was her courage--some might say fearlessness--in saying what she thought.

"If you were fortunate enough to spend time with her in the past year, you know that Clara was aware her life was coming to an end. She often said she wanted no sadness around her passing. She planned this evening with all of you in mind. As she grew closer to her death, she grew closer to the words that were the joy of her life. In the last months, some passage--a poem or quotation unknown to any one present, but clearly deeply meaningful to her--would come forth from her mouth in a strong and powerful voice belying the frailty and age of her body.

"About two months ago, I visited Clara at her home, and she was very excited. She had been poring over books of poetry and she found one that brought her great pleasure. She showed me the book but would not allow me to read it until she had spoken it aloud. As you all know, Clara was adamant that poetry be spoken aloud. So, in honor of Clara, let me do my best."

Miriam stands forward, holds her hands in a prayer, takes one deep breath and then another, and then begins her recitation,

### "Forever" by John Boyle O'Reilly (1844-1890)

Those we love truly never die,
Though year by year the sad memorial wreath,
A ring and flowers, types of life and death,
Are laid upon their graves

For death the pure life saves,
And life all pure is love; and love can reach
From heaven to earth, and nobler lessons teach
Than those by mortals read.

Well blest is he who has a dear one dead.
A friend he has whose face will never change
A dear communion that will not grow strange;
The anchor of a love is death.

The blessed sweetness of a loving breath
Will reach our cheek all fresh through weary years.
For her who died long since, ah! Waste not tears,
She's thine unto the end.

Thank God for one dear friend,
With face still radiant with the light of truth,
Whose love comes laden with the soul of youth,
Through twenty years of death.

When she finishes the room is silent for a moment until Miriam speaks again to ease us from our silent vision of Clara's unchanged face.

"There's one more reading," she says and a collective laugh fills the room. "Cousin was a true English teacher to the very end. If only you knew how she sat with all of these words, not wanting to disappoint you." Then she lifts the same Bible Clara had showed me the afternoon of my "vision" (the undelivered present to Eleanor Roosevelt) and begins reading the

Lord's Prayer. Halfway through the prayer, she closes the Bible and a gentle chorus of voices fills The Sonnet with the completion of the recitation.

"Now, I'd like to offer any of you who have something to say the chance to speak. If you have tears, please don't be ashamed, but let them be tears of joy, for that is what Clara would have wanted."

One by one they "stood up, spoke their piece, and didn't stop until they were done!" There were stories from classes, stories about Clara writing letters to friends and former students while they were in military service, stories about Clara and the ways she maneuvered around this or that principal who was seeking to dictate to her what she could or should teach.

Kellog Simpson, class of 1947, recounted how during his senior year, "The high school principal, Fulton Cosgrove, came into the room during the middle of class, and he was steaming. He had in hand a list of works he said were deemed unsuitable for young readers and gave it to Mrs. Spengler. Mrs. Spengler took that list, read it aloud to us, then taped it to the blackboard, and as Mr. Cosgrove looked on, she said she would confer extra credit to anyone who read any of the books on the list. Cosgrove was furious and demanded she stop using the books. Mrs. Spengler told him 'Mr. Cosgrove, long after your embarrassing list is nothing but sordid dust and you are gone from Larch High School, both these books and I shall still be here.'"

There were tears for Mrs. Clara Spengler: teacher, friend, and one precious life that graced Larch long enough to gather a rich blanket of affection.

As the memorial ended and the crowd trickled out, Rosalyn stopped me.

"Jake, would you mind staying on for a few minutes?

"Of course not. Something the matter? "

"No, nothing, just something that Miriam and I are confused about and thought you might be able to help. Thanks, Jake. I'll be a few minutes and then we can talk."

A few minutes pass before The Sonnet empties and Miriam and Rosalyn take me to the back of the store. We take our seats by the table and they show me a tablet with words scrawled in Clara's handwriting. Miriam speaks, "Jake, because you knew Clara and Fred, we thought you might know something about this." She hands me the tablet that reads

". . . here we are on this windy hilltop like a couple of scarecrows . . . "

"Does it mean anything to you?"

"It's familiar, but I can't say why, and the fact that it's incomplete is baffling."

"You know Clara never allowed quotations to go un-noted. We're sure it meant something to Clara because she scribbled this down a few weeks ago and said to be sure we read it when we spread her ashes. She was adamant about it. Oh, well, thought by chance you might make something of it." Then she asks, "We'll see you tomorrow at the river, yes?"

"Of course."

Then Rosalyn asks, "Where are you staying?" When I explain that I have been at the state park, she suggests that I pull behind The Sonnet for the night.

"We'll give you the key. There's a small bathroom and a clean shower. You're welcome to use it."

# CHAPTER 27

# Shall We Gather
# At The River?

**In Which** we spread our teacher's ashes at the confluence of two streams and find initials carved into a tree and unravel a mystery.

In the glory of a beautiful morning when the air is crisp, the trees proud with color, and the sun warm, nine of us gather at the confluence of Hiko Creek and the Caudell River:  Miriam, Rosalyn, Rosalyn's husband Benny, Lucy Beals (another former teacher from Larch), George Popper (Clara's last principal), and Franklin and Myrtle Johnson (former owners of the juice bar adjacent to The Sonnet), myself, and a cheerful, young minister by the name of Loudon Capshaw, also a friend and patron of Clara's. Though it's early July, Hiko Creek still surges with water, throwing a cool spray in the air as it roils against the steady heavy flow of the Caudell. While we stand in a circle around the blue ceramic urn holding Clara's ashes, listening to Minister Capshaw, an occasional trout snaps at an unwitting insect. The sound of the trout provides a welcome distraction from the serious tone of the sermon.

"Death is the gathering of our entirety. Even those whose faith assures them that dying is but another step in the eternal, face it with some trepidation. Death is a grand unknowing."

We stand on these banks thinking noble and serious thoughts about our departed teacher. She would not have wanted the mood to be somber, but it is. I'm certain we all imagine this is where Clara came to sit and day-dream, to take her mind off of the world, where perhaps she wrote or read the words she so loved. We're huddled together with no music, for Clara had instructed that the wind and the water of the river be the only sounds. (Apparently the trout did not figure in her planning.)

The Caudell narrows as it rolls past Hiko Creek. It has been eroding the bank opposite us for as long as I can remember. A small eddy forms in the river as the sermon continues, and I see some brightly colored ducks land in the green shimmer of the water. From where we stand, I can see Fred's old property hiding behind a thicket of red-twig dogwood. Listening to the somber words that cannot possibly capture the spirit of Clara Spengler's life, I drift between the scenery and the words until Minister Capshaw's voice slows to a conclusion.

"Therefore, as you take these ashes into your hands, please do so with an acceptance of your doubts or a celebration of your certainties. The woman they represent, Clara Spengler, asked us to assist her today. She asked us to return her to a place she loved, where she wishes to remain for eternity. Take her ashes in your hands and feel not the dust of an end, but the majesty of the life they once held. Don't grow sad or frightened by your actions because in you resides all she was in life, and you are here because she wished for you to hold her now."

And then, as if on command, we see it in the warmth of a July morning. We see it amongst fluttering leaves and fertile ground as Clara Spofford Spengler's dust forms a cloud engulfing us. A tree, a grand old maple whose branches have never been pruned or crowded but have grown in a majestic sweep like a cradle towards the opening of the river. We see beneath branches dipping down shaded by decades of weight and leaves and snow and gravity; a grotto or a nest, a resting place against the trunk of the tree. And on that trunk, a set of carved initials inside of a heart with letters formed by the blade of a knife whose wound has scarred and been healed over by years of sap and growth. The letters inside the heart: C.S. & F.T. Beneath the heart, a glistening plaque, reflecting the radiant summer light into our eyes, and on the plaque, the same words the two cousins asked me about last night at The Sonnet.

". . . Here we are on this windy hilltop like a pair of scarecrows . . ." T. W. FROM N.O.T.I.

Tracing the words on the plaque with her fingers, Miriam says, "It appears our mystery grows deeper. No doubt the C.S. is Auntie, and then she quoted in a voice remarkably like her aunt, 'One must never fail to cite the author of a fine quotation lest the audience give credit to you for the inspiration of another.' That quote is from Clara Spengler, but this one, does anyone recognize it?"

Rosalyn and I blushed our recollection at the same time. Any former student of Mrs. Shakespeare would have recognized these words that sat above the front blackboard of her classroom, written in large letters by the hand of a fine calligrapher. Rosalyn answers Miriam,

"Now I understand when Clara spoke of love, she meant love."

"You mean love, love, Rosalyn?" Miriam asks.

"I mean, capital L, capital O, capital V, capital E:  LOVE. And no doubt the other set of initials are your Uncle Fred's?" says Rosalyn to me.

"Not a doubt in my mind, Rosalyn. I had my suspicions last night and did a little investigating in The Sonnet after the memorial. I'll show you later at The Sonnet."

Leave it to Clara and Fred to cook up a plot twist to break up an otherwise far too serious scene. Everyone present is laughing as we take turns reaching into the urn holding the late Clara Spengler's ashes. With each grasp, the remains of a soul that breathed life for nearly a century are cast to the wind and the river that must have inspired Fred and Clara for many years.

Later at The Sonnet, it doesn't take long to find a much-read copy of The *Collected Plays of Tennessee Williams* and therein begin unraveling the details of the romance between our two relatives. N.O.T.I. stands for *The Night of the Iguana,* and the words on the plaque are spoken by the angelic painter, Hannah Jelks. Jelks is the angel, both to her dying grandfather, a poet, and to the defrocked Reverend T. Laurence Shannon, played by Richard Burton, who is cleft between the world of body and spirit, service and flesh.

Now, as we stare at the book and thumb to the section where the words are spoken, Miriam says, "No doubt, the plaque is a direct quotation from the play."

"Yes, look, it's underlined in pencil," says Rosalyn.

"But how did they do it?" asks Miriam. "Clara was married to Henry."

"True, but he died in 1960. Clara would have been forty-six, and Fred?" asks Rosalyn.

"Fred was born in 1922, you can do the math. 1960 was the same year my Mother died," I say. Then Miriam adds, "What I'm curious about is who dug out the quote?"

"You can bet it was Clara, Miriam; Uncle Fred was not the type to read Tennessee Williams in his spare time."

Then, taking the collection of plays into her hands and flipping through the pages, Rosalyn says with a sly smile, "I think we'll have to hold onto this, don't you, Miriam?"

Larch, of course, has no repertory theater, but it has video stores. In fact, there are three including one at a Texaco Station where you can get gas, pizza, and a movie without leaving your car. Texaco Video has six copies of *Speed* but no copy of *The Night of the Iguana*. The clerk, an eager and helpful teenage girl, has never heard of it, but does know that an iguana is an animal. She suggests I try looking at one of their rival stores, All Time Video, telling me, "They organize things by themes: you know, Love, Cars, Food, and there's a category called Animals: maybe it's there."

Taking her advice, I drive to All Time Video, which has *King Kong, Anaconda, Maltese Falcon, Babe, Bambi, Pharlap, Born Free, Dumbo, Gorillas in the Mist, Moby Dick,* and *Jaws,* to name a few, but no iguanas anywhere in the store. The assistant manager at All Time suggests I try looking at Movies Forever, the last of the three video stores in Larch, which does, to their credit, have a well organized section of classic films. The manager of Movies Forever wears a button that says "Ask Me" on his snappy red uniform, so I do. Surprise, he knows the film, and says he saw it in film class at the community college a few years ago, but thinks the only place that might carry it would be Film Spectacular, a video store in Endicott, twenty miles away.

"They have a lot of that back-in-the-day-stuff," he tells me. "There's a film studies class in the Community College in Endicott, so Film Spectacular has things we don't carry.

The drive to Endicott takes me east through even more new homes than there are in Larch. Despite the signs of progress, I enjoy the drive, especially as people seeing Zhitomir pass them on the road start honking and waving, and some even stick their hands out the window and give the thumbs-up sign. And, the trip is successful. They have the film, and by the looks of the box, it seldom gets checked out. There's only one glitch; the store manager is nervous about renting me the film because I have no permanent address.

"Well, I'm not supposed to do it, but I suppose if you give me your driver's license number and a twenty dollar deposit."

I agree and then he asks me about the film.

"I love it. Richard Burton and Ava Gardner go toe-to-toe with alcohol, religion, and lizards."

"Who wins?"

"The lizard!"

"Awesome, I'll watch it when you bring it back."

When I return to Larch, I call Rosalyn to let her know that I have found the film and suggest she get Miriam and Benny so we can all watch it together.

"Where, Jake, on that little television at The Sonnet?"

"No, we can watch in my truck. I have a larger television."

"Forget that, Jake. You can come over tonight for dinner and we can watch it in a house. You know, Jake, a house, with warm air, soft chairs, popcorn, drinks, a bathroom? Maybe you remember what that's like?"

I hear Rosalyn start laughing as she tells Benny what's going on.

"I'll call a few other people, if you don't mind. Loudon, George, and Lucy, they'll all enjoy it."

A few hours later we're all together at Rosalyn and Benny's house. Rosalyn is having a lot of fun at my expense. "Benny, can you get some gas-soaked rags? We want Jake to feel at home." Benny suggests she ease up, but she's having too much fun to stop. "You must meet a lot of women, huh, Jake? I mean, who can resist a man with a big truck? I remember when Fred hauled the elephant. I hope you've cleaned it since then," she chuckles.

I assure Rosalyn that I have cleaned it since then, and a few minutes later she lets up long enough to start making some pizza in the kitchen. Lucy and George arrive with Miriam, and Loudon comes a few minutes later. We start talking about the day's surprise. Lucy, who is in her mid-seventies with the energy of someone who still spends her summers hiking and bicycling around the country, clears the air at last.

"I knew about them all along. You know, Clara was young when Fred was in high school. She was only eleven years older than he was. It's not a scandal. Nothing happened until after Henry died, and it wasn't anybody's business. Teachers were expected to act like nuns when Clara began her career. A lot of hooey, that."

Then George, who speaks like a train slowing to a halt, says, "I knew too. We all knew, but like Lucy says, it wasn't anybody's business. Fred did a lot of things for the school, and the two of them always had eyes for each other. Clara told me once that she'd always loved Fred. I know, I know, you guys think that's weird, but it wasn't. It wasn't weird and it wasn't dirty." George looks at Loudon Capshaw holding a slice of pizza in his hands while he listens. "Don't look at me," says Loudon. "I didn't know Fred. I only met Clara seven years ago, but I'm not surprised. I used to go into The Sonnet and talk books with Clara. There she was, this tiny little old lady, but she'd get going on those books, and not the polite stuff either. She hated prudes. You all know that. It wasn't by chance that she kept the Henry Miller section right out front where you walked into the store."

"I always wondered about that," says Miriam.

At last I have to confess, "I never had a clue."

"Finally, he admits it," says Rosalyn. "Very funny, Rosalyn. But no, I never knew. Didn't know when I lived here, and didn't have an inkling from the letters Clara wrote me over the years."

"Which reminds me," says Miriam, "you have to get that chest. She was adamant about saving it for you. Do you know what's in it?"

"I have no idea, Miriam, but I'll come look tomorrow if that's okay."

After the pizza and conversation we settle in for the movie with its cackling puritanical Miss Fellowes, the more desperate (though less puritanical) Shannon, and the quote that we found today, spoken by the angelic Hannah Jelks.

At the film's end, speaking to no one in particular, Lucy Beals concludes what has been a two-day memorial for our departed friend.

"Damn, if that's not one heck of a piece of work. She did love words, that old bird."

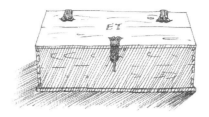

CHAPTER 28

# One Cedar Chest

In Which we open a cedar chest and reveal the remains of a life.

The next morning I drive to Clara's house where I meet Rosalyn. Sitting in front of the sofa is the chest, laid out like many other things drawn to the surface by Clara's passing. It's eerily quiet and the house has an uncomfortable stillness. Rosalyn fumbles through the kitchen to prepare a pot of tea.

Clara's things are spread out in the rooms of the house. Rosalyn explains that it was Clara herself who spent the last weeks of her life rummaging through her possessions.

"We thought she was looking for something, but she said she wasn't searching for anything in particular,  looking at things one last time."

There are papers and documents sitting in stacks on the kitchen table with notes written on top of them marked:  Accounts, Sonnet Lease, Attorney, Contacts . . . Rosalyn explains they plan to sort through things when they can.

"Not like your Uncle Fred. Wasn't he the one who had his house burnt down after he died?"

"Yes, that was Fred. Easier to disperse a gas than a solid."

"What does that mean?" asks Rosalyn.

"Oh, nothing, something Fred used to say."

When Rosalyn finishes her tea, she gets up and says, "Well, Jake, I'm off to work. Pull the door closed when you're done." Then with a kindly incisive recognition that looking inside the chest may be difficult, she says, "You going to be okay with this? I can stay if you need me to."

"That's very kind of you, Rosalyn, but I'm fine. I'll rummage through what I can and then load it into my truck. There's no rush, right?"

"Right. But no fast escapes this time, Spinner. You come by tonight for dinner with Benny and me. Okay?"

When Rosalyn leaves, I open the cedar chest and am greeted by a paper plaque that boasts, 'Keeps out moths. A Lifetime of Protection, Guaranteed!' The scent of the aged cedar fills my nostrils with the sharp and unmistakable smell of time. Why do things smell different when they age? On top of two wool blankets sits an envelope addressed "Jake," written in Clara's once-strong, familiar hand. Inside the envelope is this letter:

*Dear Jake,*

*One last letter from your old friend that I know you will read someday. I want you to know a little about the chest and its contents.*

*This chest was your mother's. Fred kept it at my house so you wouldn't stumble upon it when you were young, before he thought you were ready for it. While Eva was dying, she prepared it for you with the things she wanted you to have when you got older. She gave it to Fred and told him to save it until he thought you were ready to have it. Fred added things over the years, things he thought you might want to know about some day, like the records of the family births and deaths, and burial details and locations.*

*I think he wanted to give it to you before he died in case you had any questions, but as you know better than anyone else, things were moved to the back burner in that ever-engaged mind of his. Either that, or he thought you weren't ready. I would have passed it on to you after Fred died, but that last conversation you and I had that day at The Sonnet had me thinking you were moving forward on another path and I thought seeing all of this might complicate things for you and slow down your momentum.*

*Let me write this as clearly as I can: you were born to a fine woman and raised by a fine man after she died. There was a lot of love for you, so don't get too sad when you rummage through these things. Any collection of memories can be difficult, but there are things in here Fred spared you from. You lost your grandparents and your parents very young. I wonder if there was some blessing in that it happened before you could feel its full impact. Fred was not so blessed. He loved his parents, his sister, and you more deeply than he would ever show, but if losing them in such a short period was hard on him, raising you was not. You gave him responsibility and companionship and it helped him enjoy being alive. We're both very lucky to have had him in our lives. He was something else, wasn't he?*

*Since you left Larch, you've had quite a life, and though no one here will admit it, most of us wish we'd done something the same. We always knew you were a special child, Jake. It may have taken you a while to get rolling, but that's the way it is with some people.*

*By the way, you turned out to be a pretty good writer. Not the best of your family by any means-that would have to be your Mother-but not too bad. Keep at it, Jake, and don't worry about the wolves; their teeth aren't as sharp as they seem. Last of all: thank you for holding my hand at Fred's funeral.*

*Your loving friend, Clara*

*PS. I took the liberty of adding one thing to the chest. It's a beautiful poem and I hope you like it. I offered it to Fred after your mother died.C.*

For the second time in two days I am presented with the words of the poem, *Forever.* At The Sonnet recitation, it swept by in the moment, but today I have the chance to read it as Clara would have liked. Clara taught her students that poetry is not a silent prayer, but a song sung with the human voice. And so I read aloud:

### Forever by John Boyle O'Reilly (1844-1890)

Those we love truly never die,
Though year by year the sad memorial wreath,
A ring and flowers, types of life and death,
Are laid upon their graves.

For death the pure life saves,
And life all pure is love; and love can reach
From heaven to earth, and nobler lessons teach
Than those by mortals read.

Well blest is he who has a dear one dead:
A friend he has whose face will never change--

A dear communion that will not grow strange;
The anchor of a love is death.

The blessed sweetness of a loving breath
Will reach our cheek all fresh through weary years.
For her who died long since, ah! Waste not tears,
She's thine unto the end.

Thank God for one dear friend,
With face still radiant with the light of truth,
Whose love comes laden with the scent of youth,
Through twenty years of death.

When I finish reading the poem, I lift the two covering blankets revealing boxes within the bigger box. There is a small, smooth pine box with Fred's belongings and another hand-made cedar box with my mother's things.

Inside the cedar box are unsent letters from my mother addressed simply to Jake. They tell the story of the chest. One explains that it belonged to my mother and was given to her by my grandmother, Ariella, and grandfather, Samuel, for her wedding. The lid is inscribed with, "To Our Beautiful Eva-All that is important in a life can be held within one cedar chest. May this chest hold hope and memory, and may it travel with you through life. May all that is precious rest here."

As I read, I recall Fred explaining that his father, my grandfather, said life was meant to be lived, not accumulated. "Unless you're a mechanic with a welding torch," Fred liked to add. Apparently, I share this credo with my grandfather, and so my life's possessions fit into my truck. As a latter day nomad, I haven't gathered a lot of physical artifacts, or too many obligations.

My fingers clutch at blankets that feel soft against my skin. I lay one across my lap and drape the other over my shoulders. The blankets have their own familiar smell, the smell of leaning against my mother at the Regal, watching movies in the winter. I feel my mother near me, her warmth and her smell, and it feels as if she is sitting beside me and we're taking turns poking our fingers into the Raisinet box probing for the sweet chewy morsels. This is the first memory I have. Even as I sit recalling her so vividly, I wonder if the memory is real or something I've fashioned in my imagination?

Delving deeper into the chest, I think of "Onward," Julian's spirited slogan to move forward no matter what. I am not moving forward, but perhaps for the first time in my life, I am moving backwards. I am rolling back history and memory as I remove photos and blankets, medals and certificates, letters and locations, notes and poems, each one selected for the story they tell.

Stories require little physical space but they pack an emotional wallop. I open a small silver box that rattles when I lift it. Inside are my father's medals, which must have seemed like shiny worthless trinkets when they were sent to my mother to fill the void left by her man who never came home from war. Staring at their photographs I think of an article I wrote about war movies after showing a film to a veteran's group in Hastings, Washington. In the months before the screening, I must have watched a hundred war films, everything from glorifying films like The *Sands of Iwo Jima* and *The Longest Day* to *Full Metal Jacket* and *Coming Home*. I watched *The Best Years of Our Lives* and *Johnny Got His Gun*. In all those war films there wasn't one about a kid in the American army who spoke Hungarian and was killed under circumstances never fully explained in events leading up to the Soviet invasion of Hungary. There wasn't a film that showed him thinking about a son he would never meet but would know only from pictures. Needless to say, Mom didn't like war movies and neither do I. I hate war and its savagery.

Next I unfold a soft cloth which holds two things oddly nested together: my grandfather's straight razor, which he used working as a barber while he made his way through medical school, and a woman's hairbrush with the initials A.T. (for Ariella Tolliver). Maybe in 1952 when her parents died, my mother smelled it the way I can smell her now. Maybe she held her mother's hairbrush with its ivory handle to her nose or brushed her own hair, feeling close to her.

This is a strange Tolliver/Spinner family reunion. We're all here in this room pouring forth from this humble cedar chest, starting with my grandfather Samuel Jr., who practiced medicine out of his home with his wife, Ariella, as a nurse. Together the two of them delivered babies, dressed wounds, offered medicine, and stood vigil when necessary to the needs of anyone who called on them. Sometimes they were paid and sometimes not. Samuel Jr. lived to honor the legacy of his father, who died defending two innocent Nez Perce Indians in Larch, who were then falsely condemned and lynched by a hate-filled mob. My grandfather lived with conviction. He and his equally dedicated wife would die unfairly of the meningitis that was thought to have come home with soldiers returning from Korea in 1952. As I set the currycomb down I wonder: do all Tollivers lose their parents too young and live with that sadness?

We're all together again. I remember the day after Fred was buried when I had wandered through his empty house. Today there are no voices, only smells and a silent music playing like a slow-moving equatorial current. There are places on the certificates--dates, and locations where everyone is buried, informing me where I can find their names on headstones. I can trace a life's events from birth to graduation to death. I have the details in a small compartment in the chest. There's a velvet jewel box inside which I find my mother's gold wedding band and my father's watch (which had belonged to his father, a gift when he retired from the printing office where he worked for twenty-eight years after coming to New York). Placing the ring on my pinky, I hold the tiny watch, delicate and too small by today's standards for a man. I hold it in my hands and the gold feels cool as I stare at the glass crystal covering the clear numbers and the elegant second-wheel inset. Should I wind it? Yes, I do and the second wheel begins turning and sounds come forth. I hold the two objects in my hand, then draw them to my lips and kiss them. This is their life, the remains of two people. I should send this watch to Julian: it was his father's. Julian must remember it on his father's wrist. I feel a thread running through us, a thread of connection and loss. What is it? It isn't sadness, so much as my destiny, role, and purpose.

Digging deeper I find the folded flag that draped my father's coffin with the location of his grave at the American Cemetery in France. The flag is coarse and cold, it has no smell. He never touched it; he never saw them remove it from his coffin as they lowered him into the ground. Why wasn't he brought home? I want to believe that it doesn't matter, that where your body remains is not as important as where it traveled. I want to believe, as I set the flag aside, that I inherited the wanderer's gene from a father who left where he was raised to seek new worlds. Here are the remains of not one life but many lives, all emanating from this cedar chest given to a beloved daughter on the day of her marriage to a man with whom she would spend so little time. Now I cannot hold back tears, and I cannot pretend it is okay to be alone and wandering. Here on the bed are my mother and father and my grandparents, side by side. Here are things they made or held or wore.

Here they now accept the silent music of my tears as I sit alone, staring at a handwritten journal of unsent letters from my mother.

It is over forty years since my mother last opened this chest. At the time she was twenty years younger than I am now. The journal's paper edges are swollen slightly from years of climate changes. I open it and on the first page is a letter. "Dear Jake," it begins. The letter is three pages until the next "Dear Jake," and another and another until the pages run out. Letters from my mother, written to me in the last year of her life, written when her world was falling away and nothing remained to hold her in place.

I want to share some of the first letter with you. I want you to see how it was my fate to be a "movie man."

*Dear Jake,*

*Do you remember that I used to take you to the movies with me? We'd go on Friday or Saturday to a matinee at the Regal. Those movies were all I had to distract me from the things I felt after your father went to Europe. You would sit there mesmerized by the faces and music, and you seemed so happy there. Sometimes we'd sit through the movies twice, because you'd beg to stay and see the "people" again. That's what you'd call them, Jake, "the people on the wall."*

I read that letter and then pick up a bundle of photographs held together by the delicate chain of a silver locket. Opening the locket, I discover two ancient ticket stubs from the Lido Theater in Portland. The movie: *All About Eve, 1950*. On the back of one of the stubs in my mother's handwriting is written "First Kiss." In my father's handwriting on the other stub it says, "Forever."

There are three photos of my mother, one as a young child playing in the snow. She has a steaming cup in her hand and a smile covered with what looks to be a smear of marshmallow from her cocoa. Another is from high school. She's standing beside a friend, her head is leaning against his shoulder and her face looks tired, but in that playful way in which teenage girls are so open to their friends. You can't see the friend's face, only the shoulder of his coat. The back of this photo says "Me, tired from school." The last is another copy of the photo Fred kept on his dresser alongside the photo of his parents. This shows my mother on the day she married my father. She is standing in the hallway of our house with her wedding dress half on. She must have been taken by surprise, because the look on her face says, "You have completely embarrassed me now." Her face is so warm and playful even in this moment of embarrassment. Fred always loved this snapshot and so do I. It appears to me in dreams from time to time when I'm sleeping in Zhitomir. I see Mom getting ready for her wedding, and she says over and over, "Will someone please look for my shoes? Jake knows where they are, ask him." Then Fred appears holding a welder's visor and says he found them, but they need repairs. I know that dream means something and one of these days I'll ask someone about it. For now it's comforting to look at these photos and feel there were people who loved me. It is as the poem says: an unchanging face, the face of my mother.

I turn the page of the journal and read more.

*Dear Jake,*

*I'm sorry you never got to know your grandparents. They were loving parents to me and you would have enjoyed them. You look like your grandfather, especially when you laugh, but you remind me more of my mother and the distracted way she'd go about things. No one thought she knew what she was doing, but they were drawn to her and the things she touched shined. I wish I were more like them, Jake, and I wish they were here to take care of you now.*

*Dear Jake,*

*So often I feel you with me, inside of me, and my dreams are filled with your face and your voice. Knowing that Fred looks after you, comforts me. Fred is strong and kind. I cannot explain my absence in your life. Some people are born in the warmth of the sun and that radiance carries them through life, and some are born in the midst of a storm and the clouds seem to follow them and cast a shadow upon them.*

*When I married your father, we were so young, and his strength was for a time my light. Surely you must know that only the best of him rests in you. I saw that when you were born, I heard it in your laugh, the mysterious way that other people were drawn to you and were hypnotized by your infant eyes. I'm placing pictures in this chest so you may see him and know him in whatever way possible. Try to know him in your heart and love him the way he loved you, though he never saw you walk in this world . . ."*

There is a wedding photo of my parents. My father is wearing his army uniform and my mother a light dress. My father looks like Julian at first but then it hits me: my father looks like me, especially when I'm staring at the mirror in the morning when I shave. It is a painful surprise to see my father and mother staring back at me in this photo. I feel a tug from places and people I cannot explain. Looking at my face, my father's face in the photo, I wonder is it possible for me to know him the way my mother's letter asks me to?

*Dear Jake,*

    *Fred came by yesterday and showed me a picture of you. You've grown so much since I've seen you. Maybe I'll see you soon . . .*

Letter after letter reveals that my mother left the world too soon, overwhelmed by a deep sadness. I was born in 1952. I remember going to the movies with her. I remember looking at the screen, and sometimes looking at her face. At home her face was usually sad and distant, often washed with tears. At the movies she was distracted, even amused, and she would laugh or cry for all those on the screen and those in her own life who had been lost in such a short span. In 1958 when my mother was hospitalized, I started living with Fred. I don't remember much about it, but I do remember working hard to tune out the hushed voices people used when they'd ask Fred where Eva was. I remember the awkward feeling of explaining that my mother was in a hospital. They used the word ill, but they meant crazy, and people had a funny way of looking at you as if you might have the same disease.

As I read the letters I see a side of Fred I never did when I was young. I see how he was a devoted brother. If he didn't know much about children, he knew a lot about life. I was lucky, because the things I learned from Fred were different than what other kids learned. I learned about cars and history and about the ways in which people said one thing when they meant another. I learned to cook. I learned that the fat of the ham is the best part, learned about machines and how to make a hot fire, learned to curse joyfully, and how to listen to people, because that was something Fred did a lot of. Fred listened before he spoke and didn't feel he needed to fill up the air with his own voice. If this cedar chest holds the dates and details of so many losses, it also holds the key to understanding the benefits of traveling the winding path of the unknown.

There are a lot of winding paths in this chest. My father's flag tells the story of a man who left his home in New York City where he had lived with his family. He wanted to escape his background so he enlisted in the military, a career he barely understood. During training he met and fell in love with my mother, who had left home to 'see the world' on a six month contract, working as a clerk in the Post Exchange. How else could these two people from such different worlds come together, marry, and then conceive a child? I am the unlikely hybrid of two different worlds.

Fred took me into his home for twelve years and then returned me to the house my grandparents gave my mother. It was there I lived until Fred died. My uncle was smart; an eighteen-year-old learns well living in his own house. Throughout the decades that followed, he stayed close enough to check on me, but far enough away to lead his own life. We were the Sun and the Moon, always in each other's orbits, but standing alone.

There is more to see, but I cannot continue.

I carefully replace the contents of the chest as I found them, wanting to preserve the sequence of the hundred years of stories as if they are chapters my mother put in order for me. I take the chest out to Zhitomir and construct a small framework around it to hold it in place on the floor. I hear Fred, "You either survive or you're toast, but it all happens quickly." I've survived, but I caught a strong whiff of toast.

CHAPTER 29

# Dusting Chandeliers

In Which we make a slow exit from Larch, stopping to say goodbye, share a memory, and sample a bit of coffee culture.

I don't like goodbyes. I don't do them well. If that has a deeper psychological meaning, then I've given up trying to figure out what it is. The morning I leave Larch I step happily into Zhitomir, start up the engine, and pull on to the road. As I drive around I realize that Larch has become like so many other places I visit. Larch is the hometown I left, but it no longer holds me in its gravity. Honoring Rosalyn's request, I stop by to say goodbye to her and Benny, who are washing their car when I arrive. They wave me into the driveway, and when I stop, they turn the hose on Zhitomir.

"Might as well leave with a shine," says Benny, and we spend the next half hour washing the truck. As we work scrubbing and hosing, Rosalyn suggests I stop by Fred's old place.

"You should see it, Jake. You don't have to tell them who you are, but you should have a look."

When I finally pull out of the driveway, they wave goodbye and squirt water on Zhitomir's windshield. When I'm safely out of the reach of the hose I roll down the window and yell goodbye, to which Rosalyn yells back, "No goodbyes, Spinner. You come back and see us, and don't wait too long."

I do visit Fred's place. Using the pretense of needing some vegetables, I play the part of the curious tourist at the farm. I wasn't expecting to see Fred's tractor at work pulling a harrow between the rows of the vegetables, but there it is, still running well. For me, it's the only piece of Fred remaining on the property.

It's clear to me that there is no urgency to my "Leaving Larch" as there was before. There is no moment of truth, no foolish prosecutor, no vision of a light and a purpose. I am reflective, but content that this is where I am from, where I grew up, and from where I needed to leave.

Driving down Main Street I see newness, and it strikes me odd that I didn't notice all the changes last week when I drove in. I'm seeing what's in front of my eyes. It isn't my town anymore. I see somebody sweeping off the sidewalks in front of The Regal, its marquee boasting *Gladiator* at 6:30 and 8:45. Thinking it would be fun to stop in and take a look at the old theater, I park Zhitomir behind The Sonnet and walk the two blocks to The Regal. I introduce myself to the man who happily sets aside his broom to shake my hand and surprises me by saying, "Oh, sure, I remember you: little Jake."

When I apologize for not knowing who he is, he explains, "Of course you don't remember me; you were too young. I'm Bill Goforth, Harry's son. My dad owned The Regal. I remember you and your mom."

Bill explains that he left Larch to go away to college.

"Yes, by the time you'd have known who I was, I was long gone from here."

Curious, I ask Bill, "What brought you back?"

"I came home ten years ago. The folks still owned The Regal, but they couldn't keep it up themselves. They had one manager after another, but the good ones moved on and the others, well, that's the way it goes. Jane, my wife, and I were doing the motor home thing in the southwest when Dad's health began to fail. They needed help so we drove back to Larch, parked the motor home in their driveway, and started helping out. When Dad died a few months later, Mom said we should sell the theater, but the only people interested in buying it wanted to tear down The Regal and put in a new building. So Jane and I talked it over and decided to stay put for a while, at least until Mom passed on. Well, Mom's going strong, she'll be ninety-two next Friday and you can do a lot worse than running a movie theater."

Bill asks me what I'm doing in town and I tell him I came for Clara's funeral.

"Oh, of course, Mrs. Spengler. We were out of town at the grandson's seventeenth birthday. I would have liked to go to that. I had Mrs. Spengler, class of 1951. Who could ever forget her? I stopped in on her from time to time at the bookstore."

Bill is pleased to show me around the theater when I ask if I might have a look for old time's sakes. Stepping inside he turns on the lobby lights, making a point of flipping the switch that illuminates the lines of bulbs outlining the trim in the lobby. Between the golden chandeliers and the light pouring in through the July morning, The Regal lobby looks splendid.

Setting his broom into a closet, he takes out a long handled dust mop and as we walk around he runs the duster over things.

"I can't keep it up like in the old days. Gee, the place has needed new carpet for years, and it could use new paint, but she's still a far sight better than any shoebox theater. You must remember her, Jake. Dad made her shine."

I tell Bill I do remember well, and then I ask him how business is? He says, "I suppose our days are numbered. We own it free and clear and we're doing okay. Everybody loves going to the movies. You can watch all the videos you want at home, but you can't fall in love in front of a television set. No, we'll be okay until someone comes in and builds one of those multiplex hamster cages."

As Bill runs the duster gently over the dangling glass of the lobby chandeliers he says, "It's funny that we even came back at all, but, you know, the place kind of gets a hold of you."

When we enter the theater, a familiar warm smell, musty like cherry tobacco mixed with chocolate, comes over us.

"Don't you love that smell, Jake? Same seats too," says Bill. "Bentwood backs and high-grade corduroy. Going to stay that way, too. Do you know what they get for those new foamy jobs with the plastic cup holders? Two hundred dollars a piece. That's not going to happen here. No, we still sell popcorn for a dollar and candy for close to what it costs in the store."

We walk down the aisle and Bill points to the stage.

"Look, the same curtain and the same screen." Then we walk back up the aisle and Bill unlocks a door to a narrow set of stairs leading to the projection booth.

"I knew it! I always wanted to see what was behind this door. I used to see the door open and then a second or two later, there'd be this little shadow up in the booth behind the glass."

Entering the projection booth, Bill points to the modern projector,

"Heart of the operation. Beautiful machine, isn't it?" Bill runs his hand across the projector and sighs, "Going, going, gone. Soon enough you won't need these or even the projectionist. Digital this, digital that. They'll run a thousand theaters from a single computer."

Walking through another door in the booth, we go down a full-sized stairway that opens to the lobby. Bill asks me, "Do you remember *The Howler*, the big storm?"

"Of course, I do. I was here for the matinee and we ended up staying on."

"Me, too, how about that. It was sure blowing that night. Do you remember the pictures?"

"How could I forget? *Hud* and *Clash by Night*. Man, I ate a lot of Raisinets and popcorn."

"You too? I love Raisinets. It's not a movie without the Raisinets."

Then Bill reaches under the candy counter and pulls out a box of Raisinets and hands them to me.

"Here, gift of the Regal."

"Thanks, Bill, I'll cherish these."

"Don't cherish them too long; they go stale pretty quick." Then Bill starts talking about Paul Newman. "You know, Newman and I have the same birthday: Hud and me! That's what Jane calls me when she wants to butter me up: Hud. I like the way that sounds." Then we're standing behind the candy counter where there's a framed copy of the front page of *The Larch Post*. Bill stops and exclaims, "That was you?"

"What do you mean?"

"I think we gave you and your mother a ride home that night. I know it, I remember your mother. That's kind of weird, don't you think?" says Bill before pointing at a framed picture of Main Street in the center of a swirling snowstorm, seen only in the light coming from the lobby and marquee of The Regal. The headline says, "SNOWBOUND MASSES HUD-DLE TOGETHER IN REGAL FASHION!"

"We always got good headlines. You know my uncle owned the paper. This is weird. I mean, here you are visiting and you stop in and we have all this common ground. You know, it's kind of odd how pictures bring people together, isn't it? Even my folks, they met at the pictures."

"Mine, too."

"Amazing, don't you think, Jake?"

"Incredible, for sure. It makes me happy to hear you speak about the Howler."

Bill and I share a few more stories and he asks about Zhitomir. We compare notes from his time on the road in the motor home.

"I should of thought of it. Heck, it's such a simple idea . We had projectors back then. Why didn't I think about that?" says Bill before we say goodbye.

When I head out of town, it's eleven o'clock and my cells are craving a cup of coffee. I don't have to drive far before seeing a sign for Java Joe's Coffee Summit, which proclaims that what you get at Java Joe's is Not Only a Good Buzz:  It's Coffee Culture."

Entering Java Joe's, there isn't a whole lot of buzz buzzing at all, the place is dead except for the sound of the young man behind the counter pumping a large thermos marked "Joe's Supreme" into a tall paper cup. Stopping the pumping before reaching the top of the cup, the young man turns to me and asks, "Room for cream?"

"Yes, please." Then he places a protective sleeve over the cup, takes my money, and directs me to the counter where there is an astounding array of things with which you can embellish your coffee. There are six small thermoses marked organic cream, whole milk, soy milk, half and half, low-fat milk and nonfat milk and then a set of shakers with everything from cocoa powder, nutmeg, anise, cinnamon, to some heady aromatic concoction called Java Joe's Special Blend. There's also a bewildering collection of sweeteners from white sugar, maple sugar, cane syrup, brown sugar, to stevia and maltose nuggets called "Cave Rocks," which looks like what we used to grow in science class when I was a little kid. There are tweezers in the Cave Rocks so you can lift the little rocks into your cup. The sign at the condiment counter reminds customers:  "Java Joe's Coffee. It's Not What We Do:  It's What We Are."

Amending my cup with two teaspoons of white sugar and some organic cream, I take a seat at a small table in the back where I can stare at the traffic going by on the road. Taking my first sip, I'm happy with my Joe's Supreme. Out in the street, a car pulls up and two young men step out, walk over and stare at Zhitomir parked at the curb. Looking inside Java Joe's, they come inside and rush over to my table.

The more eager of the two reaches out a friendly hand and says, "Is that your truck?"

Taking his hand I shake and say, "Yes, my name's Jake."

"The Jake Spinner who used to do movies here?"

"Well, I don't know if I'm that Jake Spinner, but I'm Jake Spinner and I used to show movies around Larch."

"Man, this is unreal. I'm Ricky Jacobs. This is my friend, Alan Rice. We saw the truck and had to stop. We're doing what you used to. We show films at The Eagle's Club on Friday nights during the fall and winter."

Then Alan offers his hand and says, "Do you know that old timer with the battleship tattoo on his arm?"

"I'm not sure, why do you ask?"

Alan goes on, "No, you'd know this guy. I never see him except at the films. He's like outer space quiet, but he knows more about movies than about breathing. He's the one who told us about you. He said he used to come to all your films. He comes to every one of our shows."

Ricky interrupts, "Gets his bag of popcorn and takes the same seat every time. He never says a word unless you ask him about movies."

"No, I'm not sure I remember him." I answer, and then Ricky changes the topic.

"I heard you kind of flipped out and got arrested or something like that. Is that true?"

Laughing, I assure Alan it is not true, explaining to them why I left and fill them in on what I do now.

"You drive that truck everywhere?" asks Ricky.

"Everywhere that has roads."

"Unreal, man. How did you ever come up with an idea like that?" asks Alan.

"It's kind of a long story."

"Dude, we have time," says Alan. "Can I buy you a Java Joe's Super Nova?"

SECTION 6

# The Universe Is Expanding: Life's Purpose

# CHAPTER 30

# Gold Paint—Life and Times of Luella Ravan, A Ziegfeld Follies Star

**In Which** we enjoy the legacy of a feathered woman and learn of the dynamics of flying geese.

The sandwich-board sign outside Botticelli's advertises "The Finest Restaurant in Haines." Inside, over a pastry display case, stands a plaque "Third Annual Haines Fine Dining Award" confirming Botticelli's claim. The plaque also lists the "place" and "show" finishers: Stan's Drive-in Hamburgers at second followed by Nelly's Pizza at third.

Amanda, Botticelli's twentyish waitress, is quick to let you know that they will only hold the title for one year. "It's a rotation thing," Amanda said the first morning I ate there. Amanda knows because she works at Nelly's on the weekends and her father is Stan of Stan's Drive-in. "Kind of silly, if you ask me, with only three places in the whole town." When Amanda is not pouring coffee or delivering platters of food, she enjoys telling you her plans to go to art school after she "saves up."

Botticelli's owes its name to the great Italian painter, claimed as an ancestor by owner, Lu Rose. The restaurant lives up to its standing by serving a colorful palette of baked goods, perfect coffee, and butt-kicking breakfast and lunch in a ten-table diningroom that could use some decorating help from the famous painter's talents. The room is a heavy celebration of wood from its splintering plank floors to sanded bead panel walls and darkened cedar ceilings.

The windows of Botticelli's are covered with flyers announcing Pancake Breakfasts, Cub Scout Car Washes, and the Fall Steelhead Derby. This morning there's a fresh flyer for the First Annual Luella Ravan Burlesque Follies! A burlesque show in a mill town of less than a thousand people, and in the twenty-first century?

When I ask Amanda about the Follies, the ever-surprising waitress saunters across the restaurant, coffee pot in hand, to the magazine display rack and retrieves a brochure for me. "Here, read this," she says, "Luella is my inspiration." She returns to the kitchen.

The First Annual Luella Ravan Burlesque Follies has an extraordinary portrait of a barely clad woman on its cover. Feathers cover her feminine parts as she stands on a spot-lit stage (identified as *"Club des Trois Autruches)"*. The inside flap credits the portrait to Ben Ali Haggin, Painter and Scenic Designer for the Ziegfeld Follies, followed by a short biography of the Haines Follies namesake.

---

### Luella Altoona Bergstrom, a.k.a. Luella Ravan.

Luella Bergstrom was the youngest child of Raymond and Martha Bergstrom, born in 1905 in the town of Haines. Her father was the founding owner of Bergstrom Lumber, now the Weyerhaeuser Mill, and her mother ran the spacious family home her husband built for her as a wedding gift -- the "Bergstrom Mansion," as it was known 100 years ago. The Bergstom Mansion was an unlikely home to artists, dancers, and musicians, drawn by Martha's generosity to the purple and pink home which stood in radiant contrast to the aged gray, moss-covered cedar homes around it. Arthur Bergstrom donated the Mansion to the town of Haines in 1964 upon his passing at the age of one hundred. Arthur stipulated that his home be used for "the betterment of the community of Haines in honor of my late wife, Martha."

Martha was the only child of one of San Francisco's leading patrons of the arts. She came to Haines after accepting the marriage proposal of Raymond, who was visiting in San Francisco. It is said Martha agreed to return with Raymond only if he promised that any children they had would be raised with "a proper appreciation for the blessings of culture." Raymond honored his promise, though he was a man more inclined to spend his days watching logs roll through the spinning saw blades of his mill. The couple's four children, Raymond Jr. (born 1898), Henry (born 1902), Laticia (born 1903), and Luella (born 1905), were raised in a home often visited by exotic figures from the world of arts, theater, and music who had been invited west to visit the family home and made welcome by Martha.

Though all the Bergstrom children were accomplished musicians, Raymond, Jr., Henry, and Laticia spent contented lives close to Haines, maintaining the lumber empire of their family. Not so Luella who, from the privileged position of being the youngest child, spent her childhood daydreaming of achieving fame, and setting her sights outside of the home, which (she would write many years later) "spoke to me like a seductive glowing serpent."

In 1918 at the age of thirteen, Luella accompanied her mother on a train trip to New York City and received her first taste of the life she would later pursue. Martha took her daughter to the famous sites and attractions of the bustling city. At the Ziegfeld Follies she met Fanny Brice, who is said to have told the beautiful young girl, "With your name and your looks, we should introduce you to Flo. "Flo" was Florenz Ziegfeld, the Follies impresario. Upon meeting the young Luella, he was so taken by her beauty that he bowed down and kissed the child's hand, saying, "When you are old enough to join my company, I shall make you a star!" The now enchanted mother and daughter had to cut short their trip due to concerns about the great flu epidemic, but the seeds of Luella's destiny were sown. Surely the stern patriarch would have disapproved of his daughter being exposed to the temptations of New York. Had Raymond known Martha would immerse the impressionable Luella in things he disdained as "scandalous," there certainly would have been "hell to pay," as Raymond Bergstrom was fond of saying. He had his limits and was known for a fierce and volatile temper. People in Haines took him seriously.

At the age of seventeen, with her mother's secret blessing and under cover of the plausible ruse of being shipped east for finishing school, the determined Luella left Haines once again by train, not to learn how to host tea parties and sit properly, but to hold Mr. Ziegfeld to his word and become a star of the Ziegfeld Follies. This she would accomplish, though not under her own name, but as Luella Ravan, whom Ziegfeld referred to always as 'My Shining Light' (no one is certain whether Raymond ever demanded hellish payments from Mr. Ziegfeld).

Luella took to the stage with Ziegfeld celebrities Anne Pennington, Eve Tanguay, W.C. Fields, Billie Burke, Will Rogers, Sophie Tucker, and Fanny Brice. She danced across the floor of the New Amsterdam Theater for the first time at the opening of the 1923 Follies. Luella shared both art and apartment space with Muriel Stryker and, in her unpublished memoir, Luella claims it was she who first danced with the metallic gold body paint that would make Stryker such a sensation in the 1923 Follies.

Two years later, Luella left North America for the world of European clubs and cabarets, where she was courted (but never wed) by some of the most celebrated men and women in the world. Luella lived in Paris for the rest of her long life, thanks in part to the longevity genes of her father who never saw her perform. She died at the age of 98 and is buried in the Montmartre Cemetery in Paris.

In keeping with the Bergstrom Mansion's mission, we begin what we hope will become an annual celebration and tribute to the enduring stage art developed by one of Haines's Favorite Daughters who dared to go forth into the world and become something few amongst us could have imagined. Come help us celebrate!

The program for the Saturday night show:

### *Grand Opening*
*Walk of the Performers*

Act 1: *Shine On Harvest Moon Little' Delilah* (Caren Duttleman) accompanying herself on the accordion.

Act 2: *How to Bribe a Public Official*: Percy Kemper. Haines's own Will Rogers.

Act 3: Trapeze Dance: *The Fantasy Sisters* (Tina and Irina Stevens) An act of contortionism.

Act 4: *The Strongest Man in Haines*: Albert Kapuaalii. Display of amazing strength.

Act 5: Chasing the Bogey Man Home: *The 12 Harmonica Prowlers*.

Act 6: Belly Dances of the East: Lorelei Carter.

Act 7: Simultaneous goldfish juggling and poetry recitation of Robert Service's Second Settler's Story: King Philip.

Act 8: Dance of the Spitting Cobra: Alicia Diodema. (Parental supervision advised!)

### *Grand Finale:*
The Baa Baa Black Sheep Rumba: *The Haines' Chorus "Girls."*

After years on the road, stumbling upon and participating in one unlikely event after another, I should not be amazed by what I'm reading, but I am. I must confess that the life and commemoration planned for Luella Altoona Bergstrom Ravan is extraordinary. I'm not going anywhere until after this show! I wouldn't miss it for the world

Amanda serves my breakfast and asks, "What do you think?"

"What do I think? I think I'm buying a ticket. Are you going?"

"Going? I'm part of the show. I'm the designated cross-dresser."

"What is that all about?"

"I get to help my dad get into his dress. Not every girl gets to cross-dress her father; another part of the small-town charm in Haines, helping your father stuff himself into a show gown."

The next morning I'm nestled in Botticelli's drinking coffee and reading a magazine about winter steelhead fishing. Tuesday morning is not a busy day at Botticelli's. There are only three other people in the restaurant, but they are in a spirited conversation, swapping jokes and occasionally trying to quiet each other.

Amanda brings my breakfast and says, "That guy, the one telling all the jokes? He was, I mean, he is, or well, whatever ... Luella Ravan was his relative. He's a Bergstrom and he's putting on the Follies." Apparently voices carry in two directions in Botticelli's because, hearing Amanda, the threesome invite me to join them.

After carrying my plate to their table, I meet Loyal Bergstrom, Luella Ravan's great-grandnephew, and Molly and Henry Deakins, who explain that they have been listening to Loyal's latest jokes.

"Gee, I hope you're not a prude," says Molly.

"If you are, this may not be such a good idea," adds Henry.

Accepting assurances that I am not a prude, Loyal resumes his joke telling with such innocence and gentility that he might as well be holding a door open for you at a grocery store. He quickly gets me up to speed on the joke he was telling before I came to the table. It concerns a ninety-year-old sperm donor who can't unscrew the cap to the donation cup. Molly and Henry have to wipe their eyes free of tears and I replay the joke in my head hoping I'll remember to tell it to Julian the next time we speak.

Loyal, pausing for a moment to sip his coffee, explains how he mines the Internet for jokes. "I'm on JokeServe, DonRickles.com, and Humornet, not to mention all the stuff I get from my list-serve colleagues all over the country. I must get two hundred jokes every day."

"Are you a salesman?" I ask.

"Oh, heavens no," says Loyal. "I'm a minister."

"You're kidding?"

"No, he's not," says Molly. "Loyal married Henry and me twenty-three years ago in the Haines Lutheran Church." Loyal responds to that comment with an impish smile and casual shrug of his shoulders.

"Man does not live by bread alone," he says.

"Stick around here for a while and you'll find out that Bergstroms are a little different," says Henry.

Loyal then offers some explanation about his ministry and the role of humor in it. "Give your flock a chance to get upset in advance and they will, we're all pretty serious these days. So I like to take people by surprise from time to time. Keep things on the ground a little, if you know what I mean." Pointing skyward, Loyal asks me sincerely, "Jake, speaking of flocks, let me ask you something. Have you ever seen a flock of flying geese?"

"Of course," I reply. "Who hasn't?"

Then, speaking like a wizened sage, Loyal continues. "Jake, have you also noticed that one side of the formation, one side of the vee, is always longer than the other?"

"Yes, I have," I answer, poised and ready for the enlightenment I know is coming.

"Lastly, Jake, do you know why that one side is longer than the other?"

Setting him up for the punch line, I answer, "No, why?" as Molly and Henry bust out laughing and Loyal closes the joke with the answer, "More geese."

A few jokes later, Loyal proudly confirms the details of his family's history in the brochure. "It should be accurate. My sister Claire and I wrote it. Claire came up with the program idea." Loyal explains that he and his sister are two of the current board members of the Bergstrom Mansion.

"Claire has wanted to do something to honor Luella for years, but it wasn't until our Aunt Pat died that we could. Pat was the third member of the board and she was embarrassed by Luella's past. We're not going to fill her spot until after the show."

"These Follies will generate some steam, let me tell you. Have you seen the program?" asks Henry.

"Yes, I read it. I plan to come."

"Good. Do you know how to dance?" asks Molly with a wink. Amanda arrives with her coffee pot in the nick of time to hear me answer, "Well, I'm not a stripper."

"Too bad," says Molly. "Alicia wants to work a victim into the Cobra Dance. We could use another body for her."

"Dad's got another gown if you need it," adds Amanda, but I beg off becoming the Cobra's victim by explaining what I do. Loyal says he's heard about the truck from people around town.

"You certainly can't sneak around in that thing, but it sounds like an interesting way to live. You picked a good week to spend in Haines. Lady Godiva could ride down the street and people might not even toss her a towel. Normally, there's nothing to talk about, but the Follies is changing all that."

When Amanda brings the checks, Loyal grabs mine and won't let me pay, saying, "Welcome to Haines, Jake. I can promise you this: when you see the *Haines Girls* dance across that room, you will never be the same. That number is going to raise some eyebrows."

"Please, let it only be eyebrows." says Henry.

Loyal adds, "Any man with a taste for that deserves a free breakfast."

"Why is 'girls' printed in quotation marks in the brochure?" I ask Loyal, who explains that the Haines Girls are twenty-six proud citizens of Haines, half of whom will be in drag.

"It'll be a blast. My wife Bernice has been working with them for weeks. Molly made all the costumes for everyone from some sketches by Lucille she found on the Internet."

"Who's Lucille?"

"Lucille was Lady Duff-Gordon," says Molly holding her coffee pinkie extended, feigning an aristocratic air. She was a fashion designer for Ziegfeld in the twenties. Took the name Lucille as cover from the blue noses, and, get this, she was on the Titanic and survived. After our girls strut their stuff, a lot of people may wish she hadn't. Wait until you see all these people dancing around stage in big-time gowns. Whatever they may lack in coordination they make up for with enthusiasm."

"Scary thing is," says Henry, "Some of the women are worried that the men look better than they do."

"What's scarier," adds Molly, "is that some of them do!"

Then Loyal changes the subject, asking if I know anything about old films. "I mean the films themselves, the things in cans. We've got a whole bunch of them that Claire brought back from Luella's estate. When Claire flew to Paris, there wasn't much left, but she salvaged some of Aunt Luella's gowns and jewelry, as well as the films, and the portrait by Ben Ali Haggin that we're using for the program cover. Maybe you can come over to my place tonight and look at them? I'll call Claire if you'd like to go through them."

It's raining steadily that evening when Loyal picks me up at the Haines County Park. I bring along a projector, just in case, and we drive to his house, where I meet Bernice and Claire, who are excited to look over the twenty-three cans of films with titles including *Feathers and Fans with Sally, Head and Torso Jewels, Silk Streamers in Belgium for the King*, and my favorite: *Gold Paint--Avec et Sans Vêtements*. The prints are all 16mm and the cans are sealed with tape except for one.

Says Claire, "We opened that one a few years ago, but when we tried to play it the film tore, so we decided not to open any more of them until we had some help." Claire gets very serious as she slows her voice in an embarrassed whisper and says, "You know, having a famous stripper in the family can be very difficult." She slaps my knee and adds with a belly laugh, "but it's way better than having an infamous one!" If there was any doubt that Claire and Loyal are hatched from the same nest, it has vanished. Claire, having broken the ice, now starts rolling.

"Say the word 'naked' around the wrong people these days and it's like passing gas in church. Last time I checked, we all came into the world naked. All Aunt Luella did was have a little fun and make a pile of money with it. I think Luella was more frightened by wearing clothes than prancing about all free and fancy."

Claire softens her voice for a second.

"I hope you can help us with these films. I know there's something good and bawdy in them, I know it! We kind of forgot about them until we started planning the celebration. When Loyal told me about meeting you, we thought, maybe it's fate."

Pointing to the *Feathers with Sally* can, Claire says, "We're pretty sure 'Sally' is Sally Rand. We know they were friends because of all the letters. We sent the films to the university hoping they might take an interest. Maybe they'll be worth a bundle and they can fund The Luella Ravan School of Performing Arts."

Opening a few of the cans, I'm pleased to tell them the films are in decent shape even if they are old and a little brittle.

"I think they'd probably hold up to a showing or two if you're tender with them, but I suggest a cleaning before you expose them to the heat of the projector bulbs?"

"How do you clean a film, throw it in the washer?" Claire jokes.

"Almost. You spool the films through a cleaning solution that removes the oil and dust. It can't restore things perfectly but it will buy you a few more showings. I recommend you transfer them onto tape or DVD because film gets brittle with age."

"Sounds pretty complicated," says Loyal.

"Not really. Before video, every school in the country showed films and a lot of schools have the equipment. I'm sure you have a school services office. I can drop by and see what they have."

It seems like I am always driving in the rain, when the next day Zhitomir's wipers can barely keep ahead of the rain falling on the windshield as I drive to Montrose and enter the offices of Needles County School Services Administration. Dripping wet, I ask Betty Lou, the secretary sitting at the front desk (surrounded by an impressive display of family and pet photos), if there's a media technician on staff. She directs me down the hall, "Walk all the way to the end of the building. There's a door marked 'Technology.' I think they're in today. They have their own entrance so I'm not sure."

Following Betty Lou's instructions, I open the technology office door to a small shop with workbenches covered with VCRs, DVD players, overhead projectors, and a few dozen computers, printers, and copy machines that are tagged with descriptions of their problems.

Two guys look up from their work-benches squinting like moles faced with sunlight. Humorous to me, they have name patches on their coveralls identifying them as Tom and Jerry. After a minute, Tom sees that I'm carrying film cans. "Man, I haven't worked on film in a couple of years. The whole district converted to tape four years ago, sold some of the collection to this collector guy on the Internet, and then trashed the rest."

Jerry adds, "That was sad, you can't believe the stuff we had. *Deep Fat Frying, Life After High School, Dating Do's and Don'ts, How to Tune Up Your*

*1965 Chevelle, Ice Fishing on a Frozen Lake, The History of the Krapper.*
Who knows where they are now?"

I probably should tell Tom and Jerry about Lumen Desire.

Then Tom says, "Yes, and all the projectors. We had over a hundred
Bell and Howells, and even a few with big throw lenses. All gone. They put
that stuff up for sale at the state auction and I heard somebody bought the
entire lot on a sealed bid for less than a hundred dollars."

"So, what do you want to do with these films?" asks Jerry.  He listens
eagerly as I tell the story of Luella and the need to clean the films.

"Smart move," says Tom. "You can lose the whole shebang if you're not
careful. You put those on a projector and they might crumble or burn up
when you hit them with the light. I tell you what:  I don't have any right
now but I can order an emulsion that renews the celluloid. Kind of restores
some of the life to it. I know we still have the cleaner.  Jerry and I hid it
away when they surplused all the other stuff. I'll dig it out."

When I offer to pay for the emulsion, they laugh together and Jerry
says, "No, we don't pay for anything here. We write out purchase orders
and then stuff appears. If we take your money it would probably cost more
for the paper trail than the fifty bucks for the stuff in the can. No, I'll call
it in this afternoon and it'll be here tomorrow. Can you come back with
the films?"

"You bet I can. It's awfully kind of you guys to do this."

"Kind nothing," says Tom. "Those films could be worth looking at."
He makes a sweeping gesture towards the bench with all the computers on
it. "I can tell you, we get tired of working on these insidious monsters."

The next afternoon the three of us open the cans and begin spooling
the films through the emulsion. It takes about five minutes to hand crank
each film through the emulsion bath. After the bath, the films dry and the
emulsion sets.

By 5:30 the films are ready and we roll them on a cart to a little office
marked "Media Preview" on the outside. The office has a screen and some
television sets inside, but we have to use my projector to show the films.

"Hard to believe we don't have any of these anymore," says Jerry.

We cue up the first film. Most of them are around twelve minutes
long, although there are a few closer to thirty, and if the first one, *Tropical
Breeze*, is any indication of the content, sister Claire's desire for bawdy will
be fulfilled.

"Gosh," says Jerry whimsically. "Would you look at her? It's like she's floating in the wind."

"Yeah, but those scarves hide everything," laments Tom, to which Jerry responds with some sarcasm, "That's what makes it artistic."

By the time we get to *Gold Paint: Avec et Sans Vêtements*, the mystery of the title's significance has vanished along with most of Luella Ravan's clothing.

"What time is that show?" asks Tom. "I think I'm free that night."

"Yeah, me too," says Jerry.

When I return the films to Loyal and Bernice's house the next morning, I set up the projector and a screen and we start going through the films. "Holy Mother Bergstrom," says Bernice when she sees *Gold Paint*. "Loyal, I don't think Haines is quite ready for all of this, do you?" Loyal agrees with his wife, though the three of us are all taken by the stunning backgrounds of the film.

"Very realistic," says Bernice. "Natural."

"Very realistic," affirms Loyal, and then adds, "Claire is going to jump out of her skin when she sees these."

When Friday evening comes, except for the rain continuing to pelt down on Haines, the turnout looks strong for The Luella Ravan Follies. I dress in my North Dakota tuxedo, ready to show the films. Loyal and Claire have selected *Silk Streamers in Belgium* and *Feathers and Fans with Sally*, though Claire confides to me later, "I'd have shown them *Gold Paint*, to see their jaws drop."

I'm set up in the darkened space of the Bergstrom Mansion's large dining room, while the big show is slated for the large ballroom across the hall. I start showing the films to early-comers at six o'clock and I can hear the Follies cast and production crew making their final preparations. Mostly, the people who come in gaze at the screen for a few minutes and then walk out, but one old man sitting in a wheelchair stares at the screen without blinking through both films. Before leaving, he instructs his caretaker to roll him over to me.

"I always thought that girl was a looker. Should have made my move when I had the chance." Then he rolls away before stopping and turning his chair in my direction.

"That's right, one hundred and four." Then he turns the chair and rolls out of the room.

This is a night of live entertainment. At eight o'clock, with the Bergstrom Mansion ballroom packed with an audience of well over 300 people, Bernice, Loyal, and Claire kick off The Luella Ravan Follies. Loyal offers a brief prayer in honor of his great-grandparents "who had the wisdom to give birth to a daughter who would break the mold." With that the lights go down. When they come back up it is to the rousing music and parade of the entire Follies cast crossing the colorful stage. Some of the cast struggle to maintain their balance in high-heeled shoes and tight-fitting gowns, but soon enough the parade ends and the show begins. "Little" Delilah, who turns out to be a large woman with an overflowing bosom, squeezes the bellows of her tinny accordion to everyone's delight, as she sings "Shine On Harvest Moon" in a voice reminiscent of Tiny Tim's falsetto.

Percy Kemper's oration on bribing public officials has many in the audience turning their heads in the direction of a well-dressed man who squirms uncomfortably in his seat as Percy explains the ways of bribery and influence and its role in certain land use decisions.

When The Fantasy Sisters untie their licentious knot, a gasp goes up from the crowd and I wonder what life will be like for the two sisters tomorrow when they have to return to normal life.

Next up is Albert Kapuaalii who raises and lowers an impressive array of barbells, dropping one over the back of his massive body to the floor with a loud, and no doubt, expensive-to-repair thud. One wonders if "Little" Delilah" might be stronger than Albert.

Up next, The Harmonica Ramblers whose six frenetic players chase the boogieman home and, no doubt, a few cats and dogs as well. *The Ramblers* needed a little more practice, but no one cares. They receive enthusiastic applause and the evening rolls on to the next act.

Lorelei Carter takes her belly dancing very seriously. Before Lorelei takes to the stage, Molly comes out and lights two brass urns filled with incense. A smoky herbal sweetness fills the room. The lights go down, and Lorelei appears, a sensual vision in the narrow spotlight. Dazzling purple bangles radiate flashes of light from her gyrating body. The rhythmic pulse of her abdominals accompanies the bells in her hands and the bangles on her wrists.

King Phillip's juggling act is doomed from the start, having to follow the stimulating Lorelei. When one of the goldfish bowls slips from his hand and crashes to the floor, boos ring out. Fortunately, King Phillip, who has no doubt failed at this before, saves the stunned fish by placing them gently in a new vessel at the ready, to the applause and delight of the audience.

The crowd gets worked into a lather when Alicia Diodema's gyrations reflect rays of enchanting colorful stage light from her silver cobra scales. Claire swings by, taps me on the shoulder, and says, "Her husband must be the happiest man in Haines, don't you think?"

At last, we arrive at the moment the eager crowd came for. With all the cheering and catcalls, there can be no doubt that the audience came to see The Haines Chorus "Girls." As the "Girls" dance their way into position the crowd erupts. People point and holler at the stage, identifying each of their neighbors by name.

"Hey, John, where'd you learn to put on makeup like that?"

"Lucas Doerr, you're a fine looking woman."

"Yes, and the most buxom ferrier you'll ever see."

As the Haines Chorus "Girls" bumble their way through the number, a chant of "Va va va voom" rises from the room. When one of the "Girls" breaks a heel and stumbles, a shout comes from the stage, "Gosh darn, friggin pumps!" drawing uncontrollable laughter as "she" takes off "her" shoes and takes "her" place back in the line. Rising to the occasion, weeks of rehearsal pay off when the Haines "Girls" perform the show's finale, "What the Boys At Sea Want To See," which would have pleased the great Florenz Ziegfeld.

The show closes to the sustained applause of the lively crowd. In a world of annual festivals that never see a second year, I'm reserving next year's ticket in advance. The people of Haines have paid fine tribute to their "favorite daughter."

CHAPTER 31

# Noah's Ark Film Festival!

**In Which** we experience a flood of biblical proportions.

Over the weekend, as the light and energy of the Follies yields to the continuing downfall of hard rain. Haines recedes into the dreary quiet of its dark winter. "The smart ones have left," says Amanda the following Tuesday morning at Botticelli's and she must be right. There was a lot of buildup before the show, but now half the town has disappeared, including Loyal, Bernice, and Claire (who left yesterday morning for three weeks in Egypt with Loyal's church group). Amanda tells me that Botticelli's is closing for two weeks on Friday. Later in the day I have to leave my cozy spot in the Haines County Park when concerns about rising water levels shut down the campground. County Sheriff Bruce Kelly directs me to higher ground six miles away over the mountain to the town of Lucinda.

I spoke with Nina last night and told her all about the Follies and films of Luella Ravan. "You have a knack for finding things, don't you? I could use someone like you on my crew,"she tells me.

"Where do I get the application?"

"Sorry, Jake, in my work it's all about who you know."

"No point even filing a résumé then."

"I don't know," says Nina. "I've heard the sky's the limit for a man with burlesque films." Then Nina tells me she's setting up a project with French oyster growers in the Arcachon Basin who were devastated by an oil spill. "Why don't you come and visit for a while?" Nina is surprised when I tell her I'd like to do that when I finish the piece I'm working on.

"Are you writing a piece on the history of small-town burlesque?"

"No, something on the Follies. I got this idea yesterday when I saw a fisherman land a steelhead."

"What's a steelhead?" asks Nina.

"It's an ocean-going trout as big as a salmon. Highly sought after around here. I must have had fish on the brain after eating a tuna fish sandwich. I started thinking about canned fish and canned film."

"Mr. Janus," Nina interrupts, "It sounds as if you have way too much time to think."

"Yes, maybe you're right. In any case, I need a few weeks so I can park Zhitomir somewhere out of the rain for the winter, and I'll come over."

"That's good. I've been staying in a small house with enough room for a garden. It's owned by two of the oyster growers, the Courbets. They've been working oysters for sixty years and they go to the beaches each morning. Madame Courbet told me she wants to help me plant roses. She said 'you have to plant roses after looking at oysters all day.' I think she's right, Jake. I want to plant roses."

"And maybe some daphne too," I add.

"What's daphne?"

"First steelhead and now daphne. I've got some things to teach you when I get there."

Later Eric calls, and when he isn't talking about living in "Julian World," as he's started calling it, he tells me he has decided not to go to film school after all. He finished the Palau film, and it will get a showing at the Museum of Natural History, and National Geographic wants it for television! Eric also tells me he's got something else going on that "I can't jinx by talking about, so you'll have to wait to find out what it is."

After hanging up, I spend the rest of the morning sitting at my desk in Zhitomir listening to the heavy batter of rain on the roof.

It's raining so hard today that I find myself imagining the sweep of storms bringing all this water. I drift west across the mountains and reach the ocean, where the rain clouds melt into the thick and heavy grayness of the sea. I can't tell where the sea and the sky separate as I drift further west-ward to the Aleutian Archipelago, continuing northwest across the Bering Sea all the way to Siberia. As I drift against the movement of the storm I have the sense of looking for the first raindrop. I cannot find it. With my eyes closed I keep looking but fail to find it.

The next day fate's lottery deals my life an unexpected but serendipi-tous hand.

This is how the world learned of the torrential rains that changed the west, including Lucinda and Haines and the surrounding area for hundreds of miles:

From New York: ***El Nino Storms Ravage West Coast!***
From Spain: ***La Inundación!***
From London: ***Historical Deluge In American West!***
From Beijing: ***American Devastation!***
From Bangladesh: ***Tears Continue in U.S.!***

Papers all over the world picked up this *St. Louis Post Dispatch*, report:

### Surviving Flood Victims Face Uncertain Future
### as Waters Continue to Rise

National Weather Service statistics confirm what residents of the western river states already know: their lives will never be the same. A record sev-enteen inches of rain fell yesterday in some areas, bringing the month-long total to 61 inches, more than doubling the highest recorded rainfall since records have been kept.

Flooding is usually an annual inconvenience. This year it has grown into economic and personal devastation and is a potential cataclysm. Whole towns, hundreds of thousands of homes, major geographical features have been permanently destroyed, and residents weary of makeshift housing are coming to grips with what life will be like once the waters recede.

"There simply won't be any town to go back to," says Fernell Cranston, lifelong resident of Lucinda. Cranston was evacuated to the Lucinda Ar-mory's makeshift Red Cross Shelter two weeks ago for "precautionary mea-sures," but now faces the sad reality that there may be nothing left. Cranston, along with many other evacuees, had no time to prepare. "I keep thinking about a small box of photos in my living room. The day they came to get us, I had it under my arm but they told us not to bring any possessions. That's all I can think about except my iguana, Oscar. I know he's clever enough to stay ahead of the water. Probably sitting up in a big oak tree riding it out. Old Oscar will make it. I'm sure of it."

Shelter-mate Eliza Fogarty, an eight-year-old from Joseph, took no chances with her pets. She hid her guinea pig, Hazel, under her coat when her family was evacuated, and the playful rodent provides shelter residents with a welcome distraction.

Army Corps of Engineers Director General Francis Gomez, speaking after a two-hour fly-over of the flooded region, said, "We've never dealt with anything of this magnitude before. Entire drainages are being redrawn. River channels have shifted course, causing their flood plains to be reshaped."

Gomez's tour took him past the remains of the Casko Peninsula, a vast cattle grazing area that flood watchers believe has been swept down river. Even the proud Army Corps of Engineers admits that there is no way of knowing what the future will look like until the floodwaters recede.

From his temporary shelter in Van Camp, dairy farmer Ray Mosier was numb with the loss of his entire herd of 1,240 cows. "I keep thinking about them poor helpless beasts alone out there. They've given me so much and now there's nothin' I can do for them. Them cows are my life; I know everyone by name. You think of something like this happening only in the Bible. I keep praying, but I'm not sure what for. It's just that I think I should be with my cows, wherever they are."

FEMA, is amassing a team of officials and private insurance carriers to deal with the onslaught of loans, grants, and claims they expect will come after the flood. "For now, as the rains continue," Francis Gomez says philosophically, "There is nothing to do but wait. The only thing we can say for sure is that things will not be the same."


Thirty days into it, the sheriff places a call to the State Emergency Services Office (who call F.E.M.A., who call the Red Cross), alerting them to the fact that a whole bunch of people will be needing to get out of their homes, and soon.

Early this morning, I heard a knock on Zhitomir, and when I flipped the light switch there was no power. Grabbing my flashlight, I opened the door to find a sheriff who told me, "We're evacuating people from low spots along the river -- in case." Less than one hour later, I'm driving on the only paved road between Lucinda and Haines as two sheriffs' cars speed past me. A few minutes later I find out the road has been destroyed by a mudslide, and the bridge to the east has failed. Lucinda is now officially "cut off."

A mile before the slide is a small stream of cars making U-turns before a cluster of flares and red patrol-car lights. When I arrive at the roadblock, the same sheriff who alerted me earlier steps up to Zhitomir and informs me the slide is impassable. When I ask about an alternate route out of the area, he says, "I'm sorry, sir, but you're not going anywhere. The only road out of here is a gravel road over the hills, and even that is probably washed out."

As the line of cars behind me grows, the sheriff directs me back to town and the Lucinda Armory. He suggests I get a move on because they're concerned about the possibility of other slides.

Ten minutes later I pull in beside the decommissioned Lucinda Armory, occupying one full block of Lucinda's streets. The old building was once headquarters of the National Guard Unit that was relocated to Gladding, over a hundred miles away. The building still has offices, two large open rooms which once held equipment but now serve as basketball or volleyball courts six nights a week. The rooms are tall and drafty due to the high arching ceilings and even amid this momentary crisis, I find myself sizing up the space to show movies. There's a screen conveniently mounted at one end of the downstairs room and for a second I imagine a room full of soldiers howling at Rita Hayworth. Closer inspection shows the screen casing covered in dust: it probably hasn't been unfurled in years. Movies will have to wait as the growing crowd of people is gathered for orientation.

Nancy Holmgren introduces herself to the crowd of about a hundred people; most know her as Lucinda's city clerk but now learn she is also the town's designated emergency response coordinator. Nancy has a quiet competence and as she speaks the roomful of people settles calmly.

"Okay, everybody, listen please. As most of you know, our main Highway 43 is buried and it doesn't look like it's going to be unburied for some time."

"What about Fresian Road?" somebody yells. "It's a pretty good road and doesn't cross the river."

"That's true," says Nancy. "We'll send somebody to check it, but the reports we're getting on the radio aren't good. There are roads washing out and slides everywhere. We're not the only ones stranded."

Somebody asks about evacuation plans.

"It's too early to know. People, this is bigger than anything we've seen before, but at least we're high and dry. We'll know in a few hours what's going on, but for now I need you to settle in, get yourself situated for sleeping upstairs, and start getting to know each other. We may be here for a while."

Nancy goes on to explain that there are beds, cots, and blankets coming, and that for now what they want people to do is set up separate men's and women's areas upstairs in the big room. She wastes no time getting things organized and assembling crews to cook, clean, and chase down supplies from local houses and the few stores in town. She begins a roster of everyone in the building and has us write our names, ages, addresses, and any medical concerns or medications we need, and dispatches a group of teenage boys to knock at every door of every house in Lucinda and to make sure everyone is accounted for. Within an hour a makeshift city starts growing and the swelling numbers of people who come in are settled and put to work.

By eight o'clock our numbers have increased to nearly two hundred. Most of the people know each other, but there are a few other "invisible" people, as Lucinda general store owner Dave Wiggins calls them, who live by the river: the moss pickers, mushroom gatherers, and fern harvesters who are normally woven into the surrounding towns except when they surface to buy food, beer, or gas. Two hours later the rain continues as we sit eating chili from green enamel bowls with "United States Army 1948" stamped into their sides.

During the first few days most of us speak about things as if it will all be over in a couple of days. But the rain continues and the news we receive over one police radio and the television in the building manager's office tells us we are but a small part of a story that is growing larger by the hour.

Nancy holds briefings at ten and six each day. She informs us that more roads and bridges have washed out and more areas have been cut off. It becomes increasingly clear that little Lucinda is one dot in the expanding matrix of this disaster. Our numbers hold steady at 213 people.

As it settles into people's minds that we're going to be here for a while, conversations shift. People become confused. Some worry about their homes, others their pets, some simply find something to read, kick their heels up, and dig in for the duration. Nancy allays fears and reminds us twice each day that all of the county's citizens are accounted for and safe.

Oddly, I'm one of the lucky ones because I have the privacy of sleeping in Zhitomir every night. As of yesterday morning Zhitomir and the Lucinda Armory sit "officially" eighty feet above the floodwaters, but even Zhitomir is getting dank without the benefit of electricity to run the heater. I could start up the generator and warm things, but since a diesel oil furnace heats the armory and there are concerns that the fuel supply is dwindling, we may need the fuel in Zhitomir's tank. A crew armed with five-gallon fuel tanks, the one thing left over in abundance in the armory, goes each day and taps the remaining diesel fuel in the tanks of Lucinda's only gas station.

A few days into armory life, a teenage boy named Matthew sees me coming from Zhitomir and wants to know what the truck is all about. When I explain, Matthew gets excited and suggests we show a movie.

"Take people's minds off things."

When we ask Nancy, she thinks it's a great idea. Born is the Noah's Ark Film Festival, so dubbed by Matthew excited by the prospect of watching movies. He throws himself gladly into the role of "Entertainment Chief" in the armory.

Eager to get things going, we fetch a ladder so we can inspect the old screen, which rolls out supple and strong except for twenty years of must and mildew which Matthew washes away. Standing on the ladder with a sponge and bucket, he swirls white trails as he cleans the screen with acrid ammonia and water. After five minutes the screen becomes its original silvery white.

Now we have to select a film. I only have my touring collection of classics, but those should keep us going for a while. I also have some of the Luella Ravan films that Loyal and Claire lent me to transfer onto tape. I'm sure that Luella Ravan could take more than a few people's minds off these floods.

Maybe it's the hardship or the fear, or simply the necessity, but slowly a community is taking shape, and by the time all the tin bowls are filled with popcorn and I throw the switch on *The Philadelphia Story* we're actually having a pretty good time.

Over the next two weeks a lot changes. With every new downpour, the reality that life will not be the same again settles deeper into people's minds. Our eighty feet above floodwater shrinks to fifty-seven, and though no one believes we're in jeopardy, the reports of houses floating down rivers, the sloughs and slides that are making over the flood zone, give people pause to think about what's important.

Privacy falls away and people stand talking at the sinks while they wash, shave, or brush their teeth. We laugh at each other's sleepy morning faces, at how our hair is uncombed and our rumpled clothes. The younger people rally around the elderly, braiding the women's hair, shaving some of the older men, and serving them meals so they don't have to stand in line.

Day Twenty-Four in the Lucinda Armory finds us settled into our routine. We have breakfast of eggs, toast, and cereal, between 7 and 9 am. We have tuna fish or deviled ham or grilled cheese sandwiches between 12 and 1 pm and dinner is spaghetti, chili, macaroni and cheese, or ham, each night at six. Food is important, and the cooking crew has been elevated to royal status. During the mornings people tend to do clean-up chores; during the afternoon a lot of people read or remain quiet. There's a lot of sleeping. Every third day, after dinner is cleaned up, the popcorn crew makes cocoa and popcorn, and I throw another film on. Since *The Philadelphia Story*, we've seen *The African Queen*, *High Noon*, *Guys and Dolls*, and *Dial M for Murder*, not a bad program for our little refugee camp. Nancy does not allow boredom to set in. She never runs out of a cleaning project, whether mopping, polishing, or painting. The Lucinda Armory was built in 1932, and I doubt it has ever looked this good.

Home Sweet Home.

CHAPTER 32

# Playing X

**In Which** we learn the finer points of playing Scrabble: keep your tiles moving and never yield a triple!

Life has taken on a strange but not unpleasant routine in Campo Lucinda, as one of the women has dubbed the armory. Other than occasional walks to survey the ever-eroding town of Lucinda, there aren't a lot of outside activities.

It's not terribly uncomfortable and the kids seem to be having the most fun, though they get agitated when their parents attempt to organize a makeshift school. Thanks to the Red Cross, who drop out of the sky by helicopter every other day, there is a growing library of books and magazines, two more televisions that draw torpid viewers to them with nothing better to do, a group of knitters, a popular class for learning how to sketch, and an ongoing basketball game upstairs with modified rules for different mixes of teams. The game begins in the morning after the cots are cleared from the court. In the words of an eighty-year-old retired carpenter from Haines, Kyle Fulton, "Let's ride it out." Kyle says, "I seen worse than this," although when pressed for details about when, Kyle tends to beg off.

Helicopter landings are a big attraction. You never know what's coming. One day it's boxes of cookies and tomato paste, the next time it's magazines and toilet paper. This afternoon, the unmistakable sound of a chopper is heard in the distance and people start making their way to the front doors to watch the chopper land in the large yellow "helipad" we painted for them. As the chopper draws closer, the sound is deafening. It's not the normal state patrol chopper today, but a large National Guard Helicopter. A Red Cross volunteer directs the off-loading of newspapers, magazines, candy, fresh linens, and cases of food, including twelve gallons of peanut butter and some sorely needed pots and pans for the kitchen. The pans raise hope that we may get a new meal in place of the chili, spaghetti, ham, and mountains of tuna fish sandwiches. The children are excited when some toys come off, but those soon wear thin and the kids return to creating their own culture of games that are noisy, but fun to watch.

Today's biggest surprise is the arrival of a large sack of mail leaving most people stunned, especially Windy Holcom, who normally delivers the mail to a large rural route from her right-side-drive Toyota. Windy is relieved to have something to do and seizes the three bundles of mail and begins passing out letters to the recipients, or wandering the room calling out the names of those she doesn't know.

"Frank Johnson, letter from a Mrs. Ellery Boozer of Frankfurt, Kentucky . . . Mae Deegan, from Fairbanks, Alaska . . ."

When she shouts out, "Jake Spinner, General Delivery from Julian in New York City," I am thrilled. I walk over to Windy who hands me the card and says, "Somebody has a sick sense of humor." Jake's card shows Mark Spitz, the Olympic swimming champion, smiling with his gold medals around his neck and a hand-written caption, "I love floods."

*Dear Jake,*                                                   *Today*

    *Keeping track of you through the Weather Channel. Hope all is well in the flood. Don't forget to change your socks.*

                                              *Onward, Julian*

As Windy attends to her appointed rounds, one last box is carried in by one of the Red Cross staff and when Nancy opens it, a huge smile breaks across her face and, one by one, she carefully sets twenty games of Scrabble on the table in front of her.

In a few minutes a small crowd is gathered as a beehive buzz starts making its way around the room.

"It's about time, I need something to do beside read this book," shouts a quiet older woman named Alice who throws down her knitting in disgust while the woman next to her, Kay Gobbs, says, "I hate Scrabble. Couldn't they have brought Monopoly?"

"Merry Christmas to you, too, Mother Teresa!" says Alice. "Let's play!"

In a few minutes, all twenty boards are surrounded and in play. Some with a full four players, others with two, but the games bring much needed diversion and activity to Campo Lucinda.

By the end of the first day, the demand for the boards is great. In order to allocate them to all the people who want to play, two sets of cafeteria dining tables are set up with players on opposing sides and you can write your name down on a waiting list. The winners have the option of playing the next person in line, although there is some grousing about that when a few good players naturally emerge who can play all day. In order to solve that problem, someone comes up with the idea to start recording the matches and scores on a blackboard beside the tables. This quickly leads to the organization of a full-fledged tournament complete with a large bracket diagram with players' names, scores, and progression posted on the wall behind the tables. Qualifying games are held with players seeded by scoring average. What started as a simple diversion has evolved into an obsession, albeit a well-governed one. Games are heated with clusters of onlookers and there is intense concentration as players match word against word. There's even some wagering going on, although the stakes are marshmallows. Four boards are set up with modified rules for playing in Spanish and there is one board for matching bilingual players, alto, lengua, gato, abogados (played on the S at the end of huevos and on a double word score for twenty-four points plus fifty points bonus for using all the tiles: seventy-four points total) caballo, playa, tierra, salida . . .

To unify the widely divergent rules players are used to, an election is organized establishing a Rules and Proper Usage Committee. For some reason I have been elected to the committee that decides what is or isn't an acceptable word. Fortunately, my Campo Lucinda neighbors haven't discovered that I'm an awful Scrabble player and for the time being I am an influential citizen of this world because I get to arbitrate word disputes. Half of the armory is involved in the competitive daytime Scrabble tournament while later in the evenings the games are available to the more casual players.

Day Twenty-Nine, I walk into the armory for my late evening shower. With diesel now scarce, we've been asked to limit our showers to two minutes. Returning to the main room with a towel around my neck, I see a solitary woman at the Scrabble table, and even though the late-night games are less intense than during the day, I'm showered, shaved, and ready to break my losing streak. I've seen her sitting by herself for the past few nights at the boards, but didn't take much notice until this evening. As I arrive at the board, she sets her hands on the table and says to no one, "I've never seen that word before. Good play!" Then she rotates the board completely before making her next play.

When I introduce myself and ask her whether she minds if I watch, she's a little cautious until I go into the kitchen and return holding a hot cup of tea for her. Grateful for the tea, she invites me to sit down. While I was gone, she dumped the letter tiles back and now tells me, "We were practicing, but now we're ready for the real game. My name is Pearl, what's yours?"

"I'm Jake.  It's nice to meet you.  Who are you playing?"

"I'm playing X," Pearl says as if I should have known, and then she tells me it's hard for her to sleep with all the strange noises in the armory. "Sometimes, I don't need to sleep. I'm used to living alone and I'll be happy when all of this rain goes away and I can go home. The only peace I get is when everyone is asleep. Besides, I can get a board to myself when it's late."

"So, how do you play against yourself.  Do you have special rules?"

Pearl is annoyed by this question and corrects me. "I don't play against myself, I play X."

Pearl is a sinewy but clear-speaking octogenarian and she tells me she lost her husband, Earl, twelve years ago. Then in a sweet, apologetic voice she adds, "Earl wasn't much of a Scrabble player. He preferred to sit in his chair and drink. He always said 'Baby, there's nothing I enjoy in this world so much as watching you.' Earl was kind like that."

Pearl tells me she loves words and has been a Scrabble player most of her life. "I love how each game is different. Sometimes the words extend around like tentacles. I played that once, 'tentacles', added the t-a-c-l-e-s to ten but didn't score much for it. Sometimes the board gets congested with lots of in-fill. I don't enjoy that. When the board is tight, you have to know all those little words; it's too hard to play those boards. No, I much prefer when the board is wide open. I love how words appear out of nowhere when you move your tiles. That is the key, you know," she tells me in a whisper, as if yielding a secret tip before sipping her steaming tea. "One must keep one's tiles moving, see the combinations, and never, never, never, yield a triple."

Pearl informs me that she has two Scrabble sets at home, and sighs the fatalistic sigh that has become common to the armory over the past month. Her next comment tugs at my heartstrings. "Well, who knows what will be at home after this deluge passes." Then she adds, "Actually, I have two sets, but I only use my old one. I have had that set for over forty years. The box is all torn and the creases on the paper are fraying, but I like how the tiles feel and how they stick to the board. My daughter sent me a new set a few years ago, like these here, with the letters made of plastic. Can you imagine? I only use it when she visits.

"My old set feels good to me. I've kept the letters in the same brown paper sack for over thirty years. The paper on that bag is worn and supple, like an oil rag. Thousands of hands have entered the bag over the years. It is more like fabric than paper and it is amazing it does not tear."

Then, finishing her tea, she politely asks if I might leave her alone. "I need all my concentration against X, and I'm afraid I'll be nervous with you watching me."

With that, I walk out of the armory through a heavy rain and crawl into my bed in Zhitomir. That's with the Z falling on a triple letter square and fifty bonus points for "Scrabbling out," of course.

CHAPTER 33

# La Strada! The Lights Before My Eyes

**In Which** we cry for the sadness of an innocent and the loneliness of a brute.

Day Thirty-One at 11:30 am, I get a phone call from Eric and Julian as I'm sitting with a cup of rot gut reading a week-old newspaper by the Scrabble tables. "Man, Jake, I wish I were there," says Eric, who hates to miss anything.

"Maybe you can grab a canoe and make your way in."

"Do you know how to swim?" asks Julian with a bite of sarcasm before adding, "We've got a side bet going about how long you're going to be stuck there. I've got you down until 2011."

"Don't worry, Jake," says Eric. "I've got your back. I think you'll be out before the summer."

"Sounds like a parole hearing," I respond.

"You said it, not me," says Julian, and then he asks me what I'm doing to keep busy.

"I've taken up knitting. What size sweater do you wear?"

"Large will be perfect, but no synthetic fibers if you don't mind."

"All I've got is good old petroleum-derived poly, but I tell you what," I say. "I'll send you each a Campo Lucinda T-shirt when I can." Between the two of them you'd think I'm visiting Disneyworld. Hearing their voices,

I miss them, and when we hang up I start thinking of a guy I read about years ago who walked from Barrow, Alaska, to the tip of Tierra Del Fuego, South America. When a reporter asked him what he felt about completing his journey, all he said was "I'm tired and I'd like to go home." I doubt that was what he set out to discover.

I look at my watch and though I struggle with the time conversion, I'm pretty sure it's not too late to call Nina. Without much to do and nowhere to go, I'm getting a little antsy and Nina has been a source of great conversation. She answers her phone after the first ring, "Noah, how's the flood? I saw some news footage last night on the television. You're getting a lot of coverage over here."

"Coverage? That's a joke right?"

"No, what do you mean?" says Nina, laughing at her pun. She tells me that the work with the oyster farmers is coming to an end. "It doesn't sound like you'll be getting on a plane anytime soon."

"No, I don't think so. Once the rain does stop, they say it will take a least a week or two to get us out."

"Don't worry, Jake, I've got things to keep me busy for a while," and then with the tiniest bit of mystery, Nina adds, "I have something I'd like to show you over here."

"What's that?" I ask but Nina won't say more. "Something I think you should see."

Then we talk for a while about nothing in particular, content to hear each other's voices. Before hanging up, Nina says, "It's a funny thing between you and me, isn't it, the way we spend time together?" I don't say anything, frightened that she doesn't have the same feelings of enjoyment about our friendship, but she gently says, "It's good."

Phone calls with Nina are like that. Short, dense, and filled with longing. This morning the charm was greater than the density and for the first time since taking up residence in Campo Lucinda, I begin drifting off into thoughts of life after the flood. As Nina's voice hangs on the receiver and I hear goodbye, then out of nowhere, I hear Pearl admonishing another player, "Don't ever yield the triples!"

A few minutes pass before the welcome staccato of an approaching chopper excites everyone. In a moment I hear voices and there's a big commotion coming from the entrance to the armory. A blinding light blazing from the top of a news camera is following two soaking wet people as they walk. The camera follows them as they drag their beleaguered bodies into the armory showers while people scurry about finding dry clothes for them.

The news crew hangs around for a while, grabbing fifteen seconds here and there and doing short interviews with what the reporter keeps calling "flood victims." When they see the film projectors and screen, they search me out to do a brief interview about my showing films in the armory. They stick around for another half an hour before boarding their chopper to fly to the next shelter, no doubt looking for something to fill thirty seconds on this evening's news.

About an hour later, while I'm reading a magazine article about Nile crocodiles and drinking Campo Lucinda coffee, better known as Red Cross Rot Gut, someone taps me on the shoulder. I can't say anything as a familiar apparition, the locomotive man from Booker, Groat, says, "Nice to see you too, Jake," extending his hand and taking mine for a warm handshake. "Don't even ask." he says. "I was on a train with Lila," he points across the room, "She's the love of my life. We've been traveling around for a few years . . ."and with that he gushes with story after story about his life and how he met Lila at a Hobo gathering soon after leaving Booker.

"Get this, Jake; she was there with her mother. The two of them had been riding for years when her Mom decides she can't do it anymore and settles down to run a magic shop for a guy she met in Nebraska. Amazing, don't you think?"

As he speaks, all I can think of is the coffee night in Booker and the last sight of Groat's gold atlas and the unopened golden locket that hung around his neck. Groat must be reading my mind because he reaches into his pocket and fans the pages of the slightly damp atlas.

"Not going to lose my way to a little derailment."

"What about that gold locket? Are you still wearing that?"

Groat smiles and reaches around his neck, pulling out the same two chained lockets he showed us years ago. He untwines the two and pulls the golden one from around his neck and lays it open in his lap where he removes a tightly wrapped piece of paper from it. "Jake, you know I carried this around my neck for years; swore I'd never show it to anyone. Kind of held it real tight, you know, didn't want to jinx things. I remember that night in the East/West. I know you guys wanted to see this, but some things you gotta stay true to."

"But you can open it now?"

"You bet. Let me read it to you. I think you'll understand."

Groat holds the paper before him and reads,

"Until I find the love that opens my eyes to things I don't want to see, I'm not stopping. Until I see the light that stops my heart from beating, I'm not stopping. Until I find the road or the rail that holds only the truth of its promised destination, I'm not stopping.

I'm not stopping until then."

"Who wrote that?"

"I did. That's the note I left my family when I took off. No one, and I mean no one: I didn't read that to no one until I met Lila."

It's a different man sitting before me than the young hobo from Booker. Then we sit and talk and Groat tells me about The Train Wreck.

"We felt the freight-car tilt, Jake, and I don't know how or why we did it, but we fastened our arms on to some racks and held on for dear life. It was like time went into slow motion, Jake. I'm not sure we would have survived if the car went all the way over, but it didn't. It kind of slid and slid and slid and then stopped. No one knew we were inside. We were able to pry open the door enough to crawl out, and we ran up to the front where we found the engineer with a bloody gash in his head on the radio trying to get some help. He was pretty surprised to see us, but everyone was great. They finally got a helicopter out to the train and when the pilot mentioned something about a shelter where they show movies, I knew it had to be you. I knew it. They dropped us here before flying out the engineer to a hospital to fix up his head. I hope he'll be okay."

Lila joins us, carrying two plates of food, one of which she hands to Groat.

"Jake, this is my girl, Lila. Lila, this is the guy I told you about with the movie truck."

"I was having a hard time believing him," says Lila.

"Never doubt an honest hobo, Baby," says Groat, giving her a kiss on the forehead.

We talk for hours during which Groat tells me all about doings at the East/West. Vaughn married Betty after her husband Ray died. "That was a no-brainer," he says. "You should see the place. Man, it is running smoothly now. Even has real coffee. When we get out of this mess, I'm going to call Vaughn and tell him about seeing you. You and Eric are legends around there."

Groat wants to know all about Eric and he's disappointed we never got to the bears, even though he says, "Yes, I came close to hopping in with you guys, but I had a feeling, and it wasn't but a few months later that Lila and I met up outside of Lincoln." He takes Lila's hand in his in a sweet gesture of affection.

"You know, Jake, we're thinking about getting away from the trains for a while."

"You better believe we are, "says Lila. "I believe in omens and getting rolled like that is definitely an omen."

We call Eric. Groat starts speaking as soon as he picks up. "Eric! This is an old friend from Booker. Remember, coffee, locomotives?" After a pause, I hear Eric scream, "Groat?"

Over the next few days, I enjoy getting to know Groat and Lila better. Groat helps me set up the films when Matthew, the erstwhile entertainment chief, decides girls are more interesting than film projectors.

Two weeks later during breakfast, a loud cry is heard throughout the armory. "We've surpassed Noah by ten!" announces Kyle Fulton. "Yep, fifty days and fifty nights,"says Kyle, and I don't doubt he will start looking for a pair of giraffes before too long. Everyone will start looking for giraffes before long, but the good news this morning is that the cooks are making lasagna for dinner.

Around two o'clock in the afternoon, a buzz begins swirling around the armory with the rumor there's a special Red Cross shipment on the way. Why this should be a bigger deal than usual surprises me because we get supplies every few days. But today there is a buzz beyond the normal and when the rain lets up in the afternoon, we see some blue sky. There is a palpable rise in everyone's spirits. Nancy has been careful to keep a lid on our expectations. "Maybe it's ice cream, or chocolate bars," she says. Nancy reminds us that even when the rain stops, it's going to take at least a week for crews to repair the roads and get people out. Reality has changed its currency over the past seven weeks and blue sky is a welcome sight. It gives us a chance to step outside and feel the welcome rays of light on our moldering faces and mildewed skin.

At three o'clock, a helicopter arrives with containers of food, toothpaste, and soap, and enough cheese to make sure that tonight's promised lasagna will be delicious. Stepping from the helicopter is also a Red Cross counselor named Carol who has been spending time at other shelters in the region. Carol makes herself available to anyone who needs to talk about "things" as she puts it. Apparently her services are more needed than I would have anticipated. She has her hands full patiently listening to people telling their stories. I might even sign up for a few minutes. Carol's presence and the continuing improvement in the storm profile has everyone's spirits improving over the next few days.

At two o'clock on Day Fifty-Three, the sky opens up to a brilliant blue. I know the time exactly because I was lying in Zhitomir when the sun's light came streaming through the skylight directly onto my face. Whether this signals things to come or is another cruel tease is yet to be seen, but when I step outside the air is thick and warm like a barber's hot towel on your face.

Soon the temperature climbs into the sixties and people in the armory spill outside to soak up the sunshine. Carol approaches me as I stand against the warm brick wall of the armory and says, "Jake, I've got a wild idea. Can you project outside?"

"Can I?" You bet I can!"

Two hours later I park Zhitomir with its flank facing the armory. I pull out the large folding screen from its overhead cabinet and lay it out. Zhitomir has twelve hooks that fit into the grommets on the screen; four across the top, three on each side, and four on the bottom. In a few minutes (with the agile Groat and Lila's help), the screen is mounted to Zhitomir.

The setting reminds me of the first time I showed an outdoor film in Larch. It was the end of the hottest summer in history, with one hundred consecutive days in the nineties. We had a mock drive-in scheduled for Labor Day with the screen set up in a hay field where we could park cars, serve refreshments, and sell tickets from an old horse trailer. Day one hundred and one was not cloudless. It rained hard all morning and it was looking bleak for the turnout and fundraiser for the Larch Community Cemetery. We considered calling off the show, but at three o'clock the storm broke, the wind laid down, and by six o'clock when people started arriving for a chili and cornbread dinner, the field was dry and the air a comfortable eighty-two degrees. Outside projection makes you nervous, but it's always worth the worry. There is nothing in the world like throwing light on a screen beneath the stars.

Once the screen is set, Groat helps me place the projectors on a table beneath the protected arch of the armory entrance. The kitchen crew starts serving roast beef, mashed potatoes, biscuits, and gravy at six o'clock. At eight we'll throw the switch and show a repeat of *The Philadelphia Story*. It's a festive evening. At seven o'clock the air feels snug and warm like a blanket holding a bed of sleeping children. On Day Fifty-Five of this flood that will remake the lives of thousands of people, there has appeared a timelessness that only natural disasters can bring. The Lost Sons of Zhitomir Rolling Film Society is completely cued and ready to work.

After sunset, just as I'm poised to throw the switch, the distant sound of a helicopter draws suddenly closer.

Within less than a minute the helicopter hovers above the street right outside the armory and begins dropping to the ground. The chopper pop-pop-pops while aiming its spotlight on the yellow circle below. Spasmodically, the spotlight casts its beam against Zhitomir with its unlikely paintings until the helicopter lands and the engines slow to a stop. The spotlight obscures two people as they come from the chopper and cross the street. One is wheeling a dolly while the other is laden with bundles. It isn't until they walk up the steps that their faces come into focus.

Fifty-five days into the most devastating flood in the history of North America and I've finally lost my mind! Walking up the steps of Campo Lucinda is Nina Palliatti with Julian! They're wheeling a dolly with two cases: one marked 'Camcorders' and the second marked 'Battery Packs.' Both cases bear the bold stenciled letters "VPP" on them. Arriving at the top of the steps, Nina wraps her arms around me and says, "Hey, Movie Man, did we miss the show? Sorry, but we had to stop in New York." Nancy, ever in charge, comes over to walk with Julian while Nina hands me a heavy film box saying, "Here Sampan."

"No way! You guys brought a copy of *La Strada*?"

"Would you have preferred *The Road Warrior*?" says Julian. "There's nothing like Fellini to brighten the apocalypse. I couldn't send things next-day express so I had to hire the job out." Then he turns to Nancy and says, "I don't suppose there's any of that chili I've been hearing about? I'd like to eat something before that helicopter has to go. You see, there's this waitress in a Chinese restaurant…"

Delusions can shift senses, so when Nina hands me a foil bag of freshly roasted coffee beans in a Café Borghese bag, and the smell of rich, dark coffee beans wafts into my nostrils, I know I'm doomed.

"Eric thought you might need this," Nina says.

In a flash I replace *The Philadelphia Story* with *La Strada*. Goodbye Jimmy Stewart, Katherine Hepburn, Cary Grant, and aristocratic Philadelphia, hello Giulietta Masina, Anthony Quinn, Richard Basehart, and post-World War II Italy.

After *La Strada's* been going for a while, Joe Kurchen walks over to me and whispers, "Ain't that the guy who played on *Voyage to the Bottom of the Sea*? How's an 'eyetalian' get to be commander of an American submarine?" wonders Joe, a retired plumber who seven weeks ago watched his house floating down the river.

Joe stands with me behind the projectors and continues.

"Gee whiz, if this ain't the perfect thing to take your mind off of things. Will you look at these kids: they never seen anything like this. Hell, I'm 71 years old and that world was heading into oblivion when I was a kid. It was like that, you know? Used to be all it took to dazzle you was a little act, something simple, not like all the razzle dazzle everything has today. Heck, that's what it was like when I grew up. I don't think half the homes in this town had electricity when I was a kid, and if you had a telephone, wow! Most of us had to go to the drugstore to make a phone call."

Joe, no doubt, has been doing what Red Cross Carol calls "therapeutic coffee drinking," and he unfolds his world view.

"I got a theory about that *ET* and *Close Encounters*. All them hocus-pocus films about outer space and aliens and stuff. I think those films are so big because people need to believe in something beyond what's in front of their faces. No mystery, no meaning to life. You can fall into some pretty deep ruts if nothing ever overturns your apple cart. You know what I mean? Kind of like this flood. One thing's for sure: nobody's in a rut. Light speed, space travel, black holes; yeah, I read about that stuff. I even heard that guy in the wheelchair talking about what's out there. Kind of a weird show if you ask me, him stuck inside his body and knowing all that stuff about what's going on in the vastness of the universe. Kind of odd, but, you see, that's my point. Because ET has that vastness, he's not stuck in his body at all. I oughta know, because I spent enough time on my back fixing toilets to know there has to be more to life than the day to day."

Joe finally stops for a second and gazes up at the screen.

"Pathetic little thing ain't, she?" says Joe about Gelsomina on the screen before walking in the direction of the kitchen where one can only hope they will not serve him more coffee.

My delusion has stamina. I've cued up the last reel and standing beside me is Nina. In front of us is an armory of people with food in their stomachs and blankets wrapped over their shoulders, watching an innocent pixie, a brute, and a fool play out the meaning of life. Little children are piled on top of each other, surrounded by their new aunts and uncles, relatives made by the flood.

"Look at them," says Nina, "glad to be alive, glad to be warm, to have shelter and food."

I lean into the tender pressure of the warm shoulder of this woman who travels the world to ease pain and create hope. As the film closes, Zampano, the strongman of the road, the brutish vagabond who finally discovers he has a heart, is left crying on the beach because the woman whom he never gave his love to is dead. Antonina Palliatti weaves her hand into mine and whispers, "Well, Zampano, is it going to be La Strada or L'amoré?" Knowing what my reply will be, she squeezes my hand and whispers, "Mi guida la luce che vedo innanzi a me."

"What does that mean?"

"It's something my father always said, 'Mi guida la luce che vedo innanzi a me.' 'I am guided by the light in front of me.' Look, Jake, look at all the lights before our eyes.

# EPILOGUE

During my lifetime science has uncovered quite a few things. Having broken into the genetic cave, researchers find some new gene every day that they claim explains who we are and why we do what we do. But to date, no one has discovered the sequence of amino acids determining the gene for wandering. I have personally discovered that there are too many cells, too many years, and too many lives for me to stop my own travels. I don't know where I'm headed, but I do know I'm in motion and that's fine with me.

After the flood, I turned the keys to Zhitomir over to Lila and Groat. Nothing permanent of course, Groat still prefers locomotives and Lila does most of the driving, but they both love projectors.

A few weeks after the waters receded, Lila drove Nina and me to Seattle where we boarded a jet and flew to Europe. Nina had a surprise for me. She took me to see my father's grave. There, in a sad and seemingly infinite field of grave-markers surrounded by tall trees, I stood over the grave of Emil Spinner, my father. If I couldn't hear his voice, I could see his face as I held a picture from the cedar chest in my hand. At long last the three of us were together. I still feel the aching sobs in my heart as I write these words.

Eric compiled years of documentary footage and created a feature-length documentary, *Little Voices in Faraway Places,* which told of the times the two of us spent together on the road. Few films can boast of characters from bootleggers, hobos, and horse breeders to cowboys, poultry workers, and small-town mechanics, along with the most stunning collection of cafés and makeshift theaters the world has ever seen. Eric was born to make movies.

Julian is ever onward, though one has to wonder when he will slow down. He and Tanner Scofield are currently writing a script for Sophia Loren about her life, and if they don't kill each other, it will be interesting to see what comes of it. Actually, as long as it has Sophia Loren in it, it will be interesting even if they do kill each other.

I often remember what Fred told me: "Accepting change is the challenge of being alive. How we handle change is what life is all about. It can make you bitter or euphoric. Some people don't eat new foods, some don't try new machines, new medicines, whatever the new thing is, and some do. Some get heady with change, like a handsome man in a room of beautiful women. Newness holds every promise, but the only thing certain in life is change." Fred Tolliver was an amazing man and not a day passes in my life when I don't think of him.

There's one more thing I want to put in this traveler's log. It's a newspaper clipping that my mother put in the cedar chest. I can't show it to you, but the article accompanied a handsome photo of Fred with all the promise of his life before him.

Before Fred was in the service he spent one summer fighting fires in the woods. With his mechanic's abilities, naturally, when pumps or engines broke down, he was the man to fix them. Soon enough he was spared from having to wield a shovel or an ax, as long as he kept water flowing during fire-fighting operations. Fred was always proud of that work and said, "If it was a little noisy, it was at least easier on your lungs."

The article reads as follows:

### Larch Man Douses Fires; Raises Spirits With Poetry

Fred Tolliver, of Larch, spent his summer in the Olympic Peninsula as a mechanic in charge of running water pumps employed to protect the nation's forests. The recent graduate of Larch High School loves his work. "I like to watch the fire, see the flames build; it's pretty darn seductive."

Fred says the work is hard and the hours long, but the mature young man says his job is not so difficult as those on the front lines who take in the smoke and wield the heavy hoses. "By the time we get a handle on things and things start settling down, it's been a long night. The crews retreat from their posts and they're awfully tired. They've been sucking soot and spewing water with no sleep. Me, I get happy when we can finally shut the pumps down after twenty or thirty straight hours of engine noise. I like quiet."

Fred says that once the sun rises, the burned areas "look like millions of little Christmas lights through a gentle fog." Fred tells us that "From time to time, the wind whips a small fire up and they have to make sure it stays put, but otherwise all else is pretty still. You got the night sky up there, clear as can be, talking to the embers and the flickering wisps of flame in the burn. It's like a conversation between distant cousins. That's when I get that feeling and start writing something." Fred likes to capture the moments with a few choice words that he'll share with the crews over cocoa on the sleepy drive back to headquarters."

In my wallet I carry part of Fred's piece they quoted in the article. I take it out when I need to remember who I am and where I come from.

"All those flickering lights remind me I'm a little speck in the grand scheme of things. I prefer to be a speck. It leaves me free to wander, lets me breathe, lets me listen to others, lets me focus on something other than myself, and, hopefully, makes me a better person for it. I look at those lights and tell myself that's all I care about."

The last line of Fred Tolliver's poem is, "Be dynamic, remember the Titanic, and don't forget, nothing is immortal."

The End.

A F T E R W O R D   &   G R A T I T U D E

———

Bedtime Stories grew steadily over a number of years. What started as the imagined tale of an untaken trip became something much more. For that I owe a debt of gratitude to many people for their kind support, encouragement, and assistance. To Nancy and Ruby Blum, who live with me and still love me. To Nancy again, who read and re-read and re-read, always encouraging me and enjoying a cup of coffee in all the imagined cafés. To Catherine Smith, for her extraordinary ability to read and reveal what should and shouldn't be. To Tom Yohannan, longtime friend, incisive editor, and supporter. To David Campbell, my friend and talented artist who took on this project with his vast skill and talent. I am honored by his work. To Christine Coulter, an honest and capable editor whose work helped shape this book. And to all of my family and friends who create the air that sustains my life. Abrazos a todos. Any flaws in the book are mine and mine alone. All of you were perfect.

ABOUT THE AUTHOR

**Joseph Emil Blum** was born in Ohio and raised in New York. His first paid job was removing ice from a Cadillac at the age of seven. Abandoning that promising career he then went on to the care of exotic animals, life-guarding, home insulating, construction, carpentry, fisheries biology, teacher of the living and the dying, and lavender farming.
At the age of nineteen he moved to the Pacific Northwest and now lives in rural Oregon with his wife Nancy and daughter Ruby. He spends winters alternately tormented and pleased by the thundering sounds of amorous chorus frogs, and summers alternately tormented and pleased by slowly
 pitched softballs. He is very proud to have juggled fish in the Bering Sea while working aboard the world's largest fishing vessel, the Sulak: an act he believes may have facilitated the end of the Cold War, and is equally proud to have sung in a Soviet fisherman's dance band aboard the same vessel: an act that, no doubt, prolonged it.

 Bedtime Stories illustrator, **David Campbell** is an oil painter, blacksmith, metalworker, woodworker, wood carver, and organ maker. He does all with equal facility, If he were dropped into another century, even another millennium, he would not only feel comfortable, but he would prosper. He is a remarkable man.

80727051R00250

Made in the USA
Columbia, SC
20 November 2017